A Terrible Choice

Charlotte slumped against the siding and pressed the back of her hand to her forehead.

"You found the jumper, didn't you?" Theodore's voice was quiet, accusatory. "When, Charlotte? Why did you not contact me?"

"I was going to. As soon as I got off work—"

"How long have you been aware of this person?"

She sighed. "Friday. He just woke up from recovery today."

Theodore's voice lowered in pitch, and he spoke sharply. "This isn't a random jumper, is it? It's someone who—"

"He's a good man! He doesn't deserve—"

"If he's in the book, he must be neutralized! You of all people should understand that, after your father—"

"This isn't about my father!" Charlotte jerked upright. "This is about a man who may not have even done anything." Yet.

Theodore's shoulders flattened and he loomed closer to her. "But he will. Otherwise he wouldn't be in the book."

Charlotte lowered her voice and dropped her gaze to project a deferential attitude. "I'm not arguing the fact that time shouldn't be altered. But your methods... please, Theodore, let me handle this one." She forced strength into her voice. If he detected any weakness in her, he wouldn't let her. "I'll convince him to come to the House. Please, promise me you won't hurt him, you'll just send him home..."

It wouldn't be easy. Tony had tensed when she mentioned Theodore. He knew something, though maybe not the full extent of the danger. He wouldn't be easily convinced. She'd have to take care in working up to the suggestion. "Please, Theodore." She stopped before her pleading turned into begging.

Theodore's voice grew gentle again. "Who is this man, that you're willing to risk your principles, everything the Society stands for?"

"It's Tony. Tony Solomon. The man who saved my life."

Other books by Jennette Marie Powell
Time's Fugitive (January, 2012)

Jennette Marie Powell

MYTHICAL PRESS ✳ DAYTON, OHIO

MYTHICAL PRESS ✶ DAYTON, OHIO
www.mythicalpress.com

Time's Enemy

Editing by Sheri L. McGathy
Text design and cover by Jennette Marie Powell
Flood photo courtesy of Dayton Metro Library www.daytonmetrolibrary.org
Other photos used under license via www.istockphoto.com

Print ISBN 978-0-9839097-2-9
Digital ISBN 978-0-9839097-0-5
Library of Congress Control Number: 2011938411

One

THE DAY THEY WENT TO CHICHÉN ITZÁ STARTED NO DIFFERENTLY THAN THE past five of their vacation, yet Tony Solomon felt a numbing unease, the kind that sometimes came on when something bad was going to happen.

No way in hell was he going to go up that big pyramid. It'd be just his luck to fall and kill himself. *El Castillo* had existed for over a millennium without him climbing it, and it could stay that way.

Puffy clouds dotted the brilliant blue, February sky, and shimmers of heat rose from the meadow beyond the small copse of trees where Tony stood as his seven colleagues passed. A sidewise glance caught the eye of Violet Sinclair, who'd stopped a few feet away. The computer technician had won the company's charity raffle, with a spot on the executives' annual trip to Cancun as the prize. She looked away, as if Tony had caught her doing something she shouldn't.

Charlie, his brother-in-law and coworker, smacked his arm as he walked by, jerking Tony's attention off Violet. "Hey, Solomon, you coming?"

No way was Tony climbing those ninety-one steps—according to their tour guide—to stand on that narrow, unrailed platform atop the pyramid. "There's a reason that thing's closed to the public." Like people had died there. He couldn't imagine how Keith, their boss and CEO of the company, had managed to arrange a private tour of the site, which included permission to climb the pyramid.

Charlie stopped. "Everyone else is going."

If everyone else jumped off a bridge, would you? Tony put on his poker face. "You wouldn't expect Lisa to go up there."

"Lisa's not here." Tony's sister had been unable to take the week off from her job. Charlie stepped closer, a wide grin splitting his face. "Who knew? The guy who has no problem telling the boss his idea sucks, is afraid of heights."

"I told Keith the truth."

"A move like that would've gotten anyone else fired," Charlie said.

Tony couldn't argue. For some reason, the CEO had always respected his sometimes-brutal honesty. If lying to appease the boss was what it took to move up, or even remain employed, Tony didn't want the job, though he'd been more diplomatic in the meeting that morning than to say Keith's idea *sucked*.

Charlie started toward *El Castillo* then stopped. "You coming, or you too chicken-shit?"

Tony felt Violet's gaze on him again. If she didn't like heights either, she'd be his excuse to stay on the ground.

He'd invited her along when his wife Dora claimed she had a headache, and suggested he ask "that chubby girl from I.T." to take her place on the excursion. For Tony, Keith's plans to visit the ruins were a welcome departure from routine—hanging around the resort while Dora sunbathed, leaving himself with too much time to think.

"What about you?" he asked Violet.

"Are you joking? This is the chance of a lifetime. If I don't go, I'll always regret it." She twirled a lock of her long, blond hair around her index finger. A tiny breeze shifted the branches above to allow a shaft of sunlight to slip across her face, illuminating her golden brown eyes like a jar of honey sitting in a sunny kitchen window.

Charlie smirked. A good-natured smirk, but a smirk nonetheless.

Violet unwound the hair from her finger as Keith appeared beside Tony. The CEO clapped Tony on the shoulder. "Don't worry, we'll catch you if you fall. Right, Violet?"

Her words echoed through Tony's mind, drowning out her response. *If I don't, I'll regret it.* "What the hell," Tony muttered as the three started across the meadow.

As they walked, Violet sneaked a glance at Tony, then dropped back so he wouldn't notice her staring at him.

Him. Tony Solomon. After three years with the company, it was the closest they'd ever been without a desk and computer between them. Her first chance to have a conversation with more depth than the usual "What were you doing when the computer stopped responding?"

Three years of watching him whenever he walked through the tech support department to get a cup of coffee, of hearing his polite "Thanks, Violet," when she reset his password—which he forgot every time he was forced to change it. Three years of thinking of ways to put herself in his path at the office to get another glimpse of his face. Three years of longing, of trying to figure out the mystery of why something about him seemed... familiar, when nothing else did in the few, short years she could remember.

Mr. Vogel started up the steps, but Tony stopped at the bottom of the pyramid, so she did the same. She looked up at him. His gaze met hers for a brief moment.

Could he know his eyes were exactly the same shade of blue as the sky? He snatched off his glasses, peered through them, then slid them back on.

Tightness laced her chest. She was alone with him. Finally. But what would she say? *Gracious, I need a cigarette right now...*

No, I don't. Determined to stop smoking, she'd left her pack at the resort. This time she'd quit for good.

An unbidden thought of slipping into his embrace rushed into her mind, and warmth replaced the tenseness in her body. Somehow, she knew exactly how his arms would feel around her... could almost smell the clean scent of his shirt—*Tony, I'm sure we know each other...maybe you don't remember...*

Hope flared within her. Was a memory returning?

She waited. Nothing.

Just like it had been since that day years ago, when she'd awoken alone and terrified, unable to even remember her own name. She had no idea how she'd gotten into someone's garage, or how her dress had come to be covered in blood. Or whose blood it was.

Keith Lynch waved at them from the top of the pyramid. Violet looked at Tony.

She didn't know how she knew, but something—a buried snippet of recall from her unknown past—made her voice encouragement. "Just don't look down."

Tony snatched his glasses off again and wiped them, then started up the steep staircase.

Like some of the others, he crawled up on his hands and feet. Behind him, Violet took the steps in an upright crouch, mindful of her dress. Not the most practical choice for traipsing around the ruins, but she wanted to play up her positives. Its long, loose cut hid her belly and less-than-perfect thighs while displaying her cleavage to advantage. Her face heated. She shouldn't think such things. She'd worn the dress because it was comfortable, she insisted to herself. *And he's married.* Even if she had so little regard to pursue a married man, she wouldn't have a chance. Not when his wife had the figure and looks of a movie star.

By the time they reached the top, she and Tony were out of breath. Violet wiped the sweat from her brow.

Tony crept toward the square building topping the structure. "I guess that wasn't so bad." He turned around and stopped panting.

Six feet of platform at most stood between the building and the edge, and like the staircases, it lacked any kind of restraint. Violet's legs felt jittery and she wasn't typically bothered by heights, so it had to be terrifying for someone who was. She moved closer to Tony and took in the view.

Below, grass carpeted the clearing, dotted with small groups of people the size of dolls. Beyond the meadow, other stone structures broke the swath of green here and there. Buildings that had once been people's homes, markets, gathering places.

The enormity of it all sank over her like a suffocating depth of water. Ages had passed before her. Ages would follow. In the bigger scheme of things, nothing she did mattered. She'd built a life for herself from nothing. So why couldn't she figure out what Tony meant to her before—and why she was afraid to find out?

Tony flattened his back, arms, and the palms of his hands against the temple's wall and inched along it, then ducked into the doorway.

Unwilling to let him out of her sight, Violet followed him inside. Their footsteps echoed on the stone walls of the narrow corridor. She turned a sharp corner, and goose bumps rose on her arms in the cool, damp air. Or was it from Tony's nearness?

Seconds later they turned another corner and emerged on the opposite side of the pyramid. Violet started out but Tony lingered.

"Tony?" she called. "Are you—"

Another fragment of memory struck her. She gasped, didn't hear his answer.

No way, he said. It was his voice, she was sure. A vision of water, lots of it, far below...

"Violet?" His voice in the here-and-now shattered the image. "What's wrong?"

"Nothing." She swallowed. Years ago, when she'd hesitantly asked if they'd met before, he claimed they hadn't. But every cell in her body screamed otherwise. She knew him, and he'd been someone special. Someone *very* special. Then the familiar guilt crawled down her throat, forced its way deeper, whittling her thoughts down to one: sometime in her hidden past, she'd done something to him. Something terrible. Her lungs shriveled, stopping her from asking the questions whose answers she feared. "Some kind of... déjà vu," she managed. "Like I'd done something like this with you before..."

Tony's mouth lifted in a wan smile. "Trust me, if you had, I'd remember." He gripped the edge of the portal and stepped through. Staring at his feet, he crept along the wall until he stood beside Violet and Mr. Lynch.

The tour guide was in the middle of a lengthy discourse about the ancients of the ninth century who'd built the pyramid and surrounding village. Violet pretended to listen as she sneaked a furtive glance at Tony, then cast her gaze toward Mr. Lynch when she sensed Tony watching.

The CEO stood straight, arms crossed over his chest, and his face toward the tour guide, but his eyes flicked sideways, meeting Violet's. "I'll bet you've already read all about them," he said in a low voice.

"How did you know?" Violet whispered.

"I saw your book on the plane." His mouth quirked, and Violet jerked backward. His smile looked just like Tony's... or had she imagined it?

Mr. Lynch sidled toward Tony, and the resemblance leaped out. Mr. Lynch was a little taller, but aside from his graying hair and brown eyes, he could have passed for an older version of Tony. Yet— maybe it was his position in the company—she couldn't imagine having the kind of feelings for him that she had for Tony.

Tony had developed a fascination with the platform floor. She longed to wrap her arms around him and tell him it was all right. But even if he wasn't married, she doubted she'd ever be able to work up the nerve to do so much as ask him to join her for a cup of coffee after work. Push aside the feeling she couldn't shake that there was something... well, *wrong* about asking a man out, even though other women did it all the time.

She wrenched her gaze away before he caught her staring again.

Across the meadow, slabs of white stone rose in neat columns around a flat, raised platform like soldiers in formation, guarding something the mere mortals clustered at the top of the pyramid couldn't see. Another staircase, crumbled to rubble, had once led down the side of the pyramid.

"You still got that brochure?" Tony asked.

"Sure." She drew it out of her pocketbook and handed it to him.

He held it close to his face, as if trying to block the faraway ground from his view. "Wow, it says here this thing used to be a temple... they even sacrificed people here." He gazed over the view with a pained expression and started to hand the pamphlet back to Violet, when the woman from Finance stepped between them. Tony leaned back to reach around her, but his foot slipped, and he crumpled to the floor, then slid over the precipice.

Tony rolled over, then over again. He grabbed. Clutched. At anything, could hold onto nothing. His glasses flew off and skidded away. Every sharp stone jutting out from the ragged surface poked him, mocking his attempts to stop himself. A burst of pain flared in his forehead, then there was nothing but white...

A dim sensation of pressure on his ankle, then the motion stopped. "I got him!" someone said. The man's voice sounded like he was deep in a tunnel. Foggy, too indistinct to identify. Nothing but cloudy whiteness in Tony's sight. A muffled rattle of falling, crumbling stone. Shouts from above. Other voices. More hands grasping at him.

"Is he okay?"

"I don't know, he's banged up pretty bad..." More falling rocks.

"I think I saw a park ranger..."

"Tony! Tony, oh good heavens..." A woman's voice. Violet. "Tony, wake up!"

I'm awake, he said.

"Step back... everyone clear the area! Charlie—go for help! You..." Keith. Taking charge.

"Tony, please... you've got to be all right..."

Violet! Tony shouted.

She hadn't heard him. No one had. He hadn't said it out loud. Her voice faded, along with the sensation of hands on his ankles. With a strange detachment he realized his head no longer hurt.

He no longer felt anything. Only an impression of floating.

Whiteness surrounded him. There was nothing—no touch, no sound, no sight except light all around. The light grew brighter at some distant point ahead. He took two steps toward it, unsure of when he'd stood. Another step. No pain. No sadness. No fear. And somehow he knew, no questions left unanswered once he reached that light. He shielded his eyes with his hand and continued forward.

A dark speck broke the brightness.

"Daddy?" A girl's voice.

He dropped his arm. "Bethany?"

"Daddy... No!" The speck grew larger. It was her.

"I'm coming!" He started to run, then stopped. How could that be Bethany? She was dead. Had been for almost three years—

"Daddy," she called again. "Don't! Go away..."

"But..." He held up his hand so he could see the silhouette. Thick, blunt-cut hair; a lanky, young female form. But if it was, then that meant—

He looked down at himself. He could barely see his yellow knit shirt in the brightness, couldn't see his feet at all.

So this is what it feels like to die.

A lot of people had died in this place, centuries ago.

He was about to join them. To his surprise, he wasn't afraid.

"Dad?" Bethany called.

His mom would take it hard. His sister, too. His dad would deal in stoic silence as he always did. Dora'd hit the antidepressants again, but she'd move on sooner than the rest of his family.

Nothing hurt. Life wasn't that great anyway. Hadn't been since Bethany...

He started forward again, but something clamped around his wrist and pulled him back. Dizziness burst through him, and he stumbled and fell. A tingle flared in his wrist where that other hand touched him, and sparks spread through his body, then faded. The whole world spun, around and around, everywhere and nowhere...

"No!" Violet gripped Tony's wrist tighter, clutching at the stone with her other hand. She couldn't have a dizzy spell here, of all places! She was spinning, whirling through the air, ungrounded, Tony's wrist all she could feel....

A tingly feeling grew in her palm, spread out to her fingertips, then dissipated. As if something had gone from her into Tony's body.

The vertigo stopped.

Tony's wrist twitched.

"Tony?" She pressed her thumb onto the artery of his wrist and felt a weak pulse. "He's alive!" A cheer rose from the LCT executives clustered around them and the tourists gathered on the ground.

Mr. Lynch patted Tony's shoulder. "Tony? Can you hear me? Tony?"

Tony blinked. "Beth—" His eyes focused on Violet. "Violet?"

A laugh escaped her throat. "Tony! Oh, thank heavens!" Relief settled over her like a cozy blanket on a cold winter night. She looked skyward and sent up a prayer of thanks.

Tony was the only clue she had to her past, her only possibility of finding out what happened all those years ago.

The only man she loved.

In the face of his death, she could admit it, if only to herself. It didn't matter if he was married and she could never tell him, didn't matter if he couldn't return her feelings and there could never be anything more between them. He was alive.

He shifted in her grasp. A flush crept into his skin, and sweat mingled with the blood on his forehead. He struggled to sit.

"Tony, what are you—"

"Lie down," Mr. Lynch ordered.

"Burning up," Tony said. "Get me—"

"Before you fall the rest the way," Mr. Lynch finished.

"—out of the sun." Tony sat, then pulled his feet beneath him and yanked his wrist out of Violet's hand. With a grunt, he rolled over and settled his foot onto a protruding stone, then began to climb back up the pyramid.

Mr. Lynch yelled again to stay put, but Tony kept climbing. All Violet could do was watch in slack-jawed astonishment and scoot out of Mr. Lynch's way as he scrambled after Tony.

Something amazing had happened. A miracle. People didn't get conked on the head and almost die—then recover and stand up a few minutes later. She could have sworn Tony's pulse had stopped. She lifted the hand she'd held onto him with, and waggled her fingers. Something had passed between them. Something incredible, in the midst of that horrible dizzy spell, the worst one she'd ever had. Something—

No. It was nothing. Just coincidence. Odd things sometimes happened with head injuries. Maybe Tony's wasn't as bad as it had seemed, and he hadn't been as close to death as she thought. She'd just lost the pulse for a minute. The tingle, the dizziness was just a worse occurrence of the occasional vertigo she'd suffered as long as she could remember.

She clambered up the pyramid after him.

Above, Tony pulled himself over the edge of the platform, then rose on wobbly legs. Violet scrambled to reach him. He swayed, stabilized, then stumbled the few steps into the stone building. Outside, Mr. Lynch yelled at someone on the ground to go for medical help.

Tony was leaning against the wall to one side of the doorway when Violet stepped inside the structure. "Good heavens, what on earth are you doing?"

"Had to..." He panted. "...get out of that sun."

"You should sit down. The medics will be here soon."

"I'm okay." His voice was stronger.

"You were knocked unconscious. You're—"

"I'm fine." Strong enough now to stand without support, he patted the stone wall and regarded it with a studious gaze.

"Wonder what it was like back then?" the woman from Finance mused from somewhere behind Violet.

The ancient Mayans were the least of Violet's concerns. What was keeping the paramedics? The tour guide had assured them it wouldn't be long—

"Violet?" Mr. Lynch yelled from outside.

She leaned out. "What did you say, sir?"

An ambulance pulled up to the foot of the pyramid as Lynch hoisted himself over the ledge. He stood and brushed himself off.

"Started to slide a bit there—what's he doing?"

"Tony?" Violet turned to go back inside when the vertigo came back, making her lurch to one side. *No... Not again!* She groped at the wall, anything to save herself from a mishap like Tony's.

The dizziness subsided. She gripped the edge of the doorway and walked inside.

No one was there. "Tony?"

He must've gone through the temple. She navigated the short corridor and emerged on the pyramid's opposite side.

No Tony.

Tourists milled around on the ground, pointing upward and shielding their eyes. The others in the LCT group clustered behind Mr. Lynch, wearing expressions of puzzled concern. Violet walked along the building to a third side of the structure. "Tony?"

"Violet!"

She jumped. Mr. Lynch exited the doorway behind her "Where is he?"

"I don't know. I stepped out, and when I came back in, he was gone."

"The paramedics are here. Check over there, I'll look here... he might've fallen again."

She searched the platform, went through the transverse passage of the temple, then walked around to the first side, where Tony had fallen. Seconds later Mr. Lynch emerged from the opposite side. "He's not—"

"Sir?" The paramedics drew up beside Mr. Lynch. "Where is the injured person?"

"He went in there for a minute, and then..." He lifted his hands, palms up.

"It's almost like he... disappeared," Violet said. "Vanished."

Another dizzy spell. Tony pressed his hands against the side of the temple. Thank God he was inside and couldn't fall again. For a second he thought he was going to puke, then the vertigo passed.

He slumped against the wall for a minute, the stone cool against his cheek and palms, then pushed himself off. The simple action took an incredible effort. Man, was he tired. Maybe he hadn't died there on the slope, but something sure as hell was wrong. Good thing the medics were on their way.

He took three steps to the temple's doorway, holding himself up with a hand on the wall. With the uncertainty of a man twice his thirty-six years, he wobbled and moved, but this time it was because of weakness and the strange, intense fatigue. God, he felt like hell. "Violet?"

No answer. "Keith?" Tony wrenched himself through the door. "Charlie?"

The platform was empty. Where had everyone gone?

He clutched the edge of the portal, panting. Man, did his head hurt. Like someone had swung a sledgehammer into his forehead. He slowly pulled himself around to the outside of the temple, more bumps and bruises announcing their presence with each move.

He leaned against the doorway. Even that took an incredible amount of strength. What the hell had happened to him?

His fall explained his pounding head and bruises. He'd thought he was dead for sure. But then someone had latched onto him and pulled him away from that light—

Bethany. He'd seen her. Then something pulled him back, like it wasn't his time to go after all.

But the weird tingly feeling that had come from the person's hands (Violet's?) and the dizziness... He'd watched a TV show about near-death experiences one time, but no one had mentioned anything like that.

Freaky things could happen with a brain injury. Like a guy on the news last summer who got hit in the head with a baseball, seemed fine other than a bad headache, then dropped dead six hours later. Maybe he was suffering hallucinations.

"Violet!" His voice was weak. He collapsed against the little building. The cry of a bird overhead made him look up.

Black and red painted stripes circled the top edge of the temple. The air in his lungs froze.

Those stripes hadn't been there before.

His gaze traveled down the unblemished staircase leading down the pyramid's clean, limestone side, clear even without his glasses.

No way. He was seeing things. That staircase had been ravaged beyond use. Maybe he'd emerged on one of the two restored sides. Sweat rolled down his face, its moistness cool in the breeze.

Someone shouted from below. He looked at the ground. Big mistake. He flattened himself against the wall and concentrated on its solid surface. Why had he let Charlie goad him into coming up here? Then a worse thought hit him. What if, for some reason, the medics couldn't come after him? Maybe they were already out on another call. Somehow he'd have to climb down those ninety-one steps by himself.

Steps that hadn't been there before. He hadn't gone more than a few strides into the temple, and he'd come out the same side. The sun was in the same position it had been before he went inside. But below, trees and vegetation blanketed what had been a meadow. A moss-darkened, stone roof topped the rows of columns he'd seen.

Tiny, brown blurs moved toward the pyramid. More yelling.

A hallucination. It had to be. Tony blinked twice, hard. *Wake up!*

Four people rushed up the steps, shouting angry-sounding words he couldn't understand. Blurs of brown coalesced into other colors. Red. Yellow. Spots of blue and green. On long tunics, not the T-shirts and shorts the people should have been wearing.

He'd been knocked out. Come to for just long enough to crawl back to the pyramid's summit. Those voices were really Violet, Keith, others in their group. Maybe the paramedics.

When the men reached him, two grabbed his arms and yanked him off the wall. Their guttural words sounded nothing like the Spanish he'd grown used to hearing the past few days.

He jerked his arm away. "Hey!" He twisted in their grasp, but their grip tightened, and the other two moved forward. "Let me go!"

He tried to fling his body to the wall behind him.

The men's harsh shrieks cracked in his ears. One man slapped him. Hard. His face stung.

"Hey—" Disbelief locked his jaw as the other two men grabbed his wrists and ankles, their sharp fingernails digging into his skin. Tony bucked against them. "Get off me!"

A man wearing a beaded necklace and a dark, fur cape loomed before him. He growled something threatening, then gripped a wad of Tony's shirt as if trying to tear Tony's heart out. Agitated jabbers ensued among the four men. The leader barked something incomprehensible and released Tony's shirt with a jerk. The hands on Tony's limbs tightened, and the men lifted him.

Dreaming, Tony reminded himself. The medics were probably loading him into the ambulance. But did they have to be so rough? And why couldn't he wake up?

He must've been injured pretty badly. His head no longer hurt, but maybe unconsciousness was his body's way of protecting itself. *Relax. Make the medics' job easier.*

The men half-dragged, half-led him around the corner of the pyramid to a side of the temple he hadn't seen. Huge, twin snake statues flanked the triple entryway. Did their menacing, fang-filled jaws hint at his own fate? Before his mind could process an answer, the men jerked him upright.

He hung in the men's grasp, too weak to resist further. The man in the animal pelt—probably a priest, the way the others deferred to him—walked around Tony, studied him, pawed at his clothing. He stopped, faced Tony, and drew a stone knife from a sheath at his waist. Murmurings rose from below.

The man gripped the knife in his fist with the blade pointing down. Fear crawled down Tony's throat as the man brought the knife closer, until the sharp, stone tip touched the placket of Tony's shirt. He wet his lips. *It's the paramedics. Doctors.*

The man drew the knife down, slicing Tony's shirt to the hem. The blade barely touched his skin. *What the—?* The two men beside him ripped the shirt off his back and tossed it to the floor, then the leader began to saw at the waistband of Tony's shorts.

The medics were cutting his clothing off. Looking for—or treating—other injuries. Injuries serious enough his mind had blocked them out in his semi-dream state.

A cut down each leg brought his shorts down. Next, the men lifted his feet and yanked his shoes off, then his socks, twisting an already-sore ankle. Shouts and catcalls from the ground told Tony a crowd had gathered. No, a two-way radio in the ambulance, the noise of traffic as it hurtled toward the hospital.

The priest peered at Tony's briefs with a cocked head and squinting eyes. Despite his rationalizations, Tony's groin clenched at the unpleasant sensation of reliving the old standing-in-the-school-hallway-in-your-underwear dream. The man with the knife growled something, then drew the blade up one of Tony's hips, then the other. Tony's underwear fell away, then the men dragged him to the edge of the platform.

A breeze caressed his naked body, oddly cold despite the blazing sun. *Dreaming, dreaming, dreaming.* He must be messed up really bad. Tony shut his eyes to stop the queasiness that rose in his belly when he saw how far away the ground was. His captors raised his arms, holding him upright as if presenting him to the multitude. A roar rose from the crowd.

Just a dream. And even if it wasn't, he was too tired and in too much pain to give a damn. *Just let me lie down.*

To his surprise, the dream granted his wish. The men yanked him through the portal and tossed him onto a raised, stone slab. Three of them held him down, then a strap of some kind bit into his right wrist as a man lashed it to the cool, hard stone.

The medics were tying him to a body board. At least he was out of the baking sun. He didn't struggle as the men bound each of his other limbs.

How badly had he been hurt? And when would they reach the hospital?

The thumping behind his brain grew louder. Drums. His headache returned, thumping in time.

What was happening? Maybe he was in surgery, and the doctors had a radio playing. Something with a heavy beat. It was filtering into his dream, and the yelling was conversation in the O.R. The drums and shouting stopped.

The man in the fur cape leaned over him, silhouetted in the three sunlit squares of the doorway. Strings of shells and stone beads rattled in his dark hair as he swayed from side to side and chanted. The four other men loomed behind him and did the same.

What were they doing in that operating room Tony couldn't see? What if he was having major surgery? He'd read about patients who'd been partly knocked out, enough they couldn't move or speak, but could feel every cut, every stitch. He felt each touch of the men's hands on his body, the swish of air as the priest's headdress swirled around.

The chanting stopped. The other men backed out of Tony's view. The priest thrust his arms skyward as he addressed the people below.

Sweat ran down the sides of Tony's forehead despite the shade. This had to be the most vivid dream he'd ever had. He opened his mouth to shout, speak, make any kind of noise but his throat had gone dry and nothing came out.

The leader fell silent and lowered his arms. Two of the other men reappeared at his sides. On the edge of Tony's vision, one raised a weapon that looked like a battle-axe. Dark stains—blood—flecked the stone blade. The tip of Tony's tongue pressed the back of his teeth.

They were going to behead him.

Wake up—wake up—wake up! Tony commanded himself but his body again refused to obey. *You're dreaming,* he reminded himself, but he was getting harder to convince. He shut his mouth, willing the saliva to flow so he could tell them he wasn't knocked out.

Trepidation crawled over his skin like a colony of insects as the leader uttered a word, then held something above Tony's sternum. The flint dagger.

This was no dream. It was the worst fucking nightmare he'd ever had.

Tony squeezed his eyes shut. *Wakeupwakeupwakeup!*

He opened his eyes.

The man in the animal skin held the dagger high above Tony, then in a single swift motion, plunged it into his chest.

The crack of bones. Blinding pain. Blood spurting everywhere. Screams. His own. Someone jammed a hand into Tony's chest, groping around. A high, keening wail. Himself.

Then merciful darkness.

Two

Tony vaguely remembered the nurse checking on him, giving him painkillers. An older man in a lab coat asked him questions like what was his name, and please count to ten, and how many fingers was he holding up.

"What is your day of birth?" the doctor asked in accented English.

"May first." Scratching sounds came from the nurse scribbling on a clipboard. "In Dayton, Ohio," Tony added. Maybe it would give him some kind of extra credit and make them leave him alone. Damn, he was tired.

Someone shouted from the hallway and they hurried away.

Tony's neck itched.

He started to lift his arm to scratch, but it was so heavy, he couldn't. He tried again. Shards of pain burst through his ribcage, like a dagger slicing through skin and muscle. The vise-grip on his brain tightened. He clenched his jaw and forced the leaden arm up farther.

A raised ridge marred the smooth skin of his neck. As he ran his fingertips over it, images burst through his mind *(huge stone axe... Mayan priest... flint knife)* in rapid succession.

His arm fell to the bed. *What the hell was that?* Beneath his ribs, pressure warred with the lightness one feels on a roller coaster the second before it plunges over the hill. "Excuse me?" he croaked.

The nurse returned to his bed. "Yes, Señior Solomon?"

"What's this... my neck?"

Her face twisted in puzzlement. "You don't know? Look like old injury to me."

Old injury? What was she talking about? "But I've never—what happened to me? What's wrong—"

She gave him a sympathetic smile. "You had bad fall, bruised ribs. Doctors say you are lucky man."

No wonder it felt like he'd been stomped on. "But why am I so tired?" And weak? And *(huge stone axe, knife ripping into him)* where had that come from?

"The pain meds. You feel better soon. Relax."

So the ancient Mayans had to have been a dream. But not all of it. He'd been injured. "But what happened to me?"

"You don't remember?"

He gripped the cool, cotton sheet, his hands damp. Panic speared his chest and spread until tendrils of ice lanced through his body. He did remember. But which of the images racing through his mind were memories, and which were only dreams?

He came to for brief periods throughout the next several days. Mostly he slept, his body so tired it was a monumental effort to lift his arm and scratch his nose. Keith had brought him his glasses, thank God. Dora visited several times. One time Tony woke and saw her and Charlie sitting in a pair of chairs pushed together, Charlie's hand resting on her knee.

Violet had come, too, during one of Tony's more lucid moments. She'd managed to find an English language bookstore, and had brought him a crime novel by one of his favorite authors. And when she'd realized his head still hurt, she'd volunteered to read to him. He'd still been in a mental fog, couldn't remember much except her low, throaty voice and her red-lipsticked lips forming the words as she read.

The memory took him back further, to Bethany's funeral, three years ago. He'd slipped out for some air, to find Violet in the parking lot, smoking. Not offering well-intentioned but meaningless platitudes like everyone inside, her lips closed around the cigarette, then released a puff of smoke while she listened to him vent about how everyone wanted him to let them know if they could "do anything" for him and Dora. "Nothing anyone can do," Violet had said, then she'd let him bum a cigarette off her, even though he hadn't smoked in years. A small act of kindness, like reading to him.

He squinted at Dora, who sat in the chair beside his bed reading a newspaper on her lap as she twisted her wedding ring around her finger. It never would have occurred to her to read to him.

"Hey." Tony pushed aside the image of his brother-in-law being a little too friendly with her. Must've been conjured up by his painkiller-fogged mind.

Dora looked up with a start. "You're awake."

"How long was I out?" Tony clutched the sheet beneath his hand—less tired now, but still weak.

"You've been mostly unconscious for nearly a week," she said. "The doctors are baffled—it's almost like you've been in and out of a coma, but they say the brain waves are more like you were in a really deep sleep. Like an animal in hibernation. Your temperature was low, and your pulse got so slow... nothing they did helped. They were afraid you wouldn't wake up. But then everything returned to normal this morning." She turned up her hands.

Tony's gaze traveled down the bed. What did all the weird stats mean? He definitely wasn't dead. But almost a week? "Then everyone else—"

"Left two days ago." Her fingers stilled, then she rose and walked around the other, empty bed. "Next year will be better."

He heard her unspoken words. *Another vacation ruined.* Last year, he'd had food poisoning. "Sorry," he grumbled. "It's not like I planned it."

Dora stopped her pacing, and drew a perfectly manicured nail around the Gucci watch he'd given her for Christmas a few years before. "I didn't mean..." Her expression was sympathetic, but he caught the hesitation in her reply.

She walked toward him. He focused on the ceiling. With his glasses on, he could see a chipped spot in the light fixture's frosted coating.

Dora walked back around the other bed. "They want to keep you another day for observation, then—if there's no change—they said you might as well go home."

"You mean transfer to a hospital in Dayton?"

"No." She stopped at his side. "We might have them re-run the tests, just to make sure. But they won't check you in when no one can find anything wrong with you, other than how tired you are."

She kept pacing back and forth along the empty bed. "You look a hundred times better than yesterday." She finally stopped and took the chair, staring down at her hands. The newspaper on her lap crackled as she twisted her wedding ring. "I don't know if I could stand it... losing you, after Bethany..."

Tony's throat swelled. He tipped his chin up. Bethany. Their only daughter. The day after his fall was the first time he'd gone a whole day without thinking of her, since the night nearly three years before, when she'd left a party with a couple of guys no one knew. Ironic— ever since she'd been diagnosed with diabetes at age five, he'd feared that would be what killed her. Not being murdered—

Bethany. He'd seen her. Heard her calling for him. In his dreams, before he woke up and crawled to the temple. Before the ancient natives killed him.

He remembered it with a clarity unlike anything he'd ever recalled in a dream. The silhouette of a young woman in the middle of that light. He'd barely been able to see her face in the incredible brightness, but it was her. Just as he remembered, forever frozen at age fourteen. Except she was even more beautiful. He'd wanted so badly to go to her...

A shout in the hallway yanked him out of his reverie. A woman yelled something in Spanish from the hallway.

"What the hell?" Tony muttered.

People in the corridor argued. An authoritative voice spoke a few sharp words, then the door opened.

A man wearing a beige, police-style hat marked *Seguiridad* approached Dora. "This person say he is family—"

A Mexican man burst in past the guard, gesturing wildly as he rapidly spoke in Spanish. As his eyes registered Tony's slack-jawed confusion, he switched to English. "My name is Luis Ramon DeSantiago. I am your brother." He approached the bed and reached for Tony.

"I don't have any brothers." Tony recoiled as Dora yelled for security.

"But you do. In Saturn Society—"

A guard appeared and grabbed him by the elbows. "¡Fuera de aquí!"

"Get him out of here!" Dora rose, clutching her newspaper. The intruder resisted, still facing Tony as a second guard arrived and the two dragged him to the door. "I must tell him what happened... beheaded..." DeSantiago's words faded as the guards thrust him out the door, slamming it behind them.

Dora huffed as she returned to her chair. "Hopefully that's the last of them."

"Last of what?" Tony's gaze darted to the door. "What's going on?"

"Reporters. Most of them gave up yesterday or the day before, but there's still a few persistent ones hanging around."

"What are you talking about?" Holy shit, what happened?

She regarded Tony with a solemn expression. "Don't you remember?"

"Remember what?"

"What happened at the ruins."

"I fell down and busted my head."

Dora made an exaggerated blink. "That's more than the doctor thought you'd recall. What else do you remember?"

"I was knocked out for a minute, then... I was burning up." Like his body had been made of paper, and the sun's blazing rays were about to set him aflame. "I pulled myself up the side and went into that little building…"

"And then?"

Images of the brightly clad Mayans of his dream burst through his mind. A blood-encrusted, stone battle-axe. The priest and his knife. Tony's stomach grew queasy. "Nothing," He turned up his hands.

"Dr. Santos says that's pretty common with head injury, not to remember what happened immediately before or after."

Just a dream. "So why are reporters hounding us?" He swallowed, his throat dry. "What did happen?"

She twisted her ring, then dropped her hands to her lap. "That woman…"

"What woman?"

"The I.T. girl. The heavy one."

"Violet," Tony said.

Her nose wrinkled for a fraction of a second. "Yes. She said after you fell and she caught you, you…"

"I what?"

"You… died."

Tony snorted. "Obviously she was mistaken."

"She insisted she lost your pulse for a few seconds."

"Then what?"

"Like you said, you came to, got up, and went inside the little building at the top. Like you were hardly hurt at all."

"Right." He remembered hearing Thelma from Finance asking the tour guide about the ancients who'd built the pyramid. "But then…?"

"She said she stepped out for a second, and when she turned around you were…" Dora held up her hands. "Gone."

"Gone?" A feeling swept over him of standing on a precipice with nowhere to go but over the edge. People did not just disappear. "But that's—"

"Crazy, I know. But they went over every inch of that pyramid. They even unlocked the gate into the chambers beneath it and searched in there. Then, a half hour later, there you were, inside the building at the top. Covered in blood, and not a stitch of clothing."

Naked. Blood. He squeezed his eyes closed, trying to shut out the sounds of his own screams, the image of blood fountaining from his chest as the priest slammed the knife down, in the second before he'd passed out. "Was it mine?" There had to be a logical explanation.

"Of course it was yours!" She slumped back in her chair and looked down, pressed her fingers to her forehead. "I'm sorry. It's just that—"

"What about my clothes?" His skin tingled at the memory of the men cutting off his shirt, shorts and underwear.

Dora's face hardened. "I imagine some little beggar brat picked them up. Made a nice haul on your gym shoes alone, I'm sure. Those things cost over a hundred—" She pressed her hand to her forehead. "I'm sorry, this is really stressful, that's all."

"Tell me about it." Covered in blood? He lifted his hand to his forehead and his fingers met with a short, raised area. He patted around it. As hard as he'd hit his head, it had healed remarkably well.

Dora shook her head. "That was just a little cut. Didn't even need stitches. Of course, any head injury can be serious—the doctor says even something small like that can kill a person, but..."

"Then where—"

"That's just it. No one knows. Other than that, you were just a little scratched and bruised up. Nothing major. Nothing that could account for so much blood." She rose and stood next to his head, peering down him. She walked to the foot of the bed, then back. "Of course, at the time, they didn't know that, so they brought you here on a body board."

When the men had tied him down to the altar in his dream. "And then?"

"When they cleaned you up... nothing. No open wounds, nowhere all that blood could've come from. Except for this weird scar around your throat..." She reached down and brushed a finger across his Adam's apple.

His hand flew up and clamped around her wrist *(huge stone axe)*. She snatched her hand away. "Does it hurt?"

"No. It just... what is it?"

He slowly lifted his fingers to his neck, but the instant he felt the thick, raised ridge, images of the axe, and blood, lots of it, burst through his mind again as a ripping, burning sensation built in his chest.

His hand dropped to the bed. "Is it... what does it look like?"

Dora's lips tightened. "It goes about halfway around your neck. Thick, like it was made with a... I don't know, a big blade of some sort. But the strangest thing is it looks... old. Like it happened years ago. Same with the one on your chest."

One on his—holy shit. This was way too weird.

He sat up. Man, he was so tired. Finally, he swung his legs over the side of the bed. "Help me." He reached for Dora.

"What do you need? I'll call the nurse—"

"No, just help me to the john." He had dim memories of being walked to the bathroom every now and then throughout the week. "The doctors said moving around will make me get better sooner."

She took his hand and helped him up.

He let go, then kept still for a moment. When he was sure he could stand unassisted, he shuffled to the bathroom and shut the door.

His legs wobbled. He clutched the sink, but thankfully, his feet remained planted on the cool tile. Before, it had been all he could do to take care of his needs before he collapsed, but he was getting stronger. He loosened his grip on the sink and studied his reflection in the mirror.

No trace remained of the tan he'd begun to acquire before his fall. His eyes stood out stark and bright blue against his pale skin. Dark circles rimmed his eyes beneath of his glasses.

He touched the bump above his eye, then his gaze traveled down to his throat.

A thick, silvery line ringed his neck, just like Dora had described. He ran a finger along it, but snatched his hand away as the images from his dream assaulted him once more. He forced the memories away and concentrated on the mirror.

The feeling of standing on a cliff returned, but this time the dirt was crumbling beneath his toes and he was plunging toward the distant ground. The scar was as thick as a pencil. A cut that could have been made by a big, stone axe. His so-called brother's words flashed through Tony's mind. *Beheaded...* Did the guy know something he didn't?

He fumbled at the ties of his hospital gown, until all but the top came undone, then pulled the fabric aside to expose his chest.

Dread filled him when the mirror confirmed his suspicion.

A jagged L-shaped scar marred his chest to the left of his sternum. Right where the priest in his dreams had driven the dagger into him. Like the line around his throat, it was lightened with age.

The Mayan priests... the axe and knife... the blood... what if it had all somehow been real?

Tony couldn't breathe. The second he'd pulled the black turtleneck over his head, the suffocation, the images of the stone axe, the priest looming over him, knife in hand—

Tony scrambled to get the shirt off, clawed at the armholes, clutched at the neck, then finally grabbed the hem and yanked it back over his head. Relief sluiced over him as his living room came back into view.

He fought to catch his breath. "I can't... wear this."

Dora stared, her chin lowered, then snatched the shirt from his hands with a sigh.

She stepped back, her brows furrowed as she studied the scar. "I think Thelma knows a good plastic surgeon—"

"No."

Tony couldn't do it. The thought of someone taking a knife to his throat made him want to curl into a ball and hide. He didn't care how highly skilled a surgeon they found, no one was cutting into him.

Whatever had happened to him, some part of it was real. To obliterate the evidence would be like covering up the discovery of a vital part of himself. Pretending nothing weird had happened at the ruins. Lying.

And the scar was his only proof he wasn't one hundred percent insane. "People will get used to it." Eventually. It had been a week since they'd gotten home, and his stomach still lurched every time he looked in the mirror.

Dora stuffed the shirt back into the bag and snapped her briefcase shut as the doorbell rang. "You're still too weak to return to work." He wanted to argue with her but she was right. He'd gotten up only an hour ago and all he'd done was watch sports news. Same thing he did every weekend or day off, but already he felt like taking a nap. Dora bent over him to brush her lips across his in a cursory kiss, then hustled out the back door as his sister Lisa sailed in the front.

Tony frowned after his wife. Dora had enough sick leave to stay with him instead of calling his sister, but of course she wanted to get back to work. He could almost understand, might have been tempted to do the same had the situation been reversed. Work was what they both did best.

Lisa leaned on the back of the recliner opposite him. "How'd your latest tests come out?"

"Everything's within normal range."

"I think you should get a second opinion."

"I've already gotten a second opinion. And a third, and a fourth." He'd been to the hospital a dozen times since he'd come home. They'd poked him, prodded him, hooked him up to monitors and run him through machines, some more than once. They still didn't have a clue what happened. Nothing to explain his extreme fatigue, or the temporary slowing of his metabolism, pulse and all.

"Maybe you should try the Cleveland Clinic."

"No." He'd been through enough. All he wanted was to go back to work and for things to get back to normal.

"But Tony—"

"I'm fine now, so what's the point?"

His sister's bespectacled blue gaze, so like his own, met his. "The point is that people don't hibernate. Metabolisms don't just drop for a week, then return to normal for no reason—"

"Look, if you just came over here to argue with me, then leave. I'm fine, okay?"

"Yeah, like you were fine after Bethany..." Lisa walked around Dora's recliner and sat.

"My blood pressure's fine." After he'd complained of daily headaches at their weekly dinner at their parents' a couple years ago, their mom had coerced Tony into seeing a doctor, who'd discovered his high blood pressure. By paying a little more attention to what he ate and making use of the company's exercise room, he'd quickly gotten it under control. "I haven't even had any headaches."

"Well, I guess that's good." Lisa grabbed the stack of newspapers from the coffee table and tidied them, putting the *Dayton Daily News* on the bottom, then the *Wall Street Journal*.

"I'm going back to work Monday," Tony said.

She stopped shuffling papers and frowned. "I don't think—"

"I'm fine," he insisted. "I sit at a desk all day. If I get worn out, I'll leave early. I'll feel better once I get back to work."

Lisa moved to Dora's magazine rack next to the recliner and pulled the magazines out. "Tony, you'll feel better when you get on with your life, not just get back to work. I mean, do your job, sure, but—"

"What do you mean, get on with my life?"

She tilted her head, leaned forward slightly. "You know, ever since Bethany."

At least Lisa said her name. His mother never did, like it was a forbidden word. Like he couldn't handle it. "I was getting on with my life just fine until this—"

"No you're not." Lisa's face grew stern. "You're going through the motions. Have been for three years, now."

He dragged himself off the couch and walked to the window. Behind him, Lisa shuffled through the magazines. "Hey, it's the dog lady," Tony said.

"Huh?" Lisa had begun to sort the magazines into three piles: one for *Redbook*, one for *Newsweek*, one for *Cosmopolitan*. He used to do the same thing himself until Dora said it drove her nuts and made him stop.

"She used to walk her dog up our street every now and then. No one around here has any idea who she is, she never talks to anyone. Just smiles. Probably been a good couple years since I've seen her." The tall, leggy blonde walked past the house, taking tiny steps as if to match those of the little white terrier at the end of a delicate-looking leash. "Last time, she had a dachshund." Like they'd had when they were kids. "Remember Sammy?" He forced a laugh. "You always hated it when Mom called him a wiener dog."

Lisa slid a *Cosmo* onto the stack of *Redbooks*. "Tony, what I said. Think about it."

"Put the *Newsweeks* on this side, and *Redbook* closest to her chair. *Cosmo* goes in the middle," Tony said. That was how he'd always done it.

"Tony Solomon, you will not change the subject on me." But she did as he asked.

"Then stop trying to judge me." Tony's face went slack. "You haven't followed a hearse up the hill to the cemetery with your kid inside..." He looked away and focused on the dog lady before the memory overwhelmed him. "I'm definitely going back to work Monday—"

The front storm door slammed. Tony and Lisa looked at each other, then Lisa jumped up and ran to the foyer. "Who is it?" Tony called as the door opened and shut.

Lisa returned, clutching a folded newspaper, which she thrust at Tony.

Tony groaned as soon as he glimpsed the masthead. *The National Weekly Star*, one of the last of the grocery store tabloids. As he took the paper, a card fluttered to the floor. "Who left it?

Lisa shrugged. "All I saw was a little blue car driving away."

Tony made a face at a grainy image of himself superimposed upon a jungle scene of scantily clad natives dancing around him, *El Castillo* in the background. *But they weren't dressed like that; they wore colorful robes and animal skins...*

In the dream, he corrected himself, resisting an urge to scratch his neck.

Disappearing Man Actually a Time Traveler, the headline read. "You've got to be kidding," Tony said.

"One of the more creative ones I've seen." Lisa grabbed one of Dora's *Cosmos* and flipped through it while Tony skimmed the article.

It began with a summary of his fall on the pyramid and subsequent disappearance. "One minute he was there, and the next he wasn't. It was like he disappeared into thin air," a woman (unnamed, of course) from a tour group stated. A description of the ensuing half-hour manhunt followed, then the weird stuff began.

"Tony Solomon didn't just disappear, he traveled back in time," the article quoted an also-unnamed anthropologist. When Tony read the next paragraph his skin grew clammy.

While not widely publicized, sources say a stone dagger, a never-before-seen artifact, was found lying beside the unconscious Tony Solomon. Its style and the decorative carvings on its handle link it to the Chichén Itzá population of approximately 900 A.D. It has been theorized that Solomon was captured by the prehistoric Mayans and sacrificed as an enemy. It's no wonder, as he had been wearing clothing typical of a modern American tourist.

"The priests and assistants would have stripped off his clothing, secured him to the altar, and cut out his heart as an offering to their gods," stated the researcher in his exclusive interview with the Star. "In addition, such sacrifices were often beheaded. The fact that Mr. Solomon was found totally nude and drenched in his own blood bears out this hypothesis."

With shaking hands Tony lowered the paper to his lap.

Lisa glanced up. "You all right?"

"Yeah... just tired." He pushed the paper off his lap. Time travel. Sacrifice. *No way.* The tabloid slid off the couch with a muffled crinkle. Lisa snatched it from the floor and added it to the stack of other newspapers on the coffee table, then bent to retrieve the scrap of paper she'd dropped when Tony took the tabloid. "This fell out of—"

Tony snatched the slip of paper. The plain, white business card bore a stylized image of a pocket watch with a Saturn ring, flanked by three stars. Beneath it, elegant, engraved-look type read *The Saturn Society, Charles F. Everly, Watchkeeper.* The card listed a Harrison Street address in Dayton, along with a phone number and web address.

Tony turned the card over, where someone had scrawled a handwritten note.

It's all real—we can help you. Call or stop by anytime.

Chad Everly

Tony snorted. He'd heard of this Saturn Society, but where?

He crushed the card, twisted around, and tossed it at the trash can just inside the kitchen doorway, where he made a perfect basket.

Help? Yeah, right. Whoever this Chad Everly guy was, and whatever this Saturn Society was, Tony did not need their help.

Three

ON MONDAY MORNING, BERNIE'S BAGEL & DELI WAS A GAUNTLET OF glances and whispers, of people staring, then ducking behind their newspapers. The normally comforting aroma of toast and cinnamon coffee soured in Tony's stomach.

He was a freak. The guy who disappeared. Or if one believed the tabloids, a time traveler.

Tony tried to ignore the stares as he approached the counter and studied the menu board, even though he knew the offerings and prices by heart, especially the most important: Specialty bagel with gourmet cream cheese, $4.00.

"Yo, Tony!" A stocky African-American man bustled out from behind the counter and grabbed Tony's hand. "How ya doin'?"

"Not bad, considering."

"Well, it's sure good to see you in here again." Bernie gave Tony's hand a brief shake. "What's it been, three weeks? After seeing the paper—"

Tony couldn't suppress a groan.

"Hey Jack!" Bernie yelled over his shoulder. "Hazelnut with extra cream, sesame with veggie! And the paper."

Tony waited while Jack fetched his coffee and the *Dayton Daily News*. Bernie took the next patron's order, and Tony finally relaxed when Jack slid a bagel onto a paper plate. Tony pulled out his wallet.

Bernie waved him off. "Today's on me."

Tony's hand paused in mid-air. "Thanks."

Bernie turned to ring up another customer, so Tony shoved his wallet back into his pocket, grabbed his tray, then headed for his usual table.

Two people were already sitting there.

Shit. Today, of all days, he needed the consistency, the sameness. Needed to sit at his table by the storefront window, just like he had almost every workday for the past three years, watching the traffic and people walking by on Seventh Street while he savored his coffee and perused the *Dayton Daily*.

"You okay, Tony?" Bernie said.

"Huh? Uh, yeah." He'd have to make do with the table on the other side of the door.

He'd just taken a seat when Bernie pulled out the other chair and joined him. "So what really happened to you in Mexico?"

"What did you hear—or read?"

The deli owner shrugged. "You fell down, busted your head, totally disappear, then show up a half hour later in a bloody freakin' mess."

"Then you know as much as I do."

"You're shittin' me," Bernie said, a little too loudly for Tony's comfort. Tony glanced around the restaurant. A man staring at him from the next table dove behind his newspaper.

"You don't remember nothin', huh?" Bernie asked.

"Nope. I blacked out, and the next thing I know, I'm in the hospital feeling like I just went ten rounds with King Kong."

"Man, that's bad news." Bernie squinted and leaned closer, his gaze locked on Tony's neck.

"I have no clue how it happened," Tony answered before Bernie could ask.

"No shit? That's wicked, man."

Tony fingered his collar, barely touching the scar. Sometimes he forgot about it until someone eyed him for a second too long. "It looks a lot worse than it is." It was, except for—

(Huge stone axe) He squeezed his coffee cup until it started to buckle, then forced himself to relax.

Bernie glanced at the growing line at the cash register and stood.

"Gotta run. Glad you're back." He hurried to the counter and resumed barking orders at Jack.

Tony propped his legs on the chair Bernie had vacated. He sipped his coffee and skimmed the first few pages of the paper, relieved to see that military action and a local crack house bust had replaced him in the headlines.

The return to routine comforted him, even without his regular table. The first bite of sesame-with-veggie was a godsend. He glanced at his watch. Seven thirty-three. He had to hurry. Keith didn't care if his execs weren't perfectly punctual, but it bothered Tony to be even a minute late.

He skimmed the headlines of the recent uprisings in Africa and the latest skirmishes in the Middle East while he finished off his bagel's upper half and started on the lower, just like he always did.

Something yipped from near the counter. Tony looked up.

A furry, white face peered out from a woman's handbag, the little terrier's bright, black eyes seemingly focused on Tony. The woman flipped a lock of long, blond hair over her shoulder as she reached into her bag, and recognition jolted Tony. The dog lady! He'd wait until she sat, then he'd go up to her, introduce himself, and ask her where he'd seen her, other than walking through his neighborhood. Or if she got her order to go, he'd catch her on her way out—

As she pulled her wallet from the handbag, the dog wriggled and popped over the bag's side. "Baby!" The woman crouched and grabbed, but the dog slipped through her grasp.

The woman rushed after it as it wove between tables toward the door. Tony tossed his newspaper down and leaped up to help, as other patrons did the same.

People scrambled as the dog dashed under chairs and between legs. "Baby! Here!" the dog lady shouted.

A white blur zipped toward Tony's table, and he bent, poised to catch it when someone opened the door to come in.

Tony grabbed. Soft fur slid through his fingers, but something caught. As he rose, the dog lady burst past—"Baby!"—and out the door.

Tony looked at what was in his hand. A blue, rhinestone-studded, leather collar. He reached for the door when vertigo burst through him. He caught the door frame and steadied himself as it passed, then hurried out. "Hey!"

A few patrons who'd followed the dog lady outside stood scattered along the sidewalk between Bernie's and the parking garage, gazing around with bewildered expressions. Tony ran up to the woman who'd been sitting at his usual table. "Where'd she go?"

The woman pointed to the parking garage. "She went that way." Her shoulders lifted, and she turned up her hands. "Then it's like, she disappeared."

Tony froze when he got off the parking garage elevator after work.

Someone was skulking around his car. The fourth floor was deserted, not unusual for after seven on a Thursday evening.

Tony slowly walked forward, squinting to see if he recognized the man.

The guy crept around the metallic blue Buick's front end. A little on the short side, olive-skinned, with a goatee and dark hair in a ponytail, wearing suede pants and a white, lace-up shirt, like he was Latino Daniel Boone or something.

Tony punched a button on his key fob, making the car's headlights flash. "Hey!"

The man straightened, then a smile slid across his face as Tony approached.

Apprehension stirred in Tony's gut. His footsteps rang on the concrete floor in short, sharp claps. *Just fucking great.* Probably another reporter, trying for a follow-up article.

Thankfully, the days had grown less eventful as Tony's first week back at work went on. Tony had left the dog collar at Bernie's, but the dog lady never returned. And as he'd predicted, the stares and questions had grown less frequent with each day. His energy had returned to normal, and so had everything else—or so he'd hoped.

He jammed his hand into his pocket as he neared his car, hoping the interloper would assume he carried a weapon.

"Tony Solomon?" The man held out a hand, revealing a shiny, silver dagger hanging from one side of his belt, and a pistol in a tooled leather holster on the other. "Are you Tony?" The man's smile was friendly. Too friendly.

Tony grabbed the cell phone in his pocket, thumb poised to speed-dial 9-1-1. "Who the hell are you?"

The man thrust his hand at Tony. "I'm with the Saturn—"

"I talked to the *Dayton Daily* last week." Tony released the phone and fingered his key chain.

"I'm not a reporter." The guy dug into his pocket and held out a business card.

Tony took the card but didn't look at it.

The man's smile remained fixed on his face. "My name's Chad Everly. I'm with—"

Tony's face went slack. "You're the one who left that tabloid at my house." He squeezed his keys. "What do you want?"

Everly's smile remained steady except for a contrite relaxing of his features for a fraction of a second. "Well, actually, that was my assistant. I was... *away* at the time, but she knew I wanted to talk to you. You're one of the highest-profile inductions we've had in years—"

"Induction?"

Everly held up a hand. "What we call when someone becomes one of us. My counterpart in Cancun tried to see you, but he couldn't get past security."

His self-proclaimed brother. Tony's face twisted. "What are you talking about?" He took a step backward. If that whack job wasn't standing between him and his car, Tony would've jumped in and gotten the hell away.

"I'm with an organization called the Saturn Society. We research time travel."

Tony's mouth clamped shut. Definitely nuts.

Everly walked around to Tony's other side. "I know what happened to you in Mexico."

Tony watched him, not wanting to blink. "What do you want?" The top of his head tingled. Why was he encouraging the guy? His fingers twitched on the car keys.

The man's gaze settled on Tony's neck, making Tony wish he were a turtle and could pull it in. "You were beheaded, weren't you?" Everly asked. "That must've been unpleasant."

Unpleasant? The tingle in Tony's scalp grew into an itch. He forced himself not to scratch. What did this guy know? And how? Those people in Mexico had tied him down, driven a knife into his chest, and presumably chopped off his head, and this guy thought it was *unpleasant?* Then Tony caught himself. What was he thinking? "Beheaded?" He forced a laugh, but it sounded fake. "If I was beheaded, how the hell am I standing here now?"

Everly tilted his head, his smile patronizing, as if explaining the obvious to a child. "You can't die before you're born, can you?" Tony stepped back. The man went on. "When you die in the past, it brings you back to the present—"

"That's the most ridiculous thing I've ever heard."

Everly looked at the ground, chuckling. "Denial. We've all gone through it." He looked up, meeting Tony's eyes. "But once you accept it, you'll see. Time travel's one of the greatest—"

"Time travel? You've been reading too many tabloids."

"That's what happened, you know. You went back—"

"Yeah, sure. I got bonked on the head and went back in time. Hah."

Everly laughed. "That only happens in books and movies. No, it's the power of your own mind that took you back." His face grew solemn. "Look, I know you're confused and frightened. But we can help you. Once you learn about time travel, you'll find it's incredible." He stepped closer, spreading his hands in an encompassing gesture. "Any time, any place, all at your disposal. All you have to do is... imagine." The smile took over his face again, and Tony's world narrowed to nothing but that lustrous grin hovering in a vacuum, inches from his face.

A car went past on its way to the exit, its breeze chill on Tony's clammy skin. He took another step backward. "You're a fucking lunatic." He jammed the business card into his pocket, punched the unlock button on his key chain, and pushed past Everly to yank the car door open.

"No I'm not, and neither are you." Everly's voice was calm. "Call me or stop by when you want to talk."

Time travel? Tony snorted. "Yeah, right." He slid behind the wheel. "I don't think so."

"You'll come." Everly leaned closer as Tony's hand froze on the car door handle. "Because like it or not, you're one of us."

Dora sat on the family room sofa, talking on the phone when Tony walked in. "Listen, that's him now. Yes, I'll tell him." She tossed the phone onto the end table as if it burned her hand.

"Who was that?" Tony put down the boxes of takeout food he'd picked up, after he'd convinced himself Everly was either a nutcase or a reporter who'd hoped a more creative cover story would catch Tony off guard.

"Charlie. He called to ask how you were doing."

"Isn't he out of town this week?"

She nodded. "He says he's glad you're feeling better."

Tony hung up his coat. "You had dinner yet? I picked up Happy Hunan on the way home."

"I had a late lunch. Just stick mine in the fridge."

He did, then brought his into the family room to eat while he watched the news.

"Did you pick up the dry cleaning?" Dora asked.

Tony grimaced. *Damn.* "I forgot."

"Oh. I was planning to wear my teal suit for the divisional accountants' meeting tomorrow." She sighed. "I guess I'll come up with something else."

He flopped into the recliner and watched her out of the corner of his eye as he ate. She grabbed a copy of *Cosmo* out of the magazine rack. With two closets full of clothes, why did she need the teal suit? Besides, she'd change her mind three times before she left for work in the morning anyway. He voiced neither of these thoughts. It would only cause a confrontation. "Another reporter waylaid me in the parking garage today," he said instead.

"Uh-huh," Dora said, her attention on *Cosmo*.

"This guy was a real weirdo..."

Dora flipped through her magazine without looking up.

Why bother?

Their marriage wasn't bad by any means, but it seemed all they did together any more was sit in front of the television. It had grown worse after Bethany's death, as Dora coped by taking pills and sleeping her grief away, Tony by working late and traveling, or trying to lose himself on the golf course.

They didn't fight. They didn't talk. They didn't... much of anything. Except sit and watch TV.

He slurped down his food, trying to pay attention to the news, but he couldn't keep his mind off Everly. *All you have to do is imagine...*

Yeah, right. The guy was a nut, someone who'd read too many sensational stories. On TV, the newscasters mourned a community activist who had been killed two years before on that date. The murderer had never been caught.

If Tony believed that crackpot in the parking garage, he could go back. Find out who'd done it. Tony's lip curled. Yeah, right, go back two years. What had Everly said? *Any time, any place, all at your disposal.* Why would he want to go back in time? Living through it once was enough.

He stole another glance at Dora, who was still engrossed in her magazine. "...on March eighteen, two years ago," the newscaster said. *March eighteen, two years ago, huh?* Vertigo seized him. He gripped the armrests on the recliner to remain upright. His head wobbled, then the feeling passed.

"Tony? Are you all right?" Dora said, a glass of wine halfway to her mouth.

Huh? Tony searched the area around her chair. She hadn't been drinking wine a moment ago, and the magazine she'd been reading was now nowhere in sight. And she'd been wearing a green blouse, not a light blue sweater.

What the hell? "Yeah, I'm fine." Maybe her glass had been sitting on the end table beside her and he hadn't noticed. Maybe she'd dropped the magazine on the floor beside her chair, where he couldn't see.

But what about her clothes? Maybe that Everly guy with his talk of time travel had shook Tony up more than he thought. Or maybe he'd imagined the green outfit. He let out a big sigh and hauled himself up from the recliner, amazed at how difficult it was. He hadn't been this tired since his first few days in the hospital. "Man, I don't know what it is, but all of a sudden I'm totally wiped out. I think I'll hit the bed early tonight."

He trudged down the hall, stopping to lean against the doorframe leading into his bedroom. What was going on with him? Maybe something was still wrong, never mind that the doctors had never been able to figure out anything.

The five steps to his bed seemed like a mile. Like the first time he'd walked to the john at the hospital in Cancun.

He lay on the bed. Just for a few minutes to muster up some energy. Then he'd get up, brush his teeth and get undressed—and pray he didn't sleep for five days this time.

Dora did a double take when Tony stumbled into the bathroom the next morning. "You really were tired last night, weren't you?"

He reached down to slip off his underwear, but his hand met with the metal and leather of his belt instead. He looked down. He'd slept in his clothes. "Damn, I guess I was."

He patted down the front of his light blue oxford-cloth shirt, touched the logo of one of LCT's technology contract firms embroidered on the pocket. Then he brushed a hand over his casual, relaxed-cut pants.

Not the dress shirt and slacks he'd worn the day before.

"You're not coming down with something, are you?"

"I- I don't think so." Tony undid his belt and undressed to shower. The different outfit was freaky, but physically, he felt fine. Whatever its cause, his heavy sleep had rejuvenated him.

The water woke him the rest of the way. He lathered up his hands and started to wash.

When he slid his hand over his chest, he noticed something else.

No raised line where the scar was.

The soap slipped out of his hand. He looked down at his chest, but without his glasses, couldn't see anything but a light blur of hair and bubbles.

He felt around again. His hand slid smoothly over his chest.

The scar was gone.

He reached up to his neck. The skin was smooth beneath his sudsy fingers. *No way.* He jerked his hand back to his chest, felt around. No scar. He drew his hand around his neck three times. Nothing but a day's growth of beard. As if the scar had never existed.

"Hope your meeting goes well," Dora called. "See you later."

"Uh, yeah, sure." Her blurry shape moved across the textured glass of the shower stall door. Tony looked down at his chest, then picked up the soap. Both scars, gone. "Dora?"

No answer. She'd already left. He quickly rinsed off and stepped out of the shower.

He grabbed his glasses and checked the mirror. No scars.

A quick glance at his watch lying next to the sink told him he didn't have time to ponder the matter if he wanted to make the eight-fifteen leadership meeting on time.

He threw on some underwear then strode to the closet and grabbed the first pair of pants he touched. He hesitated. Where were his dress slacks? He flipped through a dozen pairs of casual trousers, several of which he could've sworn were too tight and Dora had given to AMVETS. Finally he found his suits, way in the back, and grabbed a navy one he was sure she'd gotten rid of ages ago.

For the hell of it, he slipped the pants on. They fit.

While he knotted his tie, he stared in the mirror at his unblemished neck with growing unease. Was he cracking up? Had he imagined the last three weeks?

He put his socks and shoes on. He was glad the ugly scars were gone, but what did it all mean? Then a frightening, yet exhilarating thought struck him. Maybe he hadn't dreamed he'd met a horrible death at the hands of the ancient Mayans. Maybe he'd dreamed it all. The trip to the ruins, the hospital, his scars. Everything. Including that kook Everly in the parking garage.

There was no other logical explanation.

Pleased he'd figured it out—and relieved his mind had conjured those unpleasant past three weeks—he combed his hair (*wasn't there a little gray yesterday?*), washed his glasses, and headed for the kitchen to grab his briefcase.

A piece of paper lay on the table next to it. He picked it up. An e-ticket airline itinerary. For him, leaving Dayton at 7:55 A.M. for New York, and returning at 11:18 that night. *What the hell?* He wasn't traveling that week. Then he read the itinerary again. *Huh?* The ticket was for two years ago. To the day.

He'd probably had a one-day meeting with one of the LCT ad agencies there. One they no longer used, since Tony had convinced Keith there was plenty of talent to be found in Dayton without the cost and hassle of travel.

He always gave Dora his itinerary when he traveled. Maybe she'd cleaned out her attaché after he went to bed, and found the printout wedged inside a pocket she seldom used.

He wadded it up and tossed it in the trash.

At Bernie's, his unease grew when he walked right up to the counter. No line. How long had it been since he'd seen that? And fewer than half the tables occupied?

He searched for the pudgy, black guy who'd become his occasional sports bar buddy in the two years since opening the deli on Seventh Street, but Bernie was nowhere in sight. Then a tray full of fresh bagels, carried by a pair of dark hands, appeared in the doorway.

"Hey, Bernie," Tony called.

Bernie put the tray down, revealing a much thinner frame than Tony remembered. "Hey, yourself. What can I get you?"

What the hell? Did Bernie have a skinnier twin? Tony drew back. Bernie didn't have a brother, only sisters. Then what—

His friend gave him a pointed stare. "Uh... the usual, of course," Tony said.

"Which is?" Bernie leaned on the counter.

Tony gave a little laugh. "Come on, Bernie."

Bernie's brows lowered. "I got dozens of customers who all got a usual. What'll you have?"

Tony chewed the inside of his lip. How the hell had Bernie dropped fifty pounds since yesterday? "Ah... sesame with veggie and a large hazelnut coffee, extra cream. And the *Dayton Daily News.*"

He drew out his wallet as Bernie punched the keys on the cash register. "Three sixty."

"Three—you running a special?" He gazed up at the wall menu. Sure enough, it read "Specialty bagel with gourmet cream cheese, $3.60." His stomach rolled. His usual had gone up to four dollars over a year ago—

"Hey." Bernie held out his hand, palm up. "Three-sixty. You don't like it, you can—"

"No! No, that's fine." Tony yanked out a five and dropped it on the counter.

"Hey, Christie," Bernie yelled. "Sesame with veggie!"

Christie? Must be new. Tony watched the blonde scoop out the cream cheese as Bernie grabbed the coffeepot and filled a large cup. How had he lost all that weight? Even surgery couldn't take off fifty pounds in a day.

Bernie pushed his order across the counter and turned to the next customer. Tony forced an impassive face as he reached for his tray.

He'd go to his table and read the paper, just like he always did. And when he got up to leave, Jack would be back, Bernie would yell good-bye to him, and everything would be back to normal. He was imagining things.

Bernie shot Tony a dirty look. Tony grabbed his tray and headed for his usual table by the window. It wasn't unlike Bernie to mess with him. Only it was usually something like "Sorry, Tony, we're out of sesame today, how 'bout onion instead?" knowing Tony hated onion. Then when Tony had resigned himself to plain, Bernie'd laugh and pull out a bin full of fresh sesame bagels. *Must just be having a bad day.*

Tony sat at his table—thankfully unoccupied—and propped his feet up. Whatever had pissed Bernie off, he'd get over it.

Tony took a bite of bagel then flipped the paper over to skim the headlines. *Thousands of Filipinos Flee Volcano. Activist's Death not an Accident. Warmer Weather to Return this Weekend.* Tony did a double take. Activist? Frowning, he skimmed the story. According to the article, the crusader had been killed last night—not two years ago. And the volcano story sounded oddly familiar, too.

He started to turn the page to read the rest of the article about the activist. Maybe it was a reprint, but on the front page? His hand stopped mid-flip.

No. No, no, no! The bite of bagel in his mouth turned to concrete. He stopped chewing, his tongue dry. His stomach bottomed, and the bite of bagel threatened to choke him.

The date beneath his finger read March 19. Two years ago.

Four

I HAVE NOT GONE BACK IN TIME. I HAVE NOT GONE BACK IN TIME. I HAVE not gone back in time. Tony walked down the street to the office. Everything would be okay once he got there. He'd misread the date in the paper. Imagined Bernie's weight loss. Maybe Bernie'd fired Jack—sometimes the kid slacked—and that's why he'd been so brusque.

But things got weirder when Tony reached the office. The receptionist gave him a puzzled look as he walked past her desk.

"Hi, Sarah," he said. *Weird.* Her hair had definitely been grayer the day before. She must have colored it, but hadn't done a very good job, for some of the gray still showed.

"Tony? I thought you were out today. Miss your flight?"

Flight? *The itinerary.* He mumbled something about changed plans and hurried to his office. Once inside, he shut the door, something he rarely did.

He walked to his desk, dreading what he'd find.

Breathe in. Breathe out. Stop and think.

He decided to do what he always did as soon as he arrived at work. His stomach settled a little as he hung up his coat on the middle hook behind the door, sat at his desk, and turned on the computer to check email.

The computer rejected his password.

He tried again, typing slowly to ensure he didn't fat-finger it. No go. After a third failure, he grabbed the phone and punched in Violet's number.

A man answered. "I.T. Support, Pete speaking."

Tony scrutinized the display on his phone. He'd dialed the right number. Maybe Violet had gone to the john. "Is Violet around?"

"Violet? You must have the wrong number, sir. This is I.T. Support—"

"Yeah, I know. Is Violet there, please?" He twisted the phone cord in his fingers. He always forgot his new password after he changed it each month, and Violet gave him less shit about it than the other techs, so he preferred to deal with her.

"Um, the only Violet I know is in food services. Is there something I can help you with?"

Food services. Where she worked two years ago.

By the time Pete reset the password, Tony had the phone cord wrapped so tightly around his wrist it was starting to cut off his circulation.

The calendar view in his email program displayed March from two years ago, and showed him as out of the office for the meeting in New York.

He grabbed the phone and punched in the ad agency's number, but as he waited for someone to answer, a horrible thought occurred to him. What if another Tony Solomon, a two-years-ago-version, had caught the flight as scheduled, and was already there? *Damn.* He pressed his palm to his forehead.

He started to hang up, but the agency receptionist answered. He explained that he'd missed the plane.

"No problem, Mr. Solomon," she said. "I'll let them know."

Tony exhaled as he hung up. *Well, that's one question answered.* One down and about a million to go.

Throughout the morning he pushed his chair away from his desk every now and then, closed his eyes, and concentrated on the present—or rather, two years in the future, if he'd really gone back in time. He concentrated on the one thing in his office that would have changed—his desk calendar, which should have been *Dilbert*, but now featured *The Simpsons*—which his Grandma Anderson had given him for Christmas, a year before she passed away—which should have been last year.

Nothing happened.

So much for that Everly guy's "all you have to do is imagine."

On the other hand, dreams didn't usually make sense.

Maybe he had to let the dream—or so he hoped it was—run its course. By eleven he could no longer ignore his growling stomach, so he headed for the cafeteria.

The room was empty aside from two employees at a table by the far window, where a few stray snowflakes fluttered to the flat roof of the building next door. Violet stood behind the cafeteria counter's glass hood. *Oh, no.* Tony's steps faltered, his appetite vanished, but she'd already seen him. "Hello, Mr. Solomon." She flashed him a wide smile. "Chili or vegetable soup?"

He forced a chuckle. "Violet, I told you you could call me To—" One of the men by the window rose to get a napkin. Tony did a double take. Keith had fired Bentley over a year ago.

"Mr.—Tony?" Violet's lips turned up a fraction. She tipped her chin down, then brought her gaze up to meet his. Warmth radiated from the half-circles of her golden-brown eyes showing beneath her thick lashes. "Chili or vegetable?"

"Oh, sorry. Chili, please."

Weird. Violet knew he always chose chili. He felt like he should say something more. Keith had told him she was the one who'd grabbed his ankle when he fell on the pyramid, possibly saving his life.

But the Violet who now ladled chili into his bowl hadn't yet gone to Mexico, wasn't yet the woman who'd come to his hospital room and read to him. A kindness he couldn't forget.

At least she hadn't changed. She wore her white chef's apron over a blouse and red plaid skirt that was dressier than her job demanded, her long hair pinned up in a bun. "Would you like anything else?"

Yeah, how about some sense to this crazy day, please. But Tony simply thanked her for the food and paid, then took it back to his office.

He hardly tasted the chili as he sat at his desk, with his two-year-old calendar staring him in the face. Had he traveled in time? Maybe that Everly guy wasn't such a nut after all. What if it was real?

It was like he'd stumbled onto a line in the sand, and he, ordinary-guy Tony Solomon, had just stepped over it.

My God, what have I gotten into?

What if he was stuck, and had to relive the entire two years?

Bethany was still dead; her murder had still happened. Those two years had slipped by in a mire of work, golf and boring nights watching meaningless television.

Everly! Tony jerked out of the slump he'd fallen into and dug out his wallet, where he'd stuck the card out of habit.

But none of the thirteen cards inside were Everly's. *Idiot.* Of course it wouldn't be in this wallet. Because if he'd really gone back in time two years, he hadn't yet met the man.

We can help you, Everly had said.

Maybe it was time to find out. But first, Tony would do a little research, and make sure it wasn't a scam.

He turned to his computer and did a search for the Saturn Society. The first hit was for a non-profit organization dedicated to the study of time travel.

He clicked the link. It existed all right, and "Find a Society House" returned the same Harrison Street address he remembered from Everly's card. A map pinpointed it in the neighborhood known as the Ghetto, between downtown and the University of Dayton. The rest of the information on the site was useless and vague, or required a login.

Tony grabbed the phone and started to punch in the number beside the listing, then hesitated.

In this time, Everly would have no idea who he was. He wouldn't give out much information by phone, if any. Tony hung up, then grabbed his coat. He'd use his lunch hour to check out this Saturn Society, whatever it was. And figure out what Everly had meant when he'd told Tony "Like it or not, you're one of us."

Storm clouds were gathering overhead as Tony left the office, but Harrison Street wasn't far. He could check the place out and be back before bad weather hit.

He parked across the street from the red brick Victorian house. The three-story structure loomed above him as he crossed the road. 140 Harrison Street's well-maintained exterior and tidy front lawn contrasted sharply with the surrounding properties. Two of the windows on the second floor had been filled in, judging by the rectangles of lighter brick.

A dark cloud drifted across the sun, and a sense of foreboding settled over him, like he was about to be tossed into a den of lions.

He gave himself a mental shake. It's just a house, for God's sake!

His legs wouldn't move. *Why am I here?* a little voice inside his head asked.

To get some answers, dammit!

But he still wouldn't—or couldn't—move. *No reason to be here. What am I doing?*

He took a step closer to the porch, but that other... *presence* inside his head—he could think of no other way to describe it—continued to balk. *What the hell?*

He stopped trying to force himself to move and stared down at the pocked cement of the sidewalk. A line of ants trailed busily into a raised, dirt anthill in a crack. On the street, a big, black SUV approached. Slowly, as if the driver were looking for something,

Or watching him.

Tony glanced up. Wasn't that Keith Lynch's truck?

The SUV trundled past, not slowly enough for Tony to get a glimpse of the driver.

Don't be ridiculous. What would Keith be doing in this neighborhood?

This time travel stuff was weirding him out, making him paranoid. *Go to the house. See what it's all about.*

No reason to be here, he argued with himself. *Go back to the office.*

It was as if two of him resided in his head at once. A past-self and a present-self? Or rather, a present-self and a future-self?

Crazy.

So is standing here like an idiot, his resistant self said.

A white, lace curtain fluttered in one of the house's first floor windows.

Someone was watching him.

Leave. Now. Before they think you're casing the joint and call the cops.

His legs obeyed the small voice, and he strode back down the sidewalk toward his car.

As he stepped off the curb, the black SUV came careening around the corner.

All Tony saw was the silver grille and a Cadillac emblem bearing down on him.

As Tony emerged from the elevator on the parking garage's fourth floor—after six again—a black SUV trundled down the spiral exit ramp from the floor above.

Tony tensed. Had whoever it was come back for him, after his near miss in front of the Saturn Society house?

He waited while the truck rolled down another loop, and as he glimpsed the Ford emblem on its tailgate, he let out his breath.

On the way home, he picked up dinner at Happy Hunan. He could eat Chinese almost every day, but Dora...

Depending on her mood, she'd complain or tell him to save it for tomorrow. Either way she'd say something if he brought Chinese takeout two days in a row. *If* he'd actually done so. Two years ago, he might not have. One way to find out.

When he got home, a silver Lexus sat in the driveway, blocking him out of the garage. Charlie's. *What the hell?* Lisa had choir practice at church every Tuesday night. And they never showed up at Tony's house unannounced.

Unless... He remembered the hospital in Mexico. Charlie sitting with Dora, his hand on her knee. But if he'd really gone back in time, that hadn't happened yet. And he still wasn't sure he hadn't imagined it. Maybe Lisa's choir practice had been canceled.

He parked beside Charlie's car and walked to the front door, conscious of placing one foot in front of the other, unable to get the picture of Charlie and Dora out of his mind. His wife and Charlie. *Oh, come on!* He was still freaked out by all the weird, two-years-ago stuff, not to mention almost getting run down by that SUV on Harrison Street. Maybe Dora had made plans with Lisa and Charlie, and hadn't mentioned it since Tony had expected to be out of town.

His hand trembled as he placed it on the doorknob and slowly turned it. At a gentle push, the door swung open without its usual squeal.

He took a hesitant step inside, then another. The carpet muffled his footsteps through the foyer. Before he turned the corner, a familiar giggle made him stop. It wasn't his sister's.

Dread lanced through his middle like a giant fist strangling him. *God, no.* They had to be watching TV. Laughing at some stupid sitcom.

More giggling. "That tickles," Dora said.

"A bad tickle, or a good one?" Charlie's voice.

"Mmm.... good. Very good." Dora sighed.

Tony put a hand to the wall and leaned on it. He could feel his heartbeat in his throat. *No.* He was imagining this. And the date on the paper. His email. Dora's blue sweater. Everything.

"Mm," Dora said. "Oh, yes." Louder. "Don't stop, it feels so good."

It couldn't be. No. They wouldn't. They couldn't. *Turn around, walk out. Then come back in.*

Tony's feet didn't obey. Instead, he continued to the living room, unable to take a breath, feeling like someone had punched him in the chest.

Finally a big gulp of air rushed into his lungs. He forced his feet to move until he rounded the corner.

Dora lay on the couch, facing him, but Charlie hovered over her, blocking her from view. Lisa was nowhere in sight. His brother-in-law wore nothing but his underwear and socks. Dora's bra, blouse and skirt lay in a heap on the floor, mingled with the rest of Charlie's clothing. Tony's mouth slid open as the other man bent over his wife to suckle on her breast. The bag of food fell from his hand and struck the floor with a muted crash.

Dora jerked upright, pushing Charlie back. Her eyes met Tony's. The color drained from her face. "Oh my God."

Charlie turned around. "Oh fuck." His face fell slack.

Tony's mouth moved but nothing came out.

"It's not what it looks like!" Charlie leaped off the couch and faced Tony, raising his hands, palms out.

Tony found his voice. "Then what is it? You're telling me you're not fucking my wife?"

"Wh- what are you doing here?" Dora whimpered. A ball of fire formed in Tony's chest, one he didn't know if he wanted to hurl at her or at his brother-in-law. *You fucking bastard.* Unable to speak, he clenched his fist. Wanted to deck Charlie, send him flying across the room. Dora huddled in a ball at the far end of the couch. Tony lowered his hand. The bastard wasn't worth it.

Charlie mumbled something. Tony spied a wallet and keys on the coffee table. He strode over and picked them up, then threw them at Charlie. They hit his chest and slid to his feet. Tony spoke quietly. "Get the hell out of my house."

Charlie scooped them up along with his clothes and bolted out the door.

Tony stared at the door. Dora moved off the couch and crouched on the floor, picking up her blouse. "I can't believe this!" Tony watched her with his mouth open, more words to say but none came out for several seconds. "I can not. Fucking. Believe this," he finally repeated.

"I- I can explain." She struggled to slip her arm into the blouse.

"You're fucking your goddamn boss—my sister's husband!—while I'm conveniently out of town and she's at church, for God's sake. What's to explain?" His fists curled and uncurled.

"Tony, I..." Her arm finally found the sleeve. "I'm sorry. I'm so sorry. I was just... always alone, and he stopped by—"

"This isn't the first time, is it?"

She stopped fumbling at the buttons and looked down. "No," she whimpered. A choked sniffle came from her.

Tony muttered a few more choice words then whirled around. Vegetable lo mein squished beneath his foot as he walked out the door, which Charlie had failed to shut.

"Tony! Wait!" Dora yelled. He opened his car door. She ran into the driveway, clutching her blouse shut. "Please... we can talk—"

He stopped. "I can't." She should've talked a long time ago. Who knew, maybe there'd been others besides Charlie.

Tony got in the car and slammed the door. He couldn't deal with her now. Talk could come later.

Bang. Bang. Bang. The sound crept into Tony's dream. He was firing a gun; although he couldn't see the target, didn't even know what he was firing at. The gun fired again *(Bang! Bang!)* and again—

He jerked awake. Squinting, he peered around the room. The setting sun speared splashes of light on cream-colored walls with kids' pictures. His parents' house, where he'd gone to sleep off his night spent with a bottle of Crown Royal in a motel, having forgotten that his folks were in Vegas. They went every year in March for their birthdays, which were a week apart.

Bang. Bang. It was someone knocking on the door. "Tony!"

His sister.

He heaved himself off the couch. As soon as he yanked the door open, Lisa stumbled inside and threw her arms around him, burying her face in his chest. "Charlie told me everything." Her shoulders shook, and Tony patted her back, unsure of what else to do or what to say. "He... he stayed with a friend last night, but I know he'll come home after work, and I.... I just needed to be away." She pulled back. "Where've you been? I tried to call..."

Tony's mouth tightened. "I left my phone in the car." Because if Dora had tried to call him, he didn't want to talk to her. Although when he'd gotten into his car at the motel that morning, there had been no need to worry—the only missed calls were Lisa's. Which he'd planned to return after he got some sleep.

Lisa followed him into the living room, where he sank back into the sofa. She perched on the edge of their dad's leather recliner. "What are you going to do?"

"I don't know. Right now, all I know is I feel like hell." Tony covered his eyes with his arm.

"You look like it too." She sniffed, and her upper lip twitched. Tony rolled over, facing the sofa back, but the lecture never came. The leather rustled as she stood. "Why don't I see what they've got to eat around here."

Ten minutes later he woke to the scent of hamburger and the clink of Lisa setting two plates on his mom's glass-top coffee table. His head throbbed in protest as he heaved himself upright and mumbled his thanks to his sister. As he ate, his headache abated.

Lisa sat in the recliner, elbows braced on her knees. "Charlie called me from work today," she said as Tony took the last bite of his burger. She'd only taken two bites of hers. "He wants to go to counseling."

Tony lifted an eyebrow. "Do you?"

"I don't know." She picked at a hangnail. "But it's not about me."

Tony managed a nod. Lisa's sons were fifteen and seventeen; Bethany was right between them... or had been.

"I never had a clue. He said he was working late, and..." Lisa rested her forehead on her hand. "I believed him." She looked up. "Did you? Have any idea, I mean?"

Tony popped a potato chip into his mouth, never taking his gaze off his plate. "Yeah, but I didn't think anything of it at the time."

"When?"

"When I—" A chunk of potato chip he thought he'd swallowed lodged in his throat. He took a swig of Coke, and the chip washed down. He wiped his mouth on his sleeve. "They came to—" He started coughing, unable to stop.

Lisa jumped up and slapped him on the back. "Are you okay?"

He took a deep breath. "I saw them..." *In the hospital. In Mexico,* he wanted to say, but the words wouldn't come out, as if some unseen force were preventing it.

Like at the Saturn Society. The other presence—his past self, or rather, the Tony that belonged in this time, who hadn't yet time-traveled, and wouldn't let him—

"You saw them..." Lisa made a rolling motion with her hand.

"Together. I can't remember where." The lie stung his throat, even though the truth wouldn't come out. Didn't make sense, and wouldn't for another two years. "Charlie... he had his hand on Dora's knee, thought I wasn't looking." Tony let out a breath. At least he'd been able to say that much. He studied his shoes. "In a way, I can't blame her. I mean, ever since Bethany... Dora said I was never there. And she was right."

"Maybe. But what's my husband's excuse?" Lisa went on about how she knew she'd probably be better off without Charlie if it weren't for the boys. Tony listened and nodded, then his jaw went slack.

The walls had changed. Instead of the cream color they'd been before, they now gleamed reddish-brown in the setting sun slanting through the window. And where did Lisa go?

Tony leaned on the armrest to get up, and his hand met with woven cloth. He looked down. An old-fashioned floral print. Not the brown leather he'd been sitting in before—

Lisa rose from the recliner—where she hadn't been a second ago—and collected the dishes. "I'm sorry, I'm sitting here blathering. You've got to be tired."

Tony's mouth snapped shut. The walls were once again cream-colored, and the furniture, back to the old leather stuff.

And his headache was back.

Lisa disappeared into the kitchen. Water ran and dishes clinked. Hoping to dull the pounding of his head, Tony lay back down on the sofa, facing out. The walls remained cream-colored.

He hadn't imagined the change. That maroon color was what his mom had painted them—or *would* paint them, after she retired a year from now, and bought the new furniture with the floral print—

Vertigo displaced his headache, and when the room stopped spinning, the maroon walls and floral furniture were back.

Tony blinked. The colors didn't change.

His headache was gone. So were the sounds of his sister loading the dishwasher. "Lisa?"

The house was silent except for the whir of the furnace. "Lisa?" He stood, and caught a glimpse of his slacks—

What the hell? They were tan, but he'd been wearing navy, the same clothes he wore to work yesterday.

He ran into the kitchen. "Lisa?"

The room was empty, and table and counters were clean. More telling, the room no longer smelled of Lisa's cooking.

Could he have—? Feeling like he'd swallowed a balloon, Tony hurried back to the living room, grabbed the remote, and turned on the TV. The cable news station was already on, and a quick glance at the ticker scrolling across the bottom of the screen confirmed his suspicion.

He'd returned to the present. *Thank God.*

But why was he at his parents' house then, too?

As soon as he thought the question, the answer ticked into place. He'd stopped by on his way home from the office to water the plants, and started to lie down for a nap.

Which was starting to sound really good, come to think of it. Almost like the other night, when he'd slept in his clothes, then woke to find it was two years ago.

Damn, he'd better get home, get to bed before he did *that* again. Maybe, just maybe, the whole thing with Dora and Charlie was just a bad dream.

He could hope.

By the time Tony pulled into his driveway all he could think of was bed. He reached up to hit the garage door opener button. His thumb pressed into the felt surface of the sun visor. He felt around, but nothing was clipped there.

He mumbled a curse as he stopped the car in front of the garage door, then opened the car door so the dome light would come on. Damn thing must have fallen down somehow.

He groped on the floor, then bent down to check under the seat. No garage door remote. He turned off the ignition and thought about searching some more, but all he wanted to do was go to bed. He stared down at the concrete driveway. He could almost lie down there. He forced himself to walk to the front door, fighting back images of the last time (two years ago?) he'd done the same thing.

The door was locked, but Dora had left the porch light on. He dug his keys out of his pocket and thumbed through them.

The house key wasn't there. He must have missed it. He leaned against the wall, almost too tired to stand, and flipped through them a second time, then a third.

No house key. What the hell was going on?

Too tired to ponder it further, he pressed the doorbell.

Dora opened the door. "Tony?" Her head tilted to one side, her nose wrinkled. "What are you doing here?"

"I live here, remember?"

Dora's upper lip curled, her brows pressed down. "What are you talking about? Look, if you're—"

"Dora, I don't know what kind of game you're playing, but it's not funny. Come on, let me by." He pushed past her and started to take his coat off.

Dora's gaze followed him, her eyes narrowed. "Tony, what are you doing? Look, if something's wrong, I'll call your sister to come get you, but you've got to leave. I'm expecting company."

He froze with his arm halfway out of his coat sleeve. "*I've* got to leave? I don't think so. And don't go calling Lisa, I'm fine, just tired." Too tired to care what "company" she referred to. Plans in which he obviously hadn't been included.

"Then get out of my house."

"*Your* house?"

She stepped back toward the still-ajar door. "Yes, *my* house. As you agreed to in the divorce, remember?"

Five

Tony sat in the driveway—*HER* driveway. What the hell was he going to do now?

He looked down at his left hand. No wedding band. He hadn't even noticed.

He was divorced. Had been for over a year, he realized. Was Dora's affair the cause? As soon as his mind formed the question, he knew it had been part, but not all. They'd tried to work things out like Charlie and Lisa had, but all a month of counseling did was prove Tony and Dora were never right for each other. Then another revelation struck him: being divorced disturbed him much less than the fact that Dora had told him to go home—and he had no idea where home was.

His driver's license. *Of course.* The fatigue must be clouding his mind. He pulled out his wallet and hoped he'd updated his license after moving out.

1531 Rambling Ivy Trail, wherever that was. With a Patterson Hills address. He shoved the wallet back into his pocket and started the car, hoping he found it before he fell asleep at the wheel.

He'd pulled out of his—or rather, Dora's—street before he realized he did know where Rambling Ivy Trail was. Luckily, it wasn't far.

By the time he reached the Glenhaven Forest Apartment complex ten minutes later, he remembered he had a two-bedroom apartment on the ground level, and that he always parked in the end slot in the carport. He spent little time there other than to sleep. Most evenings he worked late, or hung out at Mulroney's Pub in the shopping center on the other side of the woods behind the complex.

Mulroney's had two walls of TVs, cheap beer, and the servers knew when to be chatty and when to leave a guy alone and keep the beer coming.

Not that the price of the beer mattered, because Tony also remembered he'd made good money in the stock market. Not anything like Keith Lynch, but he'd made enough to set himself up for a nice retirement. At the time he hadn't known why he'd bought the stocks... intuition was too mild a term. Compulsion was closer, like some kind of benign possession. Later, it had made him sell his investments and buy the apartment complex where he now lived—right before the market tanked.

Himself, from the future. "My God," he whispered. He'd relived the past to ensure his financial security. Had Lynch experienced the same kind of intuition?

Come on, Solomon. Keith just had good business instincts—and so did Tony. Lynch only gambled with larger stakes.

After several misses, Tony managed to jam his key into the keyhole and stumbled into the apartment. He flung his coat down and dragged himself down the hallway and through the first door, only to bump into his computer desk, then bang his elbow on a file cabinet. Swearing, he lurched out of his home office and found the bedroom.

He woke thirteen hours later *(what's up with that?)*, fully clothed. Thankfully, it was Saturday, so he didn't need to worry about work. The first thing he did was turn on the TV, to the news, where the reporters were talking about a guy in Texas who'd found a live grasshopper as big as his hand, a species thought to be long extinct. The ticker at the bottom of the screen read March 21. With the correct year.

His fingers twitched on the TV remote, and he couldn't stop jiggling his foot.

He had to do something, get out of the sterile apartment with its neutral, brown carpet and bland, off-white walls that the department-store paintings his mom and sister had bought did little to liven.

Unable to come up with a better idea, he took the ten-minute hike through the woods behind the apartment complex to Mulroney's, where he went straight to his usual barstool, three down from the waitress rails, next to... Bernie from the bagel shop?

The memories slid into place, like a movie he'd already seen or a book he'd forgotten he'd read before. One of those small-world things, he and the deli owner had become friends. Or bar buddies, at least. The comfort in routine shaved away a bit of Tony's unease.

"Tony, my man!" Bernie said. "Where you been? I was about to come lookin' for you, not like you to stay away."

Tony tipped his head from side to side as he slid onto his barstool. "I've been busy."

He'd just ordered a beer when a whoosh of vinyl announced someone taking the barstool on his other side. He glanced over. Mandy, another regular, known at Mulroney's as Randy Mandy for her habit of taking guys out to the parking lot for a quick roll in the back of her minivan. He quickly turned back to Bernie.

"Hi Tony," the woman said. She scooted forward in her seat. Tony didn't remember ever introducing himself to her, but he mumbled a hello to be polite, keeping his gaze focused on the TV above the bar.

The bartender set a beer in front of him. Before he could get his wallet out, Mandy leaned forward and dropped a bill on the bar. "I got his."

"Thanks." Tony lifted his beer, then pretended to be engrossed in the game, responding to Mandy's pointless chit-chat just enough to be polite.

By halftime, he couldn't take any more. He searched for help, but Bernie's half-full beer sat in front of an empty barstool. Must've gone to the john. Tony hurried to the men's room, more to get away than because he had to go.

Bernie exited the restroom as Tony reached it. "Here, you might need this." He pressed something into Tony's hand.

Tony uncurled his fist. A condom. He started to say something, but his friend had already headed back to the bar.

Tony returned to another beer and a smiling Mandy. Bernie whispered in his ear. "You can thank me later."

Tony snorted. "I don't think—"

Bernie kept his voice low, although Mandy had turned to converse with another woman sitting a few seats down. "Come on man, time to get back in the saddle."

As soon as the game ended, Tony made an excuse and bolted for the door. As he walked out, movement caught his eye.

At the strip mall's other end, a woman with blunt-cut, blond hair walked a German Shepherd.

The dog lady? Tony squinted. Yep, it was her. She'd gotten a haircut since the time he'd seen her at Bernie's, after he'd returned from Mexico.

The memory filtered in. In his changed past, he'd still gone. Alone. So had Dora. He'd still fallen, still had that

(big stone knife)

horrible nightmare.

He touched his neck, drawing his finger around the scar.

Violet had spent the most time with him in those early, hazy days in the hospital. But to his surprise, Dora had volunteered to remain in Mexico when the others returned home. They had been married for sixteen years after all, she'd said.

The dog lady made a chirping sound at the shepherd, and slowed by the pet shop, still several stores down from Tony. Something about her reminded him of someone he knew, but he couldn't pinpoint who. Then he remembered the collar, from the little Yorkie that had jumped out of her handbag. "Hey!"

She lifted her hand in acknowledgment, then walked into the store.

He ran down the sidewalk, almost barreling into a guy coming out of the laundromat.

In the pet store, he checked the aisles for dog beds, toys, and food. All were deserted. He raced down the next aisle, even though it was all fish stuff, then scanned the rest of the store. The only other shopper was an elderly lady buying birdseed.

He hurried to the checkout. "I'm looking for a woman who just came in—tall, with short, blond hair, walking a German shepherd..."

The girl at the register shook her head, brows pressed down, and pointed to the birdseed woman, who was pushing her cart out the door. "She's the only person who's come in since my shift started an hour ago."

Tony rushed out the door. Had he been mistaken? Maybe the dog lady had walked around the building. He ran to the corner of the strip mall, then around back, but no one was there.

Defeated, he trekked through the woods toward home.

What was the deal with the dog lady? Who was she, and how did she just... *disappear?* And who did she remind him—

He stopped in the middle of the trail. Her hair, that was it. It was the same shade of blond, the same cut Bethany had worn when—

Bethany. A chill raced down his body. He'd gone back two years and changed the past. Why not try for three?

When Tony arrived at the house near the Ghetto, a strange sense of déjà vu settled over him.

He'd been there before. A vague memory filtered into his mind of stopping there, not last spring, but the year before. He hadn't known why he came, and hadn't gone inside.

This time he knew why he'd come to the Saturn Society house. To learn about time travel. To learn how to go back three years and save his daughter.

After leaving Mulroney's, he'd sat in his apartment for over an hour, trying to jump back three years. But nothing happened.

As if the one time had been a fluke.

Everly hadn't answered his phone, so Tony had decided to take him up on his "stop by anytime" offer.

Time travel. He snorted. Part of him still didn't want to believe it, yet the recent events were making it harder and harder not to. He stopped on the sidewalk in front of the house.

Oh, for crying out loud. Supposedly it was a research organization, nothing more.

The place looked deserted. According to the web site, the organization was huge, with offices—or houses, rather—all over the world. If Everly was gone, maybe Tony would try the Columbus location.

He forced himself to climb the three steps to the porch and strode to the front door. He paused as he reached for the doorknob and read the brass plaque beside it.

THE SATURN SOCIETY

DAYTON HOUSE

EST. 1914

He peered at the door's frosted glass top panel. A light he hadn't seen from the street glowed inside. He gripped the doorknob and turned it with more force than necessary.

The door opened without a sound. Tony's shoes tapped on the marble tile. A banker's lamp atop an antique mahogany desk in the foyer was the source of the light. The computer monitor beside it looked out of place.

A young woman with Ben Franklin glasses and stubby, black ponytails yanked her granny-boot-clad feet off the desk as she lowered the paperback novel she'd been reading. "Can I help you?" She spoke loudly, as if he stood across a large room instead of right in front of her. A brass placard beside the computer identified her as Taylor Gressman.

"I'm here to see Chad Everly." Tony gazed around. The place reeked of old money, with its expensive-looking, burgundy and forest green striped wallpaper, dark wood chair railing, and elegant landscape paintings in ornate frames. "He told me to stop by."

Her face slackened. "Oh, crap. Chad's away until—hey, you're the guy who was in the papers a few weeks ago, aren't you?" Her blue eyes gleamed behind her glasses.

Tony's mouth tightened. "Yes."

"I knew it. I knew from that line on your neck." She leaned forward, squinting. "Did they really cut off your head?"

Tony took a step back. "I- I don't—"

"You don't remember? That happens a lot. Well, I know Cha—Mr.

Everly does want to see you." She rose, tossing her book onto the desk. "Crappy book. They didn't have a clue what it was like back then."

Tony drew his head back slightly. Did she?

"Tell you what, you can wait in the conference room, and I'll see if I can get hold of him."

She led Tony up the stairs, down a long corridor, past a restroom, then by a bigger room that reminded him of a hospital ward. Although he saw no medical equipment, four sheet-covered cots flanked the wall in a tidy row. His pace slowed. He hung back to get another glimpse. Did they conduct research on human subjects here? "What's that room for?"

"That's our recovery room. Every Society House has one—"

"Recovery?" Muscles knotted in his stomach. "From what?"

"From time travel." She led him to another door at the end of the hall, across from an odd little alcove with an old, rotary-dial phone on a waist-high shelf.

Realizing he must look like a moron, he shut his mouth.

She tipped her head down and peered at him over her glasses. "Don't you get, like, totally wiped out when you go to the past or come back?"

That was a good way to describe the fatigue that had fallen over him as soon as he'd gone back two years, when he'd noticed Dora's suddenly-different clothes. Mexico had been worse, although he'd attributed that to his injuries. "I guess so."

"So when you go back in time, or come back to the present, do it here and we'll take care of you. Handy, huh?" She opened the door opposite the alcove.

"You mean this is something... other people can do?"

She gave him a patronizing expression, like she was explaining something to a small child. "Well, yeah."

Tony followed her into the room. She motioned to the round, wooden table in its center and four accompanying, straight-backed chairs. "Have a seat."

"So, uh..." So many questions. "When I go to the past, how do I come back—" Tony began.

"Unnnngh!" A groan came from the hallway.

"Oh crap." The woman jumped for the door, but not fast enough to keep the moan's source from Tony's view.

"Unngh! Uhhhh!" The man lurched around the doorframe, his vacant eyes unfocused, his mouth slack. Wispy, gray hair covered his almost-bald head. "Huhhhhhh-uhhh!" A string of spittle slipped from the corner of his mouth.

Tony recoiled. Good God, what kind of research did they do?

Taylor grabbed the man's gnarled hand. "Come on Fred, let's get you back to your room. It's almost time for *Jerry Springer.*" She dragged him away. More groans, higher-pitched. "I'll be back," she called to Tony, pulling the door shut. The moans grew more insistent as they faded.

Pressure built in Tony's chest. Was that what happened to their research subjects? He folded his hands at his waist, gripping the left tightly with the right. Maybe he should leave. He could sneak out while that girl was taking care of Fred—whoever he was.

No. He'd come for answers, and he was going to get them. The suspicion that the girl was up to something was only him not wanting to admit that there was something to this time travel stuff. If she tried to pull anything funny, he could force his way past her if he had to.

He studied his surroundings. It wasn't much of a conference room, lacking the lush appointments of the entryway. Scratches marred the table and credenza along the side wall. The desk lamp on the latter did little to illuminate the windowless room.

He took a chair, hoping the woman would return soon. There wasn't so much as a year-old copy of *People* to read. Above the credenza hung a silver relief image of the planet Saturn, flanked by three stars. Above it, a banner proclaimed Learn—Observe—Preserve.

Across the room, an institutional wall clock broke the expanse of wall where the bricked-in windows were, and beside it hung a plain calendar turned to March of the current year. The only other decoration in the room was a trio of framed, old-fashioned photographs on the wall opposite the credenza. In one, a stolid gentleman in a derby hat handed a paper to a white-haired, black man in similar attire. The middle photo showed the exterior of the house, before the two second story windows had been bricked over. In the third, two men posed in front of a frame building with "Goodwin's Smoke Shop - 140 Harrison Street" painted on the plate glass window. An antique car stood in front of it. Someone had scrawled a date in spidery, old-fashioned script across the bottom: 26 February, 1913. The little store must've been what was there before the Saturn Society house.

"Hey Chad, it's Taylor," the woman said from down the hall, her voice loud enough Tony didn't have to strain to hear. "I wanted to let you know that Tony Solomon just showed up. I'm going to go ahead and give him the test, so call me when you get this... bye."

She appeared a minute later with a sheaf of papers in hand, and sat in the chair across from Tony. "I couldn't get hold of Chad, but I know he'll want me to go over this stuff with you." She slid the papers across the table, along with a pen.

Tony picked up the top sheet. The heading read "Saturn Society," with "Membership Application" below it. "What is this Saturn Society, anyway?" He flipped through the papers. "I'd never heard of it until Everly came up to me in the parking garage."

"Not surprising. We keep a low profile."

"What hap- who was that man who came in here a few minutes ago? Is he—"

"Don't worry about him." She dismissed Tony's question with a wave. "He's... a ward of the Society. Nothing to concern yourself with."

Tony frowned at the door, then at Taylor. "I thought this was a research organization." The more he thought about it, the less scientific the place looked.

Taylor chewed her lower lip. "Well... sort of. That's our public face, so we can do stuff like own property and have bank accounts."

"You don't research time travel, then?"

"We *do* it. As for research, we keep records and stuff, like what we see when we go into the past, what happens there. Ways we die, how we heal—"

"You what?" He stared down at his hands. Could his sacrifice and death have been real? "You mean... I really died? This shit's for real?"

"As real as you and me sitting here."

"You can do this?"

"Sure. Though the farthest back I've ever been is 1927. Way cool. I tell you, people back then knew how to party—"

"How far back can you—can other people go?"

"Depends on the individual. Some people can go back centuries, others only decades." She crossed her legs, bumping one of his. "There's a limit, of course. Something to do with the expansion of the universe—jump back too far, and the earth's orbit will have been different enough that you'd warp into empty space. If your destination isn't habitable, you don't warp at all. Prevents us from warping inside of a wall or a mountain, stuff like that."

"Habitable" wasn't a word Tony would use to describe the world of the ancient Mayans, though perhaps if one weren't being sacrificed... "So you warp into the same physical location you are in the present?"

"Exactly."

"What about the future?"

She pressed her lips inward. "Can't be done."

"How do you know?"

She turned her hands palms-up. "How can you go somewhere when you can't visualize it? Sure, we get visitors from the future every now and then, but they don't tell us much. Don't want to take the chance they might change something, you know."

"But surely someone's tried."

"A lot of people have. Most of them don't go anywhere. The few who managed to jump never returned."

Which didn't worry Tony. He wasn't interested in visiting the future. All he wanted to do was warp into the past a few years and keep Bethany from getting in that car. "So how many people are in this organization?"

The girl's eyes rolled up to her left. "Maybe nine or ten thousand, world wide. Several hundred here in the United States."

"How long has this organization been around?"

She settled back in her chair, as if relieved he'd finally asked an easy question. "The Society was founded back in the fifteenth century. By Spanish missionaries in Mexico, I think, but no one's sure since most of the records from back then were destroyed by the Church, and most of us now aren't powerful enough to go back that far."

"Powerful enough? What do you mean?"

"The farther back you go, the more brain power it takes."

"Huh?" Tony's brows drew together. The power of your own mind, Everly had said.

"Well, yeah, how do you think it works? You know, we only use something like, what, ten percent of our brains? And all time is, is perception, isn't it? Anyway, the Society—"

"So what you're telling me is that the farther into the past you go, the more mental energy it takes."

She cocked her head. "Well yeah. Isn't it that way for you?"

"I don't even know how I got this... this thing. How—"

"You died, right?"

Tony's eyes darted to the credenza, to his lap, to the door. He remembered what Dora had told him in the hospital. *You lost your pulse.* "I guess I might have for a second."

"Did you have a near-death experience? You know, the tunnel, the bright lights...?"

"I might have." It wasn't just a dream. Hell's bells, he'd died. Died and come back. With something... *extra.*

His eyelids itched. His tie was too tight. He ran a finger around the inside of his collar. "What's that got to do—"

"People usually get it during a near-death experience. Something to do with the brain impulses and chemicals released when the body's about to shut down and then doesn't, or something happens so you live after all. If someone who can time travel touches you at that moment, boom. You're one of us."

One of them? Good God. "You make it sound like... vampires, almost." The thought made him queasy, though he wasn't sure why. It wasn't like he'd developed a sudden urge to suck blood.

The girl drew herself straighter in her chair. "Vampires? I never thought of it that way. That's cool!"

Who could've passed him the ability? Dozens of people had touched him as he lay on the side of the pyramid. Keith. Violet. Other people from the office. Dozens of strangers. Could one of his coworkers be keeping a tremendous secret like this?

He'd probably never know. It wasn't the sort of thing one brought up over chili at lunch, or at the bar after work. "So what makes you... go back in time then? Everly said something about..." He felt stupid saying something so absurd. "The power of the mind." She leaned her elbows on the table, her chin propped on her hands, so he went on. "The other day, I was just thinking about some time in the past, and then, next thing I know, it's two years ago, whether I wanted it to be or not."

She put her hands down and nodded. "It gets easier."

"And I got really dizzy for a few seconds."

"Right, that happens when you warp in time. Anyway, the Society was formed back in the 1600s to be like, a support group or something. Because you couldn't talk to just anyone about time travel, you know. They got executed, burned at the stake and stuff. People thought they were witches, or heretics."

"I can imagine." Tony pushed away the memory of the ancient Mayans slashing his clothes off.

"Yeah. But with the Saturn Society, they could band together, protect themselves, share knowledge and so on. We've got houses like this one all over the world, so we can help each other. And find new people like you."

Something like relief settled over Tony's insides. Everly was legit. Now all Tony had to do was find out how he could go back three years and prevent his daughter's murder. But as he opened his mouth to ask, Taylor rose. "Listen, I have some stuff I need to do for Chad, so I have to get back to my desk. Why don't you go ahead and get started on this, okay?"

"Yeah, sure." He read over the top page of the stack in front of him and started to skim through it. Standard stuff—name, address, birthday, where he worked. "Hey, I have another question."

Taylor paused in the doorway.

"I heard you say something about a test. Is there some sort of initiation for this thing?"

She waved at the floor. "Oh, it'll be easy for you. I wouldn't worry about it."

"But—"

She left, pulling the door shut behind her.

"Wait!" Tony jumped up as the doorknob clicked. He grasped it, but it wouldn't turn.

She'd locked him in.

Six

"HEY!" TONY YELLED. "OPEN THE DOOR! I'M LOCKED IN!"

Not so much as a footstep echoed in the hall. "Hey! Let me out!" He banged on the door.

No response.

Taylor Gressman hadn't locked him in by mistake.

Further pounding and shouting got him nothing but sore knuckles and a scratchy throat. Even threats of a lawsuit got no response.

He walked across the room. He'd seen no one else in the building besides the severely disadvantaged Fred. If she didn't let him out, he was screwed.

He sat at the table and skimmed over the rest of the form. Questions regarding his income and assets. He didn't like where that was going.

No thank you. The group was probably a scam, one of those white-collar cults who fleeced members out of their life savings, then disappeared. But the idea that time travel was possible, and others could do it...

No, it had to be a con, and the woman a clever actress. They'd probably read the account in the *National Weekly Star*.

The last page of the forms listed a series of provisions with a line below for him to sign, indicating his agreement to abide by them.

Agreement to maintain silence. Pretty simple. The Society wanted their members to keep this time travel stuff hush-hush. No problem there, Tony didn't exactly want to be tossed into a rubber room.

Political and religious neutrality. When visiting the past, he was supposed to blend in with the society and culture—and if their beliefs didn't mesh with his own, he was to keep his mouth shut. *Makes sense.* God knew how many throughout history had died for practicing the wrong religion, or claiming allegiance to the wrong king. He could deal with that. He hadn't so much as stepped inside a church or temple since Bethany's funeral. He continued reading.

Non-intervention. *Society members are expressly forbidden from interfering in or deliberately changing the past. Any act, no matter how small or inconsequential, can have disastrous, ripple effects. By signing below, the Society member acknowledges that he/she is aware that the consequences for doing so can be severe, up to and including death. Deliberate manipulation of the past for personal benefit will in no case be tolerated.*

Tony's stomach churned, then the slow burn of indigestion rose up his throat.

He couldn't sign the papers. Couldn't agree not to do the one thing he desperately wanted. Even if he didn't fear the consequences from the Saturn Society—after all, how would they know?—he wouldn't sign an agreement he had no intention of keeping. And if locking people up was how the Society went about signing up new members, he wanted no part of them.

But how would he get out? The door was solid wood, old and heavy. It would take some serious blows from a sledge hammer or axe before it broke.

Then he remembered his cell phone. All the weird stuff was getting to him. He pulled the phone out and punched the speed dial number for the office.

Silence. He looked at the phone and scowled. No service. *What the hell?* He shoved the phone back into his pocket and walked back toward the table. Was that someone talking from the distant bowels of the house? Taylor? He pounded on the door again. "Hey! Let me out of here, goddammit!"

No one came.

He paced around the windowless room. No doors besides the one through which he'd entered. He looked up. The solid plaster ceiling offered no way to break through either.

Nothing to eat, although someone had left a pitcher of water on the credenza. Not even a place to go to the john. He was screwed. In a final, half-hearted attempt to get Taylor's attention, he pounded on the door and shouted once more. No response.

He returned to the table and stretched out in a chair, propping his feet on another. Nothing to do but wait and hope she let him out before he had to take a whiz on the carpet.

He tore each sheet of paper into tiny shreds. *Fuck 'em.* Pounded on the door and yelled again, with the same result as before.

A little after five, he heard the front door slam shut. He jumped up and pounded on the door again, screaming.

Still nothing.

She'd left him.

What was he going to do? He was trapped until she came back. It was Friday, too. What if she didn't return until Monday? What if she never came back at all?

He'd starve. It might be months before someone found him—

Come on, Solomon, you're letting your imagination get the best of you. Someone would come eventually. But the prospect of being locked up in there the entire weekend was looking more likely.

There had to be a way out. He jumped up, strode to the credenza, and threw open the top right drawer. Empty. Ditto for the two below it.

The center cabinet held a pillow and a pair of blankets. Under the blankets lurked an antique-looking covered dish about the size of a casserole. Huh? He scratched the back of his neck, then stopped mid-scratch. A chamber pot. How long were they planning to keep him there? And where was he supposed to dump it, should he have to use it?

He flung open the top left drawer. A couple pencils rolled forward and hit a can opener. He picked up the latter. If he couldn't find anything better, he could use it to break through the plaster wall. Blank papers lay in the middle drawer. Nothing he could use to pick the lock. Hope dwindling, he pulled the bottom drawer's handle.

A yellowed certificate in a wooden frame lay inside. He picked it up and read.

The Saturn Society
Certificate of Highest Achievement
Presented this Seventeenth day of October, 1954 to
Theodore Pippin
In recognition of loyal service and dedication in finding,
apprehending, and stopping those whose actions unjustly
influence the flow of time.

Tony glanced at the photo of the two men. The certificate was the award the black man was accepting. He must be Pippin.

Tony replaced the certificate and shoved the drawer closed.

As if knowing his situation, his stomach growled, even though he wasn't hungry. The body could live for many days without food. People went on hunger strikes for weeks. But the pitcher of water wouldn't last long.

And he had other things to do. His job. Sunday night supper with his parents and Lisa's family. Watching college basketball playoffs.

Oh, who was he kidding? Other than his job, he had nothing important to do. But even if he had food, books, even TV, a weekend spent locked in a tiny room wasn't his idea of fun.

He started back for the table, then stopped. Maybe he could warp in time. Back to before Taylor Gressman was there.

It was worth a shot.

Mental energy, that's what she said it took. And all he had to do was imagine...

Last week he'd jumped back to two years ago. He could do it again.

He concentrated, waiting for the dizziness to hit.

Nothing happened.

He tried again, squeezed his eyes shut, imagined himself full of psychic energy, thought about two years ago.

Still nothing.

He tried other years. Four years ago. Ten years. Fifteen. One. The dizziness never came, and the room remained unchanged. And locked.

Maybe he'd never traveled in time after all. The thought relieved him, but he wasn't looking forward to digging through that heavy plaster wall with a can opener.

Could be he wasn't imagining hard enough. His gaze lit on the photograph of Theodore Pippin receiving his award. *Okay, 1954, what the hell.* He tried again. Lightheadedness swept over him, but only for a second. Could've been wishful thinking.

Perhaps it would help if he pictured the room as it was five decades ago. That woman had said something about visualizing. He studied the photo. It had been taken in that very room. Pippin stood beside the little table, with the credenza behind him. Striped wallpaper covered the walls, and an unremarkable still life painting behind him made it look like flowers were growing out of his hat—

The vertigo swept through Tony. He stumbled and grabbed for a chair, then looked down as his balance stabilized.

The worn, wall-to-wall carpet had given way to hardwood floor with an oriental rug beneath the table. The painting he'd seen in the photo had replaced the photographs. And someone had taped flyers all over the striped, papered walls. At least three dozen, each with a mug shot, like wanted posters.

He stepped closer to one, and saw that was exactly what they were. *Sought by the Saturn Society,* the headings read.

Thoughts of escape left him while he scanned the bills. Some were men, some women. Some young, some old. White, black, Asian, Hispanic, Native American...

Below each picture was a name, a date of birth (some of which were in Tony's future—one was in 2022), and the reason they were wanted. Most of these were "For disruption of the time-space continuum." Below that, a line read "Capabilities," and had four check boxes beside it, labeled Minimal, Average, High, and Exceptional. All but a few were Average.

He'd walked halfway around the room when one flyer made his heart stop for a second. The name below the photo was Tony Solomon.

He froze, an icy fist clamped around his throat. He couldn't breathe. Couldn't see anything but his own face, starting at him from between a beard and longish, unkempt hair.

He stepped closer, conscious of his footfalls on the wooden floor. *No way.* It had to be another Tony Solomon. He'd never let his hair get like that, or wear a beard. He'd tried to grow one before, and it always itched like hell to the point he shaved it off before it ever filled in. But despite the differences, the features behind the man's oval, wire-rim glasses were frighteningly familiar, as were the glasses themselves.

The man in the photo had more gray in his hair, too. But the date of birth was May first. Tony's birthday. Under "Capabilities," the checkbox next to "Exceptional" was marked. The physical description matched too, except Tony weighed more than the flyer noted by a good twenty pounds. Too close to be a coincidence.

Somewhere a door slammed. Footsteps approached in the hallway. "Hello?" a man called.

Tony glanced around. What would the guy do if he caught him? Keep him locked up, or worse? His legs seemed made of rubber, but he forced them to move and ran to the door, hoping to catch the man by surprise and rush past him to freedom.

He gripped the doorknob and tried to turn it. Still locked. A phone rang, a clanging, metallic sound. Probably in that little alcove across the hall. He pressed his ear to the thick, wooden door. Something clicked. "Pippin," the man said.

Holy shit, the guy in the picture.

Tony's body went rigid. He glanced across the room at his own face, staring balefully from the wanted poster. He wanted to sit down, stretch his legs out, and take a nap.

"...got to go, I have a visitor," Pippin said. "I'll get back to you..."

Rock formed in Tony's chest. The guy was coming for him, no time for a nap. And there he was, one of the Society's most wanted.

He'd have to warp back further, before the Saturn Society arrived in Dayton.

The plaque by the door had said established nineteen fourteen. Tony fought the increasing urge to sit down—hell, even the floor was starting to look good—and squeezed his eyes shut. He would warp to the Smoke Shop that had been on the site before the Saturn Society House. He was on the second floor, so he'd likely wind up in the shop's attic. He'd leave when the store closed for the night. Hopefully they wouldn't have a guard dog.

He heard the clang of the phone being replaced on its hook, then footsteps.

Nineteen-thirteen, nineteen-thirteen! He squeezed his eyes shut. Imagined a deserted attic. Bare rafters overhead in a sloped roof. Maybe some crates of tobacco. He gripped the doorframe, and this time was prepared when the dizzy spell hit.

When it passed, he opened his eyes. Too dark to see anything. The room was cool, but not uncomfortably so. A roaring sound came from all around him, and a light, woodsy smell of tobacco permeated the room.

Thunder cracked. The roar was rain pelting the roof. In the burst of lightning that followed he saw hulking, square crates and boxes. He'd made it.

He rose to take a look around, swearing when he bumped his head on the low, slanted ceiling. He rubbed the sore spot as his eyes adjusted to the dim light coming from a low window in the gable end of the attic. A feeling of accomplishment spread through him. He'd done it. Gone back in time of his own will, escaped the prison where that Taylor girl had locked him. Escaped Theodore Pippin and God knew what.

He gazed around the room, then moved slowly toward the middle of the room, where a gap in the crates could indicate an exit. But each step took more of an effort, his body growing heavier by the second. Lightning flashed, and dust swirled at his feet. The attic obviously wasn't frequented regularly. He squinted toward the window in the gable end. Had he seen a pile of blankets over there?

A stairwell descended from the center of the attic. Heat wafted up from it. A crack of light showed around the shut door at the foot of the stairs, and voices drifted from beyond. He'd sneak out later, then warp home from outside.

But he had to rest first. Must be that mental energy thing. He forced himself to take another step.

At the other end of the room, he found an old quilt draped over a crate. He snatched the quilt and laid it on the floor behind a couple more crates that would block him from view should someone come upstairs. He lay down and pulled the blanket around him. It smelled musty, but as weary as he was, it could've stunk like a skunk and he wouldn't have cared. A man's voice drifted from downstairs. "Thanky, sir, and have yourself a nice Easter!"

"Be better if this rain would stop," a second man said. "Least it's Friday." He said something else Tony didn't hear, then a door slammed.

The rain's steady drumming started to lull him to sleep almost instantly. Hopefully, no one would find him before he woke.

The whistles woke Charlotte before dawn on Tuesday morning. They stopped for a few seconds, then started up again, strident even above the steady beating of rain on the roof. In the brief pauses she heard church bells ringing, every bell in town from the sound of it. "Papa?" She tumbled out of bed. "Mabel?"

The other bed in the room she shared with her sister creaked and a loud sigh told her the noise had roused the older girl too. "Mabel? What's going on?" Charlotte asked.

"Don't know. But it isn't good."

Charlotte bit back a retort. She might be only nine, but she wasn't a dunce. Sometimes Mabel didn't seem to realize that.

They stumbled downstairs, where their father stood at a window, watching the rain.

Mabel's eyes went round. "We're going to get flooded, aren't we?"

"Flooded?" Charlotte twisted a strand of wavy blond hair around a finger.

Their father turned from the window, an unlit pipe in his hand. "I don't think we have anything to worry about here, girls. But I suspect those closer to the river will have to move to higher ground soon, if they haven't already."

Mabel jerked open the pantry and peered inside. "Perhaps we'd better lay in some food."

"Nonsense," Papa told her. More a mother than a sister, fifteen-year-old Mabel worried over the slightest thing. Charlotte let out the breath she hadn't realized she'd been holding. "The high water won't reach here," Papa said. "It didn't in ninety-eight." As soon as he spoke, the whistles stopped. "See? Probably a false alarm. Why don't you girls go get a little more rest before it's time to get ready for school."

An hour later the whistles started up again. It was still pouring outside as Charlotte dressed and rushed downstairs. Mabel told her a neighbor boy had stopped over, bearing news that school was canceled due to the threat of high water.

As soon as Charlotte sat, Mabel pushed a plate of eggs and bacon across the table to her, then handed her a glass of water. Charlotte held it up, one eyebrow raised. "No milk?"

Mabel shook her head. "The milkman must be running late this morning."

"Where's Papa?" Charlotte asked. "And Dewey?" It was unusual for their little brother to sleep past dawn, even when the skies were gray and rainy.

She had scarcely finished eating when Mabel pressed a few coins into one hand and thrust an umbrella at the other. "Get some bread and cheese."

By the time Charlotte reached Henry's Market, Seventh and Harrison Streets were filled with water, enough to cover her shoes. The din of the whistles and bells continued.

But inside the shop, it was dry. Struggling to close the awkward umbrella, she walked up to the counter.

"Why hello, Charlotte," Mr. Henry said. "What can I do for you today?"

"Mabel wanted me to fetch some bread, sir. And do you have any cheese?"

"I've some cheese in the back, but the bakery wagon hasn't come yet." He placed a curled finger on his chin. "Should've been here an hour ago... I wonder what's keeping him?" He turned a smile to Charlotte but it looked fake. "Oh well, I'm sure he'll be here soon. Do you want to wait? You can come sit back here if you like."

Charlotte thanked him and hopped onto the stool behind the counter.

She watched him scurry back and forth, tidying shelves and stacking canned goods in a display.

Then she saw the water. "Mr. Henry?"

He looked down. A rivulet of brown water had seeped in under the door and was stretching toward the dry goods aisle. "Oh, mercy... I guess we'd better start moving things off the lower shelves... I heard it was getting bad up north, but I never thought we'd get water here."

Charlotte jumped off the stool to help him stack the lighter merchandise on the counter.

By the time they cleared the bottom shelf of the first aisle, the water was up to her ankles, and icy cold. Mr. Henry had just ordered her back to the stool when a man in a top hat entered, along with a surge of more water. "The levee's broken!"

"How bad is it?" Mr. Henry asked.

The water was already several feet deep up north, the man told them. "I was at the coffee shop, eating breakfast... the owner's wife rang the shop and told us to get out of there, said it was like a wall of water coming down the street!" He shot another glance at the door. "Be here before you know it—"

Charlotte looked down. The water was already inching up to the first rung on the legs of her stool.

By noon the water had chased them onto the counter, then up to the attic. Ringing her family to let them know she was safe—and find out if they were—was out of the question, for the phones were out by the time she thought of it. The lights followed soon after.

She crouched next to the lone window above the store's porch roof and watched the torrent of muddy river that East Seventh Street had become. The water carried all kinds of things by—furniture, crates full of groceries, pianos, even automobiles. Lots of wood, she hoped from the lumberyard, but some looked as if it had been part of houses. The poor horses were the worst. They bucked and struggled, and made horrendous shrieks, but Charlotte doubted they'd be able to swim far in the fierce current.

She rubbed her hands up and down her arms. Lordy, it was cold. All up and down the street, as far as she could see, faces lined the windows. Some of them might have been shouting, but the noise of the rushing water and driving rain made it impossible to hear. Henry's Market creaked and groaned from the constant buffeting of the river's forceful current. Objects caught in its rush banged hard against the market walls.

Mr. Henry and the other man spoke in low whispers. She thought she heard Mr. Henry say "don't think she can take much more of this." Charlotte didn't think he was talking about her.

Something banged into the shop, shaking the building hard enough Charlotte stumbled. The two men examined the rafters. "We've got to get out of here," said the man in the top hat.

"Mr. Henry?" Charlotte forced her voice to be steady. "Is the store going to fall apart?"

He'd grabbed a rope and was coiling it over an arm while the other man helped gather it up. "I don't know, Charlotte." His voice was grim. "But if it does, we'll be long gone by then."

Something made a loud crash nearby. Charlotte hurried back to the window in time to see the waters hurl an upside-down streetcar against the corner saloon across the street. The building's wooden walls crumpled inward as if they were made of paper. Charlotte watched, too horror-stricken to do anything but open her mouth, as the tavern splintered into bits. Lumber swirled in a huge whirlpool where Harrison Street crossed Seventh. The streetcar broke free of the debris, and with the help of the endless, rushing water, tumbled across Seventh Street. Charlotte sucked in a breath. "Mr. Henry!"

The streetcar was headed right for the market.

Seven

An inhuman shriek jolted Tony awake. His gaze darted across sloped rafters, to the end of a long room where dim light filtered through a dusty, mud-spattered window. Church bells rang amidst the roar of hard rain, and whistles were going off everywhere, but they weren't what woke him. He clutched the quilt. Where was he?

He sat up. Then the scream came again. Outside. It started as a loud groan, then escalated to a grating, high-pitched howl that cut to his soul.

It went on and on then faded as whatever it was passed. Tony threw off his blanket and scooted to the nearby window.

A torrent of muddy water coursed through the alley below, coming halfway up the doorway of the warehouse across the street. He'd never seen so much water where it wasn't supposed to be. "Holy Noah's Ark!"

He stood, then regretted it when his head smacked into a rafter. With a curse, he rubbed the sore spot as his memories of the previous day fell into place. The Saturn Society. Taylor Gressman. The wanted posters and Theodore Pippin. Goodwin's Smoke Shop in 1913.

What had he warped into? He twisted around to search the rafters, as if answers hid in their dim recesses. The only reply was the beating rain. Then it hit him. March, 1913. He'd escaped the Saturn Society only to wind up in the middle of the worst natural disaster in Ohio's history.

The horrible shrieks started again. He crouched and peered out the window. In the raging waters, a horse struggled to swim, its reins caught on the crossbar of a streetlamp. The yellowish-brown waters came to within a couple feet of the light globes. The horse raised its head, its lips drawn back over its teeth, and let out another ear-piercing cry. Tony cringed. A wooden crate bumped the helpless animal, knocking it free, then the current carried the crate and the horse away.

The view out the other window was much the same. A barrel floated by. Small, dark shapes clung to it. Rats.

Tony leaned against the window, the glass cold against his hand and forehead, and stared in morbid fascination at the water below. The rain churned its rushing surface between pieces of broken furniture, crates and unidentifiable flotsam. Bumps and clunks came from below, probably furnishings, floating around in the shop's lower level.

He slumped against the gable wall. His stomach hollowed. How would he get out of that attic and find a place to warp safely home? He didn't know how long Dayton had remained flooded. Had he traded one prison for another?

He walked to the stairwell and peered down. It was half-filled with water. Icy cold, judging from the temperature in the attic. There'd be no escape by that route.

He'd have to warp from the attic, then. But...

His first warp had been on the pyramid at Chichén Itzá. He'd later warped in his living room, and this time, wound up in... he sniffed. A light, earthy smell hung in the motionless air. Tobacco. The smoke shop.

He remembered Taylor Gressman telling him he traveled only through time. His physical location didn't change.

Which meant he'd wind up right back in the Saturn Society's locked conference room.

He stared out the window. He had to get back to his own time. No telling what might happen to him if he remained in 1913. Hundreds of people had died—*would* die—in that flood.

He clenched his fists, shut his eyes, and pictured the windowless room where he'd been imprisoned in the present. Imagined the credenza, the beat-up conference table and the photos. Maybe that woman had come back and unlocked the door. Conscious of his heart banging in his ribcage, he waited for dizziness to hit.

He squeezed his fists and closed his eyes. *Come on!* He opened his eyes. The attic room remained unchanged.

He concentrated again. Nothing. After several minutes he gave up.

He was stuck. In the midst of a flood, in an attic, a century in the past. When he'd gone back two years, he hadn't been able to return to the present at first. Of course then, he hadn't realized what had happened until he'd been in the past for several hours. But even once he'd begun to accept it, no amount of wishing had taken him back until a day later, when his parents' furniture was different and the walls started to change color, as if the present had begun to break through. Anxiety ballooned in his chest. How long would he have to wait?

Fear sluiced down his body like the rain on the tin roofs. What if the dizziness never came and he was never able to return home? His parents would never know what happened to him. Nor would Lisa or the boys... even Dora.

He had to get back. Somehow.

He moved to the window, his fingers unable to decide whether to form fists or clutch at the window jambs. His breath formed a foggy circle on the glass. Another loud crash, then a few seconds later, a piano floated by, followed by a mass of splintered lumber that had once been a building.

The water swirled and eddied around the debris, lodging it between a telephone pole and the Smoke Shop. In the pile of wood beneath his window, a broken sign read *ry's Market*. They wouldn't be doing business any time soon.

Something moved in the wreckage.

Tony leaned closer, and his fingers found purchase on the window frame. His hair clung to the moist glass. *Oh, no.* He shifted again for a better view.

A small arm sheathed in a clinging, ruffled sleeve emerged from the water, and little fingers clutched at one of the larger pieces of wood.

Slipped.

Grasped again, lost purchase.

A little girl. "Oh my God." His voice echoed in the empty reaches of the rafters. The child groped again, failed to latch on, started to slide.

He had to do something.

He grabbed the window sash's blackened handle and pulled. Stuck tight. With a grunt he leaned upward and pulled harder. "Come on, open, dammit!" The sash didn't move.

He could barely hear a thin, plaintive wail over the rushing water.

He pulled his sleeve down over his fist and was about to break the window when his gaze lit on a piece of tarnished brass atop the window's center rail. Locked. He gripped the protrusion, tried to twist it. It moved a tiny bit, enough for him to wedge his hand behind it, get better leverage. Finally it flipped around with a thunk. He grabbed the sash handle, yanked upward, and this time the window obeyed.

The girl's cry reached him again. Helplessness pinned his feet to the floor. Fear he wouldn't reach her in time mocked him. He'd have to climb out onto that haphazard pile of wood. One misstep could plunge him into the icy, raging current. Compared to this, the pyramid in Mexico was nothing. If he didn't go out there, that little girl would die.

He yanked off his suit jacket. Cold as he was, it would only get in the way. "Hang on!" He climbed over the sash. She tried to grab hold of a broken timber. Missed. Then slipped into the water.

"No!" Despair stung him. The same way it had the night Bethany hadn't come home, and a state trooper rang their doorbell. Tony had known his daughter was dead before the man said a word. "Hang on!" This little girl had a chance. "I'm coming!"

He lowered himself onto the pile of debris. The wind buffeted him, and the wood shifted and cracked as he planted his feet on it. He picked his way across the rain-slicked wood to where the girl had fallen. The rivers pushed at the hulk of the former storefront and dislodged a plank or chunk here and there, forcing him to retrace his path and find a new route twice. Finally he reached the spot where she'd gone under, and knelt down to peer into the floodwaters' murky depths.

The water was so muddy it was opaque. Hopelessness ate at his soul, but he kept searching. The driftwood settled again, and he stumbled. He caught himself and picked his way a few steps to his left, praying the current hadn't carried her away. Then he spotted a swath of dark blue—her coat. He crawled to it, reached into the chill water, and grabbed an arm.

He pulled. When she started to come out, he almost lost his balance. Bracing one leg against a piece of drift, he shifted until he was over the small body. He wrapped his arms around the child and lifted her to his waist as he straightened. Icy water poured off her coat.

She could have already drowned. *No!* He couldn't think that way. Whatever it took, no matter what the risk, he'd save her. He laid her on one of the larger boards and pressed his finger to her wrist. "No..." His voice came out a croak. He made a choking sound and lowered his chin. Too late. He'd taken too long, let fear make him hesitate. He started to relax his grip on the small wrist when vertigo burst through him. Was he going home? He stumbled, barely caught himself, and gripped the child's wrist tighter. His hand tingled where he held her, like a thousand needles pricking his skin. The sensation moved up his arm and through his body, then dissipated. The vertigo passed.

No warp. He still clutched the child's wrist. It was still raining, and the muddy river still swamped the Dayton, Ohio of a century in his past. There was nothing he could do for the kid. Despair stabbed him as he started to let go of her. Then... was that a pulse?

He squeezed her wrist tighter. Felt it again. She was alive.

Her head lolled to the side, and water drained out of her mouth. He did a quick visual survey for injuries. Thankfully, he found nothing more serious than a few scrapes and bruises on her ankles, hands and face.

He rolled her onto her back. "Hey." He grasped a small shoulder and gently shook. Cold pinpricks formed on his back where rain was seeping through his shirt. Her eyes remained closed, and her muddy hair lay plastered to her head in a tangled mass.

She lay still. No rise and fall of the chest. Had he pulled her out of there just to watch her die? He pressed two fingers to the side of her neck. The pulse was weak, but there.

He leaned over her to confirm no breath escaped from her mouth or nose, then straightened and gazed over her inert form, trying to remember the sequence of actions they'd taught in the first aid class he'd taken at work last year.

Somewhere, a father would be looking for this little girl.

Tony would do anything he could to spare another man the grief he'd gone through.

Watching her chest, he tipped the girl's head back, pinched her nose shut, and puffed two short breaths into her mouth.

It rose with each breath. Good. He sat up.

Her chest didn't rise again.

He breathed into her a second time, checked for motion afterward.

Still nothing. He felt her carotid artery, and her pulse beat faintly beneath his fingertip.

He leaned down and gave two more short breaths. "Come on, breathe, dammit!"

This time he thought her chest expanded a tiny bit. He waited. There, it went up again. Her eyelids quivered, and a shudder racked her body.

"Hey!" He grasped her shoulder and shook. After he made sure she was still breathing, he shook her other shoulder. "Hey kid, wake up!"

Her mouth opened, and she let out a spastic, gurgling cough as her eyelids slid open, revealing round, brown eyes like a frightened doe's.

He'd seen those eyes before. But where?

"Mama?" she whispered.

"It's all right, honey." Tony's heart knotted. She made a little whimpering sound. Another shudder convulsed through her. "You're going to be okay." She had to be freezing. He was, and he wasn't as wet.

"Mama..." she repeated, louder.

"I'm sorry honey, but I don't know where your mama is," Tony said softly. "We'll find her as soon as we can." First he had to make sure she didn't succumb to hypothermia. "Let's get you inside and out of those wet clothes before you freeze."

"Ma- ma..." The little girl's gaze darted around, focused on Tony, then at the raging floodwaters a few feet away. Her lower lip trembled, and she panted in shallow gulps. "Wa- waaaAAAAAHHHHer!" she shrieked. "No! No water! NO WATER! NO! NOOOOOOOOOOOOO!" Tony reached for her and scooped her into his arms. Her screams faded into unintelligible blubbering. "Please don't... no! Water! Please..."

Tony cradled the girl's head against his chest. "It's all right, baby, it's all right. You're safe now. It's all right." Finally, she quieted. "Let's get you inside, okay?" Her head shifted against him in what he hoped was a nod.

Driftwood shifted beneath him as he hoisted her over his shoulder and painstakingly made his way back to the Smoke Shop, trying to hurry and get her inside before the whole pile gave way and the river claimed them both. She held still while he pushed her through the open window, then boosted himself through.

She struggled to sit. "Mama?" She searched the attic.

"Oh, God," Tony murmured. Had the poor kid just watched her mother drown? "Your mama's not here, honey. But we'll find her." Alive, he hoped. And soon, too. Not only for the little girl's sake, but he didn't know if he could handle another meltdown.

"She went... to heaven," the girl said. "A long time ago."

Some of the tension slipped off Tony's bones. "We've got to get you out of these wet things, okay?" He unbuttoned her coat, grateful the child hadn't just seen her mother swept away by the river. But what was he going to do with her?

She leaned over so he could more easily pull off her dripping coat. "Th- thank you, sir."

"I'm just glad I was able get to you." He knelt, leaned back on his ankles and gave his best shot at a don't-worry-it's-going-to-be-all-right smile, but the expression faded as the girl continued to shiver. "Can you get undressed? There's a blanket over there, I'll go get it."

She looked down at herself, then brought a pair of shaking hands to the buttons on her dress. He jumped up and slammed the window shut, then dashed across the attic and grabbed the quilt he'd slept on, ignoring the chill settling into his own body.

He waited as she fumbled around the neck of her dress. Her fingertips had a bluish cast, and slipped over the tiny button.

He had to help her. The longer it took for her to get dry and warm, the more she was at risk for hypothermia. "Is it okay if I help?" Tony reached for the buttons.

Her golden brown eyes went round, but not fearful. Finally, the girl nodded.

Letting a stranger undress her felt funny. Even Charlotte's papa hadn't done that since she was little. But the man was right, so she let him unbutton her wet dress.

"What's your name?" He worked the next button free.

"Ch- Charlotte. Charlotte Henderson," she said through chattering teeth. "What's yours?"

His hands went still, as if he had to think about it. "Tony Solomon."

"It's very nice to meet you, Mr. Solomon."

The corners of his mouth turned up a little. "I don't know about nice, considering the situation, but I'm glad to meet you, too." He undid the last button and sat back on his ankles. "Can you get your clothes off the rest of the way?"

"I- I think so."

He scooted around so he faced away from her. "When you're done, wrap up in that blanket."

"Y- yes, Mr. Solomon."

"You can call me Tony."

He sat with his back to her while she worked to pull the soaked dress over her head. "My papa says it's disrespectful to call adults by their Christian names."

"You and I will probably get to be real good friends by the time we get out of here. So under the circumstances, I think it's okay."

"My name's really Dorothy." Talking helped warm her insides. "Charlotte's my middle name, but my mama's—"

"No way." He turned around, and his eyes got really big like she'd grown wings or a tail. Then, as if he'd suddenly remembered she had her dress half off, he quickly faced away again.

"Why do you say that?" Why didn't he believe her?

"That's my ex-wife's name."

"Wha-"

"Dorothy Henderson. My ex-wife," he repeated. Charlotte wiggled out of her slip. "That was her name before we got married. Only her middle name's Carol. And everyone calls her Dora because she doesn't like Dorothy. Or Carol."

"My grandma's the only other Dorothy Henderson I know," Charlotte said.

"Probably no relation, Dora's family's not from around here." He half-turned. "Charlotte's a pretty name."

"Thank you, sir." How funny that she had the same name as his wife. She pulled her stockings off. Her shoes had come off after she fell into the water. She hoped Papa wasn't angry that she'd lost them. Her bloomers were wet too, but she left them on. Mr. Solomon was saying something about the rain. Her papa would say it was idle chatter, but she was grateful the man kept talking. He was trying to make her feel better, to help her forget the horrible cold and wet. She pulled the quilt around her.

Tony watched the corner of it slide along the floor. "You covered up?"

"Yes, sir."

He scooted around and studied her. "You're still freezing." He motioned her toward him. She crawled over. He snatched a jacket off the floor next to him and piled it over the quilt. Then he sat, Indian-style, and motioned with his hands. "Come here." He wanted her to sit with him. When she moved closer, he pulled her onto his lap and wrapped his arms around her. "This'll be the best way to get you warm." He lowered his chin so it rested on top of her head.

He was warm, but she couldn't stop shivering. Keeping one arm around her, he swiped his glasses off with the other hand, rubbed them on the quilt, then pushed them back on.

She wriggled in the quilt until she could twist around.

He was a handsome man, though not quite what she would picture as a hero. His dark hair stuck up sort of funny, and he acted nervous, like Dewey did after he told Papa a fib. Mr. Solomon's oval-shaped, gold glasses were just like Papa's, only shinier, but something about his clothes wasn't quite right. He wore a nice shirt and trousers, like those her papa wore to the office, but no vest, and the tie that hung loosely knotted below his neck was fatter than Papa's. His collar had pointy corners, and was shorter than it should be. But strangest of all was the pale, thick scar around his neck.

He caught her staring. "Feeling better?"

She'd almost stopped shivering. "Yes, sir." He looked like he expected her to say something, so she asked the first thing she thought of. "Do you have family out in that?"

He had to think about it. "Yeah. Distant relatives. I'm not sure exactly where they live. What about you?"

"My papa's at work. He works in a big office on First Street. Mabel—that's my sister—and my brother Dewey—they were still at home when I went to the store..." She stuck a hand out of the blanket and twirled it in her damp hair. "I hope they're all right." Her voice was shaky.

"I'm sure they're fine."

"And Mr. Henry."

"Who's he?"

"He owns the market... before the water tore it to pieces." She told him about her morning up to the time she fell into the water near the building they now sat inside. "I was sure I was a goner, 'cause I don't know how to swim." All that horrid, yucky water swirling around her... she couldn't breathe... then the water swallowed her, every move trapped her further, and it was so cold... She shivered.

Then everything had become bright, so bright she couldn't see anything. Nothing except her mama in the middle of all that light...

Tony rubbed his hands up and down her back. "How old are you?" He said it quickly, as if he was trying to change the subject.

"Nine." She was glad he'd made her think of something besides the awful water and how cold she was.

"You look older."

"Everyone says that. I'm tall for my age."

"What grade are you in?"

"Fourth. I'm supposed to be in third, but last year it was too easy and they let me skip a grade."

"You must be really smart."

"I am," Charlotte said. "Papa says I'm pre- preco..."

His mouth twitched, like he was trying not to laugh. "Precocious?"

"Yes! That's it."

"What's your favorite subject in school?"

It was hard to choose. She liked them all, even math. "Science, I think. Or maybe reading. Because a good book can take you anywhere. That's what my teacher says."

"She's right."

"I like everything about school, except for Sammy Schmidt and John Oliver. They're boys in my class. They make fun of me and call me Too-Tall-Charlotte. But Miss Jessup—she's our teacher—she makes them clean erasers if she hears. She's really nice. She tells us lots of good stories, and... when I told her I want to be an inventor when I grow up, she didn't tell me it was foolish and girls are supposed to get married and have children, like Uncle Curtis says. Miss Jessup says women can do anything if we put our minds to it."

"Your teacher's right," Tony said.

"She does lots of work for women's suffer—so women can vote," Charlotte said. "Papa and Uncle Curtis say it's nonsense, that women don't belong at voting places."

Mr. Solomon lifted his hand and brushed a clump of stray hair our of her face. "Well, I disagree. And I have a feeling your teacher's efforts will pay off before long. By the time you're old enough to vote, I bet you'll be able to."

"Really?" Charlotte searched his face for a sign he was joking.

"I think so." He shifted her on his lap.

They talked about all sorts of things—Charlotte's papa, Dewey, and bossy Mabel, Mr. Solomon's—Tony's—job in a big office building. He said he helped people find smarter ways—what a funny thing to say—to run their businesses. He'd traveled all over the world. He'd even flown in an airplane!

"Wow! Do you know the Wrights?" A friend of Uncle Curtis' knew them, and one time he took Charlotte out to Huffman Field to watch them fly. It was the most amazing thing she'd ever seen.

"Uh... not personally."

"I wish I could fly in an aeroplane," Charlotte said.

"Maybe you will someday. I bet they'll keep building bigger and faster planes. Ones that can carry hundreds of people, and fly over the ocean in just a few hours."

"Woooooow!" Charlotte drew the word out. Maybe she'd get to go flying one day. Maybe she'd get to help build better airplanes. "Papa tells me I have an overactive imagination when I say things like that." She twisted around so she could see Tony's face. Even behind the glasses, his eyes were as blue as the sky on a pretty day. "Do you have any children?"

"I used to have a little girl."

"Used to?"

A little muscle in his chin twitched. "Yeah. She ah, was killed in a car accident."

"Oh." Something in his voice told her he wasn't telling the whole truth, but she shouldn't ask any more questions about it. "My mama died when I was three. She had consumption."

Tony's fingers twiddled in the quilt, as if searching for something to grab. He gazed out the window, then into the far corner of the attic, where it was darkest. "Sucks, doesn't it." His voice came out harsh.

"Sucks?" Charlotte searched his face. He had a funny way of

talking, and his words didn't make sense.

"I mean it's... hard to deal with." His hands stilled on the quilt over her hips.

She snuggled closer against him. "What was she like? Your little girl?"

His arm tightened around her, and in the long silence the rain drumming on the roof and the water rushing by outside seemed to grow louder.

"She was beautiful." His voice went soft. "At least she was to me." He blinked a lot, fast.

"I'm sorry," Charlotte mumbled. It was what people always said when they learned about Mama.

"Yeah, me too." He fingered the edge of his glasses. "She liked to read, like you. And she liked to draw, though I think she knew she wasn't very good at it. She did well in school when she wanted to. She played basketball, too. And when she grew up, she wanted to be a compu- uh, a mathematician."

"Golly! Papa would say that's foolishness, like me wanting to be an inventor."

"Why does he say that?"

"Because I'm a girl." She tried not to pout.

"So?"

"Because... I don't know. You don't think it's foolish?"

"Not at all." He rubbed his hand up and down the quilt where it covered her arm. "Women can do anything. Even be ast- uh, pilots. Aviators."

"Like Harriet Quimby," Charlotte breathed.

"Sure. Maybe someday we'll even have a woman president. Are you warmer now?"

"Yes, thank you."

"Good. Because I have to put you down." He scooted her off his lap. "I've got to get something to drink." He rose and walked to the nearest crate. "If I could just find something to catch some rainwater in..."

She settled against the wooden box and pulled the blanket and his jacket tightly around herself, then craned her neck and turned around. He picked at the crate's lid. "Damn thing's nailed tighter'n hell." He moved to another crate a few feet away, then the next.

"What are you looking for?" Charlotte asked.

"A screwdriver, crowbar, something to open this with."

"I'll help." Clutching his jacket and the quilt to her with one hand, she rose and tiptoed around the staircase hole. Water filled it up to the second step from the top.

At the other end of the attic, she found a box full of fascinating junk—ashtrays, empty candle holders, electrical wires. But before she reached it something shiny on the floor near the window caught her eye. A copper coin. She reached for it—

"Aha," Tony said. Charlotte's head flipped around. He'd found a crate someone had already opened.

He lifted the lid and held up a red and white, soup-can-sized canister of tobacco. The kind her papa bought. "Perfect." He pulled the lid off and dumped the tobacco into the opened crate. "Sorry, Mr. Goodwin, but we need some water." He walked to the window, eased it open, then wedged the can under the sash. "Now we wait." He scooped Charlotte's dress off the floor and carried it to the stairwell, leaving a wet trail.

"What are you doing?" She gripped her quilt tighter.

"Laying these out to dry." He held her dress over the opening and wrung the water out, then spread it on the floor. He did the same with her coat. "They'll take a while to dry in this cold, but there's not much else we can do." He returned to the window and sat, watching the tobacco can as if that would make it fill faster. Charlotte started to join him when she remembered the coin on the floor.

She picked it up. A quarter. Finding a penny was supposed to be lucky, so a quarter must be even luckier. She hoped it was. They needed all the luck they could get.

She frowned as she held it up to the light coming in from the window. It looked like a quarter, but the picture on it was all wrong. Instead of Lady Liberty, it had a picture of George Washington, with IN GOD WE TRUST beside his head. But it said QUARTER DOLLAR right beneath him.

She flipped the coin over, and the other side was even stranger. It showed an outline of Ohio, with the Wrights' aeroplane, and a man wearing what looked like a big, puffy diving suit. Above the aeroplane it said "Birthplace of Aviation Pioneers."

She'd never seen a quarter like that. She turned it again and angled it.

At the top it said OHIO 1803. She supposed that was all right, for that was when Ohio became a state; they'd learned that in school. But what could the number on the bottom mean? It should be the year the coin was made, but that couldn't be right. 2002 was almost a hundred years away! She scooted closer to the window and tilted the quarter in the light, in case she'd read it wrong.

It still read 2002. She squinched up her nose. It must mean something else, or it had to be a mistake.

She looked at Tony. He stared out the window, hadn't seen her. She closed her fist around the quarter. Maybe it was his. Giving it back was the right thing to do, but she didn't want to.

She searched the floor. Maybe she could find more funny money. There were no more coins in sight, but a thick square of brown leather lay next to one of the crates. A billfold. Probably Mr. Solomon's. She picked it up, and it flipped open.

From a white card with typing on it, a photo of someone stared back at her. Him. In color. When she tipped it in the light from the window, tiny rainbows danced around a circle thing beside it. She gasped.

Tony's head snapped around. He sat frozen with a dumbfounded look on his face, like something important had just happened, but he didn't know what to do. When he spoke, he drew out the words slowly. "Oh... shit."

"It's beautiful," Charlotte breathed. Unable to tear her gaze away, she studied the strange card. Ohio Driver License, it said across the top. He strode across the attic and snatched the wallet out of her hand before she could read further. "Mr. Solomon?" she asked as he jammed it into his pocket. "What's the pretty card for?"

"It's, uh..." His teeth pressed at the tip of his tongue.

"Mr.—Tony? Where are you from?"

He clamped his mouth shut for a second before he answered. "Not far from here."

She wasn't sure she believed him. "I've never seen anything like that before." Pictures were just black and white and gray unless someone colored them... but his photograph looked... *real*. And what made the rainbows? "Where did you get it?"

He stared out the window, and his own image from the 1954 wanted poster flashed through his mind. "You wouldn't believe me if I told you."

Sought by the Society for disruption of the fabric of time and space. If the kid found out he was from the future, would he be violating their non-involvement directive?

"Yes I would." She gave him a smile to light up the room, revealing a gap between her front teeth that somehow made her even cuter.

Relief and apprehension warred in Tony's gut. He'd already come close to slipping up a couple times—once, by starting to say Bethany wanted to be a computer programmer, and again when he almost said astronaut.

Charlotte's silent gaze implored him. She *would* believe him, no matter what he told her. Her big brown eyes met his. Why were they so familiar? It was going to drive him nuts until he figured it out. With a sigh, he lowered himself to the floor next to her.

She held one hand curled in a fist, and slowly opened it when she saw him looking. "I found this, too," she said in a small voice. "Is it yours?"

He studied the coin lying in her palm. "Yeah." He squinted to read the date. 2002. *Shit.* What must she think?

"It's a real quarter, isn't it?"

Her eyes were so solemn, her face so earnest beneath the bedraggled hair. He'd never been a good liar. "Yeah. It's real."

She stared up at him, waiting. So trusting.

He'd seen her studying his clothing. Men's fashion hadn't changed a great deal in the past century, but there were still minor details that had to be off. Good thing small, round glasses were in style when he got his–if he'd worn the plastic-rim ones he used to have, she'd really find him strange.

The hell with it. Tell her the truth. After all, it wasn't like anyone would believe her if she told. They'd put it down to—what had she said? An overactive imagination. Sure.

He sat beside her, turning the wallet over in his hands. What should he say? *I'm from a hundred years in the future, Charlotte. That's how I know about airplanes, and...* The wallet flipped open, revealing his license. He slid it out of its clear pocket and handed it to her. "Here."

"What is it?" She tilted it back and forth.

He explained he had to have it to be allowed to drive a car. "It's so pretty," she said in an awed voice. "How did they get all those colors on you? Did someone paint it?"

He shook his head. "Read it. And tell me what you think."

She continued to turn the card around, and over, flexed it between her hands. "Why, it's made of something like... picture film. Only harder."

Her hands finally stilled as she examined the card further. "Anton J. Solomon, fifteen thirty-one Rambling Ivy Trail, Patter—" She looked up. "Where's Patterson Hills?"

"Not far from here. It's called something different now. I don't remember what."

She turned back to the card. "Birthdate..." She flipped the card over, and over again, then scrubbed at his birthday with a finger. "Your card has a mistake on it. Like the quarter."

"It's not a mistake."

"But..."

A series of emotions played across her face. Intense concentration. Bewilderment. Disbelief. Wonder. "But... if this is right, you won't even be born for... for a long time."

"That's right."

"You mean..." Her jaw slowly slid open. "You're from the future?"

He nodded slowly.

"But…" She looked at him, then at the card, then back again. "That sounds like something out of one of Miss Jessup's books."

He leaned back against a crate. "Let me guess. H.G. Wells?"

She gulped. "How did you know?"

Tony pulled one knee up to his chest. "People still read him in the twenty-first century."

"Twenty-first century?" She jumped up, holding the blanket, and ran to the window, angling her neck to see. Then she scurried to the other end of the attic, and did the same. "Where's your time machine?"

"I don't have one." He squinted at the floor. "I'm just now beginning to figure it out, but apparently it's some sort of psychic phenomenon."

She took three slow steps toward him. "What's a psychic…"

"Powers of the mind." Damn, was he actually saying this? And she believed it? He had trouble believing it himself, but the longer he remained in 1913, and the more he talked to her, the more real it became. "You probably shouldn't tell anyone, or they might throw you in the loony bin."

"Do they have loony bins in the future?"

"Yeah, but no one calls them that and only people who're considered dangerous go there." Yeah. Like someone who could transform history.

Charlotte sat and scooted close to him. "What are things like in the future?" She turned her oddly familiar, honey-brown eyes to his. "When do women get to vote?"

"Nineteen twenty."

She held out the 2002 quarter. "Why is there a diver on it?"

He took the quarter and they studied it together. "It's not a diver. He's an astronaut."

"What's an astronaut?"

In for a quarter, in for a hundred bucks. He tried his best to explain space travel. "The first man to orbit the earth and the first man to walk on the moon are both from Ohio. That's why there's an astronaut on our quarter." He told her about airplanes that could carry hundreds of people, and about automated teller machines, radio and television, air conditioning.

The questions continued. She sat in the circle of his arms and stared up at him with rapt devotion. She was there, alive, for him to speak to, because he'd pulled her from the water. The knowledge gave him a heady feeling. In saving her life he'd done something important. Something that might make up for letting Bethany go to that party, a small atonement of sorts.

The girl reminded him of Bethany when she was young and full of questions, back before she figured out he didn't know everything. Charlotte was old enough to know better, but hadn't yet developed the attitude that anyone over thirty was clueless. If she wanted to be an inventor, he had no doubt she'd succeed, provided her family didn't discourage her.

He found that once he started answering her questions, he didn't want to stop, even when they were about Bethany. Especially when they were about Bethany. It was the acknowledgment he needed, craved, that his daughter had been a special person, that her memory lived on.

He explained that the distant relatives he thought lived in the flooded area were his great-grandparents. Even his grandma hadn't been born yet.

He avoided the subject of war, fearing if he told her World War I would start in Europe the following summer, he could influence the course of history and contribute to his disturbance of the fabric of space and time that so concerned the Saturn Society. And although he didn't want to attempt an explanation of computers, he did show her his cell phone.

Too bad the battery was dead. Even though he couldn't call anyone with no service, he wouldn't mind taking a few pictures, so he could have proof later that he'd really been to 1913. Although that was probably against the Society Code, too. "It won't work in this time," he said with a dry laugh. "Or we could phone for rescue."

The comment sobered Charlotte. "Tony? How many people will die in this flood?"

He pulled her close against him before he answered. "I'm not sure, but I'm afraid quite a few." He thought about her freaking out when she regained consciousness. Better change the subject. "By the way, what day is it?"

"Tuesday. March twenty-fifth."

It had been Friday when he'd warped, he remembered the shop-keeper downstairs saying so. His head flopped back against the crate. "I've slept for over three days." No wonder his phone was dead.

Charlotte drew herself up straighter. "Three days?" Her mouth formed an *O*.

The two of them sat watching the rain, which had slowed to a light sprinkle. Not much else to do, with no way out of the attic. A couple times during the afternoon, boats hurtled down the current the next street over, strange, flat, makeshift crafts. By the time Tony got the window open to yell, the boats had disappeared.

Charlotte's shoulders slumped. "They'll never hear us, the water's so loud."

Tony pressed his lips together. "Guess all we can do is keep trying."

Charlotte stared at the floor, her gaze unfocused, then her head snapped up. "I know! We could build a raft."

"How?" Tony frowned at the wooden crates. "I don't exactly see any tools lying around."

"Well, let's look again." Charlotte clutched the blanket below her neck and strode to the opened crate. While she dug through the tins of tobacco, Tony searched the floor.

"Nothing in here." With a sigh, she let the lid fall and moved to the next crate. In her shifting shadow, something under the front eave caught the faint sunlight seeping through the window. Charlotte glimpsed it at the same moment as Tony. "A screwdriver!"

Maybe there was hope after all.

By late afternoon, Tony's hands were blistered and sore from using the screwdriver to pry apart a half-dozen crates. Charlotte was trying to lash the lids together with some electrical cords she'd found in a box of junk. Tony wasn't optimistic that they'd be able to build anything seaworthy, but working at it at least kept Charlotte occupied.

The waters had continued to rise, and lapped at the first step below the attic floor. The door of the warehouse across the street was completely submerged, and the pile of debris Charlotte had ridden in with had grown smaller as the water carried pieces away and encroached on the remains.

They tried to ignore their growling stomachs. Thank God the tobacco came in tins, or they'd have to worry about dehydration, too.

"Tony?" Charlotte squirmed. "I have to go."

"Go—" Then he realized. "Oh. Uh, I guess you'll have to use a tobacco tin." They hadn't found anything larger, so that would have to do for a toilet.

He emptied a can, handed it to her, and waited while she scurried behind a couple crates.

By saving the child's life, he'd taken on an awesome responsibility, though one he was glad to have. He'd stay with her, keep her safe until they found her family.

And if they didn't?

He'd take her home with him. *As if.* He almost made a face at the absurd turn his thoughts had taken. For all he knew, he was trapped, destined to live the rest of his life nearly a hundred years earlier than he should have. Even if he did manage to get back to the twenty-first century, he doubted he'd be able to drag someone else along.

But what if he could?

They'd have a great time. He'd take her places—the zoo, the kids' Discovery Museum, to movies. He wouldn't travel so much. Screw his job, if he had more important things to do. Even if it was just hanging out at home and watching T.V.

If only he'd realized that when Bethany had been little. But he'd gone along with Dora's urgings, chased the American dream, the illusion of success.

If fate gave him a second chance with this child, he wouldn't screw up. He wouldn't forget to tell her he cared. Wouldn't blow off her birthday party because he had to leave town on business. He'd introduce her to cartoons and Barbie dolls and video games. Maybe she'd play sports, like Bethany.

They'd go to the park and he'd teach her to shoot hoops...

He heard her slide the window open and pour something out. "Tony... come look." She stood at the window in the far end of the attic. He walked over so he could see where she pointed.

From somewhere beyond the warehouse across the street, a thick plume of smoke rose into the air.

"Fire," Tony whispered. He slowly lowered his hand until it rested on her shoulder. "Who'd have thought, in all this rain." Fortunately, it was far away. If fire reached the Smoke Shop, the place would go up like a box of matches.

Then something exploded, with a boom that reverberated through the attic, knocking Tony and Charlotte to the floor.

Eight

CHARLOTTE SCREAMED. TONY PUSHED HIMSELF OFF THE FLOOR. "HOLY shit, what was that?"

Trembling, Charlotte crawled into his arms. "I think it was a few streets over."

He stroked her back and rocked as they both stared out the window. Chunks of flaming wood rained into the water. Most of it extinguished the instant it hit the rushing flow, but one big chunk of roof burned until it floated down the street and out of view.

Charlotte's arms snaked out of the blanket and gripped Tony around the waist. "I'm scared."

He pulled her close. "It's okay, honey. I'm scared, too." The kid amazed him. After all she'd been through, she was just now admitting she was scared?

Small blazes sprung up in the vicinity of the blast. Tony and Charlotte were safe as long as the wind blew in the opposite direction from the Smoke Shop.

Throughout the afternoon, more little boats went by. None came close enough to hail except for one already full of refugees. Tony threw open the window and he and Charlotte hollered as loud as they could, but the man with the oars shook his head apologetically as the craft disappeared around a corner.

Charlotte wandered to the other side of the attic, where she'd found Tony's wallet, and amused herself by digging through a box of electrical junk she'd found. She examined each item with the eye of a jeweler assessing the value of a gemstone. Tony couldn't help smiling. She had the curiosity to go with her aspirations, no doubt there.

As he watched, the enormity of what he'd done struck him.

He'd zipped a century into the past. Into a time where it was commonplace—expected, even—for a father to discourage ambitions like Charlotte's. A time when a woman who worked outside the home was in the minority. When many would call a little girl's wish to be an inventor foolish.

But he'd also fallen into a time when Dayton was in its glory days of industry and innovation. The age of the Wright Brothers, Charles Kettering, and cash registers. A far cry from Tony's own time, where many equated Dayton, Ohio with *boring*.

After seeing the city streets filled with over twelve feet of water, he'd never look at them the same way.

When night fell, the darkness was nearly absolute. Only the lurid glow of distant fires illuminated the sky. Tony and Charlotte huddled at the window, hoped and prayed the fires didn't come nearer. Once in a while, something else blew up, and plumes of flame shot skyward.

"Tony?" Charlotte's voice was small in the dark attic. "What's making all the fires?"

"My guess is the weight of the water on the streets is rupturing the gas lines beneath them. Then someone lights a match and next thing you know..."

Shivering in his arms, she sneezed three times. She'd been doing that a lot, and Tony feared she might be getting sick. He rubbed her back, though it couldn't do much to warm her.

Eventually, she fell asleep in his arms. Her legs and arms twitched, and she made little mewling sounds as if she were back in the water, struggling to swim. Unwilling to wake her, Tony stayed where he was, sitting with his back against a crate, his feet propped on the lashed-together skids that were their poor attempt at raft building.

In the second story windows of the warehouse across the alley, a match flared. It snuffed out a second later, followed by the crack of a gunshot.

The church bells had just rung ten o'clock the next morning when Charlotte saw the fire down the street. She pressed her forehead to the window, barely able to feel the glass against her numb skin. Would she ever be warm again? Tony's hands felt like chunks of ice when he held her.

Sometimes he paced. One time Charlotte counted nine round trips. When he sat beside her, he stared out the window, his eyes unfocused. "Tony? Are you all right?"

He slid an arm around her, but kept staring outside. "Yeah." She wasn't sure she believed him, especially the way he jumped whenever someone shot a gun nearby. "Trying to get the rescuers' attention," he muttered. That's what he'd said at night, when the gunshots woke her.

He rubbed her arms over the blanket. "Man, what I wouldn't give for a hot cup of coffee and one of Bernie's sesame bagels."

Charlotte twisted to look up at him. "I don't know what bagels are, but I wish we had some, too." They'd given up on the rafts when they'd run out of electrical cord. The planks they'd been able to tie together wouldn't be enough to hold Charlotte by herself, let alone the two of them.

The rain had finally stopped, and the water was beginning to recede. By noon almost half of the door across the alley showed above the floodwaters. Downtown, fires still burned.

Charlotte clutched the blanket to her body and walked to the crate where he'd laid her clothes to dry.

Her dress was still damp. She wasn't sure what they'd do or how they'd escape if the fires came near, but she didn't want to be caught wearing only her bloomers and a blanket. She grabbed her clothes, then started to sneak behind a crate to pull them on when something sparkled on the floor.

Tony' quarter. She'd slid it beneath her dress while he wasn't paying attention.

She sneaked a glance at him. He was still looking out the window. Surely he wouldn't mind if she kept the quarter. He'd told her they weren't worth much in his time.

But to Charlotte the quarter was something magical. It was real, he'd told her so. And so were the other coins he'd shown her, and his tiny, square telephone, and the Ohio Driver License.

The quarter was proof that he wasn't batty, that he really had come from the future.

He'd come back in time a hundred years to rescue her.

Maybe that meant she'd grow up to be someone important.

The idea settled over her like a fuzzy blanket. She slipped behind the crate and dressed, then pocketed the coin.

She'd barely donned her stockings when the biggest explosion yet rocked the building. She clapped her hands over her ears, unable to suppress a wail. Tony threw himself to the floor. "Holy shit!" Outside, wood splintered and popped. He pulled himself up and rushed to the window, but Charlotte beat him to it.

"Tony..." Her voice was shaky. "It's right next door!" Orange flames reflected in the glass windows of the warehouse door across the alley, where they'd marked the water's progress.

"God, we've got to get out of here." He ran to the opposite end of the attic, then doubled back as she caught up with him.

"What are we going to do?"

"I don't know." He stared out at the water, deep and raging. "There's no way we could swim for it—"

She ran to the other window. "Tony, look!"

Down the street, a man had climbed the telegraph pole where more debris from Henry's Market had lodged. He walked on the lowest wire like a tightrope, clasping the wire above, while people watched from the second story windows of the house behind him.

Why hadn't she thought of that? With the power out everywhere, they wouldn't have to worry about getting electrocuted.

"No way." Tony's eyes were huge behind his glasses. The man on the wires was now over a street away, making his way to the big hill by the fairgrounds, and safety. A woman started up the pole, her skirt clinging to her legs, and a man waiting on the rooftop boosted a little boy to his shoulders. "Tony, we can get out! We're saved! All we have to do is climb that pile—"

"No." His jaw went slack.

"But Tony—"

"No. Fucking. Way." He nodded with each word.

Charlotte didn't know what *fuck* meant, but when Dewey said it once, Papa had washed his mouth out with soap, so it must be really bad. Lots of adults were probably saying bad words now.

"No way," Tony whispered again.

Charlotte peered at the window across the street. In its reflection, the flames outside the warehouse had made it across the alley and were licking at the roof of the smoke shop. She sniffed. It was getting smoky in the attic. "But Tony, the fire..."

He stared ahead. His mouth moved but no sound came out.

He was scared. Really scared. Maybe as scared as she'd been when the streetcar had come tumbling toward Henry's Market. But she'd refused to cry, until the piece of wood she'd floated on wedged against the building they were in now, and her hand slipped, and she knew she'd made it only to wind up in all that nasty, cold water anyway. Then she'd started to cry. But she'd been brave until then. Sometimes you needed to be brave and only think about what you had to do. That's what Papa'd said when Mama was sick.

This was another of those times. But now she had to be brave for Tony, too.

"Tony? You know the future, don't you?" He didn't answer. "Will this building be here? After the water goes down?"

Tony recalled the plaque on the Saturn Society house's front porch. It had been built in 1914, the year following the flood. His voice cracked. "I don't think so."

He gripped the window jamb. He hated his phobia of heights, hated how Lisa had always laughed when they were kids and he refused to go on the high rides at the amusement park. He hated the ribbing he'd taken from coworkers when he'd turned down the window office on the ninth floor, even though he'd insisted Tina Watterson had been there longer and deserved first crack at it. He hated how Charlie had to cajole him into going up the pyramid at Chichén Itzá, even though Tony's bad feeling had turned out to be spot-on. But he'd never hated his fear like he did now, when it stood between life and death. Not only his own, but a little girl's.

He stared at the wires, high above the rampaging water. *No, please no. Let there be some other way. Anything.*

Charlotte coughed. Gray smoke filled the air, and it was getting thicker. "Please, Tony. I know you're scared..."

He crossed his arms over his chest, more to stop himself from shaking than for anything else. He lacked the strength to lie and say he wasn't afraid. "There has to be another way..."

He regarded Charlotte for a long moment. The crackle of the flames had crescendoed to a roar. Her eyes met his, beseeching, pleading, sympathetic in quiet desperation.

Somebody's baby.

What if it was Bethany? What if the situation were reversed, and some other man had held Tony's baby's life in his hands?

To hell with his stupid phobia.

He moved to the window, and studied the debris that had been Henry's Market, then examined the telephone pole and wires.

They'd be wet and slippery. He and Charlotte could fall and die.

Taylor Gressman's words floated through his mind. *Oh, we keep records. How we die, how we heal...*

He pressed his fingertips to the scar on his neck. He'd died in Mexico. And returned to the present.

If he were alone, he might take his chances and remain in the burning building. But Charlotte was too small to hold on above and walk the wires by herself.

He was responsible for her. He hadn't pulled her from the water to leave her at the mercy of fire.

He threw open the sash. "Come on."

She trembled as she climbed over the sill. Was it from the cold, or the fearsome journey upon which they were about to embark? Tony followed, then dropped to the wood behind her.

They crept to the telephone pole. Tony glanced back at the tobacco store. The smoke had grown denser, and he thought he saw an orange flicker in the window.

His eyes traveled up the splintery, wooden pole. Metal spikes protruded from it every few feet down both sides, forming a ladder. *Put one hand on this rung, then your other hand on that one, foot up...*

His limbs didn't obey, his body frozen.

"Tony..." Charlotte didn't whine. Her voice held no accusation. She wasn't afraid.

He had to do it. Maybe he'd fall and die. But they'd definitely die if they stayed.

"You're going to have to ride piggy-back." Tony crouched down, his back to the child. "Climb on." He grabbed her legs and hoisted her up higher. She locked her arms around his neck and pressed her legs into his sides. Her weight settled on him like a yoke, oddly comforting as it urged him onward. "Hold on tight. And whatever you do, don't let go."

"I won't." Her voice was thin and strained. Behind them, the crackling and popping grew louder. Had the smoke thickened while he'd stood there waffling? With a grimace, he gripped the spikes and pulled himself up, grunting under Charlotte's added weight.

He stared straight into the telephone pole as he climbed. His breath came in short bursts. He looked up only enough to see the next pair of spikes. Finally, he reached the point where the first cable crossed the pole, then climbed upward until he could grab the upper wire.

He slowly let go of the metal protrusion and flexed his hand. It was already stiff from clutching the cold, metal spikes so tightly.

The wires dipped in gentle scallops from pole to pole. Three streets away, a corner pub's porch roof extended close enough they'd be able to hop onto it from the wire. He counted the poles between them and the tavern. Seven.

Seven hundred feet between them and safety.

It might as well have been seven miles.

Then he looked down. Big mistake.

Far below—it was only fifteen feet or so, but it seemed like a hundred—the turgid, brown river burst by. Death above, death below, death behind them.

"Hurry, Tony!" Charlotte's voice was firm and strong. Facing death in three forms, the kid was braver than he'd ever thought about being.

Her legs gripped his middle tighter. He flew in planes all the time. He could do this.

He clenched his jaw, grabbed the cable above, and slid his foot sideways onto the lower one. With his feet perpendicular to the wire, the heels of his dress shoes hooked around it.

He gripped the wire so hard he half expected it to cut his hand. For the first time in years, Tony prayed. *Please, God, get me through this... if not for me, for her.*

He started across. *One foot in front of the other.* He kept his feet angled on the wires, and concentrated on the next pole, impossibly distant.

By the time he reached it, he'd gotten the hang of the tightrope act. From the upstairs window of a nearby house people cheered and bolstered his spirits.

He let go of the cable with one hand. His jaw rigid, he swallowed a string of expletives as he swung around the pole. Charlotte tensed. He picked his foot up, gripped the wire on the other side, then clutched the splintery surface of the post with his left hand as he scooted the rest of the way around. He reached for the wire again with his left hand. His legs wobbled. Charlotte gasped.

We're dead. This is it...

He fumbled for the cable, then miraculously found it. *Don't look down...*

He'd made it this far. Damned if he was going to fall now.

Somehow, they made it across two more poles. After they crossed the fourth, it started to snow. The wires grew more slippery. Every few seconds Tony slowed and checked to make sure his shoes were planted on the wire. *Don't look down, don't look down!* He could no longer feel his feet or his hands, and Charlotte shivered so hard he feared she'd fall off his back.

Halfway to the fifth pole he slipped. *Damn damn damn!* He hung on to the wire above as his left foot flailed for purchase. Charlotte bit back a wail, then he regained his footing.

He inched along without lifting his feet again. The world narrowed until it was nothing but his numb hands on the wire above, his feet sliding on the one below, and the weight of Charlotte on his back. Nothing but the need to move forward. *One foot in front of the other, don't look down!*

"Hello there!" a man called from below.

Tony stopped. He couldn't move. Couldn't take the chance he'd slip again.

"It's a boat!" Charlotte said.

Tony let his gaze travel downward, then wished he hadn't when he saw how far away the boat was. "Ohhh, shit," he mumbled. Charlotte's grip tightened around his neck.

"Just a little farther, there, and we've got you." The man stood in one of those odd flat-bottomed boats. Another passenger clung to the telephone pole Tony was trying to reach, and held the boat stable in the rapid flow of water.

"Thank God," Tony breathed.

He barely remembered the descent down the spike ladder. His foot touched the blessed, wooden surface of the boat's bottom, and Charlotte slid off his back. One of the men reached for him, grabbed his arm and guided him into the craft. "Steady, there, fellow," said the man holding on to the telephone pole. "We've got to pick up a few more, then we'll head for the cash... get you some warm food, dry place to rest."

Tony didn't know what the guy meant by the cash, but he didn't care. He'd give them all the money he had, if that's what they wanted. As long as he was on the ground. His head slumped to his knees as the boat slid away with the current. He palmed the wooden plank of the seat beside him. Wood. Solid. His whole body shook, but it wasn't until a small arm linked through his that he realized he was sobbing. "It's okay Tony," Charlotte said. "You know what?" She snuggled close to him. "You're a real hero."

"The cash" referred to The National Cash Register Company, which had transformed into a huge rescue and relief operation. Tony spent the next two weeks there, working with the Ohio National Guard. He fell into bed every night, aching from physical labor he wasn't used to, but he slept better than he had since before his divorce. When he got home—if he ever did—he'd have to start hitting the apartment complex's workout room on a regular basis.

Staying busy helped keep his mind off the things he missed. People and places he feared might be gone from his life forever. His parents. Lisa and her family. The bagel shop. Bernie and the guys at Mulroney's. People at work. Violet, and build-your-own tacos on Wednesdays at the cafeteria. Television. Cell phone service and the Internet. His electric razor—even though it wasn't fashionable, he was growing a beard. He didn't have much choice when the sight of the straight razors at the barber shop made him break into a sweat, reminded him of things he'd rather not think of *(stone knife)*.

His latest assignment was building wooden walkways in a temporary camp for the homeless. He bent over to hammer nails into a plank—not fun, when he'd had a hellacious headache for the past two days, and aspirin from the relief center's infirmary did little to help. On top of that, he'd been catching weird glimpses of home— fleeting images of modern cars and trucks, One Dayton Centre rising from downtown, the new University of Dayton buildings where the tent city had been a second before. But no matter how hard he concentrated, the views always disappeared, and home never materialized. Probably nothing more than wishful thinking—

Footsteps stopped behind him, jerking him back to reality. "Tony?"

He turned to see a little girl in a blue sailor dress. Her waist-length, wavy blond hair blew in the breeze, catching the sunlight, and when she gave him a gap-toothed smile, it was like the sun coming out from behind a cloud. "Charlotte?"

She rushed for him and gave him a big hug, then stepped back. He set his hammer down, amazed at the difference clean, dry clothes and hair made. He hadn't seen her since they'd parted at the rescue operations, and her sister had arrived and practically had to drag her away from him.

She twirled a lock of hair around a finger. "I hardly recognized you with your—" he began, but the words stopped when he realized who her honey-colored eyes and her warm expression reminded him of. Violet.

Say something, Solomon, you're staring like an idiot. Something about her hair. Yeah. "You look a lot different now that the river's washed out of your hair." Not brilliant, but adequate. She giggled. Tony squinted at the row of square tents behind her. "How are you doing—your family's all okay, I hope?"

She gave a vigorous nod. "Papa and Dewey are cleaning the mud out of our house." She wadded a clump of skirt in her hand, like she wanted to say something else, but wasn't sure how to ask. "Tony... why were you looking at me funny?"

"You... now that you're all cleaned up... you remind me of someone I know."

"Someone from the future? Your time?"

He glanced around. None of the other workers were within earshot. "Yeah."

"Do you miss her?"

"Yeah." He did miss Violet. And a lot of other people.

The girl sidled toward the edge of the walkway, then back again, studying the planks as if inspecting Tony's handiwork. "Does she look a lot like me?"

Tony gripped the hammer tighter. "She probably did when she was a little girl. But she's older, thirty or so."

An "a-ha" grin spread across Charlotte's face. "Maybe she's my daughter."

Tony chuckled. Warmth rose in his chest and spread through his ribs. "That would make her at least sixty or seventy years old in my time. But it's possible she's your granddaughter. Or maybe your great-granddaughter." The resemblance amazed him. Especially her eyes. They were the same shape, the same golden shade of brown. "If I ever get to see her again, I'll ask her."

Charlotte fingered her hair, separated a lock, then wrapped it around her thumb. "Tony... why did you come here?"

He raised his hammer. "To help build the camp."

"No, I mean to 1913."

"Oh. I didn't do it on purpose, but..." He'd told her he came from the future. No reason not to tell her the truth. "Bad people locked me up, and it was the only way out."

Her fingers twitched. "You didn't come back in time to save me?"

His jaw stiffened. "'Fraid not. But I'm glad I was here so I could. Why?"

"It's silly." She studied the strands of hair curled around her finger. "I thought it was maybe because... you knew about me in the future, and I'd be someone special, do something—"

"Charlotte..." He grasped her hand. "You are special." She lifted her head and the corners of her mouth again tipped up.

In the distance a woman called her name. "I have to go." Charlotte slid her hand out of his. "I'll never forget you."

The woman called again and Charlotte ran off, leaving Tony alone. He watched the corner where she'd disappeared for several minutes before he turned back to his work.

As he reached for another nail, a flash of light made him look up.

Where the neighboring section of the tent city had been, was now a parking lot full of shiny, modern Chevys, Hondas, Fords, Toyotas. Passenger cars, SUVs, vans, and pickups. "Oh my God," he whispered.

He jumped to his feet and raced for the cars, stumbling as the vertigo hit.

Nine

DRIPPING SOUNDS. CLICKING AND WHEEZING. THE FAINT CACKLE OF television from near Tony's hand—the speaker unit in his bedrail. *Hospital.* Again.

Footsteps clicked on the tile from the doorway. That was what had awakened him. He willed his head to move. The effort was like trying to roll a boulder, but he managed to turn to his right. In another bed a few feet away, tubes and wires snaked around a motionless, withered form. A light blanket of relief settled over Tony. The machines were hooked up to his roommate, not him.

And he'd made it back from the past.

On his other side, vinyl crackled as someone sat in the guest chair. "Next time, come back to the House before you jump," the visitor said. A man. Not his dad or Charlie. Not Bernie. Tony forced his head around.

Everly! Tony opened his mouth but nothing came out. Everly's mild smirk spread to reveal his even teeth. "That way you won't have to deal with doctors poking at you, trying to figure out what's wrong when you're just tired. No bums finding you passed out at a bus stop and calling the cops. Our recovery room's much more restful than this hospital—"

"You!" Tony managed to gasp. The memory of the wanted posters in the 1950s-era Society House brought a cold sheen of sweat to his brow. What would Everly do to him?

"Easy there," Everly said. "How are you feeling, Tony?"

Tony tried to force words from his dry throat. Everly seemed kind.

Not someone trying to apprehend a criminal. But how could the man be so nonchalant? "I could sue you," Tony gasped.

Everly's eyebrows raised a fraction of an inch. "For what?"

"You locked me up. You—"

"I didn't lock you up." The smile remained.

"That girl—"

Everly's face settled into smug satisfaction. "Oh yes, I'm afraid I have to apologize for Taylor's... overzealousness. But I doubt you would have undergone the test voluntarily, and it was vital that you complete the First Rite of Initiation. Which you passed with flying colors, by the way—"

"First Rite! But I—" Tony panted, trying to catch his breath.

Everly crossed his elbows over his chest. "If you want to sue us, be my guest. You won't be able to prove a thing."

"I could have you arrested." Tony reached for the remote unit with the nurse call button.

Everly snatched the remote out of reach. "Come on Tony, hear me out." Tony went limp. He lacked the strength to grapple for the remote or shout for help. Everly was right, he wouldn't be able to prove a damn thing.

Everly held up a hand. "Look, I realize our methods seem... extreme, but the test is necessary. We have to be sure you're the real deal—that you really can move through time. We have to have proof that you have the mental faculties, the problem-solving aptitude to deal with it, and the moral fabric to only use your abilities in accordance with the Society's strictures."

"Why—"

"You'd be amazed at how many have tried to infiltrate the Society. Researchers, thrill-seekers... the government... especially military types. They'd love to find out how we do it—and exploit it, change the face of history. Which is strictly prohibited by the Society Code. But we can go over that later." He squared himself in the chair, his hands on his knees. His constant grin reminded Tony of the Cheshire cat from *Alice in Wonderland*. "So, tell me about your trip. Where—or I should say when—did you go?"

"Nine..." Tony's voice came out a dry whisper.

Everly filled a cup from the pitcher on the bedside table. Water splashed over the rim as ice cubes plopped into the cup. He handed it to Tony.

Tony downed the water then wiped his mouth with the back of his hand. *The wanted flyer.* Panic rushed down his body. There he was, lying in the hospital with scarcely enough energy to lift his arm, much less escape.

"Tony?" Everly said.

"I don't care to discuss this with you."

The ubiquitous grin widened. "It's okay. I'm like you, remember?"

Uh-huh. Except Everly's face wasn't on a wanted poster.

"It's not like I'm going to toss you in a rubber room."

Tony ran his finger and thumb over the edge of the sheet. The other man's face bore no malice or deceit, and Tony considered himself a decent judge of people. The panicky feeling ebbed.

Maybe Everly didn't know about the wanted posters.

What the hell. "Nineteen thirteen." Tony's voice was getting stronger, and his anger at being trapped against his will was returning with his strength.

"Oh, shit. I was afraid of that." Everly's grin disappeared. "The flood."

"Yeah, the flood."

"Oh, man. I'm sorry—"

"Sorry?" Tony clutched the bed rails and pulled himself forward. "I froze my ass off, about starved—and you're *sorry?*"

Everly turned his palms up. "What would you have me do, Tony? Is it money you want? Because if you join the Society, you'll never want for anything in that regard." His smile reappeared. "Do you want to make it not happen? You can, though I don't recommend it. And you'd have to wait until next year—"

"Next year?"

Everly lowered his hands and tipped his head to one side. "You jump in time, not in space. So the earth's at the same point in orbit around the sun. Which means you always go back to the same date, give or take a little, in a different year."

"And when I come back?"

"Same thing. If you've been there for two weeks, you return to the present two weeks later."

Tony had already figured that part out. His sister told him their mom had almost wound up in the hospital, too, with the stress of her son being missing for three weeks.

No more unscheduled visits to the past. Not worth the risk.

He ran a mental calculation. He could go to the Saturn Society house on March twenty-first next year, make the jump again, only to a less eventful year. Or better yet, not at all. "You mean I can... un-do my trip back to 1913?"

"If you want to—"

"No." Tony picked up his cup and twirled it around, making a piece of ice circle its bottom.

He'd done something important in 1913. Because of him, little Charlotte Henderson had survived the flood, gone on to live—he hoped—a full, happy life.

He'd done something meaningful. If he relived the experience, he wouldn't change a thing.

Except maybe the trip over the wires.

He set the cup down. "I saved a kid's life. I don't want to un-do that."

Everly's grin disappeared. "You what?"

"Saved a little girl's life—"

"That's what I thought you said. Oh, Jeez."

"What's wro—"

"You changed history."

"Oh..." Shit. The non-intervention edict he'd read on the membership form. What if Charlotte was the reason Tony was on that wanted flyer? "The kid was drowning!" He picked up his cup again, gripping it tightly enough the sides started to collapse. "There was no way I could just stand there... could you?"

Everly pulled at his ponytail. "I'd like to think I could—"

"You *what?*" What kind of monster was this guy?

"Tony, do you realize what you've done? That little girl could've grown up to... oh, give birth to Hitler, maybe. Or—"

Tony sneered. "In Dayton, Ohio?"

"Okay, bad example. But you get what I'm saying? A seemingly inconsequential act could have a tremendous impact on us all, on life on earth as we know it—"

"One of her descendants could find a cure for cancer, too."

Everly's lips tightened. "Possible, but unlikely. I've heard of a lot more examples where that kind of change had done no good... and plenty of harm."

Tony dragged his finger down the cup's ridged side. If Everly had a problem with Tony's saving Charlotte, there was no way he'd condone preventing Bethany's death.

And he'd been Tony's best possible source of information.

Too bad. Tony would learn how to do what he needed with or without the Society's help. Whether Everly approved or not, Bethany should not have died. How could an innocent child being beaten, brutalized, and murdered be *meant to be?*

Maybe Charlotte Henderson wasn't meant to die that day in 1913. And what of the others he'd helped ferry to safety the next day? What purpose could there be to such an extraordinary gift, if not to fix things that shouldn't have happened? What about his warp back two years, where he'd busted Dora cheating on him, and the change in his timeline had resulted in their divorce?

"Okay, I see your point." Everly must not know about Dora, and Tony wasn't about to tell him. "But what about that little girl? Are you saying I should go back next year and not save her?" Not that he had any intention of doing so.

Everly waved at the floor. "No. Definitely not. It's bad enough to change history the first time. But in the Society's experience, going back to un-do one mistake only leads to others, often far worse. Maybe you did do a good thing, and nothing more will come of it." He didn't sound convinced. "You have to understand, changing something—no matter how small—can have serious consequences. Not from the Society, but in terms of the very structure of time." He met

Tony's gaze with an almost frightened look in his eyes. "Each time one of us makes a change, it makes a tiny tear in the fabric of time. Usually it's not noticeable." He held out his hands, turned up his palms. "What does it matter if a blade of grass—that died ten years ago—shows up in someone's yard today?" He lowered his hands, then held them in front of him and made a circling gesture. "Holes in time, if you will."

Tony's lip curled. "Holes in time?"

Everly shrugged. "Or, if you subscribe to the multiple universe theory, holes between realities. Every time you make a change, you create a new universe, a new dimension. And the division between them gets thinner. Either way, it's dangerous. Did you see that story on the news a few weeks ago, when some kid found a grasshopper— a kind that people thought was extinct?"

Tony twirled the sheet between his finger and thumb. "Sounds familiar."

"No one can say for sure, but it's pretty much accepted in the Society that that's how it happened. A hole in the fabric of time. Or between realities."

Tony'd seen the news story, right after he returned from his warp back two years, where he'd busted Dora and Charlie. And changed his own life significantly. Was the emergence of that grasshopper, a hole in time, Tony's fault? "What's one little grasshopper?"

"No big deal, right? One insect can't reproduce. But what if the holes get big enough to let more through? What if it's something bigger? What if the holes get big enough that people disappear into them? Or what if technology from the future appears here, and people misuse it? Or animal or plant life our current ecosystem can't handle?"

Tony stared down at the sheet while his mind tumbled around the possibilities. Killer mosquitoes. Bacteria. Viruses long eradicated, or stronger ones from the future. "Do these holes always happen when someone goes back? Surely people make unintentional changes all the time."

"We don't know. Like I said, most of these tears are so tiny, we don't notice them." He relaxed, crossed one ankle over the opposite knee in a square. "Look, I'm not trying to scare you. As far as we know, the big holes only happen when someone makes a big change. And that's what the Society's here for. To educate, help you learn how to deal with time travel in the safest way possible." He drew a folded sheaf of paper from the inside pocket of his vest and leaned over to hand them to Tony. "I brought these in case you'd like to consider joining us again—especially in light of your recent experience." He pushed the over-bed table across Tony's lap, then laid a pen on it.

Tony unfolded the pages. The words swam in his vision, until Everly handed Tony his glasses.

Tony shoved them on and read. It was the same form Taylor Gressman had given him.

He skimmed the questions, then the provisions requiring his agreement, and reached for the pen.

Before he could talk himself out of it, he filled in his name, address, social security number, phone number and work information. Under income, he put "enough to pay the bills."

As he completed the form, a sense of weight lifted from him, as if the sheets had been made of lead before, and had now metamorphosed into ordinary cloth. Though he didn't look up at Everly, he could feel the man's perpetual smile.

He needed this. Needed the help, the support, the guidance.

And the instruction. To help him learn—

He reached the signature line, then paused as the full implications hit him.

He couldn't sign this.

Everly raised an eyebrow. "Questions?"

Oh yeah, he had dozens, all pushing forward in Tony's mind at once. But he'd better bury the most important one in a bunch of others—which were also important. "When I was in 1913... why was I stuck there for almost three weeks? But when I went back two years, I was only there for a couple days?"

"The farther back you go, the longer it takes for the pull to hit," Everly explained.

"The pull?"

"It's the force connecting us to our own natural present. Before you came back, did you start to see things from today?"

"Yeah... sort of like a double-exposed photo. And I had a hellacious headache."

"That's the pull." The Cheshire cat grin spread across Everly's face again. "You can't stay in the past indefinitely. No matter when you go, the pull will eventually snap you back, even if you fight it. I take it you were around other people all the time?" Tony nodded. "That's why you got the headache. The pull was trying to haul you back home, but you can't warp when you're in view of linear people."

"What?"

Everly's smile came back in full force. "People who experience time in a linear fashion. Normal people. If a linear person were to see you warp, it would jar the space-time continuum, create a difference in their perception and in the generally-perceived reality."

"There were people around when they—" Tony had to bite the word out—"sacrificed me in Mexico."

"That's different. You died."

Tony's insides turned to jelly. "What?" He put the cup down on the over-bed table and dropped his hands to the sheet.

"Sure," Everly said. "You die in the past, it instantly pulls you back to your own time, healed, at least partly." Tony's jaw went slack as he remembered Everly's comment in the parking garage—*How can you die before you're born?*

In a weird way, it made sense. The idea was freeing, magical. An odd sense of relief mixed with anticipation trickled through Tony. "Let me get this straight. If I'm in the past and I find myself in a jam, I can die, and... come back?"

"As long as you've gone back to before you were born." Everly pointed up. "But you still feel the pain. You still have all the..." His gaze fixed on Tony's neck. "Unpleasantness."

Tony slid his fingers around the neckline of his hospital gown. "Okay. So if I go to the past again, I take some medication, or poison... or pack a gun, so if I get into another situation like in Mexico—"

"You can't kill yourself." Everly crossed his arms and let the silence sink in, along with his ever-present smile. *When he warps, does the smile stay behind?* "If you do, you're dead. Permanently. Plenty of Society guys have had the same idea... an easy way to get through the Second Rite. Never works, not even if you try the old fall-on-your-sword trick. It's the intention of taking your own life that seems to make the difference."

Tony snatched off his glasses, and rubbed them with a corner of sheet before putting them back on. What was this Second Rite? He'd ask after he cleared up this death thing. "What if I go back and do something I know is dangerous, like uh... doing the tightrope act on the telephone wires?"

"That's a gray area. If you're doing something dangerous because you want to die, you probably will. For good. If you're doing it for other reasons and get killed, you'll come back."

Not that it mattered to Tony. He wasn't going to go back to the past again, except to save Bethany. Which reminded him of his most pressing question. "What if I start to warp... and I don't want to?"

"That's easy," Everly said. "You warp by concentrating on how a place was at the time you want to go, right? How it looked, the sounds and smells, the feel of it.... So to stop a warp, you do the same thing—concentrate on the here-and-now, what you see right in front of you."

Tony closed his eyes and let out a breath. It was that simple. No more unpleasant, unplanned visits to two years ago. Or any time. He met Everly's gaze. "What about warping within my own lifetime?" Everly's smile wavered, but Tony forged on. "A couple weeks ago, I went back two years, relived two days of my past... yet when I tried to do it again, I couldn't." He lay the pen down.

Everly's smile flickered, then dimmed, but enough remained that it was still a smile. "Aren't you going to sign that?"

Tony stared down at the paper, the non-intervention clause burning like a neon light.

He needed these people. Needed their help, their support. Their information. But he couldn't sign that paper.

It would be a lie. Most people would probably go ahead and sign, even if they planned—as Tony did—to break the rules. But Tony couldn't. "I don't think I'm ready for this." He pushed the forms across the table toward Everly.

Everly's mouth drew into a hard line. "Tony... I know what you're thinking. Don't do it."

"Do what?" Tony slid his hand under the blanket and clutched at a wrinkle in the sheet beneath him.

"Your daughter. You're thinking about going back and changing—"

Tony smacked his lips, his mouth suddenly dry. "How do you know about my daughter?"

"The Society researches all prospective members." Everly's stare was relentless. "Don't do it. Don't change the past. Observe and learn. But don't change anything. Hard as it might be. Believe me, the ramifications..."

A concrete ball formed in Tony's stomach. All this mess of slipping back in time, and here Everly was, trying to take away the one good thing that could come of it. Tony's baby, back in his life... He could feel the solidness of her slim body in his arms when he hugged her after a game, feel the cool skin of her forehead as he kissed her goodnight...

Everly's voice softened. "Tony, if you do this, you're playing God. Not to mention the dangers of the time-distortion holes. What gives you the right to determine what should and what shouldn't have happened—"

Something snapped in Tony's hand. He looked down. He'd picked up the plastic cup and squeezed until it cracked.

Everly rose and moved to the bed. "You're not the first one who's thought about changing the past, you know. Taylor said you saw Fred at the House—"

"The guy who was wandering around drooling?"

Everly nodded, his mouth pressed in a hard, straight line. "We make sure all his needs are met—"

Tony gripped a wad of sheet. "The guy's a zombie! What did you do to him?" He let go of the sheet. Gripped it again. Let it go. Smoothed it. Rolled a wrinkle between his finger and thumb.

Everly faced the TV, his eyes unfocused. "A combination of surgery and medication." He turned to Tony. "Those who did it, did what they felt had to be done. He violated the Code. And he would have done so again—"

"What did he do?"

"Influenced his ancestors' investments back in the twenties. Then when everyone else lost their asses, Fred's grandpa raked it in, thanks to Fred's knowledge of the future. Bad enough to change the past at all, but for such blatant personal benefit..." His gaze hardened, its threat unmistakable.

Tony inwardly cringed under its intensity. He made a pretense of studying the cracked cup in his hand. Holy shit, what if they found out about his own investments? He hadn't been greedy, just made a couple of wise decisions.

Resolve settled over him like a new fallen snow. He'd save Bethany. But he'd make sure Everly—and any other Saturn Society people—never found out. All he had to do was figure out how.

Ten

CHARLOTTE FINGERED THE QUARTER ON ITS GOLD CHAIN AROUND HER NECK as she hopped the trolley at Fourth and Main. Theodore had given her the necklace last week as a gift for her sixteenth birthday—and also in honor of her passing the First Rite. She'd drilled a hole through the coin, then secured it to the necklace with a wire loop. Somehow, putting the two together seemed fitting.

She'd had no difficulty escaping from that locked room in the Saturn Society house into 1901. The proprietor of the Smoke Shop had been surprised when she emerged from his attic, but luckily she'd convinced him she hadn't stolen anything, and he let her leave.

Her trip to 1901 had been far less unpleasant than her childhood forays into the late nineteenth century, when she'd been chased by horrid, dirty tramps, then caught by the police who took her to the girls' home where the matrons rapped her knuckles and worked the girls from dawn to dusk. Neither journey was one she cared to repeat.

She soon reached Mr. Pippin's elegant Society House at 140 South Harrison Street. She always enjoyed going to the House and spending time with Mr. Pippin, ever since the day he'd shown up on Papa's front porch when she was ten, claiming he was a psychiatrist, who'd read about her disappearances in the papers and thought he could help. After her three trips back in time, Papa was so distraught that he hadn't even cared that "Doctor" Pippin was colored. Mr. Pippin later told her he wasn't a physician, it was only a story he'd fabricated so Papa would let him "treat" her.

Mr. Pippin had told her all about how time travel worked, and most important, how to stop if she felt herself starting to jump when she didn't want to. To this day, Papa believed something horrific had befallen Charlotte during her early disappearances (she'd once heard him and Uncle Curtis talking about "white slavers"), and she'd made up the time travel story to forget about what had really happened. On Mr. Pippin's instruction, she'd stopped correcting Papa, and let him believe what he wanted. It was easier.

She flung the door open and burst into the House. As she expected, her mentor sat at his desk in the vestibule, poring over an album of photographs he'd compiled over the past several years—time criminals, men and women who'd committed selfish acts of change in the past. Although the green banker's lamp's light didn't reach the elegant green and maroon striped wall paper, it reflected brightly on the mahogany desk and illuminated the tome before him. He glanced up. "Good afternoon, Charlotte."

She returned his greeting. "Look." She lifted the quarter on its chain out of her dress.

Mr. Pippin stood, squinting. "Ah yes, the coin from the future." He was the only person she'd shown it to besides Dewey. He leaned closer. "Sensible way to keep it hidden."

"Of course, Mr.—Theodore." He'd recently told her to call him by his Christian name.

He gave her a thin, barely-there smile, the only kind he seemed capable of since the day his wife Nellie Mae had disappeared three years earlier. He patted the book. "Look through this new edition, and familiarize yourself with these miscreants, should you chance to happen upon any of them."

Charlotte dutifully sat in his vacated desk chair and studied the photographs as he retired to the parlor to read the newspaper. Their last visitor—a writer from the 1970s researching prohibition and bootlegging—had left over a week ago.

She tried to memorize the faces before her, along with the accompanying details that would help identify the criminals.

"Well, that one's gone," she murmured. Alan Fishel, born in 1926. Not even a gleam in his father's eye now, in 1920. Yet Fishel had been caught by the watchkeeper in New York City a month ago, as noted in the book. Traveling back in time to buy stock in an attempt to get rich. She remembered hearing the news at the time from a jubilant Theodore.

What had become of Mr. Fishel?

Her thoughts turned to Nellie Mae Pippin, and her heart clenched. There had been no one kinder than the dark-skinned woman who used to bake cookies in honor of Charlotte's afternoons with Theodore, who'd shared hours of quiet wisdom and companionship with a motherless girl. Her words of advice and knowledge hadn't been about time travel, or even science, but about people, the world, and life. Then Nellie had disappeared in a time-distortion. No one knew where—or when—she went, if she was alive, or if she even existed anywhere, in any time, at all.

Actions like Fishel's caused those ripples in time. He deserved whatever punishment the Society had dealt him.

Charlotte turned another page and scrutinized the photo, then gave the next page the same careful study. She'd do whatever it took to prevent others from using their gift in ways that caused the sort of time-rifts that had taken Nellie Mae. She'd do whatever Theodore asked, to help him eradicate these people before they could do even greater damage.

Charlotte flipped the next page, and her heart doubled a beat as the name on the printed page burned into her vision. Chills coursed down her limbs despite the lack of a breeze in the Society House's warm vestibule.

Tony Solomon. The man who'd saved her life. Who'd listened to her talk of her dreams and ambitions without laughter or scorn. The man whom, as a child, she'd thought she'd marry someday.

No. It's not my Tony. But the name was his. The man in the photo wore a beard and long, unkempt hair. Not the Tony she remembered. *It could be another Tony Solomon.* Neither name was that unusual.

In a pig's eye. The glasses were the same as those the man she'd met in the attic had worn seven years ago when they'd been trapped in the attic. So was his expression of wary concern.

She drew away from the book, the smell of new paper and ink rising from the page as she dragged her hand across it. Dread swelled inside her as she remembered what he'd said the last time she saw him, when he was working at the refugee camp. *Bad people locked me up.* What had Tony done?

Tony rapped on the door to Dewey Henderson's room at the Whispering Pines Nursing Center. Charlotte's brother was alive, over a hundred years old, and Tony's closest link to her.

Seeing the old man in the flesh would prove that Tony's experience in 1913 was real, that he really had been a hero.

He'd researched her. There had been newspaper articles about her disappearances, and references to "tall tales of time travel" on Lydia's genealogy site.

Charlotte had been a time traveler, too. If he could go back and visit her, she'd tell him how to warp within his own lifetime. He'd saved her life. Surely she wouldn't refuse him such a small favor.

"Who's 'ere?" a gravelly voice called.

"My name's Tony Solomon. I spoke to your granddaughter." He leaned close to the door and strained to hear activity.

"Hang on a minute..."

The old guy probably didn't move too quickly. It amazed Tony that he lived in an assisted living room instead of the full nursing section. Tony picked at his sleeve as he waited. A spot of something stained the cuff of his sport coat. Probably salad dressing, from yesterday's lunch meeting with Keith Lynch, where the CEO had informed Tony that he was putting him on an indefinite leave of absence. Tony had started to argue, but then Lisa had called, cutting the conversation short. As if his sister had ESP, and had known Tony had needed some sense talked into him. As she'd pointed out, he was lucky he still had a job after disappearing without notice for three weeks. He'd told the doctors he couldn't remember where he'd been. Keith wanted him to take some time off to get his life sorted out.

Strange thing was, the day he got out of the hospital, Tony could've sworn he'd seen Keith's SUV in the parking lot at the apartment. Then Keith had shown up at Mulroney's, and he hadn't given even a hint of his plans.

The enforced leave would have stung a lot more without the income from the apartment complex and most of all, Tony's plan to prevent Bethany's death. Being off work for a few months would give him more time to spend with her once he got her back.

Finally, Mr. Henderson's door swung open.

Henderson slouched in a wheelchair, his head listed to one side. *Oh man, let this be one of his good days.* The granddaughter had warned Tony Henderson's level of lucidity varied from day to day, sometimes hour to hour. Tony held out his hand.

The old man took it and gave it a limp shake. "What'd you say your name is again?"

"Tony Solomon."

"And you're a friend of Lydia's?" Other than his lax posture, the old man was surprisingly hale for being over a hundred years old. Then again, Tony didn't know any other centenarians for comparison.

"Actually, I just met her." It was the truth, if exchanging a few emails counted. "I was searching for information on your sister. I'm, I mean my great-grandpa—was a friend of hers." Damn, screwed up already. "I found her on Lydia's genealogy web site."

The cuckoo clock on the wall ticked away several seconds before Henderson wheeled his chair around and motioned for Tony to follow him inside. "Your great-grandpa was a friend of Mabel's, huh?" He indicated a wingback chair.

Tony slid into the proffered seat. "No, Charlotte's."

Henderson sat still, the only motion a slight wobble of his chin. He'd gone into some kind of funk. Maybe it wasn't one of his good days after all. But then Henderson fixed his rheumy brown eyes on Tony, and their sharpness told him the old man was sizing him up. "That's a name I haven't heard in a long time." He spoke softly.

Tony launched into his carefully planned story of how he found out about Charlotte. "My grandma passed away recently, and we found her father's journals in her stuff. He mentioned your sister in one of them." He spit the words out quickly, as if the falsehoods left a bitter taste in his mouth.

A faraway expression settled over Henderson's face for a long moment before he spoke. "What'd you say your name was?"

Tony repeated it.

"That was his name, too."

A tingle radiated down Tony's limbs. Henderson knew of him? "Whose name?" Tony gripped the arms of his chair, then loosened his hold before Henderson noticed. Charlotte must've told him about her rescue.

Henderson didn't reply. Tony swallowed, then continued with his story. "In my great-grandpa's journal, he wrote about saving her life in the flood. I'm named after him."

"Oh yes, heard that story a hundred times if I heard it once." Henderson's eyes sparkled. "How he pulled her outta the water when she'd done near drowned. Carried her on his back, walking over the telegraph wires though he was scared out of his wits."

You don't know half of it. Tony shifted in his seat.

"She was never the same afterward," Henderson continued. "Took to disappearing for weeks at a time."

Tony leaned forward. "You mean she ran away?" he asked, though he suspected he knew better.

The old man scowled. "Could be, but the third time... she disappeared right out of her bed." Tony fought to stop himself from squeezing the arms of his chair. "The police found her near the girls' home on Tyler Street, two weeks later. Other times, too."

"Wh- what happened to her?" Did Henderson have any idea?

"Said she went back in time."

So she *had* warped. Shock shot through Tony's center, but Henderson chuckled. "Charlotte was always... overimaginative. Whole family thought she was a little loopy. More so when she got older. Always building crazy contraptions in the basement, always..." He concentrated on Tony again. "After the third time she went away, Papa made us take turns watching her sleep. Mabel said Charlotte had never talked in her sleep before, but she did then... crazy stuff... like we were all gone and our house wasn't there."

Tony's breath caught. She had to have been terrified. He asked something a normal, rational person would. "So what really happened to her?"

Henderson slowly moved his head from side to side. "No one knew. Including Charlotte. When our father took her to a psychiatrist, all she'd say was she didn't know. Couldn't remember anything. Papa believed something terrible happened to her, and she'd concocted the time travel story to block it out. Then that other doctor showed up."

"Other doctor?"

"Another psychiatrist, I assume. Came to the house, said he'd seen the papers, knew what was wrong with her. Papa was beside himself, willing to try anything, even a colored doctor. So he took her to the fellow's house down on Harrison Street. Funny... it was in the same spot the Smoke Shop was, where she and that man—your great-grandfather—were trapped during the flood."

The Saturn Society. "Was the doctor able to help her?" Tony asked.

"Must have." Henderson's gnarled hands wrapped around each other. "The disappearing stopped after she started seeing him. And no more foolish talk of time travel. But the strangest thing was, the man never charged Papa a dime."

Tony quelled an urge to clean his glasses. "She had a normal life then?" Had she joined the Saturn Society?

Henderson snorted. "If you could call it that. Never married, though she had suitors aplenty. Could be her nutty projects and crazy talk kept the fellers from proposing..."

Henderson's words faded as the implications of the so-called doctor on Harrison Street settled into Tony's brain. The so-called "doctor" had to be Theodore Pippin. If Charlotte belonged to the Society, she might not be so willing to answer his questions. Not when the knowledge would enable him to break the Society Code.

"...too busy with her *work*." Henderson spat the words. "And running errands for the doctor. But I figure it was also because none of 'em could measure up to Tony."

Tony struggled to keep his face neutral against a whirlwind of emotions and surprise. "Wh- what do you mean?"

"Oh, she put him on a pedestal." Henderson flipped his hands over, as if washing them. "I always thought it was a lot of nonsense, she'd built him up in her mind. But once I met him myself, he was everything she said."

"When?" Flecks of dirt on Tony's glasses that might or might not be real clouded his vision. He snatched the glasses off and rubbed them furiously with the corner of his jacket. "Who?"

Henderson chuckled, a dry raspy sound. "Why, your great-grandpa, o' course. When he came to see her in thirty-three."

Tony's rubbing slowed.

"You all right, son?" Henderson said. Tony managed a nod, then slid his glasses back on. Charlotte could move through time. *He'd* given her the ability. But why had he gone back to her, when he'd vowed not to travel into the past again except to save Bethany? Had Charlotte provided the information he needed?

"Mr. Henderson? What... what did my great-grandpa do? When he visited Charlotte in 1933?"

Henderson pensively looked off to the side. "Oh, he helped out at the restaurant some—"

"Restaurant?"

"Irving's Place. Where she worked after they shut down the re-search shop." Henderson gazed somewhere above Tony. "I can re-member it like it was yesterday... helluva cook, my sister was. Then Irving went too far, and he wouldn't tolerate it—your great-grandpa, I mean—got her in trouble with Irving. 'Course, he'd already run off Elmer. So they came to me, spent a week at the ol' fishin' shack. Lordy, she was happier than I'd ever seen her..."

Lightness, fear and wonder bubbled up inside Tony. Had he and Charlotte been... more than friends? It was hard to imagine, when he'd only known her as a nine-year-old girl. What was she like as an

adult? Questions battered his mind. What had Irving done to Charlotte? And what had Tony done to Irving? And Elmer, whoever he
was? What had happened at the fishin' shack?

Henderson squinted at Tony. "Come to think, you look just like
him."

"Yeah, everyone tells me that." The lie slid out like warm syrup,
surprising Tony with its ease. He couldn't concentrate, all he could
think of was

Him?

And Charlotte?

More than friends? More than little girl and rescuer?

The real reason he'd come to visit Dewey Henderson broke
through his musings. *Bethany.*

He had to go to Charlotte. Whatever else happened between them
didn't matter. She was his best bet to find out what he needed to
know. Even if she belonged to the Society, she'd tell him. He'd saved
her life. If she was at all honorable—and he had trouble imagining
her otherwise—she'd feel she owed him. "Where did you say she
lived back then?" Tony asked.

"On Hopewell Lane, offa West Fourth. Cute little house, though
Lord knows how she afforded it on what Irving paid. They tore it
down when the highway came through. 'Course, she was long gone
by then."

Tony gripped the chair's arms. "What happened to her?" Heart attack, stroke, cancer?

Henderson's eyes grew watery. Or was it Tony's imagination? "In
thirty-three, the second time he came... She disappeared again. That
time, for good. They found a piece of her dress down by the river...
lots of blood, but no one knew what happened. Mabel thought maybe
she was mixed up with the mob. Never saw hide nor hair of your
great-grandpa again, either." He stared at the wall for a long moment, and when he resumed speaking, his voice shook. "God, I miss
her." Henderson slowly turned his head to face Tony, his brown eyes
calculating and accusing. "Unless there's something you're not telling me..."

"What?" Tony almost came out of his seat. "I mean, no. There's not! My grandpa—" What had happened to her?

"Thought it was your *great*-grandpa." Henderson's wispy hair trembled, his body otherwise rigid.

"It was," Tony insisted. "But—"

"She said she could go back in time, and he could, too. Didn't believe her, no one did. But I always wondered, ever since she showed me that quarter *he* gave her when they were stranded in that attic. And now, seeing you after all these years, not a hair on your head changed..." Henderson shook his head, slowly, deliberately. "That wasn't any great-grandfather. It was you."

Eleven

"THE NEW BOOK ARRIVED TODAY." THEODORE HELD UP THE VOLUME AS Charlotte entered the Society House. "1924" shone in gold lettering on the cover. "That fellow who jumped in last week? An Enemy."

"H- he is?" She reached for the chain hanging beneath the neckline of her dress and fingered her quarter through the fabric. *Please, don't let it be Tony.* Ever since she first saw him in the Book five years earlier, it had been a constant fear that he'd return, and Theodore would find him.

Theodore slung the book onto the vestibule desk, and Charlotte worried the quarter as he thumbed through the pages. The date on a photo he flipped past read 1991. "How on earth do we get these images?" she asked. And who determined who got into the book in the first place?

"From their contemporaries, or those of our number in the past who've observed their misdeeds." He glanced sideways as he flipped another page. She forced herself to drop her hand.

Couldn't let him see her nervousness, her fear. "Where's the justice?" *Don't let it be Tony...* "How can you simply believe, just because the image is in the book?" She'd voiced the question before, but this was the first time he'd brought in a new book and announced that an Enemy was near, an Enemy that might be—

"Ours is not to question why." His voice grew louder with each familiar phrase. "Our successors, in their wisdom, provide us with this information so that we may prevent dire consequences to their time, our time, the very fabric of time!"

Charlotte pressed herself against the wall. She couldn't just stand there, not when it might be Tony Theodore was after. "But- isn't that condemning a man without the benefit of investigation?"

"The investigation has been done! Do you have so little faith in your future peers?" Theodore pressed the book open to page 94. "There he is."

Charlotte leaned over the book. *Fred Cheltenham.* She suppressed the urge to sigh in relief.

"Another fortune hunter," Theodore spat.

Charlotte forced her breathing to slow as she studied the page. Cheltenham had been—or rather, would be—born in 1950. The picture was dated ca. 1984.

Theodore jabbed his finger at the photo. "Do you find it acceptable that this vile cur of a man gets rich by changing the past?"

Charlotte shrank away from him. "No sir."

He leaned forward, clutching the edge of the desk with both hands. "Do you prefer to look aside and allow this man to misuse his gift with no regard for the harm it does to others?" His voice boomed like a traveling revival preacher's in the Society House's foyer.

Charlotte squeezed the quarter in a fistful of dress.

"Do you think it's all right for this man to play God? To amass wealth at the expense of others? To allow the formation of time disruptions, regardless of the cost?" His breath reeked of onions and fried foods.

"N- no sir." She released the quarter. "Of course not." Charlotte dropped her hands and fumbled with a bit of skirt. This wasn't just about right and wrong, it was about Nellie Mae. But Theodore was right in his conviction to prevent others from sharing his wife's fate.

"Do you not agree that those who break the rules should pay?"

Charlotte straightened. "Of course."

He was right. They could not permit people like Fred Cheltenham to use their knowledge of the future in selfish, rash ways that allowed more time bubbles to form.

As a student of physics at the university, she knew better than most that the threat went beyond the displacement of an object here and there, or even people. Enough temporal distortions, and the fabric of time itself could unravel, resulting in chaos, the breakdown of linear life—possibly even the destruction of the universe.

It was the Saturn Society's duty to prevent that.

The thought chilled her, but strengthened her resolve. She drew up straight, and tried not to think about Tony, or how her rescuer might have earned his page in the Black Book. "H- have you invited Mr. Cheltenham to the House, sir?"

The flush seeped out of Theodore's face. "I have. He has declined our offer of hospitality. He knows what he's doing. But I am not the person to bring him in. Perhaps Dr. Caruthers." He sat at the desk, yanked a drawer open, and pulled out a thin booklet. The Society directory.

Ben Caruthers, the Society Watchkeeper from Cleveland and a renowned surgeon, shared Theodore's passion. Like Fred Cheltenham, Dr. Caruthers was white, and might more easily convince Mr. Cheltenham to come to the Society House.

Charlotte suppressed the compulsion to curl her lip as Theodore flipped through the small book. Dr. Caruthers was also a skirt chaser whose oily gaze lingered too long on her whenever he came to the Dayton House, making her feel like a specimen on display for his pleasure, and for his taking.

Charlotte wouldn't be taken. She recalled the night before, when she'd gone on an automobile ride in the country with Louie Lambert. A shiver ran up her body at the memory of the deliciously wicked feeling when he slid his hand up her leg.

She might be taken by Louie. But not by Caruthers. *Never.*

"Ah, here we go." Theodore pressed his finger to the booklet in his palm.

Dread swelled beneath Charlotte's bosom. "Perhaps I could approach Mr. Cheltenham." She didn't like the idea, but offering to help would mollify Theodore.

It worked. "Yessssss." He drew the word out "Excellent idea, Charlotte. My observations tell me he'd be more open to an overture from a lady." He clapped the directory shut as a narrow grin spread across his face, the closest he came to a genuine smile.

What had she gotten herself into?

The sounds of Al Jolson from the phonograph drifted out into the darkened laundry as Charlotte pushed the door to the back room shut, leaving the speakeasy behind. Fred—as he'd insisted she call him—gripped her hand as if he were afraid she'd reconsider leaving with him. *Not to worry.* She had a job to do. They crept around wash-tubs and wringers, until they reached the front door.

Charlotte grabbed the door handle—Fred wasn't even gentleman enough to get it—but an arm swung out from the dark corner, block-ing her. "Hold there a minute," a man whispered.

"What—" Fred began.

"Shh!" The man pressed them against the wall while a streetcar rumbled past, its wheels splashing in the puddled street. Then he dropped his arm. "Can't be too careful. Go on now, quickly."

"Ah, the feds," Fred said. As Charlotte flung open the door she caught a glimpse of his grin in the light of a nearby streetlamp. All of this was a novelty to him. He'd already told her prohibition would be repealed within ten years.

She stepped from under the eave, the drizzle instantly coating her dress.

Fred hesitated. "Damn rain'll ruin my suit," he grumbled.

"Surely you can easily afford a new one," Charlotte said. That suit probably cost more than her Papa made in a month.

Fred let out a big laugh. "That's true."

The laundry door opened, and the watchman leaned out. "Hey! Beat it, you two!"

They ambled down the sidewalk, staying under the storefront awnings as much as possible. "Hell, I can buy you a new dress... a whole closet full!"

Charlotte suppressed an unladylike snort as they stopped beneath an awning at the corner of Seventh and Main. She already had a closet full of dresses—though most had been purchased on credit, while she looked for a job. She'd find one eventually. She certainly didn't need Fred Cheltenham's charity. But she made herself give him a broad smile.

"Did I tell you I'm a dentist?" he asked.

"Yes, you did."

He peered at her mouth. "I could fix your teeth, you know."

The boor. "That's nice." She fisted a wad of soggy skirt. Time to do what she must. "Did you have a place in mind to go?"

He took her hand. "Well, since I'm not from around here, I thought... maybe we could go back to your place?"

Charlotte stifled a gasp. The nerve. Did he think her no better than a street trollop? Perhaps the nicest girls didn't congregate in the back room of Bushmiller's Laundry, but still... She swallowed her retort as logic returned. Morals were undoubtedly looser in 1984. Insulting as it was, Fred's suggestion made her job easier.

She injected enthusiasm into her voice. "Why... that's a capital idea!" The perfect opportunity. "But my father would question my bringing a strange man—"

"I'm staying at the Gibbons Hotel—"

"Oh, goodness no. My sister's best friend works there. I couldn't take the chance she's on tonight... why, the talk! I know someplace better."

"And where might that be?" His eyebrows bounced up twice as a suggestive smile shot across his face.

"My employer's, right down the street." The fabrication slid into place as she spoke. "A lovely house. They do some sort of research there, and often entertain overnight guests."

"Research?"

"Some psychiatric thing, I think. They're quite secretive about it, but the pay's good, so I don't ask. No one's in tonight, so it would be the perfect place for a little..." She stroked her finger down his hand. "...dalliance."

Fred slid an arm around her shoulders. "Then let's go."

Revulsion rose in her gullet for playing the coquette. Sure, she let Louie take a few liberties, especially when the drink flowed freely at some of those racy parties he took her to. Fred wasn't an unattractive fellow. But she was Louie's girl.

The drizzle stopped, so they walked the rest of the way. She resisted the urge to squirm when Fred's arm slipped to her waist. If Mabel or Papa knew! She tried not to think of Louie, or how angry he'd be if he found she'd allowed another man to see her home. But it served the Society's purpose.

Besides, Louie would never know. This was his poker night. Thanks to the rain, the street was deserted, so she need not fear someone she knew seeing her.

"What exactly do you do at this research place?" Fred asked.

"I'm a secretary."

"Hard to believe a pretty girl like you isn't married by—how old are you, anyway?"

"Twenty-one. I just graduated from university. Too busy studying to find a husband, I'm afraid." Which had been true, until she'd met Louie at an off-campus party.

"What did you study? Literature, I'll bet."

Charlotte laughed, genuinely this time. "Physics."

Fred eyed her, his brows pressed down. "No shit? Why're you a secretary, then? Surely you can find something better."

"I would love to find a position in research and development, but no one wants to hire a woman." She turned up her hands, glad for the excuse to slip from under Fred's arm. "They all figure I'll quit to get married and have babies."

Fred chuckled. "I'd hire you if I could stick around."

"Why can't you?" Charlotte pressed, curious to hear his explanation.

"I'm just here temporarily. Business."

"What sort of business?" Could she trip him up?

"Investing."

They stopped at the corner of Tyler Street while a lone automobile passed. Charlotte glanced behind her. In Castle's Fine Jewelry's window, diamonds and silver twinkled in the streetlamp's light. Fred turned and followed her gaze, then let his eyes travel up her. "Too bad they aren't open. That pearl necklace would look great on you." He drew a finger across the base of her neck.

"Oh, you're too kind." She leaned toward the street, and he took her hand, casting a backward glance as they walked away.

"Perhaps we can come back tomorrow."

She brought her palm to the base of her throat. "Really, I couldn't."

"You'd do well to take it. Times won't always be so good."

She slowed as they stepped up the curb and continued toward Harrison Street. "What on earth do you mean?"

"Five years from now, the stock market's going to tank. There'll be a run on the banks. People'll lose everything—"

"How would you know such a thing?"

He smiled sidewise at her.

"If I didn't know better, I'd... I'd think you know the future," she said. "But that's impossible, of course."

"What if I told you it wasn't?"

"That's preposterous! That's something only for fantastic stories." Charlotte tried to tamp down her growing unease.

"It's true. I do know the future. Because I come from it." He stopped and turned, as if trying to heighten the drama.

Charlotte regarded him through narrowed eyes, feigning what she hoped was a convincing look of disbelief. "All right, what year did you come here from?"

"1984."

"Really. And what are things like then?"

They started to walk again. Fred regaled her with tales of television, space travel and computers. Charlotte did her best to look surprised, though she remembered hearing of such things from Tony like it had been yesterday.

Though Fred spoke of fascinating things like microwave ovens and nuclear bombs, his frequent asides to talk about himself and his attitude of superiority grew tiresome. Relief swept over Charlotte when they approached the Society House.

She was up the steps before she realized he was no longer beside her. She turned to see him staring up at the house, his mouth hanging open. "This... is where you work?"

"Is something wrong?" Drat it all, he recognized the House from his own time. It likely hadn't changed a great deal.

He hesitated, still gaping at the House. She stepped down from the porch and joined him on the walk. "There's no one here at this hour." She tried to sound reassuring.

"There's a light in that second floor window," he said.

Charlotte took his hand in hers, and stroked it with the other. "My boss forgets to turn them off sometimes." She lowered her voice, hoping to inject a suggestive tone. "We'll be quite alone, I assure you."

He met her eyes, and the corners of his mouth tipped up. "What are we waiting for, then?"

She felt his breath, hot on her neck as she unlocked the front door. This was too easy.

Fred glanced around nervously as he stepped into the foyer, but said nothing. She flipped on the entry light, so Theodore, hiding in the garage, would know she'd arrived with their quarry. "Shall we go sit in the parlor? Perhaps there's a good program on the radio."

Fred's eyes gleamed. "Lead the way, babe."

She let him grasp her fingers as she led him around the corner, giggling like an infatuated schoolgirl. Her laughter rang false to her own ears, but Fred made a playful swipe at her hand when she pulled it away to tune the radio.

She sat on the sofa, expecting him to take the chair, but he sat beside her.

Charlotte kept her gaze focused on the radio, the lacy wallpaper, the delicate doily on the back of Theodore's overstuffed chair. She made idle chit-chat about the music, but Fred scooted close, and when he slid his arm over her shoulders, the words she'd planned to say flew out of her mind. "Did I tell you you're a very attractive lady?" His mouth stretched into a leer.

She fought the urge to recoil from the smell of gin on his breath, relived she'd dumped her own into a laundry tub when no one was looking. She needed to keep her edge.

"Why, yes, you did." She glanced at the door. What was keeping Theodore? She tittered, hoping Fred would mistake her nervousness for flirtation.

He stroked her arm. "You were the foxiest babe at that party."

"Is that how they say one's attractive in 1984?"

He laughed, and before she knew what was happening, he grabbed her and pulled her against him, pressing his lips to hers in a wet, sloppy kiss.

Bile rose in Charlotte's throat. *Theodore! Where are you?*

Fred drew back. "What's wrong? I thought you wanted..."

Whatever it takes. She had to keep Mr. Cheltenham here until Theodore could trap him. She swallowed. "I was just... surprised, that's all." She slid her hand onto his knee, closed her eyes, and leaned close, bracing herself for his slobbery mouth. *Pretend he's Louie.*

It helped, enabling her to feign enjoyment. Until she realized the face in her imagination wasn't Louie's.

It was Tony's.

She almost drew back in surprise, but Fred's arms crushed her against him. She tried to conjure Louie's face in her mind but could only see Tony. *Why on earth?*

The Black Book, of course. She was simply overwrought at having seen him in it again, for the fourth year in a row. Come to think of it, Louie bore him more than a passing resemblance. How had she not noticed before?

Fred pulled away, his brows lowered. "Are you okay?"

She forced a smile. "Of course. Why—"

"You seem a little... preoccupied."

She fanned herself. "It's not every day I meet someone like you." How much longer would she have to keep up this charade?

Fred opened his mouth to respond when the front door flew open. "What the—You said—" He started to rise, but his chance of escape disappeared when Theodore appeared in the entrance to the parlor, flanked by... Dr. Caruthers?

"Sit down, Mr. Cheltenham," Theodore said. "You'll be here a while." They advanced on Fred. "Excellent work, Charlotte."

Caruthers pushed Fred down on the sofa. "Yes, terrific job." He smirked at Charlotte, his eyes glittering.

Charlotte's insides turned in on themselves, and she fled to the other side of the room. Fred's head whipped around, from Theodore, to Caruthers, and back. "Who are you? What do you want?" To Charlotte, "You! You sold me out! You bi—"

"You have broken the Society Code, Mr. Cheltenham," Theodore said. "You've been warned not to tamper with the past to suit your own purposes, and you've willfully disregarded those warnings—"

"That's a crock!" He rose and tried to push them aside. "I haven't done a thing—" Caruthers shoved him back down and sat on him. Fred's limbs flailed, his fingers clawed at empty air, but his efforts were as ineffectual as his muffled shouts. Theodore drew a flask and a handkerchief out of his pocket, uncorked the flask and held the handkerchief to it as he upended it. As he pressed the cloth over Fred's nose and mouth, Fred's motions became slow and feeble, then he went still.

Caruthers slowly rose. "Time to take him downstairs?" A grin spread across his face like a joker in a deck of cards.

A chill rushed down Charlotte. What had she done?

Theodore walked around Cheltenham's inert form, poking and prodding the captive. "Yes. We must get him taken care of before he revives."

Charlotte shrank into a corner as the two men lifted Fred's arms and dragged him toward the parlor doorway. Caruthers paused as he passed her. "You've done well, Charlotte. I'll make sure you're re-warded." He moved on, but as he yanked the unconscious Fred around the corner, he gave her a long look, one of those that made her feel raw and exposed, like he could see through her clothes.

"Serving the Society is reward enough," she forced out.

"Well said, Charlotte," Theodore grunted.

She pressed her back against the wall, anxious to be out of Caruthers' sight. When the sounds of Fred's shoes dragging the floor receded, she peeled herself off the wall. She stumbled twice as she made her way to the sofa.

She sat, clasping one hand with the other, then switching them. She couldn't stop shaking, though the room was warm. Something sweet-smelling lingered in the air. The anesthetic, though she doubted it was the cause of her sudden malaise. It hadn't affected Theodore or Caruthers.

She made herself stop wringing her hands. *You're being silly!* She'd done something good, something necessary. Theodore was proud of her. Caruthers, too, though she doubted she'd want his promised reward.

What would they do to Fred? Curiosity finished off her misgivings. This was the first time she'd been present when Theodore made an apprehension. What was the Treatment that rendered the enemies of time harmless?

Her shakes gone, she got up and walked to the parlor entrance. The hallway was deserted, though scuff marks from Fred's shoes marred the hardwood floors. She followed their trail to the stairwell leading into the basement.

She tiptoed down the steps, hoping none creaked. She flinched when one did, then scanned the dim cellar. Her ears pricked at a faint snap coming from the storage area at the other end of the basement. She clutched the handrail, the wood cool in her grip, then continued down the stairs.

The damp, chill air raised goose bumps on her arms. The still silence amplified her footsteps, then someone shouted from behind a closed door. The storage area.

It had been locked as long as she could remember. Theodore had told her there was nothing inside except extra coal, which he'd taken to keeping since the shortage in '18.

She crept to the big wooden door and stopped, her back to the wall beside the jamb. She could make out Theodore's and Caruthers' voices, but not their words. Slowly, she leaned around the doorframe.

Not one lump of coal lay inside. Her breath caught.

Their backs to her, Theodore and Dr. Caruthers stood before a long, metal table. Both men had donned white surgical gowns. Theodore applied more of whatever was in the flask—chloroform, probably—to the handkerchief, then pressed it back over Fred's nose and mouth. At the table's other end, thick leather straps bound Fred's ankles. When Theodore shifted to the side, Charlotte saw more restraints around Fred's wrists.

"Ready?" Caruthers asked. "Scalpel, then." Theodore handed him an instrument from a tray of tools on a stand beside him.

Charlotte clutched her quarter through her dress, its edges biting into her palm. She should leave.

Caruthers brought the scalpel to Fred's forehead. Her curiosity warring with apprehension, Charlotte leaned to the side, trying to see around Caruthers, when an inhuman shriek issued from the table.

She cringed. Caruthers barked a command at Theodore, who grabbed the flask off the side table and tipped it over the handkerchief covering Fred's nose.

The screaming died down. Charlotte relaxed, then let go of her quarter and leaned close to the doorframe again.

Caruthers lifted the scalpel again. "No more time travel for you," he said in a haughty voice, ending in a chuckle. Not an ordinary laugh, as one might at comical motion picture show or a joke, but more of a cackle.

Her skin felt like ice crystals were forming on it. What on earth were they doing to the man? *This must be what demons sound like.* She stood, transfixed. She couldn't see around the two Society men, but from Dr. Caruthers' motions, it looked like he was sawing Fred's head open.

He held a bloody hand out to Theodore, but his request drowned in another wail from Fred.

Charlotte bolted for the stairs and didn't stop until she reached the front door. More shrieks drifted up from the basement.

She threw open the door and burst outside. She couldn't listen to that horrible noise and know she'd been part of the cause. She ran down the sidewalk until she reached a trolley stop several houses down.

Trying to catch her breath, she sat on the bench. Wetness soaked through her skirt. She'd forgotten it rained earlier.

The world was wet and black, the streetlights making distorted reflections on the pavement. She could see nothing but the afterimage of Fred's face, could hear nothing but his cries and Caruthers' voice echoing in her head.

She wasn't sure which was worse.

Someone was watching him. Tony couldn't see them, but he could feel it. Rain smacked his face as he exited the parking garage and scanned the street. Earlier when he'd gone to visit Dewey Henderson, the sun had been shining in a cloudless blue sky, typical of Ohio's capricious, spring weather.

But no one lurked in the shadows, and no one peered over the concrete half-walls of the parking garage. Tony plodded down Seventh Street toward Bernie's, though the deli was dark and closed. He'd brought an umbrella, but it was in his authentic, vintage suitcase. It would look strange if he jumped with it open, only to arrive to a beautiful, sunny evening in 1933.

A noise behind him made him stop and turn around.

The sidewalk was empty. Strange, it had sounded like a footfall amidst the rumble of traffic on I-75 and the splatter of rain striking the pavement. Tony moved on.

As he slipped into the alley behind the deli, he squeezed the brown leather suitcase's handle more tightly. He'd borrowed it from his great aunt Louise, along with the double-breasted, gray pinstripe suit and fedora he wore. Luckily, his long gone Uncle Abe had been close to Tony's size, maybe an inch or so shorter. Hopefully, the narrow band of his socks that showed above his shoes wouldn't draw attention.

He stopped by a dumpster and looked around. Someone ducked away from the parking garage's second level wall. He hadn't imagined it.

That fluid movement, the salt-and-pepper hair, reminded him of someone. Keith Lynch.

He frowned. Why would Keith be skulking around Seventh Street, a block away from the office, after nine p.m.?

It's not him. He was imagining things again.

Tony looked back, then ducked behind the dumpster in case the person reappeared. He imagined the back wall of Bernie's, decades newer, the bricks cleaner, the dumpster replaced by metal cans. The dizziness built, and he let it take him.

Cool droplets struck his hand as the vertigo faded, leaving him in an alley that looked just as he'd imagined it, flanked by a parking lot full of boxy, Model-T type cars.

He raised his hand to open the suitcase, but it lifted too easily.

The suitcase was gone, leaving only the hard, wooden handle in his grasp.

Twelve

DIZZINESS SWAMPED CHARLOTTE AS SHE REACHED FOR THE PASSENGER door of Elmer's car. *No!* She grabbed the door handle, focused on the here and now, as Theodore had taught her... the cool metal of the Model T's door beneath her fingers, the bits of rust flaking from its fifteen-year-old finish, the rain striking her hand in tiny, cold spots...

"Charlotte?" Elmer said from somewhere far away, beyond the spinning and whirling.

Here-and-now, here-and now, she couldn't jump, not now... *Focus!* The smell of the moist earth, the crispness of the rain in the spring-time night. She concentrated on the signs across the street, noting that Castle's Fine Jewelry was going out of business. Rain had seeped through the frayed awning, causing the paint on the signs to run. Had it been only ten—no, nine years ago—that Fred Cheltenham had offered to buy her something from there? Charlotte concentrated on the dripping letters, focused on the rainbow-ringed streetlamps in the hazy mist—

"Charlotte? Are you all right?" Elmer's hand, damp and clammy, closed over her arm as he opened the car door with his other hand. She lowered herself the rest of the way into the car.

The ground settled beneath her. "I'm fine... just a little tired," she lied. Silly goose! Even if she wanted to, she couldn't have jumped with Elmer watching. She scooted over, the cracked leather seat squeaking under her damp skirt.

He shut the car door behind her.

Someone else had jumped. Who?

Theodore always informed her before he jumped, so she could monitor the Society House in his absence.

Elmer's umbrella bobbed over the car's hood as he cranked the starter. Pity he couldn't afford anything better, but it was more than Charlotte had. A pang shot through her. It had been over a year since she'd driven, and she missed it. It still saddened her to think of the Chevy she'd sold to pay her rent after Dayton Kitchen Products Research went under, taking her job with it. The position as a cook she'd found soon after wasn't enough to pay all the bills, even though the Society paid for the telephone Theodore insisted she have.

Finally, the Ford roared to life, and Elmer climbed in.

Queasiness brewed in Charlotte's belly during the quiet ride home. Whoever had jumped was not her concern. Theodore would see to him or her.

"Penny for your thoughts?" Elmer asked.

"I doubt they're worth that much." She cast him a wan smile and made a vague comment about the movie they'd just seen. Bland and ordinary, already forgettable.

Not unlike Elmer. He was a nice enough fellow, and not unpleasant to look at, but this was the fifth time she'd been out with him, and he had nothing more compelling to converse about than the weather or the show. Was this all there was?

It was a relief when the car rumbled to a stop in front of her house, the rain-slicked Room for Rent sign gleaming balefully in the Ford's headlamps. Elmer opened the car door, took her arm, and walked her to the house.

She pulled her sweater around her as he unlatched the front gate and moved toward the little bungalow she'd rented four years ago, right before the stock market crashed. Her insides dropped a little at her realization they'd soon reach her front porch, where Elmer would want to kiss her.

He'd kissed her the last couple times they'd gone out, with all the ardor of a man saying goodnight to his mother. It was like laying her lips on a slab of meat, with as little appeal.

"Life's not like the movies, Charlotte," Mabel had told her after she'd introduced Charlotte to Elmer, a friend of her husband's. "You're practically an old maid."

Charlotte was nearly thirty. Maybe Mabel was right, and it was time she put aside fantasies of love and passion and settled down with a practical man.

Elmer was polite, and he treated her well. He had a good job at the paint factory. And his attention was easily ensnared by the radio, enough that he might not notice if a woman slipped down to the basement from time to time when there was no laundry to do. He might not realize she was building things and mixing powders in said basement.

She tried to conjure some interest in him as they proceeded up the walk. *It will be fine if he kisses me.* The movie had been enjoyable and romantic. Despite the light sprinkle, a warm breeze caressed the hem of her skirt. A pleasant May evening before the heat and humidity of summer set in. A nice enough night that Elmer might sit on the porch swing with her to smoke a cigarette, and listen to Ozzie Nelson drifting out though the open window. He'd tell her to fix him a cup of tea. She'd do it, though it made her feel like she was at work and Elmer a customer. He wouldn't stay long, as he had to rise early in the morning.

They walked up the three steps to her porch, then Charlotte stopped.

A long, black mass lay in the porch swing. She clutched Elmer's arm.

"What is it?" His voice held a note of impatience.

"Someone's on my swing," she said quietly.

"Wait here." Before she could protest, Elmer extracted his arm and approached the swing. "Hello!" He shook the form within, but the man barely stirred.

Dread lanced through Charlotte's chest. Was he dead? She haltingly walked forward.

"Some derelict." Derision filled Elmer's voice. "Out cold." He took her arm again and steered her toward the steps. "Wait in the car. I'll go in and phone the police."

"I'm perfectly capable of ringing them myself." Charlotte jerked her arm out of his and marched toward the swing, but she stopped short, her gaze drawn to the man in the swing. The porch light glinted off the gold rim of his glasses. She took a step closer, and her foot bumped something. A gray fedora, lying on the porch floor, beside the wooden railing. She picked it up, its dampness chill in her hands. "He doesn't look like a derelict." The man was dressed too well, his water-darkened, gray pinstriped suit appropriate for church, a wedding, or a night out dancing. She sniffed the air. No liquor odor. "I don't think he's drunk." Something about him struck her as familiar.

She moved closer, and gasped when she saw the strange scar ringing his neck above his collar. "Tony!"

Excitement rushed through her, a good-exciting as she would have said when she was a girl. The kind she felt when a project worked after months of trial and error. The kind she felt when she completed a particularly arduous equation.

The kind she'd felt with Louie Lambert in the back seat of his car.

It was unmistakably Tony.

He hadn't aged at all since she'd seen him twenty years ago. It was he who had jumped. She clutched the hat to her chest with both hands, barely aware of Elmer's footfalls behind her.

"You know this man?"

The hat slid from her hands and hit the porch with a muted plop. She crouched beside Tony and pressed her fingers to the side of his neck, above the scar. A slow but steady pulse beat beneath her hand. Relief trickled down her insides. Her eyes roved over his handsome face, serene in recovery sleep. Elmer remained behind her. "Who is he?"

"A friend." She reluctantly pulled her hand away. Tony's head lolled toward her as she bumped the swing. "He saved my life. In the flood."

The rain intensified a notch, drumming on the tin roof of the Paulson's house next door. Elmer shifted his feet. "Do you want me to go in and call a doctor?"

Charlotte whirled around. "No!" Doctors wouldn't be able to help

Tony. They hadn't been able to help her when she started going off to the past soon after the flood. "No," she repeated. "I... I don't think he's ill. And I can't afford a doctor anyway." She rose and faced Elmer. "He just needs to rest. Please, help me carry him inside."

Go inside, ring Theodore, her conscience urged, but she ignored it. She bent to slide Tony off the swing but Elmer hesitated. "This is highly... irregular," he said.

You shouldn't do this! the little voice admonished. "Please, Elmer." She spoke softly. "I know what's wrong with him. It's happened to me before. He'll sleep for a day or so, then he'll be fine. There's no sense wasting money on a doctor." She would call Theodore in the morning. No point in waking him at such a late hour.

Elmer drew back. "You mean that strange childhood condition you spoke of? When you disappeared, then remembered nothing?"

"Yes. Don't worry, it's not contagious." At least not in this situation. She shoved Theodore and the Society out of her mind, crouched and wedged a hand beneath Tony's back.

After a couple of seconds, Elmer moved to her side. "I'll get him, you get his legs—no, get the door first." He waited while Charlotte pushed the door open, then slipped his hands under Tony's armpits. Charlotte dashed back across the porch and gripped Tony's ankles, and the two of them carried him inside. "Where...?" Elmer asked with a grunt.

"The spare room." Charlotte labored to cross the threshold, then finally, they deposited Tony on the narrow bed her boarders used. "Perhaps it's just as well I haven't found a tenant." The sparse, plain room held nothing but the bed, a lowboy, and a single lamp, but her boarders never complained.

Elmer wiped his brow. "I still think we should call a doctor. I have credit, if you need—"

"I won't have you running up a bill, and he doesn't need a doctor." She could phone Theodore, claim he was a doctor, as he himself had done twenty years earlier. But Elmer would find it odd when a colored doctor arrived. Her voice softened. "Please, Elmer, I know you're trying to do the right thing, but... believe me, this is what he needs."

Elmer backed away and straightened his tie. "You're not going to let him stay here?" His inflection made it sound more like an order than a question.

Tony lay motionless except for the slight rise and fall of his chest. "What else would I do?" Charlotte asked. "Of course he'll stay here."

"I can't stay with you," Elmer said.

"Of course you can't. Nor would I expect you to—"

"You can't just take a strange man into your house."

"He saved my life! It's the least I can do for him."

Elmer let out a humph. "Well, I don't like it. People will talk—"

"The Paulson's can't see my front porch from their house, and Ida's long in bed by now." Charlotte didn't care what the neighbors thought. All that mattered was taking care of Tony. She bent to pull off his shoes.

"What are you doing?" Elmer asked.

"We have to get him out of these wet things." Mesmerized by Tony's inert form, she dropped the shoes on the floor with a clunk as she rose. "Could you...?" She backed toward the door.

"You want me to undress him?"

Charlotte put a hand on her hip. "We can hardly leave him to sleep in that sopping wet suit." Elmer's expression softened. Charlotte backed out the door. "Just bring his clothes out and I'll hang them in the bathroom to dry." She pulled the door shut and waited in the hall.

Rustles and the occasional grunt issued from the room. "Jumpin' Jiminy!" Elmer said.

Charlotte moved closer to the door. "Is something wrong?"

"No, nothing... but this fellow has the strangest set of drawers I've ever seen, and his socks..."

"What about them?"

Another grunt and more rustles, then Elmer emerged from the room. He thrust a wadded ball of fabric at her. "Elmer?" What was so unusual about Tony's clothes?

"His socks... all stretchy. Stay up all by themselves. And his drawers..." He cocked his head at the armload of clothing. "Have to be mighty uncomfortable. Tight around the waist..." His eyes met hers and his face reddened. "Nothing a lady need concern herself with. It's getting late, I must be going. If you're sure you'll be all right with him—"

"I'll be fine." She moved toward the front door and hoped Elmer would take the hint.

He followed. "I'm not comfortable with the idea... a strange man in your home..."

"Consider him nothing more than another boarder," Charlotte said. "Which is exactly how I'll explain—"

"But a man, Charlotte?"

"It's been two months since Sally left. At this point I can hardly be choosy." If only Tony could be a boarder. Her butter and egg money was long gone. She still owed Theodore what she'd borrowed last month, when her landlord had threatened eviction. The last thing she wanted was to become further indebted to the Society.

Elmer nodded and paused with his hand on the doorknob. "I had a pleasant time this evening."

"I did, too," Charlotte said. Pleasant? Was that what an evening with a gentleman was supposed to be? "Thank you again for the show." She rested a hand on the doorframe.

Elmer started to lean toward her, then glanced at the still-ajar door to the second bedroom. "Until Tuesday, then." He walked out the door.

Charlotte pushed it closed behind him, then sagged against it. Why couldn't Elmer be more... exciting? Or at least interesting? Maybe real life wasn't like the movies, but Dewey and his wife enjoyed being together. Mr. and Mrs. Paulson next door looked at each other and laughed together like they didn't find each other's company merely pleasant, but fun. Magical.

She carried Tony's wet clothes into the bathroom and draped them over the bathtub. Nothing unusual in the jacket, trousers, shirt or tie. He'd taken care to dress appropriately to the era. Except for the socks...

She held one up. Black, a soft knit fabric, with gold thread woven into the heel. She pulled at it and it stretched four or five inches. She gasped. What wondrous material was it made of? She released the toe, and the sock returned to the same shape it held before. "Mercy!" She would have to ask Tony about his socks when he woke. Ideas spun in her mind. The practical things that could be made with such fabric! Garters would become obsolete. Surely there was money to be made—

She couldn't. It wouldn't exactly be violating Society law, but it might cause Tony—

She had to check on him. Elmer wouldn't approve of her approaching an almost-nude man, but he'd never know.

Drawn like a stray dog to food, she walked to Tony's side, and gazed down upon the sleeping form. "What am I going to do with you?"

The question was rhetorical. He'd wake once he'd slept off the effects of the jump, then Theodore would serve him a punishment suitable for whatever transgression had earned him a place in the Black Book, and that would be the end of it. Or Theodore would deal Tony a swift and—she hoped—painless death, and let Tony's contemporaries handle it when he returned, alive, to his own time.

She didn't want Theodore—or anyone—to handle it. Whatever ill he'd done, Tony had saved her life. At the least, she owed him the opportunity to defend himself.

Her hand went to the hollow between her breasts. Heavens, she'd forgotten he was so handsome. She fingered the quarter. It hadn't come off her neck since she'd hung it on the chain Theodore had given her years ago.

Twenty years ago, the coin had been magical. Shining, silver proof that time travel was real, and so then, must be Tony's claim that she could do anything, be anything.

She'd believed him. She'd chased that dream for a while, gotten close enough to touch it when she'd gained a position in the inventions department at Dayton Kitchen Products Research. In a field dominated by men, she'd dared to take her place among them, to prove that she, too, could contribute to the world and make people's lives better. Then her chance at glory had slipped away like a hot air balloon, its moorings cut by the depression.

All she had left was the quarter.

It was a lifeline, a link through the decades to the man to whom she would always hold a connection, no matter how tenuous. A sign that someday, he'd come back to her, bringing with him her dreams renewed.

Only now, she was a woman harboring a fugitive.

Tony took a deep, shuddering breath, but didn't wake. Charlotte couldn't move, couldn't tear her eyes from him. As she watched the rise and fall of his chest, his criminal past—or future, as it might be—slipped away, and he once again became the man from the future who'd come back to save her. A man whose knowledge Charlotte desperately wanted, no matter how much she knew she shouldn't.

She had to see those drawers.

She leaned forward, then stopped. Heavens, what was she thinking? Nothing a lady should concern herself with, indeed.

It's purely scientific, her rational self argued.

In a pig's eye.

Curiosity warred with propriety. He was in recovery sleep, he'd never know if she took a tiny peek. A chance to learn something of the future, nothing more.

Curiosity won. She leaned over and peeled back the quilt.

A zing shot through her that had nothing to do with Tony's clothing. A zing she never felt with Elmer. But why?

Scientific reasons. She studied the undergarments. Elmer had left Tony's ordinary, sleeveless undershirt on. She pressed her palm to his chest, let her hand rest over his heartbeat. Had to assure herself he wasn't wet to the skin.

While her proper side protested, she pushed the covers back until she revealed the strange drawers.

The soft, white cotton clung to Tony's hips. Didn't cover the tops of his legs at all. She drew a finger along the odd, blue-striped waistband. Elastic! Just like suspenders. How clever clothing was in the future! The underpants fit snugly, though she doubted Elmer's assumption they'd be uncomfortable. They even had a flap over—

Her face heated, and she yanked the blankets back over him. Good heavens, what was she doing?

From the living room, the dome clock atop the radio cabinet chimed twelve times. She had to get to bed. Had to be at work by six. If she was late again, Irving would fire her.

She'd grown weary by the time she and Elmer reached home, but she couldn't think about sleeping now, not with Tony lying in her spare room—

The cats! She tore her eyes off Tony and hurried to the kitchen.

She set out scraps from the restaurant for the alley cats every night. The poor dears had to be starved. She set the plate of leftover stew—mostly vegetables—on her back stoop then returned to the spare bedroom. She lingered beside the bed and contemplated Tony, unsure of what to do. *Call Theodore.*

She couldn't.

But you should.

Tomorrow would be soon enough. The niggling little voice was annoying, so she forced her mind to blank.

He looked so peaceful lying there, his strange spiky, unkempt hair—not slicked back like most gentlemen's—the only visible clue that he didn't belong. What would Theodore do to him? Surely not the Treatment. *Lord have mercy, no!* Her fingers twisted in her skirt. Many of the Black Book peoples' crimes were egregious enough they got the Treatment immediately. The lucky ones were killed, though she'd heard in other times and places the death sentence had fallen out of fashion.

Tony had saved her life. She couldn't call Theodore.

But you must. It was her duty to the Society. When Tony had saved her life, he'd plunged her into a terrifying world where she could disappear any time, to eras full of danger, times when no one knew her. The Society had given Charlotte her life back. Theodore had taught her how to control the frightening tendency to slip in time, and how to stay grounded in the present.

He would have felt the jump; it was a matter of time until he tracked Tony down himself anyway.

Bed, it was time for bed. Her feet dragged as she left the room.

She'd just buttoned her nightgown when the telephone rang. She'd always considered it an extravagance, but Theodore insisted on being able to contact her at any time, so she let the Society pay for it. She hurried to the kitchen to answer it.

"Charlotte?"

She let out her breath. "Hello, Theodore."

"I apologize for ringing you at this hour but I had to know if it was you who jumped."

Tell him! She forced a light chuckle. "Well, now you know. You know I hardly ever—"

"I know dear." A hint of underlying Southern accent crept into his cultured voice. "But we must be ever vigilant for those who would manipulate time to serve their own ends."

She sighed. "Yes, Theodore." Sometimes he could be fanatical about chasing down those he called the enemies of time. His personal crusade. She shot a glance toward the hallway, where a known Enemy lay recovering.

"You'll keep an eye out and let me know?"

"Of course."

He bid her good night and hung up. She replaced the phone, then leaned against the wall. She should have said something.

She couldn't. Not when he could very well condemn Tony to the Treatment.

Images of Fred Cheltenham assaulted her, the ones that still haunted her dreams on occasion. She'd returned to the House a few days after she'd run away that night, before the pull claimed Fred and returned him to his own time. She'd never forget his drooling mouth and vacant eyes, void of thought.

She couldn't let the man to whom she owed her life fall victim to such a fate.

Yet she owed Theodore, too. She would be vigilant. Just not in the way Theodore expected. She would stay with Tony throughout his visit to her time, keep an eye on him, make sure he didn't do anything to earn him his place in the Black Book.

But if he committed his crime in her time, she'd be the one changing history...

She pushed the thought from her mind and returned to the spare bedroom. She'd forgotten to remove Tony's glasses.

She slipped them off, folded them and lay them on the dresser. What would his odd, spiky hair feel like? Would it be bristly, like her father's beard? Tentatively, she reached out and brushed it back with her hand. It was surprisingly soft. She let her hand hover there for a second, then snatched it away as his eyes fluttered open.

They were the same brilliant blue of a summer sky that she remembered. "Tony?"

His mouth slowly slid open. "Violet?"

Thirteen

TONY HESITATED AS HE REACHED FOR THE DOOR HANDLE OF IRVING'S Restaurant. The narrow, old frame structure and its hand-lettered front window reminded him of the tobacco shop where he and Charlotte had found refuge during the flood.

But it was the sign above the door that made the enormity of what he'd done hit him like a sucker punch to the gut: *Whites Only.*

He'd gone back a century in time by will alone. A time where men still tipped their hats to women—ladies—and offered them their seats on the bus, and no one got offended. A time before civil rights, when it was acceptable to deny someone entrance to a public estab-lishment solely on the basis of race. Even an honest, respectable businessman like his friend Bernie.

An old man brushed past him and walked inside, the door's squeak jolting Tony out of his daze.

His fingers slipped on the door handle when he grabbed it.

He stared down at his sweat-moistened hands. *Man, Solomon, get a grip!*

He'd awakened in her home, instead of a hotel like he'd planned, and—who had undressed him? Charlotte? As far as he could tell, she lived alone. The thought turned his stomach to wet noodles. What a turnabout from the day he met her.

She'd left a note on the nightstand, requesting him to come to the restaurant when he woke, and said she looked forward to seeing him.

He wiped his hands across his pants, trying to get rid of the fluttery feeling in his belly.

Like he was in high school again, about to go on a date with a hot girl.

It wasn't a date. Nothing would happen, never mind what Dewey had implied. Tony was there to learn, nothing more.

He gazed around at the passers-by. No one gave him a second glance. Thanks to Great-aunt Louise's reluctance to part with any-thing—even seventy-five-year-old suits—Tony fit in with the other businessmen he'd seen during his walk to the restaurant.

He yanked open the door and strode inside.

The eight, white linen-covered tables were empty, but three men hunkered at the counter and pored over a newspaper, their backs to the door and window. Tony slid onto a stool beside them. They were grumbling about baseball, and what a sorry game the Ducks had played the other night. Some things never changed.

Where was Charlotte? Empty coffee cups sat before two of the men. They were talking about work now. Or rather, the lack of it, and how someone they knew had lost his job the other day when the plant closed.

If someone didn't take care of them soon, Irving's Restaurant might not be far behind.

As if provoked by the thought, a man's face appeared in the pass-through window. His mouth contorted into a snarl beneath the greasy, graying hair combed across his balding head. "Charlotte!" he bellowed, then disappeared.

"Coming!" a woman called. A slam behind the counter drew eve-ryone's attention, then she dashed into the dining room with a pot of coffee.

Lightness rose in Tony's chest. It was her. His knees tensed. He studied her as she reached across the counter to refill the men's cups.

The same face had leaned over him last night, a halo of short, wavy, brown hair framing her concerned expression. Those hands had held a glass of water to his lips when he awakened for a few hazy moments. The same curvy body had led him to the bathroom a couple times during his stupor, one he vaguely remembered thinking reminded him of Violet.

Charlotte filled the second customer's cup. "Oh dear, Mr. Dawson, you should have hollered for me." Her voice held a hint of the same throaty quality that characterized Violet's. When she leaned over to top off the third man's cup, the v-neck of her dress drooped to offer a view of her ample cleavage, drawing all of the men's stares. Charlotte appeared not to notice.

Her step carried an energy, and the sincerity of her words and their reflection in her eyes bespoke a life force that elevated her otherwise ordinary appearance to timeless beauty. All this in a woman who read heavy science in her free time. Tony had perused her cluttered bookshelf and found it crammed with volumes by Einstein, Hubble, others he'd never heard of.

He leaned on his hand, elbow on the counter, as she approached. "Oh! I'm so sorry, sir, I didn't hear anyone come—Tony!" Her hand tightened on the handle of the coffee carafe, and her lips parted to reveal the same gap-toothed smile that had charmed him when she was a child. "How are you feeling?"

"Good, now that I've rested." Her face brightened the room like a neon light in a smoky bar. The men stopped talking and peered sidewise at them. Tony lowered his voice. "What day is it?"

"Tuesday, May sixteenth."

She'd taken care of him for three days. "Thanks for taking me in. Honestly, I didn't mean to pass out on—"

"Think nothing of it." She waved him off. "I know what it's like."

"You do, don't you?"

She tipped her head toward the other customers as she lifted a coffee cup and saucer off the shelf. The three men resumed their talk of sports and the weather. "Coffee?" she asked.

At his nod, she filled the cup in front of him. She could've been Violet's twin. All she'd have to do was let her hair grow and color it blond, and put on some weight.

"What else would you like? You must be famished." She slid a hand-printed, paper menu toward him.

"Now that you mention it..." He skimmed the restaurant's offerings as he poured some cream—the real stuff—into his coffee. No bagels, of course. "Scrambled eggs and bacon would be great." In the 1930s, no one worried about cholesterol. A tendril of smoke curled from a cigarette as the man beside him took a puff. *Or smoking.*

He felt the men's eyes on him as he watched her depart through the kitchen door. They didn't bother to look away when he met their stares. "Morning," he said.

Two of the men grunted a response. The guy nearest Tony lay the newspaper on the counter. "Don't reckon I've seen you around before."

"I'm an old friend of Charlotte's."

For a long moment no one moved. The wall clock behind the counter ticked off several seconds. Tony pointed at the newspaper. "Mind if I look at your paper?" Brushing up on current events might help him immerse himself in the time.

The man slid it over to him. "What few jobs in it're probably taken. Then again, I don't guess you're hurtin'. You a salesman or something?"

"Something like that."

The men resumed their conversation as Tony opened the *Dayton Journal*, a newspaper which no longer existed in his time.

The man beside Tony muttered something about how long his brother had looked for work. "Lord knows when it'll get better." The other men grumbled their assents, little different than the patrons at Bernie's decades later. So ordinary, yet not.

Tony felt their stares and turned to the paper.

"Hearing Dropped when Faber Resigns" (whoever he was) read the main headline, followed by news of qualifiers in golf's National Open. Tony found the ads most intriguing of all. Engrossed, he barely heard the door open and shut when the men left. A few minutes later, Charlotte emerged from the kitchen and walked around the counter.

"Oh good, they're gone." She leaned around him to place a fragrant plate of food on the counter, then climbed onto the stool beside his. "I swear, those three are worse than a bunch of gossipy old women."

Tony popped a bite into his mouth. "Mm-hmm."

"They would've hung on every word you and I said, then gone straight home to their wives..." She reached into her apron pocket and pulled out a box of cigarettes. Chesterfields. "Of course, we need all the business we can get, so I should hardly wish them to leave once they've paid their nickels—"

Tony sucked in a bite of eggs too fast and coughed. She held a cigarette in one hand and dropped the box back into her pocket with the other. "What's wrong?"

Tony swallowed, then chuckled. "It's just funny. A nickel for coffee. Where I come from, a buck is cheap."

Charlotte's free hand flew to her chest. "A whole dollar for a cup of coffee? Why, that'd buy lunch for five here. A good lunch, too." She held the cigarette near her lips and gazed at him through a fringe of wavy hair. Her voice went soft, sultry. "Do you have a light, by any chance?"

Tony's mouth opened but nothing came out. She was hot—no, that wasn't quite it. Something about her... maybe the ease with which she spoke to him, the way her luminous eyes settled on him as if he were the only man in the world—made it hard for him to reconcile this woman and her flirtatious smile with the little girl he'd pulled out of the floodwaters.

"Tony?" She jerked the cigarette away from her mouth. "Did I say something wrong?"

Tony shook off the fog in his mind. "No, I... you know, you've grown up to be a beautiful woman." He mentally slapped himself as soon as the words tumbled out. What the hell was he doing?

She demurely turned away for a second. "About that light... or don't people do that in the twenty-first century?"

"They do, but I don't have one. I quit years ago. Or, I guess I should say, years from now?"

With a giggle, she pointed to the counter's back edge where a box of matches lay. It took him three tries to light one. He lifted it to the tip of Charlotte's cigarette as she leaned close, and a warmth burst through him that had nothing to do with the hot coffee or the match in his hand. Somehow, it seemed much different to be doing this for Charlotte, in the light of day, than for the women at Mulroney's. With them, he complied only out of politeness.

"You know smoking's bad for you?" he asked.

She pulled back and took a puff. "It is?"

"Causes all kinds of health problems. Doesn't get to be common knowledge until the sixties or seventies, though." He took a bite of scrambled eggs.

She regarded the smoldering tip. "But it's so relaxing."

"Lots of people in my—where I come from still enjoy it."

"After this morning I can certainly use it." She took another puff. The smoke formed ribboned whorls in the air. "Had a big breakfast rush just before you came in. Normally I cook, but the waitress didn't show up this morning."

Tony mumbled his sympathy. He sneaked furtive glances at her while he ate. She sat sideways on her stool, gazing out the window as she smoked. Her casual, unfeigned elegance belied the apron or the threadbare hem of the cotton print dress beneath it. She even stubbed out her cigarette with grace.

Finished with his breakfast, Tony pushed his plate away. His hat slipped forward on his head. "Oh, man," he said. She tilted her head as he swiped the hat off. "You must think I have no manners at all."

"Actually, I just thought you were very hungry." The side of her face twitched in a half-wink, half-smile. "I always was after... you know."

Tony lowered his coffee cup. "When—how long have you been able...?"

"Ever since you rescued me." She cast her eyes down. "Though most of the time I choose not to." She fidgeted with the corner of her apron.

"Why?" This was a far cry from Everly's "it's incredible... anytime, anywhere."

"It's been a long time since I've spoken of this."

"Believe me, I understand." He stared into the honeyed depths of her eyes.

"It was horrible. Those first few times... No one knew me, I had no idea what happened. The police took me to a girls' home. They were so hateful there, especially to someone... different."

She shot a nervous glance at the pass-through window. "Papa was frantic. A couple times I disappeared right out of my own bed. He was so desperate by the time Theodore showed up it didn't even matter that Theodore's colored—"

"Theodore?" Tony gripped his fork tighter. She had to mean Theodore Pippin, from the award plaque in the Society House. The man who'd made it his life's mission to hunt down and punish those who disrupted the fabric of space and time.

"I suppose you could call him my mentor of sorts." The warmth in Tony's middle vanished. She drew out her pack of Chesterfields again.

Theodore Pippin. Her mentor, of all people. Honored by the Society for capturing time-criminals.

Tony studied her face as she shook out a cigarette. She concentrated on it, frowning at the box as if trying to avoid looking at Tony.

He should find someone else to answer his questions.

She tipped the cigarette box and let the one she'd shaken out fall back in. Her eyes swept over him. "You haven't changed a bit." Her voice held a quiet amazement.

"It's only been six weeks for me."

"Six weeks?"

"Since the flood."

"Oh my." She straightened. "Then you must find this... this thing as much of a puzzle as I did at first."

"I found someone to answer some of my questions. I was hoping you could answer the rest." Should he tell her about her brother? *Better not.* Once Dewey had concluded Tony was the man he'd met with his sister, he'd grown agitated until his shouts drew the staff and they'd made Tony leave. And wouldn't there be an inherent danger in knowing one's own future? Or in Charlotte's case, lack of one? Dewey said she'd died the second time Tony came to 1933.

A future he'd make sure didn't happen. There would be no second visit.

"I'll do whatever I can to help you," Charlotte said. "Though it's been years since I've jumped to the past, or even thought about it, other than to avoid it."

"Can't say I blame you." Tony recalled his own resolve to do no more time traveling once he got Bethany back. Especially after his short trip back two years had so affected his life. Memories of another life in another timeline surfaced, one where he hadn't discovered Dora's betrayal and had remained married.

The greasy face appeared in the pass-through again. "Charlotte!" the man bellowed. "I ain't paying you to sit around and jaw with the customers! There's dishes—"

"Coming, sir!" Charlotte hopped off the stool. The man disappeared again.

"Irving, I assume?" Tony asked.

Charlotte's lips tightened as she straightened her apron.

"Nice guy," Tony commented. She snatched the empty coffee carafe off the counter and hurried through the kitchen door.

He should leave. If Charlotte knew Pippin, and he'd still been at the Society House in 1954, that meant he'd be there now. How close were Charlotte's ties to him?

Irving scowled at Charlotte as he strode into the kitchen, broom in hand, and jerked his thumb toward the dining room door. "Some dandified darkie's out front asking for you," he growled. "I told 'im his kind ain't welcome here, but he insisted. So I made 'im wait in the alley out back."

Theodore! Charlotte flung the dishrag into the sink. "I'll go talk to him." Time to pay the piper. She dashed past Irving, but not fast enough to avoid a pinch on the fanny.

Louse. She waited to rub the sore spot until she was through the door and out of Irving's view, unwilling to give him the satisfaction of even that small acknowledgment. If jobs weren't so hard to come by... Of course, she could always do like Theodore and let the Society support her. But she'd rather suffer Irving's attention than allow them to own her. It was bad enough she'd let them put her through college.

She forgot her indignity when she glimpsed Tony at the counter, bent over the newspaper. The sight stabbed her heart. How could she tell Theodore he was right there, in the restaurant? What terrible things would he do to him? She ran out the front door before Tony could hail her. Thank heavens his back was to the window. For the first time, she was glad Irving didn't permit colored in the restaurant.

"Good morning, Charlotte." Theodore tipped his hat as she slipped out the front door.

"What are you doing here?" she hissed as she led him around the corner of the building. Away from the window.

He held up a hand. "I know, I won't keep you. I'm just a little concerned. You haven't answered the telephone for the past two nights, especially after you missed dinner Sunday."

"I'm better now. Just tired." Due to Tony's presence, she'd begged off their weekly dinner at the Society House, claiming she didn't feel well. Theodore cocked his head, unconvinced. "Really, Theodore, there's nothing wrong." Nothing, if she didn't count the fact she was harboring a wanted man, and hiding him from the person to whom she owed everything beyond life itself. She started to lean on the restaurant's white, frame wall, then pulled away when she remembered how dirty it was. "It's been busy here, and after fighting off whatever bug it was I had, all I want to do when I get home is collapse with the radio and a cigarette." Which was the truth, except for the reason. For the past two days, as soon as she walked in from work, she'd taken up her post next to Tony, to be near in case he woke.

She'd avoided the telephone because she knew it was Theodore. Her loyalty to him and the Society warred with her need to repay Tony for saving her life. And she longed to talk to Tony, to let him see the woman she'd become, get to know him. "I'll have the money I owe you Friday. I'll bring it to you af—"

"I'm not concerned about the money." Theodore's voice was firm. "As you shouldn't be. There will always be a suite for you at the House, the Society takes care of its own—"

"I know, Theodore. I just want to..." Be her own person. Not be ruled by the Society any more than she had to. "...take care of myself. I won't take charity, not even from the Society. I wasn't avoiding the phone because of the money, you know me better than that."

"Yes, I do." Theodore spoke slowly. "That's why I get the idea there's more to this than you're telling me."

She slumped against the siding and pressed the back of her hand to her forehead.

"You found the jumper, didn't you?" Theodore's voice was quiet, accusatory. "When, Charlotte? Why did you not contact me?"

"I was going to. As soon as I got off work—"

"How long have you been aware of this person?"

She sighed. "Friday. He just woke up from recovery today."

Theodore's voice lowered in pitch, and he spoke sharply. "This isn't a random jumper, is it? It's someone who—"

"He's a good man! He doesn't deserve—"

"If he's in the book, he must be neutralized! You of all people should understand that, after your father—"

"This isn't about my father!" Charlotte jerked upright. "This is about a man who may not have even done anything." Yet.

Theodore's shoulders flattened and he loomed closer to her. "But he will. Otherwise he wouldn't be in the book."

Charlotte lowered her voice and dropped her gaze to project a deferential attitude. "I'm not arguing the fact that time shouldn't be altered. But your methods... please, Theodore, let me handle this one." She forced strength into her voice. If he detected any weakness in her, he wouldn't let her. "I'll convince him to come to the House. Please, promise me you won't hurt him, you'll just send him home..."

It wouldn't be easy. Tony had tensed when she mentioned Theodore. He knew something, though maybe not the full extent of the danger. He wouldn't be easily convinced. She'd have to take care in working up to the suggestion. "Please, Theodore." She stopped before her pleading turned into begging.

Theodore's voice grew gentle again. "Who is this man, that you're willing to risk your principles, everything the Society stands for?"

"It's Tony. Tony Solomon. The man who saved my life."

"I know! Let's go visit my friend Theodore." Charlotte popped a dusty-pink, bell-shaped hat on as soon as her shift at Irving's ended.

Nausea welled in Tony's stomach as he held the door for her. What was she trying to do? She couldn't have seen the wanted posters in the 1954 Society House, but were there earlier versions?

Not a chance Tony wanted to take. "Uh... I don't know, I'm kind of tired, and I could use a shower—or bath." Even though he'd taken one that morning, he preferred not to go through the rest of the day smelling of fried food.

"Oh, how rude of me! Of course we can go back to my house. Then maybe after—"

"I'm going to need some new clothes, too," Tony cut in, hoping to distract her. "I brought a suitcase, but when I got here, all I had was the broken handle."

They turned down Fourth Street, toward the river and Charlotte's house. "I've tried that before, too. There seems to be a sphere of influence, if you will, around us. Unless something's directly touching you, and within a couple of inches of your body, it stays behind when you jump."

Tony gave a rueful chuckle. "Then some homeless guy's probably got himself a week's worth of socks and underwear. And a couple of mint-condition, vintage suits. Speaking of which... who, uh, undressed me?"

A tinge of red crept into her face before she turned away. "Elmer did." She stared at a laundromat as they walked past, as if there were something fascinating reflected in its front window. "He's a... gentleman I've been seeing."

Oh yeah, the boyfriend Dewey had mentioned. The one Tony supposedly ran off.

Which he wouldn't, despite the hollow in his gut. He was there for information. Nothing more, never mind what Dewey said.

Conversation made the half-hour walk zip by. Tony told her about welfare and Social Security, and other legacies from her time that lasted into his day, all while trying not to gawk at the old-fashioned—at least, to him—cars, the newsstand huckster, the teen-age boy selling apples on the corner for a nickel apiece. Tony flipped him a dime, and he and Charlotte munched apples as they walked, juicier and sweeter than any he could remember eating. Maybe it was just in contrast to the underlying tang of pollution that curled from exhaust pipes and floated in gray clouds on the north and east sides of town, from factories long gone in Tony's time.

Charlotte listened with attentive eyes, made him feel interesting and important. In turn, she amused him with stories of her childhood, fascinated him with descriptions of projects she'd worked on at the now-defunct Kitchen Products Research Company.

Though her dreams and her life's work had become relegated to a few minutes she could snatch here and there on weekends and evenings, they were still intact, unlike his own.

Tony had called it The Plan, the product of a naïve, twenty-one-year-old's mind.

Establish management career with prestigious firm, good pay, and advancement. Check.

Get married, have kids. Been there, done that, though a little earlier than planned.

Make a million by age thirty-five. Done, with a little help from his future self.

And what did it all mean now? His one child had been taken from him in a horrible, violent way. Divorce hadn't been in The Plan, either. Time travel sure as hell hadn't been.

His achievements weren't without sacrifice. And once he'd reached them, what was left?

It was a question he didn't care to ponder at the moment. Much more pleasant to enjoy the company of a beautiful, intriguing woman, one who was alive because of him. "So what do you do for fun?" he asked.

"There are the dances every weekend. And the movies, of course. Though I'm afraid my social life isn't very active now."

She entertained him with tales of her college years, of weekdays spent studying and weekend jaunts to roadhouses or an illicit club with a laundry for a front.

"So were you a flapper, then?" he asked.

She laughed. "Well, I never took up the habit of going about with my coat and galoshes unfastened. But I've enjoyed my share of drink, and dances my papa would have never approved of. The time my sister visited... oh, the things she said to me! But then Mabel's always been dreadfully dull and proper."

They'd reached Charlotte's neighborhood. Children played in yards and on the sidewalks, on bikes and with balls. More activity than Tony ever saw around his apartment, no matter how pleasant the weather.

As they neared the house three doors down from Charlotte's, a woman burst out the front door calling her name. When they stopped at the gate, she pressed three Mason jars of green beans into Charlotte's arms. "I can't thank you enough for fixing the radio." She went on about how her husband was driving her crazy, being unable to tune in to his programs.

Tony waited while the women chatted, then they moved on to Charlotte's house. "I take it you're the neighborhood fix-it lady?" He held the gate open for her.

"So some people call me." She didn't elaborate, and he found her modesty refreshing. She waved to a boy riding past on his bicycle. "Andy there gave me a ball of tinfoil for fixing his bike a couple weeks ago."

Tony chuckled. "Tinfoil?"

"I'm sure it will come in handy. Perhaps for the sun-powered furnace."

Tony stumbled going up the steps to her porch as he did a double take. "So you did become an inventor!"

"Well, I did work at the Kitchen Products Research Company. Before it closed. Now I work at home, in the evenings. Weekends. Whenever I can spare a moment. "Things like beans and foil may not seem like much to you, but..."

"They're a lot to them," Tony finished.

"Yes. And even if something isn't much to me—like a ball of tinfoil—helping others is my way of giving back. I've been fortunate. I've had a college education, a good job—or did, until the Research closed. And way back when we were trapped, you gave me the encouragement I needed to follow my dreams."

Pride swelled in him. He'd made a difference in her life. Brief as it was, his influence had had an impact on the fascinating woman she'd become.

She has a boyfriend. Tony pushed his thoughts back to the immediate conversation. "So why's a skilled woman like you working for a dirtbag like Irving?" The guy had deliberately brushed against her more than once, and when he goosed her a couple times, Tony wanted to jump up and deck him. Once Charlotte had whirled around in surprise and spilled a cup of soup on the letch. Tony suspected it wasn't an accident.

She sighed. "It pays the rent and puts food on my table. I'm lucky to have a job at all." She stared straight ahead, as she tossed her hat onto a wall rack. Her jaw tightened.

Then she whirled around, her grimace gone. "Why don't you get your bath, then let's go shopping. One of the customers said there's a good sale at Rike's." Her smile dissipated. "Only I'm afraid I don't have enough money to buy you anything more than the most basic—"

"I have money," Tony said. Somehow the prospect of shopping seemed less distasteful since he'd be with her. "While we're at it, I'll find a place to stay—"

"You'll do nothing of the sort." A stern expression took over her face. "You did see my room for rent sign, didn't you?"

He hesitated.

She put her hands on her hips. "You need a place to stay, I have a room. Unless... Oh, dear, I imagine you must stay in much nicer places—"

"No, no." He waved sideways. "Your spare room's fine. How much is it?"

"Tony! You saved my life. I can't take—"

"The hell you can't. If I'm going to be your boarder, I'll pay the same as anyone else."

"But your money..."

The coins in the attic. His driver's license. "Irving took it, didn't he?" Tony opened his wallet and pulled out one of the 1929 ten dollar bills he'd bought on E-bay.

She studied the bill but didn't take it. "Very well. The room's six dollars a week. Includes supper."

A slow grin spread across his face. Perfect. He should have ample opportunity to ply her with questions. As long as Pippin didn't come around.

An hour later, Tony held the door open then followed her inside the big department store. Charlotte strode toward the store directory. "It's been a while since I've been here."

"Me too." No point in telling her the building would be demolished in 1999 to make way for a performing arts center.

"I can't afford to shop very often," she said in a matter-of-fact voice. "And I have adequate clothing."

He did a double take. What woman ever had enough to wear?

In the men's department, she went straight to the shelves with sale placards above them. They got off the elevator with three shirts and a week's worth of underwear and socks—all for a little over thirty dollars. Of course, that thirty dollars had cost him over two hundred to buy. He checked his watch. The entire shopping excursion had taken fifteen minutes.

"What are you looking at?" Charlotte asked as they walked toward the exit. The sparkle in her eyes told him she didn't take offense at his curious expression.

"You shop like a man."

"I knew what you needed and got it. Some women can stay here all day and not spend a dime. Not me. I've never seen the point in gawking over things you've no intention of buying."

Her logic amazed him. But her gaze traveled over the dresses as they walked through the better dresses department. "See something you like?" he asked.

"I don't need anything." She stared straight ahead.

"I didn't ask if you needed anything, I asked if you liked something. I got new clothes, you should get some too."

"But I don't—"

"I have money." He led her back toward the dresses, but she held back. "Come on." He took her hand. She hesitated. "Consider it a hostess gift," he said.

"Boarders don't give hostess gifts." She looked down at his hand clasped around hers, but didn't pull away.

"Too bad. I'm going to. Now go find something you like."

He found a chair and sat while she asked a clerk about the dress in the window display... something about violets. When she returned, her step had lost its spring.

"They don't have your size?" Tony asked.

"It's over twenty-five dollars," she whispered.

"So?"

"It's much too expensive. I don't need it."

He ran a mental calculation. If coffee was a nickel, the dress would cost over two hundred dollars in his time.

Dora wouldn't have given it a thought. "Go get the dress." She started to open her mouth, but shut it at his resolute gaze.

She came back holding a filmy white dress with a leafy floral print. Violets. Funny how a woman with such a strong resemblance to his friend from work would choose a dress bearing her namesake. "It's pretty. Don't you want to try it on?"

"It will fit." She beamed. They walked to the cashier. "Thank you, Tony," she said as the clerk rang up the sale.

"You deserve it." Tony pulled out his wallet and thumbed through it. As he yanked out a couple bills, something slipped out and hit the floor with a light snap.

"Shit." A credit card-sized calculator a trade show vendor had given him. He ignored the cashier's frown, grabbed the calculator and shoved it in his pocket.

"What is it?" Charlotte lowered her voice, glancing sideways at the clerk, who was folding the dress. "Is it a telephone?"

Tony chuckled as she took the bag from the cashier. "No." He'd left his cell phone in the car before he'd warped.

"Then what is it?" She moved toward the doors.

"It's called a calculator—like an adding machine." He pushed the door open as another shopper entered, then held it while Charlotte walked out.

"You'll show me later, won't you?"

"Yeah, sure." Why hadn't he cleaned out his wallet when he put in his 1929 money? For that matter, why hadn't he pitched the darn thing? His phone had a calculator on it. If he'd dropped the rubber Bernie had given him at Mulroney's, he might come across as immoral, but the calculator was more problematic. Showing a cell phone with a dead battery to a child hadn't seemed like a big deal. No one she told about it would have believed her. Was he tempting fate now by showing her the future?

At least the store clerk hadn't seen it. Hopefully, Charlotte would forget about it by the time they got to her home—

Yeah, right. Who was he kidding?

He tried to come up with another subject to divert her attention from the calculator, but her presence beside him muddled his thoughts.

He couldn't help sneaking glances at her as they walked down the street. They carried their bags in their outside hands, and it seemed natural to take her arm with the other.

She slid her hand down his arm and gave him a quick squeeze.

"Thank you again for the dress. It'll be lovely for the dance Saturday."

A dance. He wasn't much of a dancer, he preferred to sit and drink beer while the women danced. But the thought of walking into a crowded room, arm in arm with her in that filmy dress sent warmth through his body. As did his mental picture of her wearing it, for it was lower-cut than the frock she wore now.

"Oh dear," she said.

"What?"

"The dance. I told Elmer I'd go—"

"So?" The boyfriend. Tony dropped her arm, a sinking feeling sliding down his gut at the reminder. *It doesn't matter.*

"But I don't want to leave you alone."

"Do you usually stay home to entertain your boarders?"

"Of course not." She pretended to study a white picket fence flanking the sidewalk. The remains of the lightness in Tony's chest dissipated. He was there to get information, not have a fling. God knew Charlotte wasn't the kind of woman for a short-lived affair. She deserved someone who could give her a forever, not someone who'd get yanked to almost a hundred years in the future in a week or so. He pushed the unwelcome feelings aside and told himself he genuinely hoped Charlotte had a good time at the dance, though he had trouble believing it.

She deserved a regular guy who'd always be there for her. Not one who'd get her killed if he came back.

When they got home, Charlotte could barely restrain herself from snatching Tony's hat off and flinging it onto a hook for him. "Please, may I see your calculator now?"

"I don't—"

"Oh, how rude of me!" She pressed her palm to the neckline of her dress to brush the tip of her finger over her quarter. After his

bath, he'd had no choice but to don the clothes he'd jumped in, recovered in, then worn all day. "You probably want to change clothes,
don't you?"

"I do feel pretty grungy," he said.

"Grungy... what an interesting word."

She waited on the sofa. As soon as he changed, she should tell
him about the Saturn Society and start working on getting him to go
to the House. But Theodore had waited this long. He could wait a
little longer while she got a look at the fascinating device called a
calculator.

After a minute she rose, paced to the window, gazed out at the
street as Andy rode past, then returned to the sofa. Her eyes lit on the
letter from her landlord, lying on top of the radio, no doubt regarding
her overdue rent. She jumped up, grabbed it, and stuffed it between a
couple magazines.

She sat again. If she could figure out what made the wondrous
device work, she would be a woman ahead of her time. Smaller than
a playing card. She'd create things that would make the world a better place, make life easier for others. Not to mention herself. She'd no
longer need to suffer Irving's attentions. She'd be able to pay the rent
on time, and then some—why, she might even have money to spare,
to help Dewey and his family, who'd been struggling since his hours
had been cut at the factory.

But it's wrong! a voice inside her head shouted.

It is not, she argued with herself. She wouldn't be altering the
time stream, not if the calculator happened to fall into her lap.

But it could be why Tony was in the Black Book.

She pushed the thought into the dim recesses of her mind and
glanced at the guest room door. How long did it take a man to change
clothes? She forced herself to listen to the radio in an effort not to
think about what she might see if she went in—and worse, the fact
that she *wanted* to. Finally, the door clicked. She jumped up. "Can I—"

"I'm not sure it's a good idea." His expression was wary, like in
his photo in the Black Book.

Her face went slack. "Why?"

He walked to the sofa and sat. "You're a woman of science. An inventor. What'll you do with this knowledge?"

She sat next to him, uncaring that it wasn't proper. "Your concern is well-founded. The possibility of me developing technology before its time has serious implications, it's true. But how much knowledge could I gain from a brief look? What could be the harm?"

What could be the harm indeed, she could hear Theodore say, in a critical, sarcastic tone of voice. Or his favorite, "Learn—Observe— Preserve," the Saturn Society motto. As good a rule for dealing with the future as the past. Which was all she'd do.

Tony stared down at his hands. "I guess you're right." He slipped the calculator out of his pocket and handed it to her.

She ran her fingers over the tiny, numbered buttons, and the smooth, shiny black casing, then tapped it with her fingernail. Plastic. "How does it work?"

"Press where it says 'on.'"

She gasped. "It says zero!" Then she pressed the button with a number one on it. "Why... it's like a tiny typewriter! Except with numbers." She pushed the plus sign, some more numbers, then the equals sign. The little machine displayed the result instantly. "It's like magic!" She jabbed more numbers. "It's absolutely right, every time. It even figures square roots!" She stared at him in amazement. "How does it do that?"

"You mean how does it do the math?"

"Yes, and what makes the numbers? And what's this red panel?" The calculator wasn't the simple gadget it appeared. The tiny package contained a wealth of knowledge.

He tapped the numbers. "These are called liquid crystal displays." As he moved his arm, his hip brushed hers and sent a spark of awareness racing up her side to mingle with her excitement over the calculator. "Electricity makes the segments turn on and—"

"But how does it get electricity without a cord? Or batteries?" She squirmed.

"The batteries are very small. But it also uses light for power." Tony touched the shiny, dark red rectangle. "This is where it collects the light."

It was the answer she'd been searching for. "It's amazing! And we'll get these... when?"

"Maybe thirty, forty years from now. And not this small until several years later." He held out his hand, and she slowly placed the machine in his palm. "You said you'd show me your project?"

She led him into the cellar, scarcely able to concentrate enough to describe the sun-powered radiator as the calculator's possibilities pummeled her brain.

If she could unravel the mystery of how it stored energy, then she could solve the real challenges of her sun-powered furnace. How to regulate its temperature. How to make it usable at night, or on cloudy days.

Tony followed her into the basement, her favorite room in the house despite its constant, damp chill. Her favorite because of the workbench that ran along an entire wall, a place she could lose herself for hours. She snapped on the two metal clip lights above her creation, a welded, metal cabinet with foil-covered panels. Tony craned his neck to study the water tanks and the pipes she'd twisted around it. "I'm experimenting with water to store the sun's heat," she explained.

"I'd say you're on the right track." She searched his face. Not a hint of the veiled reservations Dewey always tried to hide when she showed him one of her projects. She seldom mentioned her work to Mabel, whose usual response was to chide her for wasting time she could better spend on something constructive, like quilting or working in the garden.

Louie had gone beyond skepticism to outright derision. Among other things, it proved he wasn't the man for her. If he hadn't broken their engagement, she would have. Elmer's lack of enthusiasm confirmed she'd best keep her activities to herself, should they eventually marry.

That prospect grew less likely the longer she spent with Tony. She let her eyes travel over him and remembered the bubbles of joy she'd felt when he took her arm in his on the way home from Rike's. So different than Elmer. Tony opened the cabinet's sealed door and ran his fingers around its smooth edges. "You might be onto something here."

"You think so?" She clasped her hands.

"Oh yeah, this is cool."

"Cool?" Her shoulders slumped. "But it's supposed to get hot. Or at least warm."

He laughed, and heaviness fell over her body like a lead jacket. It was worse than Louie's scorn. She started to turn away. "Oh, no, I mean it's neat," Tony said. "Good. *Swell.*" His face settled into a grin. "In my time, cool has another meaning besides temperature. It's a good thing."

The heaviness lifted and her lips formed a smile, as if she were a young child who'd finally learned her addition, or her poetry recitation, and he was the teacher offering praise. "Do people use these in your time?"

He hesitated. "Well..."

Her exuberance deflated. "They don't, do they?" She rested a hand on the sun-powered radiator's stainless steel top, its surface suddenly cold to the touch.

"Well, people begin to take an interest in solar energy for heating their homes in the seventies and eighties, but it doesn't really take off until twenty-ten or so."

Dejection settled over her again. "I'll never amount to anything as an inventor." She sighed.

He lay a hand on her shoulder and drew her around to face him. "I wouldn't say that." His touch sent a tingle up her arm. He slid his hand away as her eyes met his. "You could be laying the groundwork for developments that won't come until after my time."

Her sun-powered furnace wouldn't catapult her into fame and fortune—or at least away from the likes of Irving—but Tony went on about all the potential it had. Related projects and technology to which she could contribute. The kinds of companies she could approach now who might have an interest in her ideas.

Anticipation warred with unease, and she figured out why as

they trudged back upstairs to start dinner.

She'd finally met a man who believed in her. Not only believed in her work, but wanted to help her. A man who could take her ideas and sell them. Do the part she hated and, she had to admit, was hampered in by the fact she was a woman. Tony could cross barriers she couldn't. He could solicit interest in her work from men who couldn't see the innovator beneath her feminine form.

He intrigued her, intellectually. And otherwise, she had to admit. If it weren't for the fact that he belonged decades in the future, she'd want Tony to take her to the dance, not Elmer. Tony to be the one who spent his evenings with her. Tony who might ask her to marry him—

She couldn't think such things. Especially about an Enemy of Time. A man she needed to convince to go to the Society House and turn himself in.

Later. First, she'd at least fix dinner. It would hardly be civil to send him to Theodore on an empty stomach.

Fourteen

SOMEONE KNOCKED ON THE DOOR. CHARLOTTE JUMPED. ELMER! HEAVENS, she'd forgotten all about their plans.

She didn't want Elmer there. Didn't want to go out with him. She was having a far better time playing chess with Tony.

Of course, if she'd done what she should have, she'd welcome an evening at the movies with Elmer to get her mind off Tony, who would be at the Society House.

There was something about him, something she hadn't noticed as a little girl. His attentiveness, beyond rescuing and caring for her. His willingness to answer her endless questions, his—

The knock came again. Unable to delay any longer, she jumped to answer it.

Elmer brushed past her, crackling of paper. "Here." He thrust a cone-shaped bundle of newspaper at her, then dropped his hat on a chair back.

Charlotte took the flowers and gave the mixed bouquet inside a deep whiff. "Oh, they're lovely."

"Thought you might like—he's still here?" Elmer's lips drew back from his teeth like a feral dog's.

Charlotte looked at Tony, then Elmer, who continued to glare at Tony. "Elmer! Tony is my boarder." Tony approached, and she made a hasty introduction.

She fumbled for the chain beneath her collar. The men sized each other up until Tony extended his hand. "Nice to meet you."

Elmer's face tightened, but he reciprocated. "Well," he said to

Charlotte. "We'd best be going if we're to make the show on time." His narrowed gaze slid toward Tony. His lip twitched. "It isn't right. Living with a man who's not your husband—"

"I told you. He's a boarder," Charlotte repeated. "A *paying* boarder. And he saved—"

"Even if he did save your life, he should go to a hotel—"

"Which I was going to do," Tony said. Charlotte's brows drew together. "But she drives a hard bargain," he added.

Elmer went on as if Tony wasn't there. "There are rooms aplenty at the Miami, the Gibbons, the Biltmore. I'll pay you the money you'd get from him for the board—"

"You'll do no such thing!" Charlotte put her hands on her hips. "You're far from wealthy yourself. I'll—"

"You'll what? You hardly have money to pay your rent."

Charlotte's jaw clenched. Elmer didn't know how true those words were. He shot another glance at Tony, then grabbed her arm and propelled her onto the front porch.

He gazed out at the street, as if he wanted to avoid looking at her. "I was going to wait until I managed to save some money, to get you something nice, but..."

Dread lanced down Charlotte's throat. She swallowed.

"If you're having trouble making ends meet, we could get married. Move into my house. Then—"

"But I like my house."

"Mine's bigger."

"But I have so many things! I can't just pick up and move..." Her projects. He wouldn't be willing to move all that junk, as he'd called it once.

But if she did marry him...

She could have a family. No children of her own, her liaisons with Louie had confirmed she was unable. But Elmer came from a large family and had nieces and nephews, many of whom were quite fond of him. Their house would seldom be quiet.

And though Elmer didn't have a lot, she wouldn't have to worry about money.

But her work...

Pride swelled in her at the things she planned to do, ways she wanted to contribute to the betterment of society. Once that happened, money wouldn't be a problem. But the thought of spending her life with Elmer...

"It's too soon." She couldn't do it. "I'm not ready for this."

"Why the blazes not? I've been calling on you for almost two months. That's time enough."

Charlotte stared at the porch floor. Its gray paint was beginning to peel.

Elmer was a good man. He'd be good for her, provided she managed to sneak her project time in. Maybe the magic wasn't there. It didn't always happen right away. But he was right. She should have some idea by now. She lifted her head. "Elmer... I can't marry you."

Elmer drew back. "You're being hasty. I'll fetch my hat and we'll go to the show. Take some time to think about it." He whirled around, threw open the front door and strode inside, Charlotte on his heels. Elmer eyed Tony, who'd taken a sudden interest in the magazines lying on the coffee table.

Elmer slapped his hat on his head. "Regardless of what you choose, he should be gone before we return. Either he goes..." He crossed his arms over his chest. "Or I do."

A burn blossomed beneath Charlotte's ribs. Elmer had never ordered her around like that. The hairs on the back of her neck rose, then receded into a comforting warmth when Tony appeared a few feet behind her. His presence strengthened her resolve. She couldn't marry Elmer. Not now. Not ever.

Maybe being commanded like a soldier was all right for some women. But if she let him do it this time, it would continue, and the next thing she knew, she'd be nothing more than his puppet. She might as well forget about her work.

"Well?" Elmer said.

She squared her shoulders. "Enjoy the show, Elmer."

Elmer stood with his mouth agape. "Uh, uh..." Without another word, he whirled around and stomped out the door.

After a moment, Charlotte burst out laughing. "I do declare, the look on his face was priceless."

Tony joined in her mirth. "Yeah... new clothes—fifty dollars. Party dress for your girl—twenty-five dollars. Seeing her now-ex-boyfriend look like Beavis and Butthead... priceless!" They laughed until Charlotte sank into the couch, wiping her eyes.

"Tony? What's Beavis and... Butt—?"

Tony snorted back a final guffaw. "Never mind." He made his way back to the sofa and sat beside her, then half-rose as if he'd committed some kind of faux pas. But something in her face must've told him it was all right, for he sank into the cushions. He eyed her as if to ask, now what?

Her better judgment told her to move to the rocker. Or go to the kitchen, fix a cup of tea, do anything but place herself in danger of physical contact.

Physical contact she shouldn't want, but couldn't make herself stop hoping for.

Tony was everything Elmer wasn't. Educated, funny, entertaining, full of interesting stories. Wonderful to look at with his odd hairstyle that stuck up all over, combined with the studious appeal lent by his glasses. No doubt, his lovely blue eyes made the ladies in his workplace swoon.

Tony couldn't be her fellow. Not when the pull would yank him back to his own time in a couple weeks, maybe sooner. And Good Lord, he was in the Saturn Society's Black Book. Her only concern should be to get him to the Society House and let Theodore kill him and return him to his own time.

Despite her logic, her fanny remained planted on the sofa. She tried to concentrate on the radio.

Tony sensed her tension. If he said something to her now, it would only make her more nervous, so he reached for the magazine he'd feigned interest in earlier, a copy of *Time* with Charles Kettering on the cover.

Tony brushed his hand over it in amazement. To think, Kettering was still alive. Again the enormity of what Tony had done hit him, and he almost dropped the magazine.

He pawed through the other magazines on the coffee table. A few other issues of *Time*. *Amazing Stories*. Two *Life*s, complete with Rockwell-esque cover art.

He slid the Time from April—the latest one—over on the table, then placed the March issue atop it, then February, then January, the one featuring Kettering. As he reached for the *Life* magazines, quiet laughter stayed his hand.

"Tony? What on earth are you doing?"

"Uh, just tidying up." God, he was such a dweeb. He shoved the magazines into an unordered stack and sat back on the sofa.

Charlotte regarded him with a smile, not a making-fun one, but more... bemused appreciation?

Tony's hand itched to reach for hers on the cushion between them. Had she scooted closer?

Better not. Bad idea. But the perfect time to ask his questions. "Charlotte?"

"Yes?" Her golden gaze penetrated his soul. He wanted to tell her everything. About Chad Everly. About his trip two years into his own past, and his resulting divorce. About Dewey. And most of all, about Bethany.

Best to lead up to it gradually. "This time travel thing... What about the grandfather paradox?"

She drew back and blinked. "You mean if you go back in time and kill your grandfather?"

"Yeah. What happens? Do you suddenly cease to exist?" Most of the more scientific web sites he'd perused focused on time travel to the future, where the paradox wouldn't be an issue, but the science-fiction-oriented sites had raised a very real concern.

"Of course not. That's the stuff of the science fiction pulps." She nodded at the magazines on the coffee table, where he'd left a copy of *Amazing Stories* on top. "An intriguing conundrum, but it simply can't be done. Some have tried, but something always prevents the commission of the murder."

"I see."

Her voice took on a slight raise in pitch. "Goodness, I need a ciga-rette." She jumped up and grabbed one from her purse, then returned to the sofa.

Tony lost his train of thought when her lips closed around the cigarette, caressed it as she took a puff, and left the end stained pink when she pulled it away. A fierce urge to kiss those lips struck him. He wanted to fold her into his arms, pull her against him.

Are you out of your mind?

She flicked her cigarette on the ashtray on the end table, obscur-ing the hand-painted "Florida" and beach scene in the middle. He'd found it in his room when he woke, on the floor next to the bed. Had she sat beside him, smoking as she watched him sleep? A vague memory stirred of his first brief awakening in her house. She'd leaned over him, brushed back his hair. Or had he imagined it?

Charlotte fidgeted, as if she could read his thoughts. He had to get the conversation back on track. "Okay, I can go along with your can't-be-done theory. But what if, say for example, you influence the past so your parents never meet?"

"I imagine that, too, would be impossible. Circumstances would prevent it, somehow or other. Some things are simply fated to be." She brought her hand to her neckline, and toyed with a chain hidden beneath the fabric. "Only God, or the universe, or whatever higher power you believe in, knows what should be and what shouldn't. It's not for us to decide."

Her gaze lowered as she absently drew her finger around the chain. Only the radio and the hum of crickets outside broke the si-lence. Was Bethany's death fated to be?

He wouldn't believe it. Just ideological bullshit. Sure, God, the universe, or whatever might transpire to prevent a paradox, but he couldn't see where his daughter's death could be fate. A child killed—especially violently—wasn't fate, it was a couple of creeps preying on the innocent, and Bethany's own bad choice that had put her in their path. A choice Tony could change, angry words he wouldn't say—

Charlotte lifted her cigarette again.

Time to get the answer he came for. "Have you ever warped within your own lifetime?"

She paused with the cigarette halfway to her mouth, then slowly lay it in the ashtray. "A couple of times. Have you?"

Did her voice have a slight tremor in it?

"Once, I went back two years. I wouldn't mind doing it again, but I can't figure out how. Obviously I'm missing something—"

She burst out laughing, but her hand shook as she stubbed out her cigarette. "I do declare, this is hilarious!" She scooched closer to Tony, but stared at the radio.

What had gotten into her? He started to repeat his question, but she held a finger to her lip, then laughed again at the radio show host.

Tony clamped his mouth shut, then something rubbed his leg. He looked down. Her hip brushed against him.

Holy shit, was she coming on to him? Willpower fled. Bad idea or not, his arm slid behind her back, as if it had a mind of its own. The silky fabric of her dress burned into his fingertips.

She relaxed against his arm, and an arrow of excitement shot up his body. He should scoot away. But it had been so long since he'd touched a woman. So long since he'd even wanted to. It wouldn't hurt. *Just this once.*

Her face held a pink tinge that hadn't been there earlier. "Tony?" Her hand moved to her collar, then dropped lower and fumbled at her neckline. "Why did you come here?"

The question snapped his attention back to what he should be doing. And what he shouldn't. "Well..." He slipped his arm off her and smoothed his pants over his thighs.

"Of course I'm glad you did," she said. "But why now? Why not... later in 1913? Or 1920? Or some other year?"

"I didn't know where you lived then. The records are... sketchy." He took his glasses off, held them up to the light.

Her brows dipped. "But why did you come at all?"

He pulled out a shirttail and rubbed one of the lenses. Slowly, deliberately. Why did he have to be such a lousy liar? He slid the glasses back on and met her gaze. "I was curious, wanted to find out what'd become of you. Why?"

The pink in her face deepened. "I just wondered." She glanced at her cigarette case, lying on the table next to her purse. "You said you hoped I could answer your questions."

Shit, too close to the truth. Like his mom and sister, she could see through him. "Well yeah, there is that." He smoothed his pants again, molded them to his legs, pressed each wrinkle out.

"Why didn't you ask the person who answered—"

"Because he wouldn't answer any more. Not unless I joined some club... some cult he was in. And I didn't want to." All true. Why couldn't he think of some bullshit to give her?

"What kind of club? Others... like us, perhaps?" Why did she ask, when she knew all about the Saturn Society? Was she testing him?

"Supposedly. But they wanted to take my money. And I didn't agree with all this guy's beliefs." Truthful enough.

"Oh." She started to reach for her neckline again, then let her hand flop into her lap, twisted a wrinkle in her dress instead. "What... did you find problematic?"

"The idea that changing the past in any way is wrong. That you're playing God if you do. Some people would even think my saving your life was interfering in the natural order."

Looking down, she ran a finger along the seam of her skirt.

"What do you think?" he asked. "Should I have let you drown?"

"No!" She jerked her hand off the fabric. "Of course not. And I'm thankful you didn't. But if you're talking about changing the past for your own benefit..."

"I guess it depends on what one considers one's own benefit."

She jumped up and flipped off the radio. "I know! My friend Theodore would be much more qualified to answer your questions. He's usually home in the evenings, I'll go ring him to let him know we're coming."

The air in Tony's lungs froze. She was going to call Pippin.

He found his voice as she disappeared into the kitchen. "Charlotte! Wait!"

"Tony?" Charlotte asked Friday evening after the newscast. "How long does this go on?"

"How long does what go on?"

"So many people out of work."

Tony studied the wall where it met the ceiling. How much should he tell her? "A few more years." Vague enough to be safe.

Thankfully, he'd managed to talk her out of calling Pippin by faking an upset stomach, but how long would it be before she suggested it again?

They spent their waking hours together. As long as he stayed away from the topic of jumping within his own life, things were companionable. He felt contented. Surprisingly so.

Too comfortable. Especially when the pull would jerk him back to the twenty-first century in another week or so.

Especially when he was only here for answers.

And especially when he was a wanted man, and the strength of Charlotte's ties to the Society remained unclear.

"Oh my heavens. What- how does it end?" she asked.

Tony hesitated. "I don't know how much I should tell—"

"What can I do? One woman?"

"Well..." Didn't Saturn Society Code preclude sharing details of the future with people in the past? Yet if she was encouraging him to do so, maybe she wasn't in with them as deeply as he feared. Still, there had to be danger in telling.

"Is it President Roosevelt's programs?" she asked.

"That's—" He caught himself. "Yeah. The WPA, FDIC, Social Security, unemployment compensation..."

She stared at him with a rapt expression, like a student trying to absorb every shred of wisdom she could from a revered teacher. When Tony didn't continue, her eagerness melted into apprehension. "There's more, isn't there?" He didn't answer. "War," she whispered. "Isn't it?"

He drew his finger across his chin. Shit, why did he have to be so transparent? "Yeah." Might as well tell her.

She twiddled her gold chain. "When?"

A feeling he was doing something wrong gripped his chest. "Look, I don't think it's right for me to tell you stuff like this." Especially when every time he tried to get some answers, she grew evasive.

He had to push her harder, lay a guilt trip on her if that was what it took—after all, she owed him her life. But he'd raised her guard. He'd best work back to the topic slowly, get what he needed, then split. The longer he stuck around, the harder it would be to keep his hands off her.

Like now. They sat on the sofa and listened to the radio. It had already become an ingrained routine. In the mornings and early afternoons, he helped at the restaurant—Irving had grudgingly offered him a buck-fifty a day plus meals. After work, Tony helped Charlotte around the house doing things like mowing and weeding the garden. She told the nosy woman who lived next door that Tony was working off part of his board.

Evenings were the hardest. Each night, it grew more difficult to restrain himself from taking her hand or slipping his arm around her like he'd done the other night. Yet every evening it seemed they sat a little closer on the sofa as they listened to some radio show.

He wanted to touch her, God did he want to. He wanted to touch her like he hadn't touched a woman in over two years. *Why now?* And why her? Why not one of the women at the office? Why not one of those at Mulroney's?

Easy. The women at work were too much like Dora. The women at the bar were either gold diggers or just looking for a good time. His sister would say he was attracted to Charlotte because she was unavailable, and therefore safe. Maybe she was right.

But he longed to hold Charlotte in his arms, the way he had in the attic. This time, not because she was cold and frightened, but because he wanted to.

She'd been quiet all day. Her silence unnerved him, and he feared his hunch was correct, she knew something about him. But when he'd questioned her as they walked home from Irving's, she'd told him she was just worried about Elmer. She'd expected her former boy-friend to get over his anger and call on her, but he hadn't.

Guilt crawled over Tony. All his fault. "Guess you'd be at the dance right now if you hadn't blown Elmer off."

"Blown Elmer off?" Confusion knotted her forehead.

"Told him to get lost."

She stared down at her skirt and picked at a fraying thread on a buttonhole. "It was my choice, Tony."

"You sorry?"

Her jaw tightened for a second. "Not for a minute." Her voice was firm. "Elmer wasn't the man for me. I just... I hope he's all right. That he found someone else to take to the dance. And I shall miss going myself, but not because of Elmer."

"You and I could go." Tony wanted to smack himself. Where had that come from? *Too late now.* "If you don't mind going with a guy who doesn't have a clue how to dance."

A grin slid across her face. "I would be delighted!" At her reac-tion, something happy and bubbly rose inside him, along with trick-les of warning. It was too much like a date. Hell, it *was* a date.

One date couldn't hurt. Might be fun. He'd at least try to dance. To feel her waist beneath his hand, to move with her...

"I could show you a few steps," she said. "Or we could just so-cialize." The clock chimed nine times. "Oh dear, it's nine o'clock, ad-mission will be a quarter now. Elmer and I always try to get there early, then it's only a dime—"

Tony chuckled. "It's okay, I can afford it."

"Then I'd best get ready." She jumped up and dashed for her bed-room, then returned a few minutes later wearing the violet-print dress he'd bought for her. He stood. The happy-bubbly feeling solidi-fied into raw desire. "You look fantastic," he breathed. He wanted to sweep her into his arms right there. If only they had more than a week together... She twirled, and the skirt flared out in a wide circle. His eyes followed her. It wasn't the dress, but what was inside. Pride swelled in him. He'd be the envy of every guy in the place.

He tipped his head toward the door. "Shall we?"

As they reached for their hats, someone knocked on the door.

"Who on earth?" Charlotte lifted the curtains to peer out the window. "Theodore!" She dropped the curtain.

Pippin? Holy shit!

Tony's gaze darted around the room, and he almost forgot to breathe. There was no way he could escape out the side door without Pippin seeing.

Charlotte rushed to the door and reached for the knob. Tony bolted for the only other exit: the bathroom. He bolted inside and turned the lock as the front door squealed and Charlotte greeted her guest.

"Theodore! What brings you this way tonight?"

Me. Tony studied the window above the bathtub. The opening was just large enough for him to squeeze through. He leaned over the tub and tugged on the sash, but it didn't move. Great. The damn thing was stuck.

He pulled harder. The window didn't budge. Tony's head whipped toward the locked door. What would Pippin do to him?

He strained to hear Charlotte. She'd lowered her voice to a mumble. "...working on it... I need a little more time... Please..." What was she talking about?

Tony gripped the window handle and pulled again. Dried paint on the wooden frame cracked, and it gave a little. The front door clicked shut.

Footsteps came, sharp clacks on the living room's hardwood floor. One set. Charlotte's. "Tony? Are you all right?"

He released the window handle, and his adrenaline rush dissipated. Pippin was gone.

"I'm fine, just thought I'd better, uh, unload some of that coffee before we take off." Not the most graceful excuse but the best he could come up with on short notice. He regarded his trembling hands, palms up. A thick reddened stripe slashed across the right one from pulling on the window handle.

He unlocked the door. Her wide eyes and tense features contrasted with her calm voice. "Who was at the door?" he asked.

"Theodore stopped by. He was in the neighborhood, wanted to know how my project was coming—" She snapped a finger. "Oh, drat! We could have asked him your question, I didn't even think about it." She hurried to the front door, as if she was going to call Pippin back.

"No!" Tony rushed to follow. "It's okay. My question can wait." It would have to, if Pippin was around. "Actually, I'd forgotten all about it, thinking about going to the dance with you." He touched her shoulder as she reached for the doorknob. She turned around, her face bright.

It was true. He really had forgotten about Bethany for a few moments, forgotten about warping...

He couldn't let it happen again. He had to keep his eyes open, his mind on his goal—and on the threat of Pippin. That kind of lapse would land him right in the Saturn Society's lap. "Ready—" he began, but stopped mid-sentence.

They couldn't go to the dance now. Not if Pippin might still be in the neighborhood. "Uh, you know, I was really looking forward to going out, but I'm afraid I'm not feeling very well... maybe I'd better stay in tonight after all."

The lighter-than-air feeling in Charlotte's stomach snapped, dropping her back to earth. He'd wanted to take her to the dance. Enough he hadn't tried to ask his alarming question yet that evening, as he'd tried every night so far. But now... "What's wrong?" she asked.

Tony looked her in the eyes as his breathing slowed to normal, although his expression remained wary. He rubbed his stomach. "Nothing major, just a little heartburn."

"Oh dear. You're sure? Perhaps a glass of milk would help."

"Uh, sure." Although sure was the last thing he sounded, she dashed to the kitchen.

He was lying. Why? Did he know what Theodore wanted? She dumped the last of the day's bottle of milk into a glass, then hurried back to the living room.

Tony had moved to the sofa. She handed him the milk. He took a small sip, then dragged the back of his hand across his mouth. "Sorry I ruined your plans."

She shot a glance at the curtained window and sighed. "I suppose it's just as well."

He looked up, questioning. "It would look strange for me to show up with a man who's supposed to be just my boarder," she said. "Betty Clark from down the street goes every week with her sweetheart, she'd tell her mother and next thing you know... And next week, others would wonder what happened to you, why you're not there after... you know." After the pull took him away. She didn't want to think about it.

"You're right. I'm still getting used to this whole time travel deal. Coming here was easy." His thumb squeaked in the condensation as he drew it around the glass. "And the time I went back two years. That was even easier, but... I've never been able to repeat it. Why?"

"Why do you want to?" She thumbed her quarter through the fabric of her dress. The low neckline barely hid it.

She waited while he sipped his milk. Tiny sips. Like he was trying to make it last. "Tony?"

"You know, I think I've heard this song before," he said. The Waldorf-Astoria Orchestra had begun playing a melodious, slow number. She looked at Tony, then the radio, then at Tony again. She should bring up the Society, try to turn the conversation around and suggest going to the House.

Her mouth wouldn't form the words.

He stood, his eyes never leaving her, and held out a hand. "Miss Henderson, would you care to dance?"

A thousand tiny wings beat against Charlotte's heart, blowing away all thoughts of Theodore and her obligation. It was just a dance. What could be the harm? The fluttering slowed, and she forced calm into her voice. "I'd love to."

She slid her hand into his, and he led her to the center of the room. His other hand was warm on her back between her shoulder blades, and his sureness pushed away the last of her anxiety. She let him lead her in an odd, freestyle step that made up in feeling what it lacked in style. This moment could last forever. It'd never been that way with Elmer. Not even with Louie, the first and only man she'd let—No use thinking such things. She and Tony had no future. But they had tonight.

They swirled in time to the music, the feel of his hand in hers and on her shoulder sent an intoxicating warmth through her. "Did I tell you you look incredible?"

Her cheeks heated. "I believe you did. But I don't mind hearing it again." Perhaps the dress showed more than was proper. She didn't care. She turned her face back to his and reveled in the feeling that for this moment, there was only the two of them and the music. Nothing else existed. Her world began and ended in Tony's arms.

He pulled her close, enough to catch the dance-hall inspectors' notice had they gone to Triangle Park. She leaned into his shoulder and caught a whiff of the restaurant beneath a pleasant blend of his clean shirt and mildly musky man-scent. Too soon the song was over, and the orchestra picked up with a faster one.

Charlotte tipped her head. "Thank you, that was delightful." She didn't want to let him go, didn't want the emptiness, the sense of something lacking when they'd part. But she couldn't stand in the middle of the room holding his hand all night. She stepped back but Tony didn't release her. Instead, he tightened his hold and slid his other arm around her back, then drew her closer until their bodies touched. She let go of his hand, unable to do anything but look into his eyes.

"I'm sorry we didn't go to the dance," he said.

She looked down, conscious of the press of her breasts against his chest, then met his gaze again. "I'm not."

His eyes closed halfway and he lowered his head until his lips touched hers. A thrill coursed through her body as she angled her neck to meet his kiss.

His lips were soft, yet firm, and her body tingled with awareness everywhere they touched. He started to pull away, but she slid her arms around his back. He relaxed against her and did the same, his mouth still molded to hers, moving with hers. *No future. Just this moment.*

Finally he pulled back and dropped his arms. "God, I'm sorry. I had no business doing that."

Her fingers trailed down his arm as she stepped away. "Don't be sorry. I didn't try to stop you."

They moved to the sofa and sat with a wide gap between them. They stared at the radio, the way Tony said people in his time sat and watched the wondrous thing he called television.

Finally he spoke. "Look, Charlotte... maybe I should go to a hotel. I don't want to, but... Elmer may not be the man for you, but neither am I. Not when I have a week at the most to be here."

She studied her hands in her lap. Maybe he was right from a personal standpoint, but there was so much more at stake. His life, maybe his soul. She had to be the one to bring him to the Society. If she failed to keep her end of the bargain, Theodore would find Tony and make him a mindless shell of a man like Fred Cheltenham.

She'd watched Tony for four days. Tried to convince him his best chance to learn what he wanted to know lay in the Society House. He hadn't fallen for it.

He hadn't done anything wrong so far, but his questions warned her he would. She had to stop him.

Warmth crawled through her insides. He was so much more than the man who saved her life.

She studied the tip of her shoe, where a small scuff marred the black patent leather. "Maybe you're right," she said. He shifted, started to rise, but she touched his arm, stopping him. "But it's late. Stay here tonight. Go tomorrow if you must."

As soon as she got off work, they'd leave for the Society House. Forget trying to convince him. She'd insist on it. Trick him if she had to. He found her intriguing, enough to make him temporarily forget his mission. If all else failed, she'd use her "woman's wiles," as Theodore called it. *Whatever it takes.*

The close call with Pippin weighed on Tony's mind as he mopped the restaurant floor after the breakfast rush the following morning. Somehow Charlotte had managed to talk him into going with her, though it was a continual effort for Tony to keep from wanting her, watching her, touching her as she cleared tables. "Thank you again for staying through today." A coffee cup slipped in her fingers as she grabbed it, but she caught it just in time. "You don't know how much of a help you are. The new girl doesn't start until tomorrow, and Sunday's our busiest morning."

"I figured it was the least I could do, for letting me stay with you all week." His grip tightened on the mop. Charlotte's workload wasn't the real reason he stayed.

The prospect of leaving gnawed at him until he finished mopping and started gathering the table linens that needed to go to the laundry. He didn't want to leave, dammit. He'd be stuck in 1933 for at least another week. Seven long, lonely days of trying to find something to fill his time until the pull hit—

"I declare, Mr. Irving, do try to be more careful." Charlotte slipped through the kitchen door. "That's the third time today you've bumped into me. What if I'd been a customer?"

Tony barely heard the man's grumbled response. Charlotte hurried to clear a vacated table, sureness and grace in her every movement. She held her own with Irving, but her tight jaw betrayed her discomfort at his advances.

The eggs and toast Tony had eaten for breakfast sat in his stomach like a ball of hard clay. He wanted to take her away from that asshole. Give her a comfortable life where she could work on her projects all day if she wanted.

But he couldn't, not when his return would precipitate her death. He had to leave now. The longer he stayed, the harder it would be to leave. He'd tried to ask his question for five days. If she hadn't answered by now, she wasn't going to. And she kept suggesting they go to see Pippin! Didn't she know her mentor was more likely to torture, brainwash, or kill Tony, than help him?

The lump in Tony's stomach hardened into rock as he collected the napkins from the table by the window. It was more than the sense of failure, the knowledge that he was this close to getting his daughter back and he'd failed. No Bethany...

And no Charlotte. The better he'd come to know her, the easier it was to believe Dewey. Their kiss last night confirmed Tony's suspicions. Gratitude for saving her life wasn't the only reason she'd insisted he stay with her.

She wanted him as much as he wanted her.

All the more reason to get away. Spare her heart, not to mention his own. He'd split now.

He gathered the last tablecloth, then stopped to pick up a dirty plate from the counter on his way to the kitchen. His work was done. All he had to do was say goodbye to Charlotte... forever.

He nudged the kitchen door open, and the scene before him froze his blood.

Charlotte's back pressed against the edge of the sink. Irving hovered over her, gripping the countertop on each side of her. The cigarette dangling from the corner of his mouth bobbed as he spoke. "Come on babe, there's dozens of broads out there wouldn't give it a thought to have your job..."

Tony couldn't move. Charlotte shrunk back farther. "No..." Her voice was small and weak. She reached up to her neckline, fumbled with her necklace. Irving leaned closer. "Did you say no?" His lips drew into a sneer. "Come on, don't make me get ugly—"

Tony leaped forward and yanked Irving's shoulder, pulling him off of Charlotte. "You're already ugly, you sonofabitch!"

Irving whirled around. "What the—" He glared at Charlotte. "You told me there ain't nothing between you and him!"

"There's not." Tony bit the words out as he edged close to her. "And the lady said no."

Irving drew himself up, his hand clenched into a fist. "Now look here, pal!" He extended a finger and jabbed Tony's chest. "This is my place." *poke* "I'm the one in charge." *poke* "If I say she puts out or gets out, then she puts out or—"

Tony whipped off his glasses, tossed them aside and hurled his fist into Irving's face. The restaurant owner stumbled backward, clutched at a food prep table to break his fall, missed and grabbed at the edge of the hot grill instead. With a howl, he slid to the floor. "You motherfucker! Get outta here! And don't neither one of you ever set foot in here again!"

Tony scooped his glasses out of the sink where they'd landed and bolted for the back door. He was dimly aware of Charlotte's footsteps echoing in the alley behind him.

He slowed after he put a few buildings between himself and Irving's Place. The clickety-clack of Charlotte's heels pounded the gravel until she caught up with him. "Tony! Wait!"

She caught his elbow. "Where are you going?" He stopped and turned. A tiny crease formed between her eyebrows.

He surveyed the alley. He'd run in the opposite direction of Charlotte's house. "Away." Away from Irving. Away from the threat of Theodore Pippin.

And away from Charlotte.

Her shoulders shrank backward. "Please... at least come back for your things."

He hesitated. If he went with her, would he be able to leave? The temptation to pick up where he'd left off the night before might grow too great, despite the possibility of another visit from Pippin. "No. It's better this way. I've run off your boyfriend. Got you fired from your job. Fucked up your whole life. I can get new things." At his own reminder that he had money, he dug out his wallet and pulled out most of his cash. "Here, it's the least I can do for all the trouble I've caused... God, I'm so sorry..." He pressed a wad of tens into her hand and closed her fingers around it. He couldn't look at her stunned face. He swallowed hard as he turned away, then allowed himself one last glimpse.

She stared after him, her body rigid. "Tony..."

"Good—" He turned and walked toward Main Street, unable to force the rest of the word through his thick throat.

Tony paced across his room at the Gibbons, the only downtown hotel he was aware of that still existed as such in his time, although it had a different name. He threw open the window and gazed over the parking lot, already darkened by the lengthening shadows of the buildings that surrounded it on three sides.

He'd blundered around for hours after he left Charlotte, then took in a movie, something about a lion tamer. He sat through it twice—not because it was good, but because it had enough action to take the edge of his mind off Charlotte.

He paced to the door, then back to the window again. What was he thinking? He was a man who led through knowledge and order. A man who rearranged the magazines on people's coffee tables. Not the kind of guy who threw a punch without thinking. Or at all, for that matter.

Never mind that it had felt damn good.

Through Charlotte, he'd discovered his heart wasn't dead, and he could still feel excitement, anticipation and wonder. She was the first woman he'd found remotely interesting since Dora's defection.

The woman who had the answer he needed but wouldn't give it to him. Hopelessness settled over him like a new fallen snow. In his quest for knowledge, he'd failed. Was the one thing he wanted—his daughter's life—too much to ask?

He sat and took off his shoes. If he got extra sleep, maybe the mental energy he needed to bring on the pull would build sooner.

He peered around the room. Bed, dresser, nightstand. Not much different than any of those he'd stayed in on his many travels, other than the absence of a TV and phone. And quiet. At his request, the desk clerk had given him a luxury room with a private bath on the sixth floor. There were no other guests in the wing.

It would be an adequate place to live—exist—until the pull returned him to the twenty-first century. Hopefully, the room would be unoccupied in his time. After he warped, he'd check into the modern-day hotel, then crash.

He wandered back toward the door when someone knocked.

"Yes?" What the hell did someone want this late?

"Room service," a man in the hallway called.

"I didn't order anything." Tony hoped the intruder heard the irritation in his response.

"It says Room 639 right here on the order... Open faced beef sandwich with mashed potatoes, green beans, apple pie..."

Hmmm, that sounded good. Tony hadn't eaten since breakfast, hadn't been hungry, but eating might also speed the renewal of his mental energy. Better take them up on it, even if he didn't order the dinner. He yanked the door open.

The black man in the hallway wore a white server's uniform, but his hands were empty. Tony glanced down the hall in both directions. Where was the cart? "Where's the food?"

"My apologies, Mr. Solomon, but I need to talk to you—"

Tony glowered at the man. "Who are you and what do you want?" Something about him struck Tony as familiar.

"My name is Theodore Pippin."

Fear shot an icy tentacle down Tony's throat. He couldn't move. Moisture trickled down his back beneath his undershirt. God, how could he be so stupid? Charlotte and his failure had clouded his mind so much he'd forgotten all about the Saturn Society's threat.

His stupor snapped. He shoved the door, but he man blocked it with his foot. "I'm with an organization called the Saturn Society... perhaps you've heard of us?"

"Yeah, and I'm not interested." Tony leaned against the door, trying to dislodge Pippin's foot. "Get out—"

"I'm afraid it's not that simple, Mr. Solomon. Now if I could come in, we could discuss this like gentlemen..."

"There's nothing to discuss." Not with the man who'd been lauded for subduing more time-criminals than any other Society member in known history. Tony leaned harder against the door, but Pippin's foot held. "Get out of here, or I'll—" Somewhere outside, a woman shouted. He glanced at the window. Big mistake. Pippin took the opportunity to wedge himself through the door.

In Theodore's car, Charlotte panted, her throat raw from screaming. Couldn't the hotel worker emptying the trash hear her? She struggled against the ropes Theodore had used to tie her down, her sweat-dampened legs squeaking against the beige, leather seat. Theodore didn't trust her, he'd said. Couldn't leave her home and risk her getting a warning to the Enemy before he could apprehend him. She shouldn't have been surprised Theodore's patience had run out.

She screamed again, but hope splintered and lodged in her throat as the hotel worker disappeared back inside the service door.

The parking lot was deserted, the post office next door having closed hours ago. Buildings hemmed in the lot on all sides. Theodore had parked far from the entry, concealing the maroon Packard from anyone who might walk past. Most of the hotel's guests were likely in for the night—what few there were, as less than a dozen windows were lit.

She had to get out. For her own sake, if not Tony's. She might be able to convince Theodore her intentions had been honorable, but as soon as he'd phoned the hotels and located Tony at the Gibbons, he'd rung Dr. Caruthers, who was now on his way from Cleveland to help Theodore administer the Treatment. There was no telling what punishment he'd mete out to a Society member who'd harbored an Enemy. She struggled harder, but the rope didn't loosen.

Her shoulders slumped. There was no way she'd extricate herself. Unable to worry her quarter, Charlotte's fingers twiddled within her bonds. The more she struggled against Theodore's sailors' knots, the more they tightened.

Tony backed away as Pippin strode into the room. "It's late," Pippin growled. "Get your shoes—"

"Get out." Tony tried to edge around him to the door.

"We're going to the Society House," Pippin said. "We'll begin your instruction right—"

"I'm not going anywhere." Tony sidled farther to the right, keeping his eyes on Pippin. The "instruction" Pippin referred to was likely the surgery and medication Everly had told him about, that would turn him into a zombie like that Fred guy.

Pippin advanced toward him, sidestepping to place himself in Tony's path. "You must come with me. We can't have untrained folk traveling all over history—the implications are enormous, should you interact too deeply, leave something behind—"

"Get out!" Small chance anyone would hear. Tony gathered a deep breath for another shout, but Pippin leapt forward and whipped a knife from a sheath in his sleeve.

Tony froze. A vision of the ancient Mayan priest and his stone blade superimposed itself on Pippin's image. The Society man's voice was stern. "That's not an option, Mr. Solomon. You're wanted by the Saturn Society. You can come with me peacefully, or—"

"No!" Tony lunged at Pippin in an effort to disarm him, but the other man was faster and grabbed Tony's arm in an unyielding grip, then slammed him against the wall, pinning him with his body. Tony twisted beneath him. "Help! Someone, help!" he shouted, even though the wing was deserted. There was little chance of rescue.

Pippin held firm. He spoke quietly as he drew the knife back. "You leave me no choice..."

Fifteen

CHARLOTTE STRUGGLED AGAINST THE CORDS BINDING HER TO THE CAR SEAT. The ropes chafed her wrists. She scanned the hotel looming over the parking lot. Was one of those lit windows Tony's room? *Please, let him get away...* She screamed again. Though it was doubtful, maybe someone would hear through one of the open windows.

Pippin brought the blade down, but Tony jerked aside. The knife drew a shallow gash down Tony's side instead of the deeper cut the other man had obviously intended. Pain lanced along the thin trail and made Tony stumble forward.

"I'm warning you." Pippin brandished the knife. Its polished silver surface gleamed in the light from the bedside lamp. "Come peacefully, or..." He and Tony circled, dancing around each other like a pair of boxers.

He leaped toward Tony, but Tony anticipated the move and jumped away. Pippin crashed to the floor. He rolled sideways and sprang to his feet before Tony reached him.

Pippin backed away, holding the knife out. "Please, consider my—"

"I have considered," Tony said through clenched teeth. "And I'm not interested!" He lunged for Pippin again, reaching for the hand holding the knife. Pippin jerked it out of his reach.

Across the parking lot, a door slammed. The worker Charlotte had seen earlier was back, with another man. "Help!" *Please, let them come over!* "Please help me!"

Tony and Pippin faced off, each poised for the other to make the next move. Outside, another scream came from the parking lot. The woman sounded almost like... Charlotte? Both Tony and Pippin turned toward the window for a split second, but Tony recovered first. He slammed into the other man, jarring the knife out of Pippin's hand. It clattered to the floor, skidding until it landed at Tony's feet.

Tony snatched it up and pointed it at Pippin. Keeping himself between Pippin and the door, he took a step closer, brandishing the knife. *See how you like being on the other end of it, buddy.* "Now what're you going to do—"

Pippin bolted into the bathroom, and slammed the door behind him. "Go ahead and hide," Tony snarled as the lock clicked. "You can't stay in there forever."

His knees weak, he sank onto the bed, gripping the knife in both hands, afraid to blink lest Pippin emerge.

He turned the weapon over. PIPPIN 1905 was etched in the polished silver blade, below a hilt that bore a relief of the planet Saturn with three stars. What the hell was he doing, holding a man at knifepoint? He, Tony Solomon, whose worst infraction of the law in his whole life was three speeding tickets?

Vertigo engulfed him. He dropped the knife and clutched the bed. Was he warping?

As quickly as it struck, the dizziness passed. He glanced at his side. His shirt gapped in a neat slash, and a red line ran down his side beneath his arm to the waistband of his slacks.

Damn! He hadn't warped. But then why the dizzy—

A light knock came from the door. "Tony?" a woman called.

Charlotte! His head snapped up. Trembling, feminine fingers curled around the edge of the still-ajar door and she slipped in, her eyes wide.

Lightness burst through him. He jumped off the bed and ran to her. She tumbled into his arms, pulled herself against him, and buried her face in his shirt. "Thank heavens you're all right!" Without thinking, Tony pulled her close, her breath warm against his chest. "I was so afraid Theodore—"

Tony pushed her away as the lightness inside him turned to lead. What had she done? Had she led Pippin to him?

She couldn't have. "He's in the bathroom," Tony said. "How did—"

"But he jumped..." Perplexity twisted her features. Tony looked from Charlotte to the bathroom door, then back at her. "Didn't you feel it?" she asked.

"Feel what?" What was she talking about? Then it hit him. The dizzy spell right before she walked in. It was Pippin who'd warped. Tony pounded on the bathroom door. "Hey!"

"He's gone, Tony."

He rattled the doorknob and studied the lock. A simple one. He snatched a credit card from his wallet, slid it down the door jamb, and yanked the door open.

The bathroom was empty.

"Holy shit." He gaped into the vacant room, leaning on the door frame—

Charlotte gasped. "Tony, you're hurt!"

"What? Oh, that." The gash on his side. The blood had already begun to congeal. "Just a little scratch. No big deal." He stepped into the bathroom and yanked his shirt up. The action pulled at the cut and brought a fresh burst of pain. Tony sucked in a breath through his teeth.

Charlotte rushed in. "Here, let me..." She turned on the water, grabbed a washcloth and wet it. Tony clenched his jaw as she dabbed at the cut until it was clean. "This doesn't look so little to me. We ought to call for first aid but there's no time... I'll wrap it the best I can, then we'll go—"

"Go where?"

She squeezed the washcloth under the tap. The water came out brownish-pink. "We have to hurry, the hotel staff's calling the cops—"

"What?" What had she done?

"Theodore. For tying me up in the car and stealing a waiter's uniform. We have to leave before they get here, they'll delay us, and Caruthers—"

Tony braced his hands on his hips. "I'm not going anywhere. Not until I get some answers. Starting with Theodore Pippin. What is he to you?"

She dropped the washcloth into the sink, the water still running. "Tony... I was nine years old when I started to jump in time. I was scared to death. I had no idea what was happening or how to stop it. Then Theodore came and taught me how to control it. He gave me my life back. Please understand, I owe him so much..." She squeezed the water out of the washcloth once more, gripping it tightly. "Almost as much as I owe you," she whispered. "I'd never hurt you, Tony. Ever." She sniffled, then reached over the sink and shut off the water. "I—I didn't tell him where you were, he found out on his own, guessed you'd gone to a hotel. Please, believe me." She held onto the sink. Her lower lip twitched.

Tony's heart squeezed. He wanted to believe she had nothing to do with Pippin's attack. He wanted to take her into his arms again, tell her it was all right, smooth the worry lines from her face. But he needed more answers first. "Then why did you let me stay with you? When you knew he'd come after me? Why didn't you tell me to leave town?"

The water in the sink gurgled as the last of it went down the drain.

She started to fiddle with her necklace, but stopped short. Her lips parted, and the tip of her tongue poked between her teeth.

Tony walked to the hotel room door, pushed it shut and latched it, then came back and gently took hold of her arm. He led her to the bed, then lightly pressed her shoulder until she sat perched on its edge. Her voice hitched. "You... you should do something about that cut."

"It can wait." He lowered himself into the chair opposite her. "Now, tell me—"

"You're in the Black Book." Her words came fast. "It was just a matter of time before Theodore found you. If not him, someone else—"

"What's the Black Book?"

"A Society publication. The Enemies of Time. They're from here and now, and from the future. From the past, too, even though everyone knows you can't jump ahead in time. They've all done something, or will do something, to upset the balance, manipulate time to serve—"

"To serve their own ends." He pushed himself out of the chair, paced to the window, kept his back to her.

"Theodore's made it his life's mission to stop them. It's his passion, a personal crusade. And you're..." She fingered her collar. "I don't know why you're in the Black Book, but Theodore will do whatever it takes to capture you and make sure you can never do it again."

He turned to Charlotte, his face hardening. "How did he know I was here? In 1933?"

"He felt you jump. Like you did when he jumped. Theodore's so intent on finding Enemies of Time, whenever he feels someone jump, he seeks them out. To offer hospitality, since that's the Society's mission, but if... if it's someone from the Book, then... take care of them."

The flyers on the wall in the fifties. They must've been from the Black Book.

"What did you do?" Charlotte spoke barely above a whisper.

"Nothing!" His head whipped around to face her. "I've done nothing." Yet. Did his place in the book—and on that wall in 1954—mean he would achieve his goal and prevent Bethany's death, but at the cost of making himself a wanted man?

"I- I never believed you belonged in the book." She examined the

floral print of her dress and smoothed her skirt. "It must be something you've yet to do." She gave the skirt a final brush and met his
eyes. "Something I thought I could prevent, if I kept you with me. I
thought I could save you..." She pushed herself up from the bed with
care, as if the act pained her.

Tony couldn't stand it. He strode to her side and swept her into
his arms. "It's okay, baby, it's okay," he murmured into her hair. A
sense of déjà vu from their time in the attic struck him, reminded him
of when he held her and spoke the same words. The same words, yet
so different with her a grown woman. Her arms tightened around his
back. He pulled her against him, drank in her flowery fragrance and
the warmth of her body pressed against his.

Other parts of him became aware of her nearness and sprang to
life. He whirled around and walked away before she saw, then winced
when the movement pulled at the cut on his side. "Ouch! Get me a
towel, will you?"

She ran to the bathroom. Thankfully, the pain and the reminder
someone had tried to kill him diverted his body's awareness from
Charlotte's proximity. "Will he come after me again?"

"No." She handed him the towel. He unbuttoned his shirt to slide
it underneath. "He can't. Not right away. Theodore's over fifty years
old, so he had to have jumped at least that far back. Whenever he
went, he won't be able to return for at least a couple weeks, and then
there's recovery."

"Then I don't have to worry about him. By the time he gets back
I'll be long gone."

"But Dr. Caruthers—"

"Who's he?"

"From Cleveland. He's a horrible man, and he's on his way here,
right now. He'll never believe you're innocent, no matter what I say.
We have to leave." Her voice caught. "Please, Tony."

Tony crossed his arms over his chest. "I don't think so. I've tried
to get answers from you all week and every time you manage to
change the subject. I can hide myself."

"But there are others! They've all seen the Black Book—"

"So let them kill me. If I can't find out what I want to know, I might as well get sent home sooner—"

"They won't kill you." Her voice quieted and grew threatening. "They'll hurt you enough to silence you. Then they'll take you to the Society House and do terrible things... please, Tony..." A siren wailed in the distance.

The surgery and medication Everly said they'd used on that Fred guy. Tony's gut clenched. He could end up like that if he hadn't eluded Pippin.

The unease in his stomach settled like puzzle pieces falling into place. "All right. On one condition. Tell me what I need to do to—"

"There's no time!" She leaned toward the door, as if her stance would compel Tony to follow. "We have to go, now! Please, come with me, and I'll... " She made a tiny choking sound. "I'll answer all your questions. Anything you want to know." Tony didn't move. She gripped his elbow. "Tony... if Caruthers finds us..."

Tony mulled over his prospects. If he stayed at the Gibbons, Caruthers would force another confrontation. One Tony could lose, and wind up a mindless, drooling zombie.

Or he could leave. Alone. But Charlotte was right, there was no telling when or where he might run into another Society vigilante who would recognize him.

Or he could go with her.

She'd put herself on the line for him.

And she'd promised to tell him what he needed to know. "Where do you suggest we go?" He struggled to button his shirt over the towel.

"My brother owns some property in southeast Ohio. No one will find us there. If we hide out for a few days, Caruthers will go back to Cleveland."

"What about you? Won't he come back—"

"By the time he does, Theodore will have returned and recovered." She swallowed. "He'll protect me."

"And by then, I'll be gone," Tony said.

"Yes." She fingered the necklace beneath her dress. "If we get out

of here quickly. My brother's place is way out in the middle of nowhere, by the Clearwater River. There's a little cabin where we can
stay—"

"Yeah, but how are we going to get there? Sunday night, I'll
doubt we'll find a taxi, or anywhere to rent a car—"

"We can take Theodore's."

"You mean steal it?"

"I prefer the term borrow."

Tony's hands stilled on the buttons of his shirt. Him? A car thief?
Come on, Solomon, the guy tried to kill you. "Okay." Pippin deserved
to have his car stolen, and then some. Tony pulled on his jacket, glad
it hid the bulk of the towel in case they encountered anyone.

He pulled the door open, then stopped when Charlotte dashed
back to the other side of the bed. "This might come in handy." She
grabbed Pippin's knife and slid it into her purse.

The sirens grew nearer as they slipped out the door, down a service stairwell and out the back entrance.

The car's deep maroon finish gleamed, even in the dim light cast
by the parking lot's single street lamp. Shiny and new, a chrome emblem on the car's side told him it was a Packard, and judging from
the size of the engine compartment, a well-powered one. Catching
time-criminals must pay well.

They had one more problem. "Keys?" Tony asked.

"Key—oh, no, I completely forgot!" Her crestfallen expression
lasted only a second. "But maybe I can get it started without one."

"You mean hotwire it?" He glanced around the lot. Deserted.

"It seems our best option, don't you think?" She yanked open the
driver's side door. "Keep a lookout while I see what I can do." Tony
walked around the car and ran his hand over the smooth fenders
while she fumbled around beneath the dash. Hell, he didn't have a
clue how to hotwire a car, yet she acted like anyone could do it.

"Fiddlesticks!" She raised up. "I can't see a blasted thing! Grab
the lighter out of my pocketbook, will you? It's in my cigarette case.
Oh, and bring Theodore's knife, too."

Tony dug into her purse and located the filigreed, silver box beneath the knife. He returned to her side and thumbed the flint wheel.

"Over here." She held out a hand, and he placed the knife's handle in it. She groped under the dash and scraped the insulation off a wire. "Tony? Theodore keeps a toolbox in the back—he should have a pair of pliers in there." Tony got them for her, then flipped the lighter again.

The knife's polished silver caught enough light he could read the etched letters beneath the symbol. "What's the number for?"

"Number?"

"On the knife."

"Oh that. It's the year Theodore passed his Second Rite. The Society likes us to carry knives for self defense as opposed to firearms. Less likely to be anachronistic in the past."

"What's the Second—"

The car roared to life. Charlotte pulled her head from beneath the dash, straightened, then slid into the driver's seat. She pulled the car door shut without slamming it. Tony did the same on the passenger side, his question forgotten.

"We'll make a quick stop at my house to pick up a few things, then head for my brother's," she said. "I might be able to start a car without the key, but the padlock on the fishin' shack is another story."

Fishin' shack? Oh, God. It was all coming true. As much as he'd fought it, as determined as he was for it not to happen. What was it she'd said the first evening they spent together? Some things are simply fated to be. Was their doomed relationship one of them?

Fishin' Shack, read the childish, hand-lettered sign next to the cabin's door. Charlotte unlocked the door and pushed it open. Rusty hinges squealed.

Dust swirled in the shafts of sunlight streaming in through the window. Tony carried in the box of provisions they'd bought with his

1929 money, then took a moment to catch his breath. Luckily, the half-mile trek through the woods from where they'd parked Pippin's car had all been downhill, but it was still an effort, burdened with the food and supplies.

He gazed around the cabin. *Shack is right.* Its single room wasn't much bigger than his apartment's second bedroom. A dusty, but not unpleasant dry lumber smell permeated the air. A tingly sensation slid down his throat, an odd mix of trepidation and desire at the thought of sharing such close confines with Charlotte.

He set the box on the handmade wooden table. Two upturned barrel halves served as chairs. A metal tackle box rested in the front corner, along with a pair of fishing poles, a rusty shovel, and a straw broom. An ancient, wood-burning stove hulked in one back corner, and in the opposite one, the bed.

One bed. Little more than a low box containing a bumpy mattress, probably straw-filled. Charlotte would sleep there. Alone, Tony told himself. But with or without her in it, the bed looked inviting after driving most of the night.

He realized the tenseness that had gripped him for most of the ride was gone. As tricky as it had been to locate the place with the benefit of Dewey's hastily-scrawled map, the likelihood of the Society tracking them down was slim.

He unpacked the cans of food, sliding them onto a shelf by the stove. "What if they go through property records and find this place belongs to your brother?"

"They won't. Technically, it belongs to his in-laws, so there's no direct connection. It'll be the perfect place to hide until you start to feel..." She slowed in her unpacking.

"The pull."

"Yes." Her voice sounded strained. "By then, Caruthers will have concluded we're not in Dayton anymore, so we can go home and you can jump from there."

"What about Pippin? Won't he be ticked at you for helping me?"

"I'll... talk to him. Hopefully..." She ran her finger around the edge of a can she'd just unpacked. "I'll make him understand. He won't let them hurt me." She reached up to put the can away.

"You don't sound too sure."

She paused, her hand halfway to the shelf, and set the can back on the table. "I'm not. But it's the best I can hope for. He'll be hurt and angry, but Theodore loves me." Tony stopped mid-stride, his shoulders drew back. "Not like that," she said. "More like a prized student. Or the daughter he never had." She put the tomatoes on the shelf, then the remaining can of corn.

She regarded the canned goods, hands on her hips. "Well! I don't know about you, but I'm famished." Her voice held a false lightness. "Let's get some dinner started."

"Sounds good to me." Relieved at the change of subject, Tony walked to the stove and grabbed the axe. The wood bin beside it was empty. "Looks like we'll need some wood. I'll see what I can chop up."

He found a dead tree not far behind the cabin. Before long, he'd worked up a sweat. Had chopping wood been so hard when he was in the Boy Scouts? He couldn't remember. Then again, he'd had the other guys and a scoutmaster working with him.

He stopped, whipped off his shirt and blotted his forehead with it. Boy, was he out of shape. The cut on his side had split open and was bleeding again, though it only stung a little. Movement from the corner of the cabin caught his eye. Charlotte leaned against the cabin's back wall, a bemused smile on her face. "Having trouble?"

"No." He gritted his teeth and swung the axe.

Charlotte collected the wood he'd already chopped. Relief slid over him when she disappeared around the corner with it. Using a heavy tool would be safer without the distraction.

How would they occupy their days without the restaurant? No radio, no newspapers. Not even the chessboard or her projects. Nothing but each other's company.

He hoped to God it didn't rain. If the weather trapped them indoors, he wasn't sure he'd be able to keep his hands off her—

Like hell. He swung the axe harder than he needed, and splinters flew from the wood. They were both adults. He wasn't nineteen, he could control himself. If nothing else, he'd spend the week with the worst case of blue balls he'd had since he was in college.

He forced his attention to the downed tree, made himself focus on where to make the next cut. Before he knew it, he'd chopped the tree into pieces, and it lay in a neat pile.

He grabbed his shirt and wiped his forehead again, the muscles in his shoulders already protesting. Without a lawn to mow and yard work to do, he'd forgotten how cathartic physical labor could be—especially the kind where he didn't have to think too much.

Charlotte had a fire going in the circle of stones in front of the cabin by the time he brought her the rest of the wood. "It's nice out, and the stove will make it too warm inside," she explained.

"That's cool." He dropped the wood, then draped his shirt over the pump and pulled his undershirt off. "Man, I haven't worked like that in a long time. I'm going to go take a dip in—"

Charlotte gasped.

"What's wro—oh, this."

Her gaze lit on the backward L-shaped scar in the middle of his chest, then darted up to his neck for a brief second before she looked away. "I'm sorry, I'm being terribly rude."

"It's okay." He dropped the undershirt on the pump and sat on the cabin's front step. "Happened in Mexico. After I- after the first time I went back in time."

She sat beside him. "Where—or rather, when—did you go?"

Tony cracked a wry smile. She sounded like Everly. "Back to before the Europeans came, when the natives actually used the temples. I'd say over a thousand years."

"A millennium? Mercy!" She clapped a hand to her breast. "My word, I didn't know anyone could go back that far. Though I've heard it's easier in locales with a great deal of inherent spiritual energy. The power that must've taken... how long did you need to sleep off the jump?"

"I never had a chance. They killed me before I went into recovery."

She listened in rapt attention as he told her about his experience with the ancient Mayans.

"Good Lord, that's horrifying! It makes my first jumps tame in comparison."

She reached out and trailed a finger over the scar on his chest. He didn't move. He almost forgot to breathe. Shivers shot through him. Were they from the terrifying memories, or her touch?

Charlotte slowly shook her head. "You've been through so much."

Tony forced himself to speak. "Yeah, it's incredible how we heal if we get hurt in the past..." The words stopped, forgotten, as she slid her hand around his side to his back and pulled him close.

Unable to stop himself, he wrapped his arm around her, crushing her against him. Her lips parted, and he slid his other hand around the back of her neck. She tilted her head back and closed her eyes as he leaned down to capture her mouth with his.

He never wanted to stop kissing her. Never wanted to stop touching her. Her body pressed against his was a salve for all his wounds, physical and otherwise. He ran his hand down her back, wanted to slip his hand between the buttons of her dress, wished it didn't fasten so tightly. Her skin would be softer than the smoothest silk. He wanted to feel for himself, to touch it, to rub her all over. He ran his hand over her dress, up and down her back and to her side. As if of a mind of its own, his hand moved closer to where she pressed against his chest, and cupped her smooth, round breast. She trembled and pulled back from his kiss enough to let out a tiny sigh.

Tony pulled his hand away.

"Don't," she said.

"You want me to stop?"

"No," she whispered. "Don't stop."

He slid his other hand off her back and stood. "I think I'd better, or... I might not be able to." He studied the fire, the woods, the sky, anything but her.

But it had been so long. *Come on man, time to get back on the horse,* he heard in Bernie's voice.

"We can't do this," Tony said. "It's not right." *Sorry, Bernie.* "I'll only be here a few more days, then..."

She looked down, but not enough to hide the flush in her face. "You're right, of course. I- I guess I'll start dinner."

"What can I do to help?"

"I can take care of it." She rose, slipped inside the cabin and returned with a cigarette.

Tony didn't look away quickly enough to avoid seeing her lush, red lips close around the cigarette, lips he'd been kissing a moment ago, lips he desperately wanted to kiss again, before he moved on to other places—

He grabbed his shirt off the pump. "I'm going to the river." The closest he could get to a cold shower.

A cold dunk in the river wasn't enough to get his mind off Charlotte, so after his bath, he hiked downriver to the dam site. When he finally returned, Charlotte sat perched on the cabin's front stoop. Only the bowl of stew in her lap stopped him from scooping her into his arms, and it was an effort to merely sit beside her after he served himself from the pot on the campfire.

He tried to concentrate on the delicious beef stew instead of the press of her hip against his. "This is awesome. Even my mom's isn't this good."

Her answering smile chased away the lingering awkwardness. "We get a lot of compliments on it at the restaurant." Her mirth dissipated. "Or did." She stared into the campfire.

The bite of stew solidified in Tony's mouth. *Did.* Because he'd gotten her fired. They'd talked about it in the car. She'd insisted Tony had done the right thing, had thanked him for defending her honor, but he still felt guilty. His so-called defense had cost her her livelihood.

She dropped her spoon into her bowl with a clank. "Tony... don't. I told you, I hated that job. I'll find another. It will be all right."

He met her gaze, then took another bite. Jobs weren't easy to come by in these times. He ate the rest of his stew in silence, then remained on the stoop while she ate a second bowl.

She ladled the soup into her mouth with gusto, yet managed to look ladylike. He realized it was one of the things he liked about her—no comments about how she'd have to do an extra hour on the treadmill, or how the second helping would go right to her hips. Charlotte enjoyed food for the pure pleasure of it.

She caught him staring. "Penny for your thoughts?"

I want you, God, do I want you. But instead he said, "My thoughts are worth more than that aren't they?"

"A nickel, then. Perhaps even a dime." She smiled, the same flirty smile she'd given him that first day at the restaurant.

He pushed his lustful thoughts aside. *Can't go there.* Not when he'd be gone within a week, never to see her again.

It was time to get the answers she'd promised him. He placed his bowl on the ground. "What do I have to do to warp within my own lifetime?"

Her cheer vanished. She set her dishes beside his, her movements sluggish, as if he were watching on a slow motion video. "Why do you want to?" she asked in a quiet voice.

His jaw tightened. This time he wouldn't let her distract him. "You told me you'd answer my questions." She'd promised him answers, he was going to get them.

She looked at the smoldering campfire. The flames had died down, and a thin plume of smoke rose from the glowing red core of a big log. "You said you'd done it once before."

"Unintentionally."

"Where were you when you... warped?" The big log popped, and she flinched.

"You're not answering my question."

"I'm trying to explain—"

"I was sitting in the family room with my wife, watching TV. Tele—"

"Your wife? I thought you were divorced." Her eyes darted to his bare left hand.

"I am. But I wasn't then. Not until after I went back."

"You changed something." She clutched her skirt.

Tony snorted. "Yeah, you could say that."

"Wh- what happened? If you don't mind my asking."

Lisa had pressed him to talk about it many times, but he'd steered her away. Didn't want her analysis or advice, and he sure as hell didn't want to hear about the ass-kissing Charlie'd done to save their marriage.

But he wanted to tell Charlotte. She'd listen without telling him he needed to get a life. "I was supposed to go out of town that day," he said. "For business. Only I didn't know what was going on, so I missed my flight. And when I got home..."

A big smudge on the right side of his glasses marred his view of the fire's embers. He snatched the glasses off, whipped out his shirt-tail and rubbed them, then slowly slid them back on. Much better. "I walked inside, and there my wife was with my sister's husband, on the living room couch."

A vertical crease formed between Charlotte's eyebrows. "You caught them in the act?"

"Just about."

"Mercy, how awful!" She lay her hand on his arm. "I can't imagine." She turned to him, her voice flat. "And now you want to go back and make it not happen—"

"No."

Charlotte drew back and tilted her head.

"Dora and I were already too far gone. We never were right for each other." Time for some answers before she got off the subject, distracted him again. "How did I do it? How did I go back like that? I've gone back a century, no problem. But two or three years..."

She rose and grabbed a long stick, then poked at the logs with it until the fire blazed anew. Smoothing her skirt, she returned to the stoop. "After your jump, when you went back two years. After the dizzy spell and such, where were you?"

"I was in the family room..." His jaw went slack. In the same room. The same chair. He'd been in the same place—before, and after the jump. Could it be that simple?

"You ended up in the exact physical location as before you jumped, correct?"

"Yes."

"There is your answer." She retrieved their dishes as she stood. He started to ask her to elaborate—how close did he have to be to the physical space he'd occupied at the time he wanted to warp? Within several inches? A few feet? Millimeters?—but she'd already walked away.

At the hand pump he filled the big wash tub, then put it on the fire to heat. In silence, they washed the dishes.

He sneaked glances at her while they worked. Twice he caught her doing the same.

What had he done wrong? Was his question so horrible?

Her face held a firm, don't-mess-with-me resolve. He'd never find out if he waited for her to speak first.

"Why are you—" He started to say "upset" but caught himself. He knew her well enough to know she'd deny it.

"What?" she said.

"Quiet. Why are you so quiet?" Finished stacking the dishes, he took his place on the step again.

"Nothing to say."

"I find that hard to believe. In the whole week I've known you—"

"I'm worried." With a sigh she sat next to him. The little vertical crease again marred her forehead. "What are you going to do with this knowledge?"

He studied her face. She knew about Bethany. What was she like, she'd asked him that day in the attic, with a child's blunt innocence that stemmed from not knowing some subjects were supposed to be tiptoed around. "My daughter," he finally said.

Her eyes scanned the sky as she worked to remember. For her, the conversation had happened twenty years ago. "She was killed. In a car accident, if I recall..." Her chin snapped down, and her eyes grew round enough he could see almost the entire circle of brown. "Tony! You mustn't! It's—"

"It should have never happened! If there's any way I can make it not happen, by God I'm going to do it."

"Tony, some things are simply fated to be. We have no idea... it's like playing God."

"That's the same bullshit Everly gave me."

"Everly?"

"The Saturn Society guy from my time." She opened her mouth to ask something else, but Tony cut her off. "She didn't die in a car accident. She was murdered. And I'm sorry, but murder is *not* meant to be."

"You can't know that. And it's not just... bull." She spat the syllables, as if the words themselves were distasteful. "There are other dangers."

Tony wrinkled his nose. "Like what?"

She smoothed her skirt. "When we manipulate the past for our own purposes, tiny holes form. Rifts in the fabric of time. When they're small it may seem inconsequential, but—"

Tony waved her off. "Yeah, yeah, Everly told me about that, too. Supposedly things like insects can slip through. I'm not buying it."

"Tony, the danger..." Her voice grew firmer. "Your contemporary mentioned insects, but it's far more serious than that. *People* have disappeared because of these rifts—"

Tony snorted. "Undoubtedly people who wanted to disappear."

"No! Theodore—" He shot her a glare and she stopped short. "Please, Tony... This is the sort of thing that gets people in the Black Book... and rightfully so, I might add." She spoke softly, laying her hand on his arm again. "I don't want anything to happen to you."

Tony stared straight ahead, unseeing. "You have no idea what it's like, to answer the door, and it's a State Trooper standing there—" His throat swelled and cut off the rest of his words. Why had he thought she'd understand? She'd never felt the dread he had when he'd opened the door and known what the Trooper was about to tell him. Dread that burrowed beyond the bottom of his stomach, down to his toenails. Only it was worse than that.

He'd had to go to the morgue and identify her body, only to find she'd been beaten almost beyond recognition, her face swollen, bruised, bloody—they'd probably pistol whipped her—her fingernails, broken and bloodstained from her trying to fight. Cuts and bruises elsewhere, too, but mostly below the waist—

"I'm so sorry." Charlotte's soft voice yanked him out of the horrible memory. "But if you do this, you could make things worse."

Worse than his daughter being beaten and raped multiple times, then killed? "I don't see how," Tony said. "You have no idea..."

"You're right. I don't. And I never will."

"I hope you never do."

"It's not even a possibility." Her fingers curled on his arm. "I'll never have children."

The fire had again burnt down to a few glowing embers. "Sure you will," Tony said. "You'll find the right man. Get married. Have kids, if that's what you want." Stone coated the inside of his stomach. That man couldn't be him. She deserved someone to cherish her for the rest of her life, not a guy who could stay with her no more than two weeks at a time before the pull snatched him away. "You don't strike me as someone who gives up—"

"It's not that." She slid her hand away.

"What do you mean?"

She didn't answer right away, and when she did, she spoke in a monotone. "I'm not able have children."

Charlotte declined with a shudder when Tony asked her if she'd like to take a walk to the dam construction site down the river. "I don't like to get so close to the water." She'd had an aversion to water, anything larger than her bathtub, ever since that horrible day.

"You don't—oh." He shifted on his feet, then told her he'd be back in a while.

Tony understood. He didn't think it was silly, like Elmer did. The river's completely under control, Elmer had said when she didn't want to walk along the bank of the Great Miami with him a few weeks earlier.

Charlotte knew the Conservancy dams could hold back far more water than the flood had dumped on them. But it didn't matter.

By the time Tony returned, she'd washed and rewashed the dishes, and run out of things to tidy around the cabin. "How was your walk?" Her voice sounded falsely cheerful, even to herself.

"It was okay."

"I hope you took some time to think about—"

"I did."

Hope shot through her. "Then you've decided not to change the past—"

"Yeah." He disappeared around the cabin toward the privy.

Her grip tightened on the broom. He was lying. The odd twist of his features rendered him as transparent as the plate glass window at Irving's.

How had she let him talk her into telling him how to change his own past, to violate Society Code?

She never gave up so easily. Ever.

Yet this time, she'd completely given in. And in doing so, told him all he needed to know to do something that would condemn him in the Society's eyes for eternity.

They didn't speak of Tony's intentions after that. By nightfall, conversation became comfortable again. It was stuffy in the cabin, so they slept under the stars.

Charlotte had never seen so many, sparkling so bright. She glanced at Tony, who lay motionless in his bedroll on the other side of the fire. She didn't say anything. Too much romance inherent in stargazing with a man, and Tony had made it clear that was the last thing he wanted.

Once again, he'd become her hero. Though she was now the would-be savior and he the condemned, he'd saved her life again in a figurative sense. He'd awakened her to see she'd been letting her dreams die a slow death, a demise she would have hastened by accepting Elmer's hand. Tony had saved her from a life without joy. Yet what would be left after the pull took him?

Sleep eluded her. The seven points of the Big Dipper winked at her, mocked her. A cigarette. That's what she needed. It would help her relax. She pulled a blanket around her, then rose and tiptoed to the cabin.

There were only nine cigarettes in her box. She had to make them last. She'd smoke just one a day until it was time to go home. Sadness slipped over her in a thick, cottony mantle. She tried to ignore it as she lit her smoke, then stepped outside.

A brilliant light slashed the heavens. A shooting star! She gripped her cigarette. *Wish I may, wish I might...*

Silly. Nothing more than a superstition, her intellectual side scoffed. But she wished anyway. Her heart's desire, to be with Tony. Forever. Somehow, some way.

Sixteen

DECADES LATER, VIOLET SINCLAIR LAY BACK IN A LOUNGE CHAIR AND pulled her blanket more tightly around her as Timmy tossed another log into the wrought iron fire pit. "That should do it for now, huh ladies?" he asked Violet and his sister Stephanie in his slow, deliberate speech.

"It'll probably burn all night, as hot as you've stoked it." Violet pointed at the bottom of the fire pit that glowed red. In the morning, there would be a charred, black ring on Stephanie's concrete patio.

"Why didn't'cha say something?" Timmy slapped his forehead. "I know, I'll make myself useful. You girls want another beer?"

Stephanie handed him her empty bottle in response. "No thank you," Violet said. "But if you could grab my cigarettes and bring me one, I'd appreciate it." There were nine left in the pack. When they were gone, she'd quit. For good this time.

"Sure thing, Violet." He spun on one foot and loped across the patio, then disappeared into the house. The screen door slammed shut with a deafening bang behind him.

Thankfully, Stephanie wasn't in a talkative mood, leaving Violet to stare aimlessly at the sparks drifting up from the fire like miniature souls breaking free from the bonds of earth. The stars were unusually bright that night, and the Big Dipper twinkled above the cookie-cutter ranch house behind Stephanie's. A sense of déjà vu pervaded Violet.

Of course you've seen it before, silly goose!

Tony's image filled her mind. It always did when she looked at the stars, as if sometime in her obscured past, they'd shared a moment like this—

"Violet?"

Her head snapped around, the reproachful look on Stephanie's face clear in the firelight. "You're thinking about him, aren't you?"

Violet wound a lock of hair around her finger, a bad habit she'd acquired immediately after she'd sold her necklace with the Ohio quarter on it. "I can't help it." Her unfulfilled longing for Tony had been a frequent topic of conversation, especially in the days after she'd first seen his picture in the paper five years ago when he'd been promoted to vice president at LCT. It had taken her a year to land the cafeteria job, but it had been worth it, just to be near him.

Sympathy laced Stephanie's voice. "Violet... you need to move on. It's been what, three years?"

"I still say I knew him before...." Her friend would know what she meant. Before June ninth, five years ago. The first day Violet could remember.

"I still think you should give hypnosis another try. Especially since your therapist said it might help."

"I'll think about it," Violet said, more to get Stephanie to drop the subject than anything else. Hypnosis hadn't brought forth any memories the first two times. Why would it a third?

"You agreed that it was time to move on," Stephanie reminded her. "You've come so far—picking up on computers, going to school while you waitressed and worked in the cafeteria, then moving up to I.T..."

Technical work. Something Violet suspected she'd done before, too. "I know."

"You even saved up the money to get your teeth fixed. The last thing that should hold you back is a man."

"I know." Violet pressed her tongue against the back of her front teeth, where the gap used to be. Stephanie was one of the few who knew Violet hadn't done it for vanity, but because she feared whoever she'd wronged in her forgotten past might be looking for her. Between that, her lightened hair, and her weight gain—she suspected she'd been more active in her old life—they'd never find her. She hoped.

Stephanie twisted around in her chair, peering at the door. "What the fuck's taking so long to get a beer? Did he—"

"Oh dear." Violet put two fingers to her lips. "I put my cigarettes on top of the refrigerator. Timmy probably didn't see them, and went to the carryout for more. Thank heavens it's only a ten minute walk."

Stephanie snorted. "No doubt. But then, he'd go get your cigarettes even if he had to walk ten miles in a blizzard."

The front door slammed, and seconds later, Timmy bounded out the back and handed Violet a pack of cigarettes. "I had to go to the carryout down the road, but here they are."

"You shouldn't have. But thank you." She took the pack and shook out a cigarette.

"You know I'd do anything for you, Violet. If you hadn't showed up in the garage that day and helped me fix the plumbing, Vince would've beat the crap out of me. And prob'ly would've killed Steph, sooner or later."

Stephanie grimaced at the mention of her abusive ex, then flashed Timmy a smile. "Beer?"

"D'oh!" Timmy slapped himself on the forehead, then dashed inside.

Violet grabbed a stick and held it in the fire until the end caught, then lit her smoke off of that. Because of course, Timmy hadn't thought to grab her lighter, and she didn't feel like jumping up to get it herself, nor did she have the heart to ask him to.

Timmy returned with Stephanie's beer. "I saw Vince's old friend Big Bert at the carryout."

Stephanie made a face like she smelled something foul. Violet shivered.

Big Bert was the man who'd obtained Violet's birth certificate and Social Security number, in exchange for the antique gold and diamond chip necklace she'd been wearing when she woke in Stephanie's garage. She didn't want to know where he'd gotten the perfect-looking documents, or how.

"I don't think he saw me," Timmy said.

"Thank God," Stephanie muttered.

Violet's gaze drifted skyward while Timmy told his sister about a drunk guy who was hassling the clerk at the convenience store. She didn't realize their conversation had turned to her until Stephanie loudly repeated herself. "I told her she should give hypnosis another shot."

"I think she oughta ask him out," Timmy said.

Violet brought her hand to the base of her throat. "Oh mercy, I couldn't."

"Why not?" Timmy scooted closer to the fire and grabbed the stick Violet had used. "Girls ask guys out all the time."

"I know, but..." They'd had that conversation before, many times.

A shooting star streaked across the sky, its sparkling path lingering but a second.

Wish I may, wish I might... Nothing more than a meteor burning in the atmosphere as it fell to earth, but she wished anyway. To be with Tony.

Her heart surged, as if the fiery trail had stoked the flames of her feelings, drawn him closer to her than she had been since Mexico. If only her wish could come true...

Timmy poked at the fire with his stick. "You know what they always say. Nothing ventured, nothing gained."

"Flush him, or fish him out of the john," Stephanie said. "The worst he can do is say no."

"He's on leave of absence right now," Violet reminded them. Of course, she'd told them when she heard the news a couple of weeks before. "Maybe when he comes back..."

She'd do it. Ask him out. And if he said no, she'd give it up. Move on.

But maybe, just maybe, he'd say yes.

Wet. Cold. Little spots on his face, his bare chest. Tony opened his eyes to darkness, then squeezed them shut as a fat droplet struck one. He'd fallen asleep outside, but he hadn't counted on rain.

He'd have to go to the cabin. Bad enough the weather had trapped them inside most of the day. The continual effort to keep his hands off Charlotte wound him like a steel spring. Good thing she'd found that deck of cards. If the wet weather continued, they'd wear them out.

Not to mention wear down his resolve not to touch her again. Even though the weather was iffy when dusk fell, he'd decided it was his better risk and had brought his bedroll outside again.

He waited to see if the rain would slack off but instead, it rained harder. Thunder growled in the distance.

A dim light glowed in the cabin's window. Charlotte must've lit the hurricane lamp. With a yawn, he struggled out of his blankets and groped for his glasses until he found them at the base of a tree. A chill wind buffeted him as he stood, and whipped his boxer shorts. He considered running for the car, but with no moon, he'd never be able to find his way up the trail. The rain began in earnest as he gathered up the blankets and ran for the cabin.

Thunder boomed again, nearer. He stepped inside and slammed the door behind him.

Charlotte sat in the bed and sipped at a tin cup. A tendril of smoke drifted up from a cigarette perched in a metal saucer on the floor. The quilt pulled up to her lap didn't do enough to conceal her silky, white gown or the dark tips of her breasts beneath its lacy trim. Tony averted his eyes.

"I was about to come looking for you," she said.

He shook the water off his blankets, dropped them, and wiped his glasses on the hem of his boxer shorts. Thunder rattled the teakettle and stockpot on the stove. Charlotte's hand shook as she placed her cup on the floor and reached for her cigarette.

"Damn, it's as cold in here as it is outside." Tony spread his blankets by the opposite wall. Still too close to her.

"We left all the wood outside." She took a final drag on the cigarette then stubbed it out in the plate.

Tony lay his glasses on the table then sat on the floor, pulling the blankets around him. Maybe he'd be able to sleep if she blew out the lamp. "Is there some reason we need the light?"

She studied her lap, drew her fingers across the blanket stretched over her knees. "It's just that... I hate thunderstorms. Always have, ever since..." The flood, he realized. "Once in awhile I sleep through them, but usually, I get up and turn on every light in the house." She gave a nervous laugh. "Silly, isn't it?"

"Not really. Leave the lamp lit if it makes you feel better." He lay on the floor, facing away from her. By morning every dark, blurry knot in the wall would be etched into his brain. There was no way he'd be able to sleep with her only a few feet away, in that silky gown.

"Tony? Doesn't this sort of remind you of... when I was little?"

He felt her eyes on him. "Yeah." In many ways. The cold, the absolute darkness outside, the drumming of the rain on the roof.

Her uneasiness mirrored that of the child he'd met twenty years earlier. Back then, she'd been scared, and he'd gathered her into his arms, whispered words of comfort. He ached to do the same now.

But this was different. In 1913, he'd wanted to take her home, tuck her into bed, and read her a goodnight story. Now he wanted to join her there, act out some stories of their own.

Unable to stop himself, he rolled over. Bad idea. Instead of masking her tempting curves beneath the silk, his blurred vision softened the glow of the hurricane lamp, and heightened his need to reach out and touch.

"Tony... come here," she said softly.

Say something. Stay put. But his body obeyed her. He pushed his blankets off, rose and moved toward her. Toward temptation. He stopped at the side of the bed and turned his back to her, even though the evidence of his desire couldn't have escaped her. "We need to go home tomorrow." Roughness punctuated his voice.

"We can't go back yet! Dr. Caruthers will still be in Dayton, searching for us—"

"That's a chance I'll have to take. If I'd known how remote this place was, how small... this was a big mistake, coming out here." He couldn't let this... this thing between them happen. Not when it was likely the cause of her demise.

"But..." Her eyes grew round, as if she'd surprised herself. "It's not just you. He'll come after me too. After all, I helped you..."

"Then I'll go back to Dayton by myself. I'll hitch a ride, and you can come back when you think it's safe—"

"But Dr. Caruthers—"

"Fuck him. If he finds me, he finds me. I'll force him to kill me before he gets me to the Society House." He twisted around and allowed himself to look at her, as if he needed another reminder of why he had to leave. "Being here with you... it's driving me crazy."

There. The truth was out. As much as he always made it a point not to lie to others, he'd done nothing the past two days but deceive himself.

He thought he could stand up to her temptation. He thought he could control himself.

He was wrong. "I can't take it anymore."

Her warm hand circled his wrist, and she pulled him onto the bed. "Then don't."

The straw mattress crackled with his weight. Charlotte gripped his wrist tighter and pulled him to her. She wasn't about to let him go, not now; she wished not ever, but she wouldn't let herself think about that. His eyes burned dark with desire, so deep she could drown in their blue depths. Her breasts rose and fell in shallow heaves with her short, sharp breaths. "Charlotte..." he whispered.

He moved closer until her face was inches from his. Moistness on his lips gleamed in the lamplight, and the clean scent of rain lingered in his hair.

As if some invisible force had taken control of her body, she leaned nearer, powerless to resist his pull, until her lips met his. Wet, forceful, yet yielding. Softness mingled with the bristle of his day-old beard, sent electricity racing through her. He wrapped his arms around her back, his hands warm through her thin nightgown. His fingers trailed up the nape of her neck and into her hair. She shivered. A soft sigh escaped her lips, then his mouth captured them again, his tongue seeking out hers, entwining, joining.

One of her hands sneaked around his waist. She slid the other up his chest and threaded her fingers through the fine hairs around the L-shaped scar. He stiffened, and she pulled her hand away. "Does it hurt?"

"No. It's just a little... sensitive."

She tilted her head. "For someone who's literally had his heart ripped out, you have more of it than any man I know." Lightning flashed, and thunder rumbled. She kissed the scar, dragging her lips up and down it in a curious, silken line. His breath caught. Then she brought her face back up to his, and their mouths joined again.

Never taking his lips from hers, he reached up to slip the strap of her gown off her shoulder. She twisted to offer the other shoulder to him. He accepted her invitation and pushed that strap down, too.

He broke their kiss, and she straightened. The lace neckline of her gown drooped to reveal the tops of her breasts.

And her quarter.

She reached for it, but he picked it up first. "What's this?"

She wet her lips as he brought the quarter closer to his face and turned it over. "Two thousand- Holy shit! You found this in the attic, didn't you?"

She lowered her head. Maybe it was only a quarter, but she'd kept it when it belonged to him, like a common thief.

He dropped the quarter, then drew his hand up her neck and brushed his fingertips over her cheek. "I shouldn't have kept it." She spoke barely above a whisper. "But I wanted it! Wanted it to remember you by..."

He trailed a finger along the intricate links of the chain. "I'm honored... you put your memory of me on this fancy necklace..." He picked it up again. "It's beautiful. Though not as much as what's beneath it." Her heart soared. *Beautiful. Honored.* He let go of the quarter, then traced his finger alongside it and down. Slowly. Achingly. A delightful, prickly sensation followed his touch.

The heat in her face fled southward as desire enveloped her. She followed his gaze to the tops of her exposed breasts. Longing for his touch there, she tipped her chin up and closed her eyes. Instead he slid his warm, moist tongue down the side of her neck. She jumped, gasping. Her skin tingled all up and down that side of her body, and the warmth pooling in her loins turned to fire. He kissed the other side of her neck and sent matching shivers down her other side.

She wanted him to kiss her like that all over. Everywhere. It didn't matter if she never saw him again. Nothing mattered but right now.

He unfastened her nightgown, drew his fingers down her skin between each button, bringing more shivers with every touch, until the fabric fell away to reveal her breasts.

He brought his mouth to hers again, then lightly circled one taut nipple with his finger. She sighed. He thumbed its aching tip, and her sigh became a moan. He traced around her other breast and gently nipped her lower lip, then drew the tip of his tongue down her neck, her chest, and down the slope of her right breast. He kissed its tip, drew it into his mouth, twirled his tongue around it until Charlotte was sure she'd explode. "Tony..." She sucked in a thick breath as he moved to the other side. "You don't know how long I've waited for this, how long I've—"

He stopped and lifted his head. The curve of his lips and his sparkling eyes took on a feral cast. "How long?"

"As long as I've known what it is to be a woman."

Tony drew back. "How did you know I'd come back?"

"I didn't. I just dreamed." As a little girl, she'd thought she'd marry him, until she grew older and realized it was a foolish fantasy. And then she'd wasted two years of her life with that lout Louie Lambert, only belatedly realizing most of his appeal was his physical resemblance to Tony.

Tony's smile returned, smaller yet warmer. "I wondered about you, too. How you'd turned out, if you had a happy life." His eyes caressed her body. "You were a beautiful little girl. But nothing compared to the woman you are now."

A thrill ran up her insides, and she waited for him to resume his affections. But instead he shifted away and looked somewhere past her. "Charlotte... we can't do this."

The bubbles inside her popped, suddenly heavy. "Why?"

"You're not the kind of woman a guy wants for a one-night stand. You're a woman a guy would want forever." He swallowed. "And we don't have forever."

A sensation of floating on air rushed through Charlotte. *Forever.* Then she came crashing down. He was right. What kind of relationship could they have, when he belonged decades in the future?

It didn't matter. No future, no past. Nothing mattered but this moment. She squared her shoulders and curled her fingers around his wrist. "We have tonight. And probably tomorrow. Maybe longer. I'd rather have a tiny moment of happiness than forever wonder what I missed." She couldn't let him leave her in aching need. "Tony... make love to me."

He choked as he turned away. "There's nothing I'd rather do," he said in a raspy voice. "But we still have one problem." She sensed he was drawing on the last reserves of his willpower. "No protection."

"Protection?" Her expression drew into one of puzzlement.

He twisted around. "The last thing I want to do is take a chance and leave you... with a child. I won't do it."

Her insides relaxed. "Tony... I told you. I can't have children." For the first time in her life, the fact didn't sadden her.

Tony listed away and regarded her from the corner of his eye. "Are you sure?"

She cast him a wan smile then looked down at the quilt, tracing her fingers along a seam. "Quite sure. Unfortunately." If he belonged in her time, if he didn't have to go, if it weren't such an economic impracticality, she'd give anything to have his baby. But it wasn't possible. "I have... female problems. My sister does, too, she's been married for fifteen years, no children. And as for myself, well... you know I ran with a racy crowd, and... I'm not exactly innocent." She thumbed her quarter, trying to gauge his reaction.

He sat without moving. Didn't he understand what she was saying? She gulped. "There was a fellow in college..."

Tony regarded her silently. Waiting. Listening.

Her fist clenched and unclenched a wad of blanket. "I'm... I'm not... a virgin." There, she'd said it. Hated telling him, but he had a right to know.

"So?"

She released the blanket. He didn't care, and it was all right. "Well... I never became pregnant, though we never tried to prevent it. He would have married me if it did happen. But I'm glad it didn't." A lump formed in her throat. Would Tony reject her, too?

Tony gathered her into his arms, his hands warm and gentle on her back. "Maybe I'm a selfish ass, but, I'm glad, too." He swept the quilt off the bed, then leaned in to drop a trail of light, feathery kisses down her neck. His hands trailed down her front to take up where he'd left off with the gown. In seconds, he unbuttoned it the rest of the way, then slid the straps off her arms and tossed the gown onto the floor.

She never wore panties to bed. Both sat still as his gaze traveled over her body. Far from feeling exposed, she felt caressed, cherished, treasured. "You're beautiful," he whispered.

She tried to respond, but nothing came out. Finally, he stood and slipped off his drawers. "So are you," she managed.

And he was. Maybe not built like a bodybuilder, but perfect for her.

He tumbled back into bed. She lay down as he crawled toward her and positioned himself over her, then braced herself for the burst of pain she was sure would come. It had been a long time since Louie.

But instead, he rolled to the side and trailed a finger down her neck, her chest, over her breasts and down her belly until he reached between her legs. She hadn't realized how moist she'd grown until he slipped a finger inside, rubbed it in her wetness. Her hips jerked involuntarily. "Oh, my gracious!" What an incredible sensation he made just with his finger. He withdrew it and hovered over her again. She waited for him to complete the act but he surprised her once more. He clutched her hips and rolled over, holding her against him, until she straddled him. Finally he lowered her until she settled onto him. "Ohhhh," she sighed, and he made a matching groan. It didn't hurt at all. He slid inside her with surprising ease, despite the fact he was more than adequately endowed.

His hands guided her backward and forward while his hips rocked up and down. "Charlotte..." he breathed. Something inside her swelled. She could float away if he let go. Joy. Pure, unadulterated joy, like nothing she'd ever felt before. She leaned down until her breasts brushed his chest. Her nipples hardened from the sensation of grazing the fine mat of curls there. She reached up and raked her fingers through his soft hair, and their mouths came together again.

They moved together endlessly. This moment could go on forever. She'd never tire of feeling him inside her, of the warm, firm hold of his hands on her hips and roving over her body, or the heady sensation of power she felt at his every moan, each gasp, each heavy breath. She didn't think it could get any better until a tightness built down low, and she clenched around him until all of a sudden her whole body shuddered.

He held her hips firm until her spasms subsided. She brought a hand to her bosom. "Oh my heavens!"

A wide smile drew across his face, then he tensed beneath her.

"What?" she asked.

"Turn over," he rasped.

She relaxed, her body pressed to his, while he rolled her onto her back, still joined with her.

He raised up on his arms and thrust in and out of her. She lifted her hips to meet him, surprised at how much tighter it was, yet it wasn't painful, only more intense.

He moved faster and faster until he went rigid, his face tensed, and it was over. He relaxed and leaned down to kiss her, lingering for long seconds, then finally rolled off her.

They lay side by side, their hips touching. He reached for her hand, and twirled his thumb around hers. After his breathing slowed to normal, he rose and retrieved the quilt, then spread it over them, clutching her body to his. She'd almost drifted off to sleep when the lamp sputtered and went out. She listened. Heard only the pitter patter of a light rain and Tony's breathing.

"Tony?"

"Mm?"

"The storm... it's over."

But she couldn't shake the feeling that another storm—one of fear and danger and running—was just beginning.

Charlotte shivered as she blinked at the sunlight filtering in through the open door, though the cabin wasn't cold. *Whatever it takes...*

She'd been dreaming. *Theodore.* She'd been dreaming of him. She'd been talking with him, in his lushly decorated office at the Society House—of what, she didn't know, because the dream fled when she woke.

Why had she dreamed about Theodore? She sat up in bed, and the covers slipped down to reveal her naked breasts.

Warmth flooded her as memories of the night before rushed into her mind.

Tony. An eerie chill ran through her body. Good heavens, what had she done?

Whatever it takes, she heard Theodore say.

It was what he always said when he asked her help in apprehending one of Time's Enemies. All the times she'd played the floozy to entice a criminal to the Society House... A different kind of burn rose inside her at the memory. Thank heavens it had never gone further.

Until now.

Whatever it takes. Theodore would think no less of her for tempting Tony with her body.

No. Inviting Tony into her bed had nothing to do with the Society.

Nothing to do with who he was to Theodore. There was one reason she'd asked him to make love to her.

Because she wanted to.

It had been everything she'd imagined and more, a sense of two souls entwined along with their bodies in a way she'd never imagined possible.

The day seemed brighter than those that had come before, a crisp, clear portent of things to come, of contentment that went beyond simple happiness. Pure joy.

Strange, how a few days ago she'd had to push aside worries about what the neighbors would think, her allowing a man who wasn't her husband to live with her, albeit as a boarder. Yet away from the world and its judgments—not to mention Theodore and the Saturn Society—everything was right, if only for a short time. In their tiny, insular domain of the cabin and the surrounding wood, the woes of the world seemed far away. Though the cabin was primitive and lacked any luxuries, she and Tony had everything they needed—most of all, each other.

She loved him.

She tossed back the covers, jumped out of bed and hurried to the door.

A tantalizing scent of fried eggs drifted on the breeze. Outside, utensils clanged on cookware. Charlotte gripped the doorframe and peered out hesitantly.

Tony crouched next to the fire and flipped over some sliced potatoes in a frying pan. He wore only his drawers. Charlotte's hand curled and uncurled at the memory of brushing her hand up the fine hairs of his chest. And he was cooking breakfast. Her insides contracted. No man had ever done that for her, not even Papa. He'd had a housekeeper until Mabel had grown old enough to cook. Tony flipped an egg. He leaned back and startled when he saw her.

A big grin lit up his face. He'd be able to see her perfectly in the daylight with his glasses on, but Charlotte refused to shrink away. "Stand there much longer and breakfast'll be burned." His words washed away the last of her misgivings.

Her smile grew but she didn't move.

After they made love, dressed, and ate breakfast (which Tony took off the fire and reheated), he suggested going for a walk.

At her request, they took the upper trail. They walked through the wood until they neared the dam site, then sat on a log overlooking the construction site, where WPA workers shoveled gravel, dirt and river silt.

"All this is under water in my time," Tony mused. *His* time. To which the pull would soon force him to return.

"What's it like?" Charlotte asked.

Tony made a sweeping gesture. "All this is a huge lake. There's a big campground on the far end, and a marina... it's a beautiful lake. Maybe not this beautiful, but..."

"What's Dayton like?"

"The same in some ways. Different in others. The statue at First and Main's still there, and so is the old courthouse." He told her about the performing arts center that would go up where Rike's was.

"What about my house? What's it like in the twenty-first century?"

He regarded her from the side of his eye. "Gone. Torn down to make way for I-75."

Confusion washed across her face. "What's—"

"A superhighway," he explained.

She fiddled with the quarter. "What does it look like?"

"I-75? It's eight lanes—"

"No, I mean where my house was. Is."

"Concrete. Nothing but sloped concrete. The highway's above the city, and where your house sits, there's six pillars that support the road. This big." He stretched his arms into a semblance of a bear hug.

Charlotte gazed toward the dam workers. Her house, gone. She supposed that was the price of progress, something she normally favored, but the idea that she wouldn't always live there brought a sinking sensation to her belly.

Finally, they walked back down the trail. She didn't speak until they were almost to the cabin, when something else occurred to her.

"Tony? When I found you on my front porch, after I carried you in... you called me Violet. Why?"

Tony stopped and she stumbled into him. "What did you say?" he asked.

"You called me Violet."

"I did?"

She laughed, but it came out a nervous titter. "You don't remember, do you?"

"I was pretty out of it, if you'll recall." The workings of his tripped-out mind from the warp, no doubt. He said as much to Charlotte as he resumed walking. "You do look a lot like her."

"Who is she?"

"She's the one who caught me when I started to slide down the pyramid. She works in my office. She uh, helps people with technical problems." A grimace flashed across his face, as if he'd said something he wished he hadn't.

Charlotte's ears perked up. "What sort of technical things?" She drew up beside him, determined not to let him evade the question.

"Things like the calculator. It would take a while to explain."

Charlotte laughed. "I have time."

Tony slowed. "Look, I don't think it's a good idea... letting you in on technology ahead of its time—"

"What can I do? I'm just one woman. Surely I—"

"You build things in your basement. I've seen the books you read. Sometimes one person is all it takes." He shot her a stern look.

Fine, she could change the subject, then circle back around to it when he wasn't so guarded. "This Violet. Is she someone special?"

Relief slipped over Tony as they emerged in the clearing near the Fishin' Shack. "Yeah... but not in the way you are."

Warmth coated Charlotte's insides, and she couldn't stop the sappy grin from stealing onto her face.

"I was thinking of going down to the river to take a bath," he said. "Want to join me?"

Her joy dissipated at the thought of all that water, pulling at her, trapping her in its grip, sucking her under... "N- no thanks, I'll stay here."

"You sure?" She nodded. "Because we could do more than just wash."

She wanted to be with him, but she couldn't do that.

He took the fork in the trail to the river by himself.

Tony unbuttoned his shirt and had just unbuckled his belt when he remembered. *Soap.* With a sigh, he trudged back up the trail.

His breath lodged in his throat when he neared the cabin.

Charlotte bent beside the hand pump. She wore nothing but her quarter, dangling on its chain above her gorgeous, round breasts. As she rubbed a washcloth over one smooth thigh, Tony crept closer. "What are you doing?"

She jumped, snatched a towel off the pump and covered herself. "I thought you went to the river." Why was she suddenly self-conscious, when he'd seen it all?

"I forgot the soap. Why are you—"

"I'm just washing up a little."

Tony's brows lowered. "Why don't you go to the river? It's been so warm these past few days, the water's not cold at—"

"I can't." She gripped the towel tighter. Despite the warm sun, she shivered.

He rushed to her and gathered her into his arms. Her towel slid to the ground. The cool wetness seeping through his shirt felt good against his chest. She trembled. "You never learned to swim, did you?" he asked softly.

"No."

He held her for a long minute. "Come to the river with me." He held his hand, palm down, at his waist. "Only this high, even in the deepest spot. Much better than trying to wash like that."

"I don't know..." Her voice quavered. "I- I hate water."

"I'll hold you the whole time." He released her, then placed his hands on both sides of her face. "I don't want you to be afraid. Of anything."

"A- all right."

He took off his clothes, then grabbed her hand with one of his and snatched the soap with the other while she scooped up the towel. He led her to the riverbank.

He held her close as she took in the scene. A few dozen yards upstream, water danced over a series of rocks, then slowed where it deepened. She shuddered.

"It's okay." He tipped her chin up with a finger and kissed her. Just a quick one, but it was enough to finish the job of waking up other parts of him. "Ready?"

Her jaw tense, she nodded. "Don't let me go." Her features drew tight.

"I won't." He ignored the throbbing in his groin and led her into the water. Her arm wrapped around him, then squeezed tighter as they waded in deeper.

He pulled her to him, careful not to drop the soap, and let her get used to the water. Slowly her shivering subsided. "Not bad once you get used to it, huh?"

"It's... refreshing." The cool water flowed around them and made little eddies around her hips. Her gaze followed a fish the size of her foot as it swam by, its tail and fins rippling in the water. "There're fish in here!"

Tony chuckled. "It is the Fishin' Shack, after all."

"W- will they bite us?" Another fluttered past.

"They might nibble, but it doesn't hurt. Feels sort of like this..." He lightly pinched her arm. She giggled. He held her for another minute to allow her to acclimate—not so much to the temperature, for the day was warm, but to push away her fear. Finally, her trembling stopped. He rubbed the soap up and down her back, all over, then down the side of her arm. "Lift your arm."

She obeyed, and he ran the soap up the underside of her arm. Her skin glistened in the afternoon sun. So incredibly smooth. Then he brought the soap down and rubbed it over her side, around the curve of her breast. She allowed him to take a step back so he could wash her front, though she didn't let go of his other hand. Her nipples were already tensed into tight peaks. He lingered over them, eliciting a soft moan. Then he switched hands so he could wash her other side and arm. "Hold this." He handed her the soap.

"What?"

"Can't leave you all sudsy." She looked down at the water, and her eyes grew wide. "You don't have to go under. Here." He leaned close so their bodies pressed together. She trembled. "It's okay," he said softly. He scooped up a handful of water behind her back and released it over her. Then he spun her around within the circle of his arms so her back pressed against his chest, and did the same thing to her front, rubbing under her quarter between her breasts, cupping his hands over them as he rinsed.

He couldn't stop himself from twirling his thumbs over her hardened nipples. She threw her head back against him. "Oh, Tony..." She turned around and placed her hands on his waist, still clutching the soap. "I think I'm clean enough." Her eyes gleamed, and his loins tightened even more. God, he needed her. Now.

But instead he said, "No you're not. Here..."

Her eyes grew wide, but she allowed him to step back and lift one of her legs. He took the soap from her and rubbed it over her thigh. She started to shake again, her jaw tensed, but she let him extend her leg and rub the soap up and down her calf, then raised it higher, bending her knee so he could wash between her toes. She yelped. He looked up with a grin. Her shivering had stopped again, and her smile matched his. "Am I clean enough now?"

He was on fire but he shook his head.

He washed the other leg, then slowly rubbed the soap over the smooth flesh of her belly, then lower, dipping his finger into the slippery wetness where he ached to go. "Tony..." she groaned. "This is killing me."

"Me too." His voice grated. He started to toss the soap onto the grass when she grabbed his hand.

"Wait a minute." She stepped back, no longer trembling, although one hand still gripped his arm. "You haven't washed yet."

"Give me the soap then."

"Uh-uh." She lathered up his back. The slippery softness of her hands glided all over him, as he'd done to her.

Her gentle touch was almost enough to make him come undone. "Charlotte..." He could barely speak.

"Not yet."

He bit back a gasp. She continued to rub around his backside, then hesitated as she drew her hands around front. She looked up at him, eyebrows raised.

"Go ahead," he said through clenched teeth.

A smile spread across her face as she threw the soap to shore. She gently cupped his balls, slowly slid her fingers around, then up his cock. The ache grew worse with each millimeter. "My God, Charlotte, I can't take it any more."

With a giggle, she released him. "That's good, because I think we're done."

Clutching her buttocks, he pulled her against him. She hooked her feet around his waist, and he lifted her, then slowly lowered her onto him. "Oh, God," he said. She moaned. He rocked her up and down, the water splashing in time as he raised and lowered her in and out.

It wasn't long before she tightened around him, and her rhythmic squeezes made him lose control. "Tony, I love you," she said softly. Her legs released their hold and she stood in the water.

She loved him. Joy swelled in his chest, so much he thought he'd burst. He drew her into his arms and pulled her tightly against him. He wanted to tell her he loved her, too, but the words wouldn't come. Too soon, he'd have to leave her, never to return.

The passion in her eyes faded to fear. "Me, too," he managed. He backed away, never taking his eyes off her. He couldn't say it, not yet, but he was in love with her. The thought made his insides all jumpy, a happy sensation full of promise and delight. Why did he have to leave? Then he remembered what she'd said that first night. Better to have a moment of happiness than to always wonder what you missed.

She dropped his hand and stood on her own. Droplets of water sparkled on her cheeks. From splashing... or tears? She trembled. "Charlotte..." He reached for her, but she didn't take his hand. "Are you—"

"I'm fine." The corners of her mouth twitched up. "I'm not afraid. As long as you're with me." He wouldn't think about the fact that before long, he wouldn't be.

Tony did a mental calculation as he set down the tackle box, speared a fresh worm onto the hook, and tossed it in. The shouts of workers, the clangs of tools and equipment drifted to him from the dam site upriver.

Counting recovery, he'd been in 1933 for fourteen days. The last three had passed in a blur of meals shared, walks in the woods, and making love. It was like he was twenty-two again. Although neither mentioned it, they both knew time was short and it was as if they were trying to cram a lifetime of love into a few days. He wouldn't be able to stay much longer—

Awful quiet all of a sudden. Was it quitting time already? He hadn't thought it was that late. But the men's shouts had ceased, replaced by the distant whoosh of—

Traffic?

He peered toward the construction site.

A massive wall of concrete rose up from the river.

He dropped the fishing pole, and his chest constricted. The dam. Whole. Complete. With cars trundling across its crest. Minivans. Pickup trucks. A semi with McDonald's arches on its side rumbled by, quashing any doubt he might have had that this was the twenty-first century.

He squeezed his eyes shut. He couldn't go back, not here. He couldn't leave Charlotte.

The buzz of the traffic disappeared. He opened his eyes as a man in a bucket being hoisted up the half-built dam shouted to another worker on the riverbank.

Tony's muscles unclenched. He'd imagined it, that's all. Something tugged at his line, and he pulled, forcing his thoughts to bringing in dinner.

But as he tied the catfish onto some spare line, he knew better. *Fourteen days.*

Tension enveloped him again. The completed dam and twenty-first century traffic had been real. His time in 1933—and with Charlotte—was nearing an end.

Their lovemaking that night was urgent, with a quiet desperation that lacked the easygoing, languid quality of their previous encounters. Charlotte clutched Tony against her with both arms and legs, as if their physical closeness would keep him with her for all time. He tensed, and spilled into her, then brought his lips to hers, joined in every way they possibly could...

Green. Hazy, all around. Cold...

What? She broke their kiss, inhaled...

Water. She spat, choked, the coldness clawed at her from every side, each inch of her body that wasn't pressed to Tony's. She sucked in another gulp of the chill water...

Drowning! She tried to scream. No air. Couldn't breathe... Tony's grip on her tightened.

The green surrounding her grew darker...

Seventeen

CHARLOTTE STRUGGLED TO BREATHE AS HER WORLD WENT MURKY GREEN, then dark. She flailed, her thoughts an incoherent jumble, except for one

(drowning)

then the water's surface broke and she sucked in air, blessed, life-giving air—

"Charlotte?" She opened her eyes. Tony hovered over her, his face twisted with concern. "Charlotte!"

She shook her head, and tremors racked her body. "Water.... everywhere... Noooooooo...."

Tony rolled off her. She was soaked, as was the mattress beneath them. He touched his stomach, then pulled his hand back, staring at it, wide-eyed. "You... you were in the water, too?" He brushed a sopping lock of hair off her face.

She blubbered an assent. "Water... no..." She couldn't stop shivering. Couldn't shake the slimy feel of wetness on her skin, the certainty she was about to drown, just like in the flood...

Tony sat up and pulled her against him. "It's okay, it's okay." He lowered his hand to the straw mattress, and droplets of water splashed on her. Then he withdrew one of his arms—*No! He can't go now, please, not now*—and grabbed the quilt they'd shoved onto the floor in the frenzy of their lovemaking.

He wrapped the blanket around her, then held her close. Her trembling subsided as the quilt soaked up the wetness and the realization sank in that she was in bed, in the cabin, with Tony. Not drowning.

He rubbed the quilt over her back, and his gentle touch helped her regain her rational voice. "Tony... what happened?"

"I don't know... I was just... all of a sudden, there was nothing but water, everywhere."

She fisted her quarter, and the answer struck him as she voiced it. "You said this was all under water in your time."

"Oh God. The pull."

"Yes. And... It took me along." A chill coursed through her that had nothing to do with the dampness. "But- but jumping into the future isn't possible. Yet... How did you stop it?"

"The same way I stop a warp when I want to stay in the present. I concentrated on the cabin, on you, on now."

He pulled her against his chest. His warmth comforted her and soothed her fears, but her mind wouldn't stop. She couldn't have almost jumped with him. How could two people jump together? Especially when for her, it was the future?

She must have imagined it. Her mind had gone funny with her dread at his leaving, that had to be it. Yet, Tony had been in the water, too, for they both were wet...

She didn't want to think about it. All that water... She touched the damp mattress and started to tremble again. Tony held her tight. Good heavens, she needed a cigarette. She extricated herself from his arms and retrieved one from her purse. Her last.

Charlotte blinked back tears as she drove, tried to push away the knowledge that soon, Tony would leave her, most likely for good. She concentrated on navigating the curvy country road, the feel of the steering wheel in her hands, the rumble of the pavement beneath the tires. They'd been on the road an hour before she spoke. "There has to be some way we can be together..."

"I've been trying to think of one all week." Tony pressed his lips together. "It just won't work. Not with my family, especially my daughter. And if I have anything to say about it, I'll be back at my job, too."

His daughter. The probable reason he was in the Black Book. The reason he couldn't come back. Was she so selfish, to want him for herself? To want what was right? "I wish I could talk you out of this, Tony."

"I thought you understood." His voice was strained.

"I'm trying, I really am. It's just so dangerous."

"If it was your child, you'd take any risk."

"Perhaps." She stared straight ahead, resisting the urge to reach for her quarter before she downshifted to slow for a curve.

"She wasn't just murdered." Tony's voice was flat, as he if were reading from a dry, academic treatise.

"What hap—"

"She was beaten and raped. Multiple times. All before she died. If you think that was meant—"

"No!" She risked a sideways glance. Tony leaned on his hand, his elbow braced on his knee, his thumb and forefinger pressed into the corners of his eyes.

"Tony..." Her voice came out strained. She couldn't imagine what he must feel, never having had a child. The closest she came were Dewey's two daughters. "I can't... I had no idea. And..." She swallowed, forced herself to concentrate on the road. "In your situation... I'd probably do the same." In her peripheral vision, she saw him straighten, look out the window, then turn to her.

She pulled a hand off the steering wheel and reached for her quarter, twiddling the chain. "Where'd you get that, anyway?" he asked.

She squeezed the gearshift. "The quarter? From you, remember?"

"No, the necklace."

He was trying to change the subject. Fine with her. "Theodore gave it to me when I was sixteen, after I passed my First Rite."

"What is this First Rite, anyway?"

"Being able to jump at will. You go into a locked room—where the only way to escape is to jump into the past—"

"That's what they did to me, when I wound up in 1913. What's the Second Rite?"

"You have to die in the past. And come back."

Holy shit, he'd done that, too. "Have you—"

"No. I'm... I don't have the nerve. It's not the easiest thing, after all, you can't kill yourself, you can't want to die, or—"

"Or it's game over," Tony finished. He made a sharp exhale. "Ironic. The quarter from me, hanging on a chain from the guy who's trying to kill me." Or worse. He didn't say the words, but Charlotte could almost hear them.

"I think it's... fitting. You saved my life and gave me this- this time travel gift, and Theodore gave me the knowledge I needed to be able to live with it."

Tony crossed his arms over his chest. "Saving my daughter is what'll make it something I can live with."

"I still wish I could talk you out of it." She sighed. "I know it's hard to imagine, but you could make things worse."

He dropped his arms back to his sides. "Look Charlotte, your mother died from illness, right?" She nodded. "So it's not like you could go back and cure her. But if something else had killed her, wouldn't you use your gift to make it not happen?"

She blinked. *Papa...* "Tony... I have tried."

He flattened his shoulders against the seat and drew his chin back. "You have? But I thought she died from—"

"Not mama. My father."

"You told me he died shortly after the stock market crash."

"Yes." It had been so long since she'd spoken of Papa. She had to force the words out. "He hung himself."

"Oh God, I'm sorry," Tony said quietly. They passed a field of grazing cattle, the placid scene a marked contrast to the tension inside the car.

"It was all my fault," she said.

"It was? How? What did you do?"

She stared straight ahead. The road blurred. "He left a note.

'Charlotte, I should have listened to you' was all it said."

"Oh man. What—"

"When the market crashed. He lost everything. Even his house. Be- before I went back. I offered to let him move in with me, Dewey did, too, but Papa was too proud. He was living on the street, and I- I had to change that." She blinked.

"You went back and tried to warn him," Tony guessed.

She gripped the wheel tighter. He lay his hand on her leg, a spot of warmth on her suddenly chilled body. "Charlotte... I'm so sorry."

She swiped a hand across her eyes. "Not as sorry as I am. Please, Tony. Don't change the past. I don't know what might have happened had I not gone back. Perhaps he would have ended his life anyway. Or he might have pulled himself out of it. My point is, something you think is insignificant may not be. You could make things worse. Not to mention the Society—"

"What about you? Does Pippin know what you did?"

She sniffled. "He suspects. But no, he doesn't know, or I'm sure I would have been... reprimanded."

"Reprimanded? That's all?"

"Perhaps that's not the right word. Truth is, I don't know what Theodore would do. I doubt it would be a simple slap on the hand. Especially if Ben Caruthers found out."

She owed Theodore. He did know about her father. But Theodore loved her. Just this once, he'd said. Never again. He reminded her of it if she hesitated when he asked her to help apprehend a time-criminal. *Remember your duties.*

He wouldn't forgive her again if she let Tony get away

She couldn't do it. She loved Tony, and that had nothing to do with the fact that he'd saved her life. Even if she would never see him again, she couldn't hand him over to Theodore. "Tony, it's not worth it. What good will it do to get your daughter back if you're not around to be with her?"

"Why wouldn't I be around?" Did she know something he didn't?

"I mean if Theodore finds out. Or others."

A long pause. "What will they do?"

Charlotte spoke slowly, her voice quiet, her words deliberate. "They'll take you into the basement, and... I don't know exactly what their treatment entails, but by the time they're finished, you'll be nothing more than an empty shell of a man." She swallowed at the image of Fred Cheltenham, drooling and stumbling around the House. "They'll do the same to you."

He stared ahead into nothingness. "If they catch me."

"Yes."

"Then it's a chance I'll have to take."

She would never be able to get him to the Society House now, even if she wanted to. Why had she kept him with her? He'd been right, back there at the Gibbons, a week—it seemed years—ago. She should have told him to leave town. Maybe he would have managed to escape the Society's notice. And if he hadn't, his blood wouldn't be on her hands. But in trying to do the right thing, she'd deceived him. Let him think her ties to the Society were less than they were. Deluded herself into thinking she could handle the situation.

If she'd brought Tony to the House that first night, she'd hoped Theodore would have skipped the Treatment, and simply killed Tony to send him home.

That wouldn't happen now. She'd been fooling herself, trying to have it both ways—to do the right thing for the Society, but also do right by Tony. If Theodore simply killed him, he'd return to his own present, alive and able to continue muddling up time.

Theodore would never take that chance.

They rode in silence until familiar, small towns and farms east of Dayton appeared. Her spirit sagged, as if she were stuck in a dreary, gray day with no hope of seeing the sun again. "We're not far from home now." Her voice lacked inflection. She couldn't pretend she wasn't sad. "I just wish..." There was no point in continuing that train of thought.

"You know, I might be able to stick around another night," Tony said. "If you think it's safe. You're sure that Caruthers guy's gone?"

"I can't imagine he'd stay this long. He has his own House to manage."

"Good. Because I can think of much better ways to spend my last night here than looking over my shoulder."

A shaft of sunlight broke through her gloom. "Like what?"

"Like throw you down on the kitchen table and have you for dinner."

Her hands squeezed the wheel. "Too bad it's too late for dinner."

"Then I'll have you for a midnight snack." He peered at her from the corner of his eye. Prickles swept through her, her interior climate now close to tropical. "One I'd linger over," he said. "Take my time with each delectable morsel, lick you all over."

"Everywhere?" She squirmed.

"Everywhere."

She clenched her thighs. "I shall be most eager to serve—" She glanced out the window. "Oh dear, I've missed the turnoff to Dewey's house." Goodness, they'd better cool things off or her brother would know exactly what they'd been up to. One look at Tony's lap and there'd be no doubt.

Thank heavens, he composed himself by the time they pulled into Dewey's driveway, for the porch light came on as they opened the car doors.

Dewey came out and gave Charlotte a quick, one-armed hug. "Charlotte, my dear. And Tony, good to see you again. I trust you had a pleasant vacation?"

"Oh, it was wonderful!" She clasped her hands, barely able to restrain herself from jumping up and down.

"Beautiful place," Tony added as she handed Dewey the key.

"Velma and I honeymooned there, years ago," Dewey said. "Couldn't afford anything else, but then...." He looked from Charlotte to Tony. "We didn't need anything else." They responded with restrained laughs. "Went there a few times before the wedding, too." Dewey shot Charlotte a smirk, the light from the porch sparkling in his eyes. *He knows,* she realized. "Want to come in for a cup of coffee?"

"Oh, we couldn't," Charlotte said. "I'm sure the children are in bed... and I doubt you were far from it."

"True enough." Dewey chuckled as he took the borrowed blankets from them and they said their goodbyes. Could he tell the real reason she'd so hastily declined?

Flutters filled her belly as they climbed back into the car. "Tony? I thought of a way you can come back."

"Charlotte..." His voice held a warning.

She ignored it. "Dewey said we could use the cabin any time. You could jump to the Fishin' Shack and I could meet you there..." She trailed off.

His face held no enthusiasm. "It's underwater in my time, re-member?"

"Then nearby. There's no Society presence—"

"Charlotte, I don't think—"

She grasped the gearshift. "You could tell your family you're a secret government agent, and you have an assignment where you can't contact—"

Tony gazed out the window. "You forget I'm a terrible liar. And the Society would eventually follow you there to meet me." He pressed the back of his hand to his forehead. *The Pull.* She was prob-ably all that was keeping him in this time, and he was starting to get the headaches because he couldn't jump while in her sight.

"Perhaps I could take the Second Rite so they'd let me start my own House there... I'd do it for you."

Fear and worry knotted his brows. He was probably worried about the fact that he was from the future, and he might reveal too much of it to her, a woman of science. A valid concern.

She'd been unwilling to give up her work for Elmer, but for To-ny... "I'd... give up my work for you—for us, if that's what's worrying you."

"It's not."

"Then what is? If not the Society, or worry that I'll use your knowledge of the future, or your family's questioning your ab-sence..." Was it her? Had her unchaste past—and heavens, the ease with which he'd bedded her—given him the idea she was a floozy, not someone to settle down with? "I thought we had something magical, something worth—"

"We do. But... What do you think about revealing a person's future to them? Do you think it's wise? Safe?"

"What are you getting at? Do you know something about me?"

"Your brother. I've met him before."

"You have? When? I didn't think you'd gone back between the time you rescued me and now."

"I haven't. I met him in my time."

"You can't be serious. He'd be over a hundred years old!"

"He was. Charlotte... he knew who I was. And he remembered meeting me in this time." He wet his lips, then chewed on the lower one.

"He told you something about me," Charlotte guessed.

"Yeah." His jaw tensed.

"What?" She squeezed the steering wheel. "Tony..."

"I shouldn't tell you. Because it might not happen."

"Tell me. Maybe if I know... if it's something bad, maybe I can prevent it."

Tony clenched his teeth and stared out the window for a long moment before he finally answered. "He said... the second time I came back to this time... you disappeared. Like when you were a little kid, but... you never came back."

"And he concluded I died."

"Yeah. That's why I can't come back. Ever." His voice was choppy, choked. "I don't want anything to happen to you. It's not your time. Maybe I can't be with you, but... you still have a lot to do—"

"Did he say it was because of you?"

"He didn't come out and say it like that, but... yeah."

Her world crashed, her heart ground to dust beneath its weight. Tony was never coming back. She glanced up as they passed the Gibbons Hotel, where their idyllic week—the happiest in her life—had started.

The week that was drawing to an end. "Tony?"

"Hmm?"

"I say we make the most of our last night together." She squinted at him in the dim glow of the streetlamps. He looked lost in thought. "Starting with what you said you'd do as soon as we get home."

She parked in the alley behind her house. Something rustled in the bushes as they hurried to the back door. Probably one of the cats. A guilty thought that she hadn't fed them in a week slipped from her mind when Tony's fingers slid under the belt of her dress. He had the belt untied before she unlocked the door.

They tumbled inside. She took two steps into the kitchen, then hesitated when she neared the table. She paused. Turned. Heat rose in her cheeks as he approached. Her lips parted, and the tip of her tongue traced the edge of her upper teeth.

A little voice shrilled in her head. *Don't do this!*

What? How could she—

It's too dangerous! Let him go now! An unsettling suspicion reared within her that what she'd heard in the bushes wasn't a stray animal but something far more insidious

like Caruthers

and far more threatening.

Charlotte wet her lips. "No," she whimpered.

Tony stopped. "Charlotte? What's wrong?"

The little voice. The feeling of *must.* It was the same one that had told her—no, *made* her—go back and warn Papa. It was her future self, reliving this moment.

Her future self had been wrong—oh, so wrong—that other time. *Don't change anything. It won't work. Whatever will happen here, you'll only make it worse,* her now-self told the little voice, that other presence.

"Charlotte?" One of Tony's brows pressed down. "Are you okay?"

She drank in the sight of him before her. Her future-self fled, and desire rushed in to fill the void. She reached for the switch to turn off the light over the table—she hadn't had a chance to turn it off, Theodore had pulled her away so quickly—but Tony grabbed her hand. "Leave it. I want to see you. All of you."

He placed his hands on her hips and pulled her against him. Warmth seared through her dress wherever his body met with it. She ached for his touch, wanted him to feel her, taste her all over like he'd promised, from the top of her head, to her toes, and everywhere in between. She tipped her face up for a kiss, but instead of taking her mouth, he brushed aside the curls at the top of her forehead and kissed her there. His lips left a wet trail down one side of her face as he caressed her other cheek with his hand. Her heart swelled. "Oh, Tony..." He snatched his hands to her hips and pulled her against him harder.

She giggled when he ran his lips down her nose, then pressed his mouth to hers when he finally reached it. Their lips molded perfectly, wet and moving against each other, the way she longed to do with her entire body. She leaned into him but he gently pushed her back. He dragged his tongue down one side of her neck—she whimpered— then the other, making two trails of wetness that joined at the base of her neckline, above the quarter hidden beneath her dress. His teeth tugged at the top button a moment before it came free, then he drew his tongue down, around the quarter, until he came to the next one. He stepped back. "This is taking way too long."

Charlotte mumbled an agreement. Bubbles of excitement rose inside her. He flicked the rest of the buttons open with his fingers and peeled her dress away to reveal her bra, garter, and...

"Oh. My. God."

She turned a falsely-innocent smile to him, her voice higher pitched than usual. "What's wrong?" Play it for all she could, repay his delicious torture.

"You're not wearing any..." He bit down on his tongue, then loosened his belt and undid his trousers, muttering something about being ready to bust.

She glanced down at herself in mock surprise. "Oh. I didn't pack enough underwear, I'm afraid. And I didn't want to spend our last day together doing laundry." It was the truth, though she hadn't realized it would be such a delightful mistake.

"Like hell." He let his slacks fall to his ankles, whipped off his shoes and socks, then stepped out of them.

He reached behind her to undo her bra, while her gaze landed on the protrusion in his drawers. She longed to be one with him, savor this last night... She gave him her best demure smile. He grabbed her around the waist. With a grunt, he lifted her onto the table, then swiped the bra off the rest of the way.

He stepped back, and his adoring gaze made her feel like she was the most beautiful woman in the world, never mind she sat on a cheap, wooden kitchen table, wearing nothing but a hat, garter and stockings. His eyes roved over her like she was a feast, and he hadn't eaten in weeks. She drew her tongue across the inside of her lower lip.

He lavished her shoulders, her throat, her arms with his tongue, then sucked each individual finger, eliciting more delighted giggles and sighs before he turned his attention to her breasts, traced his tongue around their hyper-sensitive tips. Lord, she could never get enough of his touch... yet she had to. Take this night for all it was worth, wring every bit of pleasure from it, then she'd do the same for him.

His lips and tongue trailed down her belly, her hips, her thighs. Each touch made the happiness inside her swell. He would do anything for her. Anything to make her feel good. Anything to pleasure her.

He knelt. A man, on his knees for her, and not just any man, but the one she loved, more than she'd thought possible. But what—

She gasped when he lifted her left leg and licked the back of her knee, drew his tongue up her inner thigh, almost to—good heavens!—then stopped and did the same on her right. This time his tongue continued upward, until he slipped it into the wetness between her legs. She thought her heart stopped when jolts of electricity shot through her in undulating bliss. He drew back. Lord almighty, she'd thought he was joking when he said everywhere! But oh, my... She fell back onto her hands. "Ho- holy shit!"

"I've never heard you say that before!" His lips drew into a wide grin. "You okay?"

No one had ever touched her there, given her such pleasure. "Oh my gracious... yes!"

He dove back in, until her thighs tightened around his neck, her hips arched, she couldn't stop herself from shouting his name as her insides quivered and waves of pleasure soared through her entire body.

He stood as her breathing slowed again. "My heavens, that felt so good it should be illegal!"

"It probably is in this time."

He took her big toe into his mouth. The gentle suckling sent more sparks through her. She threaded her fingers through his hair and pulled him up. "That's enough," she said. "Now it's my turn."

A grin split his face as she hopped off the table and grabbed his hand. In the living room, she pulled him to the floor, in the center of the area rug. "This will suit my purposes better than the table." Her fingers worked the buttons of his shirt, slid it off, pushed his drawers down. Once she'd relieved him of the clothing, she pressed his shoulder. He took her lead and lay on the rug.

She dotted tiny kisses over his bristly face, his neck, his arms, his chest. The small, wet spots glistened in the light from the table lamp she'd left on... a week ago? Each touch of her lips elicited another tiny groan from him.

She hesitated when she reached below his waist. Louie had once made her take him in her mouth, like the European prostitutes had done when he was a soldier in the Great War. It had been degrading, something she felt she had to do, something dirty and horrid. But she wanted to do it to Tony, wanted to give him that pleasure and watch him squirm with delight. He wasn't demanding, she was offering, and it wasn't dirty. It was the body of the man she loved, and it was nothing but wonderful. "Should I...?" She looked up from beneath the tiny brim of the hat she still wore.

"If you want," he grated.

She drew her tongue up his smooth, silken shaft in a cool, moist line, then tentatively explored the other side—

He clamped his hand onto her shoulder. "I'm not going to last another minute if you keep that up." She pulled back, and he released her.

She knew what he wanted, and lowered herself onto him.

He held her hips and rocked slowly beneath her. Heavens, she could never be with another man, no one would ever compare. "Charlotte..." He drew his hands over her breasts, her sides, her back. She concentrated on the warm roughness of his palms. Tried to imprint them on her memory, for after tonight, memories were all she'd have left.

Too soon she clenched around him. He rolled her onto her back. She pressed against him as tightly as she could, wanting to become one with him, for their skin to bind them together. One last time would never be enough—

Her stomach lurched as dizziness swamped her. The room spun, faded into...

Concrete? Huge, round pilasters loomed behind Tony's shoulders, and roaring sounds above. Cold, roughness grated against her bare back. Still joined with her, Tony raised up, looked around. "What the hell?" A huge dark expanse above blocked the moonlight. Overhead, something rumbled. What on earth?

She grabbed Tony's shoulders. Concrete buildings to the right. To her left, streetlights cast spotted reflections on the river, its surface dimpled by rain. Something whizzed by in front of her, and a horn blared, lowering in pitch as it sped past.

A spaceship! Round, smooth, shiny. Something like she'd imagine in *Buck Rogers*, only on wheels.

No. A car. The highway, the concrete... Just like Tony described in his time. But it couldn't be! Icy claws trickled down her throat and gripped her from the inside. It wasn't possible to jump into the future!

"No way," Tony said. "No, not yet!"

Still dizzy, she squeezed her eyes shut and dug her fingernails into Tony's back. "Think about my living room!"

She opened her eyes. Almost sobbed in relief at the familiar, plaster ceiling above him and the softness of her area rug beneath her back. Then she forgot the dizziness and the strange sights as he moved above her and the sensation of their bodies joined together overwhelmed her. She clenched around him, and his body responded in kind.

He rolled off of her and they lay together on the rug, her head cradled in the hollow beneath his shoulder, his heartbeat in her ear. Her hat had come off and lay a few feet away, next to the radio. "Tony... I love you." Her voice hitched.

He didn't look at her. Probably couldn't. The side of his face blurred. I love you too, she could hear him say, although when he opened his mouth, nothing came out. She wouldn't press. He loved her, she knew he did. "Me too," he finally managed. She forced back her tears. She couldn't cry. Had to be strong. It was what he'd want.

She wasn't afraid to die. Not if she could have the comfort of drawing her last breath from within his arms. But if he returned and something happened to her, he'd feel responsible. She wouldn't ask him to bear that burden.

She wanted to remain there on the rug with him all night. All week wouldn't be long enough, but every few minutes his lips curled into a grimace, and he pressed a finger to his temple. The pull was hitting him harder. He wouldn't be able to put it off much longer, and then he'd have to get out of her sight so he could leave. For good.

Someone knocked on the door.

Her body went rigid. Who on earth would call at such a late hour? *Go away!* Whoever it was, she wouldn't let them steal one moment of what little time she had left with Tony. Thank heavens she'd left the drapes closed, though if the visitor tried, he'd probably see everything through the lacy fabric.

The insistent visitor knocked again. Louder. "Expecting someone?" Tony asked.

"No," she whispered. *Go away!*

The person at the door called out. "Charlotte!" A man. One she'd heard before. But not Dewey, or man next door. Not Theodore. The man yelled again, and a sword of fear sliced down her windpipe as recognition hit. Caruthers! "No!" Her hand clenched at Tony's chest.

"Who—" he began, but the man at the door shouted again.

"Charlotte! I know you're in there. If you don't open the door, I'm coming in!"

Tony tensed, but Charlotte lay paralyzed until the doorknob began to turn. She hadn't locked the door! Theodore had yanked her out so fast she hadn't had time.

The doorknob clicked. She rolled away, dimly aware of Tony bolting for the bedroom, slamming the door behind him. He'd be safe, the pull would take him home.

She whisked the coverlet off the sofa, had barely pulled it around herself when Dr. Caruthers entered.

His footsteps rang hollowly on the hardwood floor. "Ah, Charlotte, it's impolite not to answer the door when—"

"I was taking a bath!" She said the first thing that came to mind.

Caruthers stopped. She clutched the coverlet tighter as his dark beady eyes traveled down her body. Even though the blanket covered her, she felt raw, exposed, like a hunk of meat. She tensed, trying to stop herself from shaking under his scrutiny. "A bath?" he said.

"Y- yes, sir."

"In your stockings?"

Hellfire! How had she forgotten?

He glanced at the closed bedroom door. *Jump, Tony!* Caruthers' oily gaze returned to her, slid up and down her. "I think not. It appears you've been providing our Enemy with more than refuge." His lips drew into a sneer. "Be prepared to accept the punishment meant for him if he escapes—"

"No! It's—"

He strode past her, toward the bedroom door. Why didn't Tony jump? *Please, Tony! Hurry!*

"It's not like that at all!" She had to stall him. Trembling, she loosened her fist, and the blanket slid to the floor.

Tony crouched beside the bedroom door. Damn thing didn't even lock—but the footsteps had stopped. *Get rid of him!* he silently urged.

The walls blurred into thick, round concrete pillars—*Shit!* He couldn't warp now, not without a scrap of clothing! *Make him leave!* If she could just get the man to leave, he'd run to the kitchen, swipe his clothes and his glasses, and be gone.

His ears pricked at the man's words. "...interrupted something." The smooth, masculine voice held a threatening tone.

"It's not what it looks like, I knew you'd be watching the house, waiting for me to bring him—"

A roar rose in Tony's ears. She what?

He strained to hear her response. "...had to make him trust me—"

A lecherous laugh. "And that includes giving him all you've got?"

"You know what Theodore says. Whatever. It. Takes." She emphasized the words. Another Society law?

"Whatever it—" Laughter. "Ah, Charlotte, I never realized your dedication extended to using your body. Good work, my dear." Tony bolted upright. Had everything been a set up? The air rushed out of him. He clutched at the wall. Had he been utterly blind?

"...whatever it takes," she repeated.

"Where is he?"

"In the bedroom," she said loudly. "If he hasn't jumped already."

Footsteps rang on the wooden floor. Coming for him.

His stomach grew raw, layers peeled away as if he was suffocating from the inside out. He had to warp. Now, the hell with his clothes and glasses. He reached for the bedspread, but before he could grasp it—

The vertigo struck, fast and hard.

Tony uncurled his body, the concrete cold and wet under his bare ass. A semi rattled across the I-75 bridge overhead. Before him, Robert Drive shined darkly in the streetlights. A light fizz on the pavement... Rain.

He stood, then sagged against a concrete pillar. He needed to get to his car fast—*Charlotte... All lies. Everything*—before recovery kicked in. *She used me.* He had to get home before he passed out—*betrayed me*—and he wound up in the hospital. At least he hadn't told her he loved her. He couldn't go to the hospital, didn't have time for that, not when he had Bethany's death to prevent—

Forget Charlotte! Run for the car, be glad it's raining. He'd have a better chance of getting to the parking garage unseen, the chill breeze notwithstanding.

Ignoring the cold, he streaked across Robert Drive, skulked along the outside wall of a junkyard, darted from building to building until he reached Seventh Street. A bum slouching in a doorway shouted a guttural catcall as Tony ran by.

When he reached the parking garage, he crouched at the wall for a moment and hugged himself, trying to shake off his shivers. The cold was dissipating from his skin, the drizzle barely noticeable. But it wasn't because the weather had warmed or the wind and rain stopped. He was getting numb. Fading into recovery. He sidled along the wall, toward the attendant's booth—

Brakes squeaked behind him. He barely registered the sound of the car coming to a stop on the wet pavement before headlights burned his shadow into the parking garage wall, and flashes of blue slashed the night. *Fuck.* "Hey buddy," a man called. "Little chilly to be walking around in your birthday suit, isn't it?" Car doors opened, and footsteps approached. Tony didn't even have the energy to turn around and face the officers.

Eighteen

THE BATHWATER HAD GROWN COLD, BUT CHARLOTTE REMAINED, CURLED up with her knees drawn into her chest. She'd drawn the water scalding hot, as hot as she could bear, but it did nothing to cleanse the shame that stained her to the core. Boiling water wouldn't be hot enough to wash away the image forever burned into her brain of Caruthers' leering grin and his evil laugh as he unzipped his pants, then pinned her to the floor while he—

No! No-no-no-no, it didn't happen.

But it did.

Her gaze flicked to Theodore's Saturn Society knife lying on the edge of the tub. She'd found it on the living room floor where Tony must have dropped it when she undressed him.

Too bad she hadn't seen it until after Caruthers walked out the door. When she stopped crying enough to see, she'd grabbed it and crept to the bathroom.

Like walking, the water had hurt at first, but as it cooled, it leeched away much of her physical pain.

But nothing would ever heal her spirit after being taken and used by a man she despised. She'd never lose the sense of worthlessness and dirtiness, or forget the stab of Caruthers' laugh when he informed her it would do no good to tell anyone. No one would believe a woman who wore low-cut dresses to her restaurant job, who'd taken in a man who wasn't her husband, boarder or no. A woman who'd lost her only source of income and was surely desperate. In dropping that blanket, he said she'd asked for it, never mind she'd screamed no a hundred times. How could the neighbors not have heard?

She ran through a mental list of people who might offer some consolation, give her a shoulder to cry on. She certainly couldn't tell Mabel. She'd say it was Charlotte's fault, even if Charlotte didn't mention the blanket. Dewey might believe her, but she couldn't tell him. It was too shameful.

Theodore wouldn't blame his fellow Watchkeeper, the one who helped him dispatch and punish time criminals—one of whom Charlotte had allowed to escape.

Only Tony would believe her. He'd hit Irving for merely making lewd suggestions. Tony had told her later that in his time, what Irving had done was called sexual harassment, and it was against the law. If she told him about Caruthers, she had no doubt Tony would go to Cleveland, hunt him down and kill him—

But Tony was never coming back.

Her tears returned, and she bowed her head, resting her arms on her knees. Thank heavens Tony had the sense to stay away. The Society was too big a risk. There was nothing for him in this time except life on the run and likely capture... then life as a doddering idiot.

Better a life of misery and loneliness than that.

Her eyes lit on the knife again. Blinking away her tears, she picked it up and ran her finger over the engraved PIPPIN 1905, then drew the blade's edge across her finger, staring in fascination as a bead of blood formed, reflecting in the pallid bathroom light. She was a fallen woman, the one man who believed in her never to return.

She yanked the blade away and squeezed the handle. Tony had vowed never to come back because he didn't want her to die.

He said she had many things yet to do.

She'd chanced Caruthers' lust so Tony could escape.

If she had to make the choice again, she'd do the same.

She put the knife down. Tony wanted her to live. Even if he couldn't be with her. Perhaps some day, in a more enlightened time, she'd find a way to make Ben Caruthers pay.

After she got out of the bathtub, she threw on a dress and trudged downstairs. She returned with the solar radiator, pushed open the back door, and stumbled down the walk to the garage.

Slowly, she lowered her project to the concrete slab beside the garbage can. The impact jarred a pipe loose with a clank. It didn't matter. She stood, brushing the metallic dust from her hands. Next time Dewey stopped by with his car, he could take it to the dump. Useless junk. A chapter of her life that was now closed.

She plodded back up the walk. When she moved into the Society House, there would be no time for foolishness like the solar furnace. She'd have to help Theodore entertain guests and keep the House tidy. Do the cooking. With Charlotte there, he wouldn't need to use Society funds to pay a housekeeper.

Her landlord had been generous, letting her stay as long as he had. But with her owing June's rent on top of May's, eviction loomed near. She had nothing—thanks to Caruthers, not even her self respect. She should be thankful she had somewhere to go. She would simply have to find someplace else to be whenever Caruthers came around.

She slipped inside and wandered into the kitchen. A cup of tea might soothe her nerves and allow her to sleep. Sleep and forget, if only for a few hours. But the sight of Tony's clothes mingled with her dress on the floor brought a fresh flood of tears. She sank into a chair at the table where, such a short time ago Tony had given her more pleasure than she'd ever known. Love she'd never thought existed outside of the movies.

By the time her tears dried, she'd forgotten why she came into the kitchen. Unless it was to collect the clothing?

She rose, retrieved her dress, and draped it over a chair. Then she picked up Tony's shirt. Her insides convulsed, trying to expel another sob, but no tears were left. She slowly, lovingly folded the shirt and lay it on the table beside his glasses. She'd keep his things, in the unlikely event of his return.

She almost dropped his trousers, they were so heavy. His wallet. Unable to contain her curiosity, she pulled it out. The pants slid to the floor, forgotten.

The wallet flipped open to reveal the card Tony had shown her that long-ago day in the attic. Ohio Driver License. With his beautiful picture and rainbow-reflecting state seal. Her throat threatened to close again, but she swallowed and flipped though the booklet of flexible, clear pages.

A strange card marked VISA, with a breathtaking, silvery-rainbow bird that practically soared off the card. Mercy! What technology could create it? Next were photographs, in vivid, life-like color. The older couple had to be his parents. Then the sister he'd mentioned, with a man and two boys.

Next was a teenage girl. Her eyes looked just like Tony's. His daughter. Charlotte rubbed the photo, as if she could feel the girl's soft cheek.

Her heart twisted at the thought of the terrible end this beautiful young woman had—or would—meet. What Caruthers had done to her was nothing. She, at least, was alive and whole. The physical pain he'd inflicted on her would fade.

Tony was right. If it were her child, she'd do anything, even risk the Treatment, to spare her the tortuous death this girl had suffered.

Charlotte snapped the wallet shut and started to slide it back into Tony's pants pocket when the smooth leather slipped from her grasp. It plopped onto the floor, spilling the contents. She crouched on the floor to pick them up.

A dollar and some change. All that was left of the money he had tried to give her after the scene at Irving's. They'd spent the rest on provisions on the way to the Fishin' Shack.

A silver square, with a circle-shaped ridge. What on earth? She read the small print on the foil. A condom? Why would Tony carry such a thing? Had he come to the past intending to seduce her in exchange for information?

She squeezed the little package in her fist. He had no way of knowing she'd have his answers, no reason to think she'd fall for such a ploy. And he'd been the one who'd resisted, trying to do the honorable thing.

What they'd had was too magical, too extraordinary for it to have all been a lie. He must have another girl.

She gripped the foil square so hard the corner bit into her palm. She made herself loosen her fist, and put the condom back into his wallet. She had no right. No claim on him. Not when he wouldn't be born until decades from now. She hoped the woman made Tony happy, whoever she was. Or so Charlotte told herself.

She forced the thought away and reached for the last item. A flat, brushed-silver rectangle—the calculator!

She snatched it off the floor, unable to believe he'd left it. She drew her fingers across the cool plastic, slid them along its thin edge. How did it come apart? She had to find out. Had to see the workings behind its marvels.

You can't! The tiny machine slipped from her grasp. She reached to grab it again, but something stayed her hand. A feeling of impending doom, of evil, and destruction...

She realized what was happening. Her future self had come back to relive this moment. Just like when she'd tried to tell Papa to sell his stocks and get his money out of the bank.

Charlotte straightened, never taking her eyes off the calculator. *Destroy it. Get rid of it,* the little voice said. *Nothing good will come—*

"But my dreams are all I have left," Charlotte said in a weak voice. Tony was gone forever, along with her hopes for happiness. Caruthers had stolen her dignity, her sense of worth.

Her work could provide solace. A chance to discover something meaningful, technology to benefit humanity.

Tears spilled down her cheeks. She brushed them away, then stared at her dampened hand. Shaking.

She crouched and reached for the calculator. Her hand closed over the cool plastic

(Throw it away!)

but she didn't listen. "You don't know everything," she told her future self.

Changing the past could only result in disaster.

If Tony had left the calculator, it was meant to be. She was meant to have it. To do amazing things.

It could give meaning to her misery. Tony had told her she had much left to do with her life. But what?

Now she knew. And it all began with this tiny, marvelous device.

Tony woke to the smell of flour and ground coffee, and a cardboard box labeled THERMAL CUPS 16 OZ. staring him in the face. *What the hell?* He groped beside him for—

A pile of towels?

But no glasses.

He'd left them on Charlotte's kitchen table.

As he pushed himself off the floor, memories returned of Bernie half-carrying, half-dragging him from the police station to the storage room above the deli—

Oh yeah, he'd been arrested. For indecent exposure.

Tony's face burned. He wanted to curl into a ball and slide through the floor. A car thief in 1933, now—

He cringed. Charlotte. The memory of her betrayal flayed his heart like an expertly-wielded knife.

He couldn't think about her now. Couldn't think about Bethany, or what he'd said to her, that awful night, could only think about what he had to do. If he'd taken two and a half days to recover like he had when he'd arrived in 1933, he had to go to Dora's in two nights—no, tomorrow.

He wiped his hands over his face. It had been cool when Bernie'd dragged him up the stairs, but it was stuffy now.

Embarrassed to face his parents or Lisa, Tony had called his buddy to bail him out. It was either that, or risk being taken to the hospital when the cops wondered why he didn't wake up. They'd given him the shorts he now wore, courtesy of their lost and found bin. He jammed his hand into the pocket, pulled out a slip of paper, held it close to his face and angled to catch the light from a streetlamp, coming in through the window. A summons to court, next month.

The desire to disappear into the floor returned. He had a police record. They'd added him to their database. Fingerprinted and photographed like a common criminal.

But he *was* a criminal. A time-criminal. Maybe it was fitting.

It felt like hell.

He shoved the paper back into his pocket. He'd plead no contest, pay his fine and get it over with as fast as he could.

He felt his way downstairs to the bathroom and found the light switch. After shutting his eyes to the sudden brightness, he made his way to the sink and splashed water on his face.

A t-shirt lay draped over the sink. Tony grabbed it.

SPASTAR

AMERICA REMEMBERS

He scowled at the shirt's bold, blue lettering. What the hell was SPASTAR? A vague notion of Solar Power Array-something hovered at the edge of his mind, but didn't materialize. *Whatever.* He'd figure it out later. He shrugged into the shirt and slipped out the door.

In the dark and deserted dining room, a light burned over the counter—enough to illuminate the wall clock. 3:32 AM.

His ATM card was in his wallet, which he'd left at—his gut twisted—Charlotte's house. He'd have to get inside his apartment somehow, grab his checkbook, and go to the bank for cash to repay Bernie. Then begin the rigmarole of replacing his driver's license and credit cards. By the time he got all that taken care of, it would be time to warp back and rescue Bethany.

He made his way around the corner, the light rain making cool, wet spots on his back, not unpleasant, now that he was clothed. But when he reached the parking garage, he stopped short, his jaw slack. Graffiti-laced plywood covered all but one window of the attendant's booth, and that one was broken. Fear lanced through him. Had the garage closed while he was gone? What would they have done with his car? Where would he go? He'd locked the apartment. Curling up in the doorway didn't appeal—downtown Dayton wasn't the safest place at three-thirty a.m.

He crept around the corner. A few cars hulked in the darkness on the ground floor. A new glass enclosure surrounded the elevator and stairwell. He leaned against a pylon and let out a sigh of relief. They'd remodeled in his absence, that was all. He yanked the door handle, but nothing happened. He swore. Locked! Now what was he going to do?

Then he glimpsed a small, black square beside the doorframe. An engraved placard above it read Prepaid Parking Only, Touch to Enter. What the hell? He was paid, though. Paid through September. He pressed his finger to the square.

"Welcome, Tony Solomon," a mechanized female voice said. The door clicked.

When he emerged on the fourth floor, his eyes darted to his usual parking spot. Metallic blue gleamed in the blue-white light from energy-saver, LED bulbs overhead. His Buick, thank God. He patted his hip...

And met with the flat, cotton weave of the shorts the DPD had given him. *Shit.* No keys. They too, had been left in 1933.

He leaned against the car door, trying to figure out what to do.

Something poked his back. He turned around.

Beneath the door handle where the keyhole should be, was a little, black square. Like the one he'd pressed to enter the parking garage. He touched it.

The Buick's lights flashed, and the door clicked. He jerked his hand away as if the square had burned him, then logic kicked in. He yanked the door open and climbed into the car.

The last time he'd ridden in a car, he'd been with—

Charlotte. He squeezed his eyes shut, trying to banish her image. God, how could he have been such a fool? He'd saved her life. Shown her love, given her his heart.

And she'd repaid him by turning him in to the Saturn Society, to be brainwashed and tortured.

Tears burned in his eyes. This time there'd be no stopping them. *Fuck it, it's four a.m., lay your head on the steering wheel and have it out.* That's what Lisa would say. Just for a minute. Then he'd find the key—hadn't he left one under the mat last time he'd had an oil change?—start the car, and go home.

His head crashed against the polished plastic of the dash. "Damn!" He raised up, rubbing his forehead.

His mouth fell open, and thoughts of Charlotte ran away.

There was no steering wheel. Never had been.

He ran his hand over the smooth dash. What the hell?

He could barely make out the digital instruments beneath the smoked Plexiglas finish. Where the steering column should have been, chrome bordered an inch-square tile of black plastic.

The square looked suspiciously like the one on the door. He pressed his finger to it. A blaze of blue lit up the instrument panel, but the Buick barely made a sound—just a quiet, whirring fan, not the engine.

Great. No glasses, no wallet, and now car trouble. He gawked at the display until a disembodied, feminine voice spoke from somewhere behind him.

"Good evening, Tony. Please specify a destination."

"Huh?" Tony's head whipped around. "Who's there?"

"'Huh'… is not in my database," the voice said. He twisted to peer into the back seat. Empty. "Please specify the street address, or state another destination." The voice sounded robotic, like the prompts of an old, automated voice mail system. Not like the navigation and crash response system he'd had before. That had been a computer, too, but he couldn't see the button anywhere that would call a human being.

Tony stared through his windshield at the blank cement wall. Outwardly, his car had appeared no different, other than the lock. But inside—

The voice spoke again. "Please specify a destination. If you need help, speak the command 'Help.' If you—"

"Help." Tony's eyes darted around the car's interior. At this rate, he'd need a lot more help than the disembodied voice was likely to offer.

"Welcome to the General Motors Automated Navigation and Environmental Control System," the voice said. A computer. "Your car will start automatically when an authorized driver touches the fingerprint recognition pad. To engage the navigational system, specify your destination. This can be a street address, an intersection, or selected from a list of your commonly visited locations, if you have entered any. If the address you specify is outside the city limits of your current location, you must also specify city and state, or the zip code. You have... eleven... commonly visited locations. To hear your commonly visited locations, state the command 'Favorites.' To hear—"

"Favorites."

"Home," the computer said in a man's voice this time. His own. "Work. Bernie's." Weird to hear his car talking to him, weirder to hear it in his own voice. "Mom and Dad's. Bernie's house. Happy Hunan. Danny and Mark's. Drycleaner's. Mulroney's. Wal-Mart. The bank."

He sank into the seat. Odd, why had he spoken his nephews' names instead of simply saying "Lisa's"?

"Home," he said.

The headlights came on. Gears engaged, then the car silently backed out of the parking space and trundled down the exit ramp. Thankfully, it asked for no more instruction, for all Tony could do was sit in stunned silence as the car drove itself—probably a good thing, considering how little he could see. Fifteen minutes later, it turned into his apartment's driveway and swung into a parking slot near his unit.

Tony roused himself out of his daze as the headlights went dark and the engine shut off. Rain drummed on the roof. As smart as the damned car was, why hadn't it parked in the carport? Especially in the rain?

He climbed out and scanned the dimly lit parking lot and saw why. There was no carport. But what happened? He hadn't authorized it to be removed. Not when there was nothing wrong with it, and he got an extra fifty bucks a month from the tenants who used it.

Anger stirred in his confusion. As soon as Melinda opened the property manager's office, they were going to have a talk. She better have a damn good reason for the carport—

Shit. His steps slowed as he approached his front door. No keys— because they were in 1933 with his wallet and car keys. He'd have to

go back to the car and use its built-in satellite phone to call his overnight maintenance service—if he still had one, and if the car still had
the phone.

As he turned to walk back to the car, he stumbled over the scal-
loped, concrete blocks that outlined the flowerbeds, and stepped on
an orange marigold. At least that hadn't changed. As he steadied
himself, his gaze drifted over his front door. There was no keyhole on
the knob. No deadbolt. And a hinged metal square beside the door. He
lifted it, and sure enough, there was another black fingerprint thing.
No sooner did he touch it than the door clicked open.

He stumbled inside, slapping bare wall where there should have
been a light switch. What the hell? He stopped, patted around, up,
down, to the corner. No switch. Cars that drive themselves. No keys,
everything biometrically secured instead. The wave of the fut—

Oh God. A chill swept through him. Had he somehow returned
not to his present, but to the future?

By the dim light filtering through the patio door from the parking
lot, he made his way through the apartment and collapsed onto the
couch. It wasn't possible to warp into the future. At least it wasn't
according to the Saturn Society.

The TV remote wasn't on the coffee table where he always left it.
He dug between the couch cushions in case it had slipped down
there, when the knowledge seeped into his mind why there was no
remote. And no light switch. "Lights," he said. The floor lamp behind
him illuminated the room. "TV." The screen flared to life. 4:43 AM,
and the current date, the ticker at the bottom of the screen on the
news channel read.

He closed his eyes, and the tension flowed out of his body. He
hadn't warped into the future, just...

A changed present. But how?

He'd worry about this brave, new present later. First, he needed a
shower.

He slipped inside the stall and turned the tap. The warm water
sluicing over him felt wonderful after a week's worth of bathing in
the river.

His gut clenched. Bathing in the river. With Charlotte. The woman who'd sold him out. The woman whose betrayal made Dora's a joke. How could he have been so naïve to trust her, once he'd learned of her relationship with Pippin?

Fool. He scrubbed his eyes with a fist, and set his mind to washing.

Maybe she lied to that Caruthers guy.

If only. But she'd sounded too damn convincing.

No, she'd sold him out. He might have saved her life, but it was Pippin who'd taught her to deal with it. Pippin who'd earned her loyalty.

Pippin who'd no doubt taught her *whatever it takes*.

Tony concentrated on working his way up his feet, his legs, his chest, as if mere soap and water could soothe the sting of her betrayal. Then he reached his neck, and a chill trickled down him despite the warm water.

No familiar, raised line. He felt around. Nothing. The scar was gone. He patted down his chest. To his surprise, that scar was still there. But hadn't it been bigger?

Had his sacrifice at the hands of the ancient Mayans not happened? His memories had dimmed. He touched the scar on his chest again. It had happened. But maybe he'd died sooner, been whisked back to the present before they could chop his head off. He didn't want to think about that. He got out, dried and threw on some clothes, and returned to the living room.

He settled into the couch. A quick glance at the news assured him that the world in general had changed little. There was still war in the Middle East, politicians were still crooked, food prices were still going up.

He flipped to the local news channel. A reporter stood in front of a familiar sight—the Seventh Street parking garage. "...Dayton sniper claimed another life, the third in three weeks..."

Tony gripped the arm of the couch as the picture switched to a clip taken earlier that day, with a familiar face in a photo inset. "...victim has been identified as Robert Standley, of..."

Bob Standley? No way.

Ice twisted in Tony's gut. Standley worked for a law office next door to the LCT building, and also frequented Bernie's before work. He was the same height as Tony, had the same build the same spiked, black hair, and even wore glasses. Sometimes people mistook them for each other.

It could've been him.

Police milled around behind the reporter. "...pursued the sniper to the roof, but the man was nowhere to be found." She turned to a woman who was on the top floor during the shooting.

"I'd just gotten out of my car when I heard the gunshots," the woman said. "He came up the stairs, and I saw his gun—one of those big machine gun types-and I thought, oh, *(bleep)*. Then the cops got here and he ducked behind a car, and... he was gone. Vanished into thin air."

Like Pippin in the bathroom. Tony sat transfixed, his mouth open.

The TV returned to the reporters in the studio. "Police are considering the possibility that these shootings aren't random."

Tony's skin was clammy. What if the shooter was with the Saturn Society? Could he have been their real target?

The next big story diverted his worries. In southern California, a drunk driver operating a high-end SUV with the manual control option *(a steering wheel—optional!)* had struck an oncoming car and killed three people. Traffic had been too heavy for the other car's navigational system to avoid collision.

Automated control had nearly made DUIs a thing of the past. Few vehicles besides historical autos and racecars had steering wheels. "Put the bastard away," Tony snarled at the television. The dirtbags that had killed Bethany had driven a similar vehicle.

He mindlessly stared at the television until daylight seeped through the patio blinds. What would he do with himself until it was time to warp?

A rumble in his stomach reminded him he hadn't eaten for three days while he recovered in Bernie's storeroom. He wasn't hungry *(She lied. Everything, a lie)*, but he wandered into the kitchen anyway. He yanked open the refrigerator. Nothing in there but condiments, a congealed gallon of milk and four bottles of Miller Lite.

He glanced at the clock. 7:13 a.m. Might as well go to Bernie's, kill a little time. Just like he always did—or had, before all this crazy shit started. He slammed the refrigerator door shut and headed outside.

His car's black-tinted glass roof shone in the sunlight. A removable T-top? He hadn't noticed in the dark. Before his trip to 1933 it had been blue like the rest of the car. Strange.

Different license plate, too. Instead of the "Beautiful Ohio" image, a slogan above an American flag and a sun read SPASTAR – America Remembers. Like the t-shirt Bernie'd left him. What was SPASTAR anyway?

He thumbed the door lock and climbed inside. "Good morning, Tony," the car's electronic female voice greeted him. He settled into the driver's seat—or rather, the seat on the left, since no one actually drove any more. "Please specify a destination."

"Bernie's," he commanded. The inside of the roof was gray cloth. Not removable. As the car drove out of the apartment complex, he gazed out the window. White, louvered panels covered the roofs of the buildings. It dawned on him what was up with the roof on his car and every other one in the parking lot. And why there wasn't a carport.

Those white panels on the apartments and the black glass roofs of cars were solar collectors. His home drew on reserve power from the electric company only when a succession of cloudy days depleted the storage cells.

He stretched out in his seat and watched the countryside go by as the Buick silently zoomed toward downtown Dayton. Silent, because it was solar powered, all-electric. When he said "Help," the computer offered an interesting array of options: Select music. Adjust seat back. Adjust interior temperature. Select aromatherapy.

"Aromatherapy?"

"Aromatherapy currently unavailable," the car computer informed him. "Please replace fragrance canister, available from your favorite Buick dealer, or online."

Of course. He'd forgotten to buy one for the past year. Didn't use it much anyway. A pang of regret struck him as he folded his hands across his lap and closed his eyes. Charlotte would love this super car. She'd love his time.

But she'd chosen the Saturn Society over him. His eyes burned. He focused on the scenery.

Which wasn't very scenic. Hadn't there been a wood along this road before? Facts filtered into his brain. When he was a kid, there had been woods, then open fields full of fine, brown grasses blowing in the wind like a girl's hair.

But now all he could see were solar collectors, rows upon rows of big, white panels, the length of football fields, and taller than a man. Acres and acres of them, all belonging either to South Central Ohio Power or the military.

"Left front window down, fifty percent." The computer obliged, and fresh air rushed into the car. A little warm, but its tang of recent rain smelled refreshing.

Less pollution. Change could be good.

He was getting the hang of this technology. The more he thought about it, the more that other life—the one where cars had steering wheels and everyone paid for all their electricity—seemed like a dream.

Bernie's deli was mercifully unchanged. "Hey, Tony! Where you been?" Bernie called as Tony approached the counter. "I was startin' to think you'd wandered off again. Man, were you messed up the other night. That must've been some cruise."

Cruise? Oh right, the line he'd given everyone about why he'd be gone for three weeks. The only story he'd been able to concoct that gave him an excuse not to call his mother while he was gone. The lie had ground through his teeth like sandpaper, even though the truth would have been impossible to accept. "It was nice. Saw some gorgeous places. But yeah, it wore me out." That, at least, wasn't a lie. "I need a vacation from my vacation."

"Ain't that how it always is?" Bernie grabbed a large foam cup. "You want the usual?"

"Yeah." Oh God, yes. Anything familiar in this weird world. "Oh, and I transferred the money into your account." Unable to find a checkbook, he'd gone online and made an electronic funds transfer. He thanked Bernie again.

"No problem, man. Glad you had a good time on your trip."

Tony let out a breath of relief when more customers entered, saving him from having to answer any more questions—and tell any more lies—about a cruise he hadn't taken.

The sesame-with-veggie, Bernie's shouted orders at the help, and reading the *Dayton Daily News* at his usual table almost made Tony feel normal again. Never mind that the paper had stopped being printed years ago, and he now read it on a solar-powered, handheld computer tablet. He might have gone a whole ten minutes without thinking of Charlotte.

When he walked out of the deli, he didn't know where he was going until he stopped in front of the LCT building.

Though he was on leave of absence, he could drop in and say hello. Cheered, he pushed open the big double doors.

His feet froze in place, as if something glued them to the floor.

There was no receptionist's desk with a smiling Sarah. No gold-plated LCT logo on the wall. The lobby was empty save a few potted plants and a security station, complete with a bored-looking guard.

What the hell? Tony walked to the security desk, where a directory hung on the wall behind the guard. The man didn't look up from his computer tablet, where he was watching a rerun of some lame old sitcom. Tony scanned the list of resident businesses. A list that shouldn't be there—didn't LCT occupy the entire building?

A wad of concrete dread swelled in his stomach and grew larger the further he read. He squeezed the change in his pocket. LCT wasn't on the list at all.

Nineteen

TONY STOPPED TO FIGHT OFF A WAVE OF NAUSEA, THEN WALKED TOWARD the exit, his footsteps ringing hollowly on the marble floor. "Have a nice day," the security guard said.

Outside, Tony turned a quarter over in his pocket and stared up at the building. What happened? LCT—gone? There was no way. LCT was huge. Keith Lynch had spent two decades building his empire. Had Tony's trip to 1933 somehow changed—

Sure, that was it. Relief settled over him. With all the advances in technology in this timeline, LCT was probably bigger, too. Too big for the building on Seventh Street.

Feeling slightly better, Tony returned to his car and ordered it to take him home.

He watched the scenery go by, some different, most of it unchanged from that other timeline, the one he could now barely remember. The one without all the solar collectors, where he'd had to steer his car himself.

As soon as he got home, Tony grabbed a beer and instructed the TV—in this timeline, also his computer—to turn on. "Favorites, LCT web site.

"Entry not found," the television replied in a neutral, male voice.

What? He spoke the site's web address and got the same result. A chill built within him.

"People search... Lynch, Keith."

Long list of results. Of course, Keith Lynch wasn't an unusual name. Tony checked some of the links.

None were the Keith Lynch he knew.

He searched for other coworkers. He found Sarah, the receptionist at LCT, but she wasn't a receptionist; she was a daycare teacher. Charlie was a financial advisor with his own firm, and Dora was his business partner.

"People search... Sinclair, Violet," Tony commanded the computer, though he wasn't sure why.

No results came up for the Dayton area, so he took the computer's suggestion to switch to a national search.

There were only a few results, and none were the Violet he knew.

Like she'd never existed.

Tony gulped his beer. Had all of this been his doing? He rummaged through his mind for pieces of the past few years that were unfamiliar to him in this new, changed present.

Many aspects of his life were no different. He'd still met Dora in college. In this timeline, they'd met at a bar, instead of being introduced by Keith Lynch, when Tony and Dora were in college, and Keith was an industry advisor. They'd still married, still had Bethany. And she'd still met with the same, horrific death.

Tony had still time traveled. He'd still busted Dora with Charlie. And he'd met Charlotte in 1933, fallen for her, gotten his heart crushed to smithereens.

But Mexico didn't happen. Couldn't have, not if Keith Lynch didn't exist to have taken Tony on the trip and talked him into climbing the pyramid. Tony touched his smooth, scarless neck. But if Mexico had never happened, what had caused the scar on his chest? And how had he come into his time travel capability?

God, where did he work? He squeezed his eyes shut so hard it made a roar in his ears. An image of gray cubicle walls appeared in his mind. On one hung a poster that read " SPASTAR – America Remembers" across an American flag. Beside it, a sheet of paper listed his sales accounts.

An ad agency. Binkmann, Crook and Waters. Tony was an account executive, and one of his clients was the Solar Energy Museum. Last winter, they'd charged BCW to design promotional materials and a commemorative exhibit featuring solar energy pioneer Dorothy Charlotte Henderson.

Tony's beer slipped from his hands and bounced on the carpet, spewing foam. "Oh my God..." What had he done?

He'd interviewed her, that day in February. The same day he'd gone to the ruins at Chichén Itzá in the other timeline.

He hadn't been able to believe his luck when she'd agreed to meet with him. The centenarian Henderson hadn't spoken to anyone connected with the media in years.

On the way to the nursing home where she lived, Tony downed a whole energy drink and chain-smoked three cigarettes, then topped it off with a greasy, drive-thru hamburger in an attempt to clear the last vestiges of a hangover—an all-too-common occurrence. Hopefully, the valet wouldn't smell alcohol on him when Tony pressed this thumb to the card that would allow the man to park his car.

He crossed the vast, marble-tiled lobby that looked more like one in an upscale hotel than a nursing home, and located her room. As he knocked on her door, he popped a couple of antacid tablets while he waited for her to answer. Damn heartburn had been acting up worse than ever.

A uniformed maid let him across a plushly-carpeted sitting room to a chair that faced an antique sofa, where the surprisingly sound Miss Henderson waited. The lights from the overhead chandelier sparkled in her brown eyes.

Her comments baffled him.

"I only agreed to this because it's you, Tony." She indicated the chair, and he sat.

Her low, raspy voice took on a melancholy tone. "I've wondered for years when you'd come to see me."

Huh? "You know me?" He sure as hell had never met her.

"Oh my, yes. You were the most incredible lover..."

Tony almost leapt out of his chair. "What?" Lover? "You must have me mixed up with someone else." He forced himself to relax. She was either mistaken or crazy.

"Oh no, it was you. You've hardly changed at all." She brought her hand to her neck and dragged a finger around a worn, gold chain. "Oh dear. It hasn't happened for you yet, has it? I'm so sorry..." She sat straighter, and folded her hands in her lap. "What was it you wanted to ask me?"

"Uh..." Her outburst, and the absurd idea he could have had an affair with a woman sixty years his senior had destroyed his train of thought. Of course, the time travel thing hadn't happened to him yet at the time, and if Charlotte had explained it to him, he would have laughed and told her she read too much science fiction. He grabbed his tablet computer and skimmed some questions he'd scribbled down that morning. "How did you get started in solar energy research?"

Her gentle smile was tinged with sadness. "My schooling and early employment are well-documented. After the Kitchen Products Research shop closed—didn't make it through the Depression, you know—I continued my work at home. I was experimenting with a solar-powered radiator..." Tony's eyebrows lifted. She flashed him that disquieting smile again. "You'll see," she said.

Definitely senile. But Tony scribbled in his notepad anyway. "So that's what led to your breakthrough?"

"Oh heavens no. That would have been the..." Her face went slack, and she laid her hand on his forearm. "Please, Tony... go back. Take it away from me—"

"Go back where?" Tony drew away. *Nuttier than a four-dollar bill.*

"To 1933. Please..." Her voice quavered. "I've tried. Lord, I've tried. But I lacked the strength. The woman I was then wouldn't let me destroy my own dreams, they were all I had left after you. I couldn't do it. Couldn't change anything, not after Papa. You're the only one who can stop me..."

He shrank farther away. His heartburn worsened, then the cramp in his left arm, the one he'd ignored for days, flared in his chest and down to his fingertips...

His memories of the rest of his time with her were vague. He couldn't breathe. His chest felt like someone dropped a three-hundred pound weight on it.

Charlotte hovered over him. "Tony! Tony!" She moved faster than he'd thought a hundred-year-old woman could, and yanked a pull cord on the wall. "I need medical help..."

Her words faded, and everything washed into white. Pure, bright light. Someone called to him. Not Charlotte. *Bethany?*

Then pressure and an eerie tingle as Charlotte clutched his wrist.

The last thing he remembered was being carted out on a gurney, hearing the words *heart attack.*

In his apartment, Tony cleaned up the spilled beer, then unbuttoned his shirt. He felt down his chest. The scar was still there.

But smaller and neater than the one the ancient Mayans had inflicted. Because in this timeline, it came from heart surgery.

That tingle he'd felt when Charlotte's touch had pulled him out of the white light, and away from Bethany, was the same as the one he'd felt when he pulled Charlotte out of the floodwaters a century ago.

In this timeline, she'd passed time travel to him.

His hands dropped, shaking, as another memory surfaced. He'd researched Charlotte Henderson before he'd set up the interview. One biographer theorized that the reason she'd become so consumed by her work in the early thirties—and why she'd never married—was because she'd had her heart broken.

By a man who'd lived with her for a week as a boarder, then left her, never to return.

Tony dragged the back of his hand across his forehead. He was sweating, though it wasn't warm. Had all this change in technology happened because of him?

It hardly bothered Tony to walk past the sofa where he'd caught Dora cheating on him. Affected him little to sit in the same recliner he'd occupied so many evenings, the two of them barely speaking. His call had surprised her. But when he told her why—"to remember," he'd said—she'd welcomed him into the home that had once been his, too.

Being with her was nice, companionable in a way. But once the initial pleasantries were over, neither had much to say. They watched TV in silence, just as they had that night three years before and countless others. He realized the comfort didn't stem from lack of caring, nor was it simply the passage of time.

He'd gotten over it. Over her. Because compared to the soul-searing connection he'd felt with Charlotte, his relationship with Dora had been shallow. Comfortable, sometimes fun, and even loving, but lacking in depth.

And compared to Charlotte's betrayal, Dora's was nothing.

Bethany was all that mattered.

Trepidation grew in his belly as he settled into the recliner and thought about the night before her death, trying to ignore Charlotte's warning echoing in his mind. *You could make it worse.* He heard Everly, too. *Playing God.*

The dizziness hit instantly, and passed almost as quickly.

He glanced at Dora. Like the other time, she wore different clothes—a light green, button-down blouse instead of the knit shirt she'd had on a moment before. And Bethany—

"Where's Bethany?" he asked.

Dora gave him a strange look. "She went to that party, remember?"

Tony's heart nearly stopped. "What?"

"She went to a par—"

Tony jumped up.

"Where are you going?"

"I'm going to get her." He hurried for the back door.

"What? Why didn't you—"

He slammed the door, cutting her off. How the hell had he miscalculated? He had to get to her, now.

And hope to hell he could stave off recovery long enough.

Tony's world spun, and he had to force his eyes to stay open as he trudged through the gate in the privacy fence, searching the crowd. Recovery was hitting him. *Got to find her, got to stop her.* Young people thronged around the pool, laughing and drinking. Most held brown bottles Tony knew weren't designer sodas. A guy dove into the pool, fully clothed. No one looked over twenty.

It was just as he'd feared. Just what he'd told Bethany, when they'd fought about her going. That Ashley girl she'd taken to hanging out with was nothing but trouble; he'd known that as soon as he'd answered the door.

"Is Bethany there?" Ashley's voice held that infuriating teenage nonchalance, as if she were doing him a favor by merely speaking to him. She propped her hands on her hips, the motion nearly making her spill out of her skimpy halter top. He thought he caught a whiff of pot.

Tony fought to keep his brows level, and his face from contorting into a sneer at a girl he'd have immediately labeled a slut when he was her age. Instead, he simply told her to wait.

He met Bethany coming into the foyer. "Is Ashley here?" She started to brush past him.

He grabbed her arm, stopping her. "You're not going anywhere with that girl."

She jerked her arm away. "Yes, I am! I told her I'd be ready by six."

Tony stepped aside to block her. "You're staying home tonight. You don't need to be partying with older kids; you've got—"

"Da-ad!" She squirmed past him.

"Bethany—"

"Stop telling me what to do! I can pick my own friends, and I'm going!" She grabbed the doorknob.

Tony squeezed his hands into fists. Dora called out from the family room. "Tony? What's going on?"

"Bethany doesn't need to go—"

"He's trying to run my life, and I'm sick of it!" Bethany moved toward the door. Tony reached for her again, but she ducked under his arm. "I'm going, whether you like it or not!" She yanked the door open and stormed out.

The other girl sat in her car, talking on her cell phone.

Tony scowled at her, then at Bethany as she flounced down the porch steps. "Fine!" he snarled. "Don't call me when you wind up in a ditch!" He walked inside, slamming the door behind him.

He cringed at the memory he normally didn't let himself think about, his own eerily-prophetic words echoing in his brain. He leaned on the privacy fence, trying to steady himself as he scanned a group of kids clustered around a cooler, where a boy bent over, rummaging through its contents. Which one was the friend-of-a-friend hosting the party? And where were the parents?

His vision swam, and he almost missed her, but his subconscious must have made him do a double-take, as the boy at the cooler handed a beer to that Ashley girl. Bethany already held a beer in one hand, and in the other, a boy's hand—no, make that a young man, for there was no way the guy was under twenty.

Rich Muehlhauser. And beside him, Dwayne Cray. Tony would never forget those names. The scum who'd taken Bethany out to a field and beaten—

He'd head spun and he grabbed a tiki torch pole before he fell over. Bethany turned as she lifted her beer to her mouth, and froze with it halfway there as her eyes met Tony's. The bottle slid from her hand, crashing into bits on the concrete.

Conversations stopped in mid-sentence. "Shit," Ashley said.

Bethany rushed to Tony. "Daddy!" she hissed. "What are you doing here?"

Tony leaned on the fence to hold himself upright, which was becoming more and more of an effort. "I might ask you the same thing." She regarded him with wary eyes as he scanned the area again. "Where are the parents?"

Bethany made a pretense of looking over the crowd. "I don't know." She didn't meet his eyes.

"There aren't any here, are they?"

She didn't answer.

"Come on, time to go." Tony took a wobbly step toward the gate.

She didn't follow. "Bethany, we're leaving. Come on."

Ashley slid her arm through Cray's, and laughed. "Go home with your daddy, Bethany!" She tugged on the creep's arm. He chuckled.

Bethany put her fists on her hips. "I am not going."

"Yes, you are." He grabbed her wrist and pulled, but his hand slipped. God, why was he so fucking tired?

Bethany crossed her arms over her chest. "I'm not go—" Tony swayed. "Daddy, what's wrong?" She lunged for him, but he caught the fence before he fell. She gripped his wrist. "Are you drunk?"

"No, I'm just..." He caught his breath, clutched at the fence more tightly. "...ungodly tired."

Bethany grabbed his arm. "I'm taking you home."

"Yeah, s'long as you're not drunk." Please, let him get her away before he collapsed.

"I had one beer!"

Her sharp tone jolted Tony awake. "What are you thinking! You're diabet—"

"The computer said one drink wouldn't hurt!"

"I doubt that applies to fourteen-year-olds. For God's sake, Bethany—"

"Shut up! I hate you!"

"That's okay." Tony sagged against the fence. Let her hate him. "'Cause I love you." God, it felt good to say that.

His hand slid on the fence and he listed forward.

Her scowl went slack as her eyes grew round. "Daddy! What—"

"Gotta... get... home..."

She grabbed his wrist and propelled him toward the Buick. "You're not having another heart attack, are you? Maybe we should go to the hospital instead."

"Just... tired. Take me...home," he managed as she folded him into the passenger seat. Something else he needed to do nagged from the back of his mind, but couldn't break through the fog of impending recovery.

He barely heard Bethany order the car to take him to Dora's house as he slipped into recovery sleep, but he must have made it home and to the bedroom, because the next thing he remembered was Dora shaking him. "Tony! Wake up!"

"Huh?" He rolled over. It was still dark, and he was so tired...

"TV!" Dora commanded, and the set opposite their bed lit. "Local news." The channel switched as Bethany darkened the doorway.

Tony's head swam with interrupted recovery, and he almost drifted off again when the bed shook as Bethany climbed in beside him. She threw her arms around him. "Ashley..." she blubbered.

"What—"

"Watch." Dora pointed to the TV. Bethany trembled.

A reporter stood on a country road. Behind her, red and blue flashing lights from police cruisers slashed the darkness over an empty field. "...where police found a sixteen-year-old girl with her ankles and wrists bound. The girl, whose name was not released due to her age, was taken to Miami Valley Hospital, where she's in stable condition..."

"Ashley," Bethany said in a shaky voice.

"Huh?" Tony tried to forge through the fog as he absently patted her back. "Who's—"

"My friend, Ashley. That took me to the party. When we got home, I called her, she didn't answer. Kara said she left with those two older guys, the ones we were with when you came..." She shook and scrubbed at her eyes.

"Bethany called the police," Dora said. "She told them—"

"Shh!" Bethany sat up, her gaze fixed on the TV.

"One of the men, twenty-seven-year-old Dwayne Cray, was shot and killed in a confrontation with police," the reporter said. "The other man, twenty-nine-year-old Rich Muehlhauser, was apprehended shortly thereafter. The girl suffered numerous bruises and lesions, but she's expected to fully recover."

"My God," Dora said. "That could have been—"

Bethany looked up at Tony, the TV's flickering light reflecting in her tear-stained face. "Daddy," she sobbed. "How did you know?"

Tony pulled her close and shuddered in relief. His baby. Alive. "I just had a bad feeling."

The next day, when the pull began to hit, Tony was smart enough to drive to his apartment (which wasn't his at the time), warp back to the present from the parking lot, then stumble to the door—at which point it was his apartment.

He frowned at the flowerbed as he thumbed the fingerprint pad beside his front door. Yellow and orange marigolds filled the plot, surrounding a little round, woodcut sign. Neighborhood Beautification Award, 1997. What the hell? Had he warped further into the past instead of forward?

Oh please, no. Heart pounding, he stumbled inside. "TV. News." A quick glance at the ticker confirmed he'd jumped to the correct date. His breath rushed out in a whoosh.

He rubbed a hand down his face. Man, was he tired. Even a little jump back three years. But he'd accomplished what he wanted more than anything.

A glow settled over him as he trudged down the hall toward his bedroom. With recovery setting in, his legs moved as if through molasses, but he had to check one thing first.

He tapped the second bedroom's door open and leaned inside.

Posters of rock bands he'd never heard of adorned the wall above a brass-framed daybed. Stuffed animals congregated along the rail, and the striped, purple coverlet matched the curtains. The coat rack on the wall banished his remaining doubts. Its wooden letters spelled out B-E-T-H-A-N-Y.

He'd done it. He'd come back to the present, and his daughter was alive. If he had more energy, he'd have wanted to run around the block. Shout for joy that Bethany was alive. Warmth filled him, and everything was right with the world.

The scum who'd killed her in that other timeline had been caught, the survivor with a rap sheet so long he'd never see freedom, or get the chance to hurt another girl. Thank God Bethany had called her friend, known something was wrong, and had alerted the cops before the creeps had been able to do more than rough the girl up.

But how had Bethany known? He vaguely remembered her saying something about a "little voice" in her head, almost like the way his past self had interpreted his current self's urgings to make Bethany leave that party. Could she have—

Nah, coincidence. Had to be. Bethany was no time traveler.

He tottered into his bedroom and sank into bed as recovery numbness settled over him. A sudden chill burst through him as another thought tripped through his mind. Would Everly be able to tell what he'd done? What if the sign in the flowerbed was the result of a time bubble?

Dizziness burst through Tony on the way out to Bethany's car the following night. Stumbling, he braced himself against the car while it passed. What the hell?

Slowly, he pushed himself off the yellow Camaro, thankful he hadn't jumped. "Come on, Daddy." Bethany touched the fingerprint panel to unlock the car. His mom always complained when they were late to their weekly dinner at his parents'.

He'd felt a couple of dizzy spells earlier in the day. They'd passed quickly, but if more came, he preferred to deal with them in the passenger seat. Even though the car drove itself, his habits from the other timeline lingered.

Tony and Dora were still divorced, only in this timeline their constant bickering over Bethany had been a major factor that drove Dora into Charlie's arms. She thought Tony was overindulgent, especially when he bought Bethany a new car for her birthday. To Tony, Dora was overly permissive.

He let Bethany pick the music for the ride, some electronic dance crap he didn't see how the kids could listen to. But if that was what she wanted, it was okay with him.

She touched up her makeup while they rode. Tony couldn't believe how beautiful she was. She didn't need all that stuff on her face, though it was a lost cause to tell her so.

What had the past three years been like, in this new, Bethany's-alive timeline? He recalled basketball games (Bethany's team usually lost), having kids over to hang out or study, dropping her off at the mall to meet her friends—then, to her dismay, hanging around, though he tried to stay out of sight. He remembered holidays and birthdays, where he wanted to buy her everything. Fights he and Dora had when he wouldn't let Bethany stay out late or found fault with every boy she dated. At least he didn't have to worry about her friends. After he'd passed out—so he'd heard—and destroyed her credibility with the kids at the party, Bethany had learned they weren't friends after all and found others. Thankfully, these kids were more into movies and video games than getting wasted. They were all close to her age, too—Ashley's experience had driven home the lesson about creepy, older guys.

Yet, much was the same. The visit from Everly in the parking garage. Getting locked up in the Saturn Society's conference room. His trip to 1913, and his later trip to see Charlotte, because he'd still needed to go back in time, and make sure Bethany didn't leave that party with those guys.

Lisa's family was already at his parents' house when Tony and Bethany arrived. Charlie grunted a greeting from the sofa, where he and Tony's dad watched TV. Tony's mom threw her arms around him. "I'm so glad you made it back! I know, those cruise ships are perfectly safe, but I still worry..."

His nephew Mark approached. "Yeah, Uncle Tony, how was the cruise?"

"It was nice." The lie ate into him like drops of acid on his skin. It had been worse with Bernie, especially when he'd had to concoct an even wilder story about how he'd ended up downtown stark naked. *This woman I was sitting next to on the plane must've slipped me a mickey or something. Last thing I remember was getting on in Miami...*

Bernie's left eye had narrowed, and he'd looked at Tony sidewise but didn't press. Luckily, Tony's parents didn't read the police reports in the paper.

"Where'd your cruise go? See anything cool?" Mark asked.

Tony tried to think of something to say as his other nephew entered, with a girl in tow. "Hey, Uncle Tony, I want you to meet my girlfriend, Taylor—"

Tony's mouth slid open as he took in the black, ruffled dress, pointy shoes, and red and white striped socks. Something rolled to the bottom of his stomach. Taylor Gressman? "Nice to meet you." She held out a hand, smirking behind a smile that obviously snowed the rest of the family.

He shook her hand and mumbled a response. What was his nephew doing dating *her?* "Taylor's in my history class at Sinclair," Danny answered Tony's unspoken question. "I'd have flunked the final for sure if we hadn't studied together."

I can imagine. Tony fought the urge to wipe his suddenly clammy hands on his pants. Did the Society know what he'd done? Was Taylor there to catch him with his guard down and bring him in the way Charlotte nearly had? Before he could worry any more, his mother announced dinner. He'd have to watch the girl, be ready to jump up and run if she looked like she was going to pull something. The family filed into the kitchen and took their regular seats at the table.

Tony's mom went on about his non-communication while on the cruise. "I still can't believe you couldn't at least make one little phone call to your mother."

"I never had a chance," he said. That, at least, was the truth.

His mother frowned. Acid churned in his stomach. He couldn't lie again, not to his mom. He tried a diversionary tactic. "I, uh, met someone. A woman."

Bethany whirled around. "You never told me—"

"You did?" His mother slapped her hands on the table. "What's her name?"

"Charlotte." He wanted to shrivel up and die, remembering the ease with which the scheming woman had almost ensnared him.

The questions flew fast, from all directions. "When do we get to meet her? What's she—"

Tony held up a hand. Everyone fell silent. "It's not going to happen. Sorry, Mom."

"But why? Does she live too far away? Or—"

Bethany leaned forward. "You can have a long-distance relationship. One of my friends' parents does it, it's not like—"

"That's not it," Tony said. Best to stop this now. "On the last day of the cruise, I found out... she's married."

Well, she was, in a sense. To the Saturn Society.

A hush fell over the group. Tony's dad grunted, but no one spoke. Across the table, Taylor had taken a sudden interest in the tablecloth. Did she know? "I'm sorry, dear," his mom said. Mark and Danny mumbled agreements, and then his mom started passing the food bowls around. Gradually, conversations started about school, Mark's football team, Charlie's thoughts on the stock market that week. Safe subjects.

Taylor paid no more attention to Tony than any other guest of his nephews' would have. Still, he kept an eye on her throughout the meal, torn between wanting to get her alone so he could chew her ass for locking him in that room, yet afraid to, should his fears prove true.

As he waited to serve himself, he scanned each of their faces, everyone in their accustomed places. The same places the Solomon family and their significant others had occupied for twenty years' of Sunday dinners. His dad sat at the head of the table, and at the other end, Tony's mom. Tony sat in the middle of the three chairs with their backs to the window, Bethany on his left and Lisa's older son Mark on his right, and across from them, Charlie, Taylor and Danny—

Taylor. That's what was... off. Not that she was present, but that she sat in his sister's chair. "Where's Lisa?" he asked.

Everyone froze. Bethany dropped a spoon on the floor. All their eyes, huge, round. Horrified.

Tony flung his hands out, palms up. "What?"

His dad coughed. Charlie excused himself, shoved back his chair and left the room.

"Uh," Mark said.

No one else spoke, so Tony asked again. "Where's Lisa? Is it some secret I'm not in—"

"Daddy!" Bethany whispered, her nose wrinkled.

"What?"

"Daddy... Lisa's dead."

"What?" His voice squeaked. A high-pitched, pulsating roar in his ears drowned out her response. His breath was gone. This was not happening. He wasn't hearing this. Good thing he was sitting down, or his knees would have given out.

The rest of the meal passed in somber quiet. There was an uncharacteristic amount of leftovers, and everyone made excuses to leave soon after dinner.

"You sure you're okay?" Bethany asked as they got into the car.

"Yeah." As okay as he could be. During the ten-minute ride home, Tony cleaned his glasses three times. Lisa, dead. It couldn't be. He tried to dredge up memories, ones he didn't know he had. Had he somehow traded her life for Bethany's? It didn't make sense, yet...

Bethany's face twisted in concern. "I think we should go back to Grandma's and call the doctor—"

"No!" His head snapped around. "I'm fine. Just... this is kind of upsetting, even now."

"You've been acting weird ever since your heart attack. Then you disappear for three weeks. And now... Mom thought that cruise would be good for you, but I don't know..."

He didn't want to dredge up his own painful memories of that horrible day in July, five years ago. He wanted to hear it from her. It would make it more real, something he had no choice but to accept. "I'm... a little confused," he admitted. "How- how did she..."

She lowered her head, turned her eyes up at him. "SPASTAR?"

"What is it? I mean, I know it's a solar power plant satellite, but—"

Her eyes widened, brows raised. She jerked her head at him as she spoke. "It fell and killed thousands of people?"

Twenty

THE SKY WAS BURNING. THAT WAS THE MAIN THING TONY REMEMBERED from that day, seeing chunks of the satellite array falling, the smaller ones burning up in the atmosphere. Everyone at the office had run outside or braved the stairs and gone out on the roof. Tony had stood in the streets, watching the flaming pieces fall to the earth, unaware until the following day that one of them had killed his sister. She was the reason he'd never visited the Solar Energy Museum that was built a couple of years later.

But Tony could avoid it no longer. He got out of the car before he pulled into the museum's parking lot, and gazed at the pewter-plated, memorial plaque at the street entrance. "Dedicated to those who died after the fall of SPASTAR - July 3, 1998," he read. Eight granite arches bore over a thousand names inscribed on their polished sides.

The memorial and museum graced a flat plain north of Dayton, where the U.S. Solar Energy and Power Commission headquarters had once stood. The glass dome in the center of the museum's roof sparkled in the afternoon sun, barely noticeable amidst acres of solar collection panels.

Tony scanned the lines of names in alphabetical order. He found Lisa's on the second pillar on the east side of the drive. As if to convince himself of the horrible truth, he crouched and ran his fingers over the recessed letters. *Elisabeth Solomon Vogel.*

His research had revealed that Charlotte Henderson's innovations had helped the Dayton area become a center for solar energy research. Like in the other timestream, Dayton was also a center for aerospace development, which in this reality included solar energy-collecting satellites and power plants that hovered in geosynchronous orbits thousands of miles above the earth. SPASTAR had been positioned above the SEPC headquarters. Other parts of the Array orbited over several other U.S. cities.

Lisa had been at work, at the SEPC headquarters the morning the array broke apart and fell to earth. HQ and the nearby suburb of Sunborough were the hardest hit, struck by a flaming power transmission satellite the size of a football stadium. Rescuers had combed the debris for a week. They found only three people alive.

Years later, the cause of SPASTAR's sudden decay of orbit and subsequent fall remained a mystery. The Solar Energy and Power Commission and museum was Tony's account at the agency, but he'd never toured it. Now he knew why.

In the timeline of LCT and Keith Lynch, of coal-fired power plants and steering wheels, there had been no Solar Energy and Power Commission, and Lisa had worked at the Air Force base. Tony wished he could wake up and find it was just a nightmare.

Another horrible thought occurred to him. What if his warp back to save Bethany had brought about all these changes? He gulped for air, his chest unable to expand. His legs went rubbery, then logic returned to him with a whoosh of breath.

Bethany's death had occurred nearly two years after the fall of SPASTAR. He couldn't have changed time at that point. Yet he couldn't shake the feeling that everything came back to him, was all his fault for messing with the flow of time. Maybe Everly was right, maybe Tony was playing God.

He would never warp again. Not even if Bethany died another preventable death. If something happened to her, it would be a lesson to him. A reminder that no matter how unfair, some things were meant to be.

Bethany hadn't deserved to die. But neither had Lisa. Or sixteen thousand others.

He climbed back into the car. "Continue."

Time crawled to a stop as he stood in front of the museum entrance, the wind whistling in the field of solar collectors as he read the name over the door. The Dorothy Charlotte Henderson Museum of Solar Energy. "No. Fucking. Way."

Even though he'd known Charlotte had been a key contributor to early solar energy development, the sight of her name up there sent a shock through him.

He forced himself to open the door. Woodenly, he walked in.

He wandered down the main corridor, his mind in a fog, the entire experience dreamlike. He felt disconnected, as if his body walked through the museum without his brain directing it. Like he was watching TV, and another man who looked like him gazed at the first solar cells she'd developed. It wasn't Tony, but someone else who peered at watches, heating appliances, and home heating systems from the fifties. It wasn't Tony, but a mindless robot who skimmed the placards over early solar-powered computers.

He viewed the satellite power plant exhibit with detached interest. A pictorial display outlined the development of solar energy electricity generation in the 1940s. The display continued with pictures of the first solar power generation satellites, a miniature model of the first satellites to contain power plants that beamed electricity to the earth using radio signals, then a model of SPASTAR and its fall on Ohio, Florida, southern California and myriad other, smaller U.S. sites.

The hall emerged into a round room capped with a glass rotunda. A tour group clustered around a pedestal display in the center while a guide spoke. School-age kids, probably from a summer camp. Tony peered at the photos around the room's perimeter. He immediately recognized Charlotte as a little girl in the second one. His heart clenched. The little girl he'd pulled from the floodwaters, saved from drowning. He wrenched his gaze away and strolled around the room, aghast at the wall of homage to the "Mother of Modern Solar Energy." The woman who'd betrayed him. The woman whose work had indirectly caused the death of his sister and thousands of others.

Take it away, she'd said in the interview. SPASTAR had to be the reason. But what did she want him to take from her, and when?

Most of the photos showed Charlotte working on various projects. In one, she held up an early solar cell she'd developed. Ice formed over Tony's ribcage.

In the photo, she wore the violet-print dress he'd bought for her. Like the few other photos in which she looked at the camera, sadness pervaded her thin, close-mouthed smile, reminiscent of Mona Lisa's.

Tony skimmed over the other pictures, trying not to see Charlotte's sparkling eyes, or her face aglow with desire and happiness as she clung to him in the river, as she lay beside him in the little box bed at the Fishin' Shack, as she trembled beneath him in the living room of her home. He tried to forget her whispered professions of love—lies, all lies—and the press of her lush body against his...

The last photo was the only one in color. In it, Charlotte again wore the violet-print dress, by then faded. Gray streaked her hair and lines etched her forehead, a vertical one above her nose the most pronounced. The caption placed it in the year he was born. Even as a seventy-year-old woman, she was beautiful.

Beneath the photo, glass covered a yellowed, handwritten letter. Tony leaned closer. The note was dated August 9, 1968, right after the U.S. had taken Viet Nam with solar-powered explosive devices. Tony's head swam. Weapons? He forced himself to read the rest of the note, in which Dorothy Charlotte Henderson announced her retirement. Appalled by the use of her work to kill, she stated her intention to live the rest of her life in solitude.

Tony wandered away in shock. Before he'd gone back in time, he'd never heard of Dorothy Charlotte Henderson. What had happened? Mute horror flowed over his body, as if someone had poured a bucket of thick liquid over his head, slowing his motions, clouding his vision, dulling his senses.

Had his visit to Charlotte brought about this solar-powered new world?

He'd never know. He didn't want to know. He wouldn't warp again. He'd live with the questions, and the memory of Charlotte's warm body close to his, and her lies—

Someone bumped into him. A girl in the tour group mumbled

"sorry" and ambled away.

He rubbed his eye, and his hand came away wet. Crying. He'd been standing there, staring at her picture with tears running down his face and he didn't even realize it. He surreptitiously rubbed his cheeks, snatched off his glasses—an old pair he'd fortunately kept— and wiped them, then hung at the fringe of the school group.

"...this is what Henderson claimed started it all," the tour guide said. "We're very lucky to still have it. As you might know, much of the museum's collection was lost when SPASTAR fell. But this piece, along with a few others, was on loan to the Smithsonian at the time. If you'll follow me..." Her words faded as the group moved away.

Tony approached the glass-topped, cylindrical pedestal. He clutched the glass, mouth agape, when he saw the object inside.

His calculator.

The one he'd dropped while shopping with Charlotte. The one he'd forgotten all about. He'd left it in his wallet, in the pocket of the pants he'd left on her kitchen floor.

His hands squeaked as they slid down the glass, and he slumped to the floor, crumpled into a ball. It was his fault. All his fault...

Tony didn't remember driving—or rather, riding—home, or even leaving the museum. He didn't remember anything until he found himself traipsing down the path through the woods behind the apartment complex. His footsteps crunched in the dry leaves, and the black walnut trees loomed menacingly, as if their leafy canopy concealed something sinister. *Come on, Solomon,* Tony chided himself. *You walk through this woods all the time, there's nothing there.* The trail was the quickest way to Mulroney's, Bernie, and a cold beer. Tony could sure as hell use a drink, even though he wouldn't be warping back to re-do his week with Charlotte for almost another year. He had to get away from his apartment, away from the news that the Dayton Sniper was targeting dark-haired, white businessmen in their mid-thirties.

The crackling leaves on the trail gave out to pine needles, and when his footsteps became muffled thuds, the reason for his sense of foreboding became apparent. No birds chirped in the treetops above. No chatter of squirrels, or rustle of leaves as they leapt from tree to tree. Tony stopped.

Shards of blue sky showed through the treetops. Leaves fluttered in a light breeze, enough he could see but not hear. Then another presence settled into his mind, alien yet not... *Get off the path!*

Huh? "Who—" He cut off his own words. No one had spoken, that other... *person* in his head had. *Get off the path!*

He dove for a clump of undergrowth as a gunshot rang out. A puff of dirt rose from where the slug impacted the dry earth.

Good God, right where he'd been standing.

Move! the other presence urged. He scuttled a few feet away, toward a bush. Another shot. Twigs snapped from the bullet's passage in the underbrush where he'd just been. His throat felt full of gravel. At another urging from that other presence he ran back toward the path. Two more gunshots.

He crouched under a low-lying tree. *Okay, chill out here. But only for a minute,* the other voice in his head said. Himself, from the future. Like when he'd sold all those technology stocks right before the market bombed. He panted, the sound loud in the still woods. The little voice was silent, and his present thoughts kicked back in. *Sniper. After me. Bob Standley wasn't a random hit.* Tony dug into his pocket and whipped out his cell phone. "Police," he said in a low voice. His future self remained quiet, though Tony still sensed his presence. Leaves rustled in the treetops down the path, where he'd run from. The shooter was coming.

The emergency operator picked up. "Someone's shooting at me!" Tony tried to catch his breath. "They've fired five times—"

"Police are on the way," the operator said. "Please stay on the line..."

Move!

Tony darted for the underbrush. Another shot rang out. Closer. He squeezed the phone. "Sir? Are you all right?" Tony's hand muffled the emergency operator's voice.

"Yeah," Tony whispered. But for how long?

Sirens wailed in the distance. Guided by his future self, Tony ran in a crouch, then doubled back on the path. The gunman fired another shot. Tony's erratic route was all that was keeping him alive. "Sir?" the emergency operator said.

He crouched under a bush. "I'm here."

The sirens grew nearer. There must've been a unit already in the area. The little voice remained silent. Tony's legs were starting to cramp when blue lights flashed through the wood. Something at the entrance to the path crashed through the trees.

"Mr. Solomon!" a man yelled. The cops, thank God. Tony turned toward the voice and started to rise, then stumbled as dizziness swamped him. He was warping? Now? But the vertigo dissipated as suddenly as it had come. He struggled to his feet as two police officers tramped through the trees toward him. "Mr. Solomon! Are you all right?"

They questioned him and searched the woods for an hour. The only evidence of the sniper they found was the spent shells.

As Tony had expected. Because the sniper had warped away.

"Mr. Solomon, do you have any reason to believe you might have been targeted? Any motive someone might have?" one of the policemen asked as they emerged from the woods to the apartment parking lot where their cruiser sat.

"None," Tony said. At least none he could explain to them.

And none he could explain to himself. Unless Theodore Pippin had friends in the future.

The police reminded Tony to contact them if he saw anything suspicious, then departed. He trudged back into his apartment, no longer in the mood for a beer or company.

It was his fault. All of it. Everything that was wrong in this timeline. His fault. Maybe those snipers were executioners from the future, sent back to kill him—no, punish him, take him to the Saturn Society to be turned into a mindless zombie, his penance for leaving

the calculator in 1933. He had to go back. Had to retrieve the calculator, now. In the other timeline, there were no snipers gunning for him.
No SPASTAR. No sixteen thousand people—and his sister—dead. The
memorial, the fields full of solar collectors and the deforestation cri-
sis—everything. *All my fault.* All so totally, completely, wrong. He
had to fix it. Had to warp one last time. He couldn't put it off until
next year, couldn't simply redo his visit to Charlotte, because the calculator would still exist in 1933.

And because if he waited a year, he might not be alive.

Tony tossed and turned all night. The red glow of his alarm clock
numbers etched into his brain. 2:13. 2:17. 2:31. Light seeped around
his curtains from the apartment's parking lot, casting shadows in the
textured ceiling, patterns he'd memorized. *There has to be another
way.* The lines in the ceiling were rivers on a map, flowing on an inexorable path to nowhere.

Maybe Charlotte did lead the Society to him, but he couldn't bear
the thought of going back and ensuring her death. *You have to.*

What was it that Everly had said in the hospital, after Tony returned from 1913? Something to the effect that if he went back to
correct one mistake, he could fuck up something else, maybe make
things worse.

Charlotte had said that, too.

But he had to take the chance. He couldn't leave things the way
they were.

Dwindling rainforests and global warming, far worse in this timeline due to the deforestation brought about by the premature consumption of land for solar collectors, the technology having developed too soon, too fast. And with the fall of SPASTAR, sixteen thousand people dead.

His life played out in mental sound bites. The time when he was
a kid, playing in the park down the street from his house, and a

strange woman had scooped him into a car. "I'm not going to hurt you. We're just going for a ride," she'd said. At age ten, Tony knew better than to get into a car with a stranger, even a tall, pretty lady with long, blond hair, but a little voice in his head had told him it was OK.

Ten minutes later, the tornado ripped through, leveling the park, the homes around it, and half the city. He and the woman—she'd told him to call her Alpha—went to a McDonald's a few miles away. Then she took him to his home, which had been mercifully spared—

He bolted upright. The dog lady! The woman whose intervention had saved him from being blown away in the tornado was following him even now, decades later.

And she looked hardly any different.

There was another time, when he'd been in Boston, meeting with a client, and another driver—who looked amazingly like Alpha—had cut him off on the way to the airport, causing an accident that made him miss his flight.

A flight that went down in rural Missouri, with no survivors.

Who was Alpha? Was she from the future? And what of the little voice? The one that had compelled him to sell his stocks and buy real estate? The one that had told him where to run to elude the shooter?

Should he change the past again?

Everly's warning rang in his ears. *Chances are you'll screw things up even more.*

He had no choice. Damned if he did and damned if he didn't.

At six-thirty he got up and showered. By the time he donned a collared knit shirt and khaki shorts (ironically, the same outfit he'd worn that day in Mexico, in the other timeline), he decided on a course of action.

He'd start the day with his usual at Bernie's, his car safely ensconced in the Seventh Street parking garage. Hope and pray the guy who'd shot at him was sometime in the future, recovering, and wouldn't be gunning for him today. Hope and pray the guy was working alone.

He shoved a wad of bills into his pocket. The woman at the bank yesterday had given him an odd look—few people used cash any more but the rare coin shop didn't take thumbprint-initiated funds transfer.

The Buick's canned female voice greeted him when he climbed in. He wanted to snarl at its too-pleasant tone. "Bernie's."

The car started and backed out of Tony's parking space. "Music?" it asked.

He'd been listening to some thirties swing on the way to the museum. Something Charlotte would have liked. Hadn't noticed it on the way home, he'd been so distraught.

"Yeah." Music would be good. But not something she'd like. "Select by artist. Metallica. 'Don't Tread on Me.'"

The car complied, and heavy metal filled its interior. The anthem had come out years ago, but it seemed fitting.

Tony leaned back and closed his eyes as thoughts of Lisa rushed through his memory. The time when he was six and just gotten his first pair of glasses. Lisa was eight, and she'd faced down the bully on the school bus for him—and gotten the snot beat out of her for her trouble. Then there was the bottle of wine she and Tony had shared an hour before her wedding, when she'd been so nervous she could barely speak. The dinner she'd cooked at his parents' house, when her marriage had almost fallen apart—and Tony's had.

He thought of other people he knew who'd died in the fall of SPASTAR. A guy he went to high school with. One of his neighbors in the apartment complex, who'd been stuck in traffic. Dora's brother's wife. Everyone knew someone. In the Dayton area, most people knew several who'd died that day.

Iron formed around his heart. His feelings for Charlotte didn't matter. She'd betrayed him. Then had gone on to start a technological revolution responsible for so many deaths. If Tony's return to 1933 meant she had to die, so be it.

A bump jostled the car. Tony's eyes flipped open. Solar collectors filled the fields on both sides of the road. The one he'd noticed on the way to Bernie's the other day, that had been an undeveloped, wooded area in the other timeline.

The right timeline.

Another bump. Tony jerked upright. What the hell? The jolt came not from the road, but from behind. Something rumbled.

He whipped around.

A big, gray pickup truck bore down on him. Boxy-shaped, from the eighties. He barely had time to register the letters on its chrome grill before it drew close again and jolted him forward. "Turn right!" he yelled at the Buick.

"There is no access to the right," the calm, feminine voice informed him. Fucking automatic navigation. Not that going off the road made sense, with a four-wheel drive after him.

He twisted around again. A big, bald guy built like a football player gripped the truck's steering wheel, his lips curled into a grin as the truck drew closer. He lifted his left arm

(a gun)

and squeezed the trigger.

Tony ducked. A muffled report from behind. The back window cracked as the bullet struck.

He started to lift his head, then ducked again. The guy fired a second time. The Buick's rear window shattered, and beads of tempered glass rained onto the back seat. A few struck Tony's head. "Disengage speed control!" Tony yelled to his car.

"Automatic speed control disengaged," his car confirmed. The car gained speed. "Faster!" Tony ordered. He raised up and peered around the headrest. The pickup had fallen back but was gaining. "Faster!"

The car complied and the pickup fell farther behind. "Obstruction ahead," the Buick said, and braked.

"What?" Tony whirled around. An orange and white sign loomed in the road. "Road construction? That wasn't there yesterday!"

The car's only response was to slow and stop in front of the sign. The truck rumbled louder as it drew closer behind him.

Tony's first thought was to jump out of the car and run. He stared at the pickup as it rolled to a stop. The guy reached for the door, still smirking. Tony's logic kicked in. No businesses or homes for another mile or so. To the left and right, nothing but solar collectors. His pursuer was a big, athletic guy. He'd catch Tony before he reached the nearest solar panel.

There was only one way out.

Tony crouched out of the man's sight. He envisioned the woods that had been there before, in that other timeline. Woods that had undoubtedly had been there in 1933—he hoped.

His vision swam as dizziness engulfed him.

At her workbench in the basement, Charlotte reached for her cigarette and tried to take a puff. Air. She held the stub in front of her. The darn thing had burned out.

She should quit. So many of them burned to nothing while she worked, it was a waste of money. Saturn Society money that Theodore had lent her, along with increasing pressure to move into the House. Besides, Tony had told her smoking was bad for her.

She lay the butt back in the ashtray and picked up the calculator parts she'd neatly lined up on the workbench. Light played across the case's brushed metal face as she turned it over in her hands. Reflections glittered over the magical red squares that captured light. *So tiny.* Bubbles rose within her, miniatures of those she'd felt when Tony had come to her in the Fishin' Shack during the storm. Exquisite joy.

The bubbles popped. Tony was never coming back.

She felt like she'd stolen from him. *But I haven't.* She had the calculator because Tony left it in his pocket. If he'd tried to get his clothes—or the calculator—before he jumped home, Dr. Caruthers would have overcome him. Tony's life would have been forfeit. Or worse.

Tony wanted her to succeed as an inventor. She had important work to do, much to contribute. He'd told her so. His leaving the calculator was a sign. Something meant to be.

Even Theodore had been supportive of her renewed interest in her work, confident she'd in time repay the Society for its investment in her education. She'd begun working with copper plates while she waited for the newfangled silicon chips from a laboratory in Boston that Theodore had lent her money for. He'd even enlisted Society help in acquiring research texts.

Of course, he didn't know about the calculator.

She replayed her rationalizations as she reassembled the instrument, fearing if she didn't, she might lose some of the tiny parts. By learning from it, she wasn't fiddling with time. She hadn't asked Tony for it. And burying herself in unraveling its mysteries was the best way she could begin to fill the hole his leaving had left in her heart, the best way to mask the pain from the emotional wounds Caruthers had inflicted.

She pushed the painful memories into a dim corner of her mind and picked up Theodore's knife—she kept forgetting to return it to him—and scraped the carbon off the copper plate she'd fired, exposing a layer of oxidation beneath—

Don't!

She hesitated. What on earth? She brought the knife to the copper piece

Don't do it! It's dangerous! The world's not ready—

She lay the knife down as she recognized the feeling of compulsion. Another visit from herself, from the future. "Why should I listen to you?"

I've been there. I've seen what comes of this—

She let visions and sensations from her future self play through her mind. People using solar technology to better their lives. Military men presenting her with awards. Reporters. Fame and glory. Fortune, too. Enough money to pay Theodore back many times over. Enough to break free of the Society forever—

Get rid of it! her future self urged.

"I can't," she whispered. It was financial freedom. Her name in history books. A triumph for her, for all women.

And most of all, meaning in her otherwise empty life.

Destroy it! Or else.

"Or else what?" Her future self had made this trip to change something. Something that could result in another disaster like Papa. Perhaps worse. And Theodore would sense it. Still angry with her for letting Tony escape, he wouldn't forgive her this time. Never mind the Society money that now paid her bills and financed her work—if Theodore caught her future self influencing the past, it would be *her* in the Treatment chamber.

She was meant to do this. She picked up the copper plate and resumed scraping. Eventually, she would discover the calculator's inner workings.

The knife slipped and skittered across the back of the plate, grazing her left palm. She dropped the knife and clutched the edge of her workbench until the dizzy spell passed.

Someone had jumped. Who?

She gazed around the basement, as if the answer lay within the ceiling joists. Could it be Tony?

As soon as the question formed in her mind she discarded it. Tony wasn't coming back.

It didn't matter. Theodore would find whoever it was. It wasn't her problem. She didn't want to go to the House and meet the traveler, didn't want to see anyone.

She picked up the knife and resumed scraping.

A light drizzle greeted Tony as he hopped out of the truck at Fourth and Hopewell, and watched it rattle away. Hopefully, no one would notice the dollar's slight differences when the old farmer spent it—particularly the issue date. The guy had given him some furtive, weird looks, but Tony guessed his manners had kept him from asking about Tony's mud-soaked clothing, courtesy of a heavy rain during recovery, which he'd slept off in the woods bordering the country road where he'd warped.

He gazed around the neighborhood. The deepening twilight held a preternatural silence, though there were noises. The hum of crickets. A conversation drifting out an open window from the house on the corner.

No steady drone of air conditioners, that's what was different. That, along with the fact it was strange to see houses instead of the vast, concrete, community college that existed there in Tony's time.

Get going, get it over with. Tony walked. One foot in front of the other. One step at a time.

Humidity clung to him like a straitjacket, and when he finally convinced himself to move, it was like slogging through mud. Step by inevitable step closer to Charlotte's house. Closer to the woman who'd betrayed him. The woman whose work was responsible for thousands of deaths.

A car going the opposite direction slowed as it passed. The streetlight above cast just enough light for Tony to recognize the driver. Dewey. Tony turned down an alley—no time to chat, if Charlotte's brother happened to have recognized him.

Dewey drove on. Tony slipped out of the alley and continued to Charlotte's.

Four more houses. A tantalizing fragrance of someone's late dinner—meatloaf, perhaps—drifted through a screen door and made his stomach growl. God, he was starving. But food would have to wait. The longer it took for him to retrieve the calculator, the better the chance the Society would find him and stop him before he could get it. He quickened his pace as he passed through a streetlamp's weak pool of light.

A glowing, red dot moved inside a parked car across the street. The tang of cigarette smoke reached Tony's nose. The man inside leaned out the window, as if studying Tony, then jerked back inside. Tony walked on. The car started and pulled away from the curb with a screech, then roared away.

Tony stopped, the light, evening breeze chill on his rain-dampened skin. Had the man been watching for him? What if it was the Saturn Society?

He broke into a jog. The slap of his loafers on the pavement drew curious stares from a young couple huddled beneath an umbrella as they walked past.

What if they were with the Saturn Society?

Don't be ridiculous. Get the calculator. Then get the hell out.

Charlotte's house loomed ahead. Moonlight bathed its wooden siding in ghostly white. He forced himself to slow to a fast walk as he approached her front gate. Something rustled in the bushes beside the neighbors' house.

Saturn Society.

Stupid. Paranoid. Probably a squirrel.

Like last time. Caruthers.

He wouldn't think about that.

A cat darted out from the bushes as Tony lifted the latch. *See?* The gate creaked when he pushed it open, making him wince. He pulled it shut behind him but didn't latch it. He'd have to make a fast getaway, before Charlotte could contact Pippin and betray him again.

Hope to God, he wouldn't have to hurt her. But he would if he had to. *Whatever it takes.* Just like she'd told that Caruthers guy.

His steps resounded on the wooden porch. He lifted his fist to knock, then hesitated. Listened.

No sound except the whir of crickets and the light patter of rain dripping from the edge of Charlotte's roof.

He fingered the wallet in his pocket, his thumb squeaking on the stiff, new leather. She'd left the light on over the kitchen sink, and it cast a jaundiced, yellow glow in the window. She had to be home. He raised his hand again and gave the door three solid raps.

At the knock on the front door, Charlotte looked up from the scattered objects on her workbench. Who would be calling at such a late hour? She hadn't put the room-for-rent sign back up yet, and Theodore had given her enough money to pay the rent—this month. She wasn't in the mood for company, hadn't been since Tony had left. All she wanted to do was work.

She tried to collect her thoughts and refocus her mind on the project. Strips of red celluloid. A shiny, flat cylinder, half the size of a dime. A piece of green Bakelite with silvery lines running through it.

Her brother had surprised her when he'd stopped by. She hadn't wanted to see even him, but he'd walked in uninvited. Dewey had been able to tell she hadn't been eating, said he was worried about her. She'd almost told him about Dr. Caruthers. But sense and shame had made her let him think Tony's leaving was the sole reason she was upset. The fact she was wearing the violet print dress Tony had bought for her probably helped convince him.

She brushed a hand over the smooth fabric. Though the sleeves didn't quite cover the ugly, yellow bruises Caruthers had made on her arms when he pinned her down, it was the only thing she owned that made her feel pretty, ever since—

She pulled her hands back up to the workbench and picked up the shiny chip from inside the calculator. Hopefully, her silicon chips would arrive soon, and she'd see what it would take to replicate the calculator's cell. As she rummaged through a box of electrical odds and ends, the person at the door knocked again.

She kept digging. "Go away," she muttered. Rather late for Mrs. Paulson to be asking to borrow a cup of sugar.

Having misplaced her wire strippers, Charlotte grabbed Theodore's Saturn Society knife and shaved some insulation off a wire as the person upstairs rapped on the door again, more insistent. If she ignored them, maybe they'd give up and leave.

Twenty-one

Slow, steady footsteps clicked across the floor above her. Charlotte looked up. "Theodore?"

The footsteps moved through the living room, then into the kitchen. Charlotte frowned. It had to be him. He hadn't checked on her yet that day. "Theodore?" She shouted louder.

The footsteps stopped. He'd heard her. Why wasn't he—

What if it wasn't Theodore? Oh drat, she'd forgotten to lock the door! It could be anyone. Even—dread crawled down her spine—Dr. Caruthers. If the person had a legitimate reason to be there, they'd have answered when she called out. She clenched her jaw and grabbed Theodore's knife. If it was someone with ill intent, she'd be prepared.

She crept up the stairs, stepping carefully so they wouldn't creak. At the top, she hesitated.

The door lay slightly ajar. She started to lean forward to peek through the crack when another knock came from the front door. A sharper, more rapid knock than the first. "Charlotte!"

Theodore. But if he was outside, then who—

She peered into the kitchen.

His back to her, the man standing at the table rifled through the pile of Tony's clothes she'd never put away—

There was something familiar in his stance. Something familiar in the strong, muscled calves beneath his odd, above-the-knee knickers. She squeezed the doorknob. She'd seen that mussed, dark hair, run her hands through it...

A thrill coursed through her. "Tony!"

Tony whirled around as his hand closed over his old wallet, still in the pants pocket he'd left. In the crack of the basement door, Charlotte's brown eye caught a reflection from the light, blowing away all thoughts of her betrayal. "Char—"

The front door opened.

He tossed down the clothes and shoved the wallet into his shorts pocket.

"Charlotte?" the newcomer called from the living room.

Pippin! The front door squeaked as it opened. Tony yanked open the back door and fled.

Pippin hollered again, his voice strident through the open window. Tony hurtled down the steps, then—

His foot slipped on the wet grass, and he pitched forward onto the gravel path leading to the alley. His glasses flew off.

He spat out a mouthful of dirt, groped for his glasses, spotted the neighbors' porch light reflecting on them. He jammed them back on and leaped to his feet, his knees smarting where the gravel had gouged his skin.

Charlotte's voice drifted through the door. "I tried, but he got away... didn't have time, I don't know..."

Tony's bolted for the alley, a sensation of lead weight forming in his gut. *Sold out again.*

He stopped. Which way?

Headlights blazed from the direction of Fifth Street. A car started. Tony dashed toward Third.

Charlotte clutched her quarter. "I told you, he said he was never coming back!"

Theodore glared at her. "I'll deal with you later. I have a criminal to catch." He burst out the side door.

Tony'd said he'd never come back. Because she would die. Yet he had. She watched Theodore disappear around the Paulson's house, then pushed the screen door open and slipped out.

"Ben! This way!" Theodore shouted from ahead. *Caruthers!* Charlotte flattened herself against the side of her house as a dark green Cadillac—Caruthers'—trundled down the alley. Theodore jumped in the passenger side, slammed the door, and the car pulled away in a spray of gravel.

She sneaked around the corner of the Paulson's house, barely aware of the drizzle coating her arms. No sign of Tony. The car had slowed a few doors down, its red tail lights demon eyes in the dim alley. In a porch light's glow, she saw Theodore's face at the window as he peered out.

What could she do? Where had Tony gone? She made a fist, then looked down at her hand. She still gripped Theodore's knife. She squeezed it in grim satisfaction. As long as Tony could outrun Theodore and Caruthers, he had a chance.

But there were others. Men desperate for jobs, whom Theodore had hired to watch her house, despite her insistence Tony wasn't coming back. How long would he be able to elude them?

And would she die, like he'd said?

Tony crouched under a porch and peered through the broken lattice at the car down the alley. It stopped, and Pippin climbed out. He tramped along the side of a garage and shone a flashlight between two garbage cans. "He's got to be around here somewhere," he called to the man in the car.

They'd reach Tony's hiding place in minutes.

Tony brushed the dirt off his legs, picked a few pebbles from his knees, then dug the wallet out of his pocket.

He slid his fingers into the main compartment. Touched a couple bills, then the sharp corner of something else poked his fingertip.

He slid it out, held it up so that the semi-shiny, silver packet caught the light that filtered through the lattice from a nearby street-lamp. The condom Bernie had given him at Mulroney's. Tony had for-gotten all about it. Could've used it at the Fishin' Shack, not that one condom would have mattered as much as he and Charlotte had—He clenched his jaw at the sudden sensation of rocks lodged in his throat. She couldn't have kids anyway. And she'd betrayed him... He jammed his fingertips into the wallet's card holder, felt the raised lettering on his Visa card, the smooth laminate of his driver's license. A few coins. But—his throat hardened—no calculator.

Frantically, he shook the wallet open and flipped through the plastic pages of photos and credit cards, in case it might have gotten wedged between them. The change compartment was too small to hold the calculator but he looked anyway. Damn, damn, damn! He had to go back. What if she'd started working on it?

He shoved the wallet back into his pocket and poked his head out the gap in the lattice.

The car idled behind the next house, toward Charlotte's. Flash-lights flicked over the back lawn. A dark form skulked around the garage across the alley and rattled a door handle on it. No chance of slipping by that way. Tony leaned out farther. Toward Third Street, the alley was clear.

He'd run there, then double back to Charlotte's. He crawled from under the porch, then scrambled across the yard.

"There he is!" someone shouted from the house's side yard.

Tony dashed down the alley. Car doors slammed and the driver threw the vehicle into gear. How many of them were there?

He darted from house to garage, sneaked between garbage cans, behind bushes, in a zigzag path he hoped would throw off pursuit.

Charlotte slipped out from behind a garage and pressed her palm to the base of her neck. Theodore had almost seen her. What on earth was she doing? By following them and not helping, she'd sentenced herself to share Tony's fate.

She squeezed Theodore's knife in her fist. She wouldn't let Caruthers take her again. She'd die before she'd endure the Saturn Society's treatment. Tony would do the same, should they catch him. If he could.

She forced her gaze straight ahead as she crept down the weedy strip of grass along the thigh-high, stone retaining wall that snaked along the top of the riverbank, the light from the streetlamps along Sunset Place barely enough to see by. Over that wall the land sloped down until it met the Great Miami.

Looking at the river from a distance didn't trouble her. She could see a little sliver of it from her bedroom window in the winter, when the trees were bare. It reassured her, to be able to look out there after a storm, and see for herself that the river remained shallow and placid, thanks to the Conservancy dams built after the flood. As she moved toward it, her foot twisted on a bottle, and she flailed for the wall as she tumbled to the ground. Below, the water gleamed in a wide ribbon of black, festooned with sprinkles of light. Dams or no, it was too close. She tore her gaze away, flinching as she stood on her injured foot.

Someone fired a gun. Charlotte jumped. Had they shot Tony? She searched the murky darkness ahead. Nothing but black.

Theodore and Caruthers wouldn't shoot to kill. Not when that would send Tony back to his own time, where he might not be adequately punished. Their goal would be to injure him only enough to prevent his escape.

Another shot. A light came on in a house near Third Street. Shouts from that direction drew her onward.

She recognized Theodore's voice. "Over there!" Ben Caruthers' shouted reply, even from a distance, made her skin prickle, brought back rushing memories of pain between her legs, made the bruises on her arms burn. *Find Tony.* That was all that mattered.

She crept along the wall, ignoring her cramping foot as she kicked aside another discarded bottle. It made a loud clink against the concrete. She looked around, but none of the others were close enough to hear, thank goodness. Darn people, why couldn't they find a garbage bin? And where had Tony gone?

Tony crouched in the doorway of the closed gas station's office, and tried to catch his breath. Pippin and his cronies yelled back and forth at each other.

He'd been shot at three times in two days.

Tony had no clue what the twenty-first century snipers wanted, but with Pippin there was no doubt. Both of his shots had impacted the ground near Tony's feet.

They wanted to disable. Not kill.

So they could take him back to the Saturn Society House and turn him into a zombie. Make sure he'd never travel in time again, never mind that Tony was determined this was his last trip to the past.

The darkened, round signs atop the gas pumps reflected the streetlamps like evil eyes. "I think he's in here," someone shouted.

His back against the wall, Tony sidestepped along the building until he could peek around the corner. Flashlights bobbed in a strip of yard between two houses across Third Street, their lights ringed in the mist. A car sat at the intersection of Robert Boulevard, its headlights on, the driver no doubt waiting for direction from Pippin. Tony scanned the street in front of him, one he'd never heard of. Sunset Place, the road sign read. Must've been a casualty of I-75.

A low, stone wall ran along the other side of the deserted lane, a dividing line between the city and the blank darkness of the river bed, bisected by the Third Street bridge.

To the west, nothing moved. No cars lay in wait. The sound of voices came closer.

He had to run. Now. Or they'd trap him.

He assessed the gas station. A high fence bordered it on the back and the north. The Saturn Society awaited him on Sunset Place, as well as on Third Street to the east.

One option left. The bridge across the river, to the west. He took a deep breath, gathered his courage, and his strength. Then he bolted.

His feet slapped the pavement to the bridge. Voices behind him. His breath was short, but he had no choice but to keep running. He couldn't think about the fact he was on a bridge, a good thirty feet above the river, nothing but a waist-high metal railing between him and the empty air. Couldn't think about anything except evading the Society guys. He would run along the opposite bank, run back over at Fifth Street, circle to Charlotte's house and snag the calculator.

Panting, he slowed. Halfway across. He'd never make it if he didn't conserve his energy—

A car pulled up to the west end of the bridge, angled so it blocked most of the road. Tony stopped and whirled around. A second car appeared from the opposite direction to complete the obstruction.

He turned again. The car that had been sitting at Robert Boulevard rolled forward, then stopped at the end of the bridge. Two men—one pale, one dark-skinned—climbed out.

They walked toward him with slow, deliberate steps. They didn't need to run.

Charlotte stumbled along the wall toward Third Street, careful not to slip in the wet grass. Theodore's car straddled the lanes ahead, and two other cars parked across the river. Their headlights cast weak beams over the street. She stopped. Something moved on the bridge. Tony!

She couldn't move except to grip her quarter so tightly it cut into her palm. Theodore shouted and broke into a run for the center of the bridge.

Tony leaned over the railing—heavens, what was he doing?—and peered down.

Like he was about to jump.

Was he crazy? The river was only a few feet deep. He'd be killed.

Unless that was what he wanted...

Tony tore his gaze away from Pippin. Couldn't let them see his fear. God, how could he have been so stupid? Now he had no escape. Except...

He leaned over, forced himself to look down, over the rail.

The river below churned on its inexorable path to the Ohio. Calm, placid, it cut a dark swath, textured by the drizzle, broken only by the rippled reflections of streetlights. Images rushed through his mind in a rapid-fire slideshow. Shooting hoops with Bethany. Dora on vacation a long time ago, before too little time together had wrecked their marriage. Bethany learning of her friend's close call. Lisa, laughing at the dinner table. And Charlotte...

Electricity coursed through his body. The men's shouts muted. Below, the river darkened while the reflections on it grew sharper. Time crawled to a near standstill, and his fear disappeared as his mind tripped over the possibilities.

If he jumped, he might die.

Was thinking about it enough to make it intentional, and therefore, for good? Or would he go home? If he did, he could come back to 1933 a third time to retrieve the calculator—provided the snipers in his own time didn't get him first.

But it was only a twenty-five or thirty foot drop, so chances were he wouldn't die. Maybe he'd just get banged up, break a few bones. Then Pippin could simply drag Tony out of the river and cart him off to the House.

A car door slammed on the west end of the bridge. Approaching footsteps resounded in Tony's ears. He glanced back at Pippin, coming closer. The gun in his right hand gleamed dully in the light from the cars' headlamps.

If Tony jumped, he might escape in death.

If he didn't, his fate was certain.

He looked down at the river, and fear came crawling back. He gripped the railing, the metal icy cold despite the warm weather. He swung his legs over and sat there a second, poised over the rail.

He jumped.

Charlotte's body went rigid as Tony straddled the rail, then plunged into the water. A muted splash stung her ears. Paralyzed, her thoughts thick as molasses, she waited for the dizziness that would tell her Tony had died and jumped back to his own time.

She twirled the quarter between her thumb and index finger. Imagined the vertigo, willed it to come.

Nothing.

The water remained still and black. Tony had to be hurt. Not dead. Memories of being swept down Seventh Street assailed her. She pushed them away, gripped the rough stone retaining wall, and climbed over.

Her dress caught on a sharp edge. She pulled at it, but something held it. No time to fiddle with it. She cut it away with the knife she still held in her hand, the ripping sound unnaturally loud, then she half-stumbled, half-slid down the dewy, grassy riverbank. Mumbles and snatches of curses reached her from above. She had to get to Tony before they did, but what could she do?

She picked her way across the gravelly shoal at the water's edge as fast as she could, shoving aside remembrances of icy floodwaters, the feel of her lungs burning as she gasped for air and took in water instead. No time for fear.

Her heart almost stopped. Where was Tony? Had he drowned? He hadn't jumped in time, so he must be alive, unless... "No," she said.

He wouldn't kill himself. Not after he'd taken such risks to hide from Theodore and learn how to save his daughter. She squinted at the river where he'd gone in. Clouds obscured the moon, making it hard to see. A light splash, then gasps and choking as something broke the water's surface a few feet upstream. A dark form emerged, and an arm snaked out to clutch at gravel and weeds.

Charlotte tossed the knife down and rushed to him, grabbed his arm and pulled. "Tony!"

He sputtered and spit. "You!" he wheezed.

Wasn't he glad to see her? Why hadn't he spoken to her in her house? She gritted her teeth and pulled harder. The clouds parted, and the moon cast an eerie glow on the river's surface. With a grunt, she gave another sharp tug, and Tony came out of the water, flopped onto the gravel like a fish.

He lay panting. "How... can you... do this to me. After all I've..."

"Do what?" One of his legs twisted beneath him at an impossible angle, and blood streamed down them in dark rivulets in several places. "I saved your life!"

"I saved... *your* life. And you repay me..." His eyes drifted shut. Shouts came from above. Charlotte looked up. *Theodore*. Despair settled over her. What had she thought she'd do? Should she have let Tony drown? Regardless of whether he'd return to his own time, or die permanently?

"Get it over with." His voice was raspy. "Holler for them..."

What on earth? The moon cast sharp specks of light in his pain-filled eyes, unmarred by his glasses which must now lay at the bottom of the river. What was he thinking? Why would—

Realization dawned. "How could you think—"

"I heard." He inhaled raggedly. "Your dedication extends..." His voice dwindled to a whisper. "Even to using your body." His eyes roved over her, stopped briefly on her bruised forearms, then met her eyes, his gaze cold and accusing.

"What?" Then it sank in. He'd heard her and Caruthers. "No! I lied! To Caruthers!" If only Tony knew.

"You... seduced me. So you could give me over—"

"I tried to distract him, so you could get away!" Her throat swelled, and tears burned in her eyes. "Tony... believe me," she sobbed. "I love you. Even though you could never say it to me, I love you. I couldn't possibly make believe what we had those few days."

He regarded her for a long moment, his teeth clenched, each breath sharp and short. His eyes flicked beyond her, and she followed his gaze. "Knife," he choked. "Give it to me."

Something in his voice made her hurry over and grab it. She started to hand it to him, then hesitated. "What are you going to do?" Above, Theodore shouted. He'd seen them. In minutes, his legions would be crawling down the riverbanks, to—

"Please." Tony's voice croaked, his face contorted into a grimace as he held out a shaking hand. "If you love me... let me die. Don't let them—"

"No! You won't go back. It'll be for good—"

He dropped his arm. "And they'll hurt you instead."

She turned around. A man climbed over the retaining wall. "Yes," she whispered. She held the knife out to him. "Do what you must."

She lay the knife's shining, silver handle in his outstretched palm, but his fingers didn't close over it. "First... do one thing," Tony gasped. "Please..."

"What?" Anything. She'd do anything.

"The calculator. Destroy it. Terrible things... because of it. Your work."

"What?" She clutched the knife more tightly, its handle cool in her palm. "No..." she whimpered.

"Thousands of people. Dead. Satellites falling. All because of... Destroy it. You've got to," he begged.

"What?" Shivers coursed through her. What had—or would—she do?

"Do it!"

Tony's choked words, the pain he had to be in, tore at her. She gulped. "All right."

"Promise." His voice shook.

"I promise." The calculator didn't matter. Her work didn't matter.

She snatched his hand and curled his fingers around the knife handle. "Don't let them take you. It's Hades on earth, I've seen—"

"Better me than you," he said through clenched teeth. "I can't.
Let them do that to you." He straightened his fingers and pulled his
hand away. The knife slid to the ground. "I love you. Even if you lied
to me. Even if you betrayed me. Even though I should hate you..."

Charlotte gazed down upon his broken body, took in the pool of
blood forming beneath his hip. It had soaked through his knickers
and his strange, stretchy shirt. If he lived, the Society would subject
him to unspeakable torture, trapped inside his own mind. He was
hurt. But not badly enough to insure the speedy death that would
send him to his own time.

Theodore ran along the wall, another man close behind. Clouds
had slipped back over the moon, and he hadn't seen her yet, but she
didn't have long.

There was one thing she could do to save Tony. "You have a family. People who love you. I have no one, let them take me..." She
snatched the knife off the gravel and gripped it in both hands. "P-
please forgive me," she sobbed, and plunged the knife into his belly,
forced it up under his ribs. Pushed harder. His screams rang in her
ears, yet were muffled as if he lay in a deep pit. Heavens, she'd never
have guessed how tough the human body was, she thought with an
odd detachment. Blood spurted as she drove the knife upward. His
flesh ripped with a sickening resistance. The metallic scent of his
blood stung her nose, then sticky, warmth burned down the front of
her dress as his screams dwindled into a gurgle.

"I do," he choked as he gasped his last breath.

"Charlotte!" Theodore leaned over the retaining wall, lifted a leg
over.

Her mentor's words faded as she stared down at Tony's body. The
blood bubbled out of the slash in his stomach more slowly now, and
his eyes glazed over. Shouts from one of the other men drifted from
the wall, then she turned back to Tony's body. Good Lord, she'd
killed. Her thoughts seemed strangely distant as if they weren't her
own but came from somewhere outside herself. She'd murdered a

man. Not just any man, but the one she loved more than anything. Nausea gripped her. She curled into a ball and vomited. Nothing came up but bile. She hadn't had anything to eat since a piece of toast for breakfast. She dry-heaved again, then something flickered at the edge of her vision. Tony's form grew indistinct, as if drawn on rice paper with pencils. Shimmered like a mirage. The dizziness of someone jumping slammed her. She wobbled as she yanked the knife from his stomach, then his body faded completely.

He'd gone home. She'd accomplished her purpose. Killed the man she loved. And in doing so, she'd freed him.

She hoped.

The only indications he'd been there were black speckles of blood on the gravel, their edges blurring in the rain. Dark stains soaked her dress.

"He's gone!" one of the men yelled.

"She let him get away again!"

"I'll take care of her!" Caruthers' bellow bore a threat beyond the treatment. Theodore slid down the grassy slope of the river bank as Caruthers clambered over the wall.

She leapt to her feet and ran down the gravel along the river's edge, toward home. Once she destroyed the calculator, let them do to her what they would. Her life was over.

She cast a glance behind her. Caruthers slipped on the dewy grass, and slid into Theodore with a curse. She forced her legs to pump harder and didn't look back again.

A fall of dead trees came into view, and she stopped running to grab onto a protruding branch, used it to pull herself up the slippery riverbank. She should be close to her house, if she could make it to the top. She let go of the branch, clutched a clump of grass, and pulled herself up, until she reached the retaining wall.

She heaved herself over, gulped for air, then paused. Caruthers' shouts drifted from the river, then Theodore's, and another man she didn't know.

The back of the Paulson's garage loomed in front of her. She bolt-ed to the alley, then her feet pounded the gravel until she stopped behind her house. "She's going home!" Caruthers yelled. Closer.

She yanked open the side door and scrambled down the steps. Had to get the calculator before they got her. It didn't matter that once the Society got hold of her, she'd no longer be a threat, would no longer own the mental capacity to care for herself much less invent anything.

But she'd promised Tony.

The light still burned over her workbench. She snatched the calculator, flipped it over in her hand. Her dreams, shattered. Soon she wouldn't remember—or would she? The treatment—

"Charlotte!"

Theodore. Outside. She had to do it. Now. She gripped the little machine in both hands and tried to break it. The thing was surprisingly tough. Slowly, the hard, metal back and brushed metal face started to bend—

Upstairs, the doorknob rattled, then a squeak as the door swung open. "Charlotte, my dear," Caruthers called. "I'm most disappointed in you..."

Footsteps. The stairwell door flew open and light spilled down the stairs. Mutters from Theodore.

Her eyes flitted over the workbench. If only she'd brought the knife! Better that than—

Concrete. Images of a row of six huge, round pilasters holding the bridge up over the street before her, the roar of traffic overhead, the rumble of a big truck...

The future. She'd gone there before. She could do it again. Maybe it was certain death to jump into the future, but it was far better than the life she'd have in the Society. If there was a chance, however small, she could be with Tony... She gripped the calculator, squeezed her eyes shut, and concentrated on the scene she'd stumbled into with him...

Fluttery in her head. She could do it. She dropped the calculator into her pocket and pulled her quarter out of her dress, stared at its silvery surface between her bloodstained finger and thumb. George Washington. The astronaut. The Wright Flyer. In God We Trust. 2002.

Spinning, whirling... nothing existed but her and the quarter, and endless motion, and everywhere, nothing but gray...

Twenty-two

He wasn't dead. Death didn't have fluorescent lights above. Death didn't smell like antiseptic and bad institutional food, did it?

And surely death didn't have the mother of all heartburn.

A tinny voice squawked somewhere in the distance, paging Doctor-somebody to the nurses' station.

Death didn't have a paging system, did it?

Tony squinted at the ceiling, trying without success to focus. Things behind him dripped and clicked in time to the beat in his head. A giant fist clamped around his chest. He couldn't pull enough air into his lungs. His whole body ached.

He wasn't dead. The dead didn't feel pain.

With that thought, Tony Solomon allowed himself to slip back into welcome oblivion.

Tony reached through the hospital bed rail and gripped Bethany's hand. "Does your car have a steering wheel?" His voice sounded throaty. But decent for someone who'd just woken from time travel recovery an hour ago. Someone who'd suffered a stab wound in the gut.

Stab wound? He started to shove the sheet down to look—

"Huh?" Bethany squinched up her nose, making it wrinkle across the bridge.

He'd check his stomach later. "Does your car have a steering wheel?"

"What kind of question is that?" She cocked her head.

"Just answer me."

"Ye-es," she said in a long, drawn out inflection.

"What about July third?"

"What about it?"

That sounded positive. "What's July third?" he asked.

She lowered her chin and looked at him from under her eyelashes. She enunciated each word, as if he wasn't mentally competent. "The day before the fourth?"

Tony's head flopped back against his pillow. It never happened.

"Where's Lisa?"

Bethany gave him another well-duh look. "Probably at work."

"At the base, right?"

She half-turned and regarded him from the side of her eye. "Last I heard. Are you sure you're all—"

"Thank God." Relief washed over Tony like a swim in a cool stream on a blazing summer day. He didn't care if Bethany thought he was drugged, messed up, or just plain stupid. Everything was fixed.

"You're like, totally not making sense," she said. "They must've given you some good drugs." She glanced at the clock. "I have to go." She rose and gathered up her purse. Tony recalled she'd gotten a summer job in the mailroom at LCT. "I think Mom's coming by after she gets off work." She leaned over and kissed him, a cool, blessed spot of moisture on his cheek. He told her goodbye and he loved her, then she was out the door.

It was over. All done. Bethany was alive. Lisa was alive. No SPASTAR. No sixteen thousand people dead because of him.

He pushed the sheet down until he could grasp the hem of his hospital down and pull it up. There, under his fingers. A short, bumpy ridge maybe an inch and a half long. Already healed, no need for a bandage.

He lifted his uninjured, right arm and touched his neck. Instantly he felt the rough, raised scar. The one from the ancient Mayans' huge, stone axe.

He'd warped back into the other timeline. The right one.

When he got out of the hospital, he'd look up Charlotte Henderson on the Internet, just to make sure, but he suspected all he'd find was her great-niece's genealogy web site with its scant information and notation that Charlotte disappeared in 1933, presumed dead.

Charlotte. Dead.

Or worse. The sheet beneath him grew clammy. A drop of moisture trickled down the scar on the leg he'd broken when he'd jumped off the bridge—like the stab wound, already healed, in his return to the present. Had Pippin gotten to her, given her the punishment intended for him?

She killed herself. She'd had that knife. He had to believe that, couldn't bear the thought of Charlotte a zombie with a mind empty of anything but pain and misery.

She'd done it for him. Without regard for what they'd do to her. She loved him so much she'd killed him.

He turned his head to the side, crushed his face into the pillow. Wished he could suffocate himself in it.

The pillow grew wet beneath the side of his face. His mom had been there when he'd first come out of recovery. She'd told him a second-shift janitor at Sinclair Community College had seen him in the river and called the cops.

Why couldn't the guy have just gone on his way and let him die? Without Charlotte—

She'd given him this. Given him Bethany, by telling him how to warp within his own life. Given him the chance to fix everything he'd fucked up. He'd make what he could of his life, riddled with holes as it was.

Rumble. Buzz. Whooshing sounds. Charlotte opened her eyes and took in her surroundings as the dizziness subsided. A car passed on the street in front of her. The superhighway bridge Tony had told her about cut a darker swath across the night above, punctuated by misty-circled, orange-tinted streetlights. Something pressed into the hand she held at her breast. She unclenched her fists. Her quarter in one.

The calculator in the other.

She gasped, and it clattered to the concrete. For a long moment, all she could do was stare. Slowly, she picked it up.

She'd promised Tony she'd destroy it. Was taking it out of 1933 altogether enough?

She dropped the calculator into her pocket, but snatched her hands away at the wetness on her dress. Dark stains blotted out the beautiful violet print. Blood. Tony's.

Lightness burst through her. She'd made it to Tony's time. She'd jumped into the future, alive! Her eyes darted from side to side, searching for him. He'd be hurt, probably unconscious. She had to find him, fast. The jump would heal the worst of his injuries, but he'd still need medical attention.

She wandered across a vast plain of concrete and sadness sliced her. Everything she'd known, gone. Her home, and all those around it. She swallowed. Except for Tony. He was—fear whisked away her sorrow—in the river.

She had to go there, face the water and the danger and deception it concealed, and get him out of the river before he drowned.

She trudged across Robert Boulevard—now Robert Drive, according to an enormous green sign above the road. It was nothing more than a strip of deserted pavement. No homes. No more beautiful park in the median. Fear threatened to immobilize her. She fought it and tottered across another expanse of concrete, toward the retaining wall still atop of the riverbank. At least the foot she'd sprained no longer hurt, thanks to the jump. She had to get to Tony. Gripping the low, cement wall, she leaned over.

The black ribbon of the river flowed smoothly below. Decades later, the only difference was that more streetlights cast speckled reflections on its surface.

Enough light she should have been able to see Tony lying on the graveled shoal near the bridge support. Dread coursed down her gullet and bound her ribs as surely as if she'd been tied with rope. Had he come forward only to drown?

She had to go down there to make sure. Had to go into the water that would suck her under, steal the air from her lungs. Never mind the river was only a few feet deep, that was enough to be dangerous, Tony could be drowning while she stood there being scared.

She pushed aside her fear and stumbled down the dewy grass to the river's edge.

She crept along the water, peering in where Tony should have been. The contours of the graveled areas had changed, but not so much he would have wound up under water. He should be—she followed the lines of the bridge supports into the river—Right there. On that little, grassy rise.

She picked her way over rocks, discarded bottles and a tire, squinting at the grass and weeds.

No blood. No indentation where a body might have lain.

But where? He had to be there somewhere.

She paced up and down the water's edge, searching for any sign Tony might have been there. Blood. Footprints.

She stumbled along the rocky shoreline. *So tired...* She'd forgotten jumping sapped her energy so. She was beginning to slip into recovery. Had to find Tony. Before she collapsed.

"Tony?" Her voice was small and weak. Where was he? How could he have moved in his condition? She had to get away from the water. Wouldn't be much help to him if she fell in and drowned in recovery. "Tony..." she called. It was useless. Her voice was muffled, darkness was closing in on her. What if something had gone wrong, and he wasn't there?

Or maybe the jump had healed him more than she thought, and he'd managed to climb the riverbank. Mustering the last reserves of her strength, she did the same, Tony's image in her mind the only fuel spurring her onward.

But no body lay near the retaining wall. No one hid between the enormous supports for the highway. No Tony.

Barely able to stand, she sagged against one of the massive py-lons. "Tony?" Maybe he was in that parking lot over there, hidden among those parked cars that looked like spaceships.

Wobbling, she pushed herself off the column and staggered to-ward the parking lot as fog descended over her mind.

Her hand met with something smooth and chalky. Metal. She blinked. Heavens, she was already losing consciousness. A truck, its red paint oxidized. And she'd wind up face down on the pavement if she didn't lie down soon.

And what of Tony?

Nothing she could do, not with recovery about to overtake her. If he was still in the river, he was already dead.

She tipped her face up as tears threatened. He couldn't be dead! If he was, wouldn't his body be lying on the shore?

She blinked until her vision cleared. He must have somehow managed to get away.

Phone the police. Yes, that's what she'd do. If someone had picked up Tony, they'd know. Surely there was a telephone some-where in one of those big concrete buildings down the street, where a massive, cement sign read Sinclair Community College.

She could make it. If she rested a moment, maybe she could stave off recovery long enough to go there and ring the police.

She glanced at the truck she was leaning against. A pickup truck. With its tailgate down, leaving the way open to a nice, flat, relatively clean place to lie—

Bed...

Charlotte, think! You can't just lie down in someone's truck! She pushed herself off the truck, but listed to the side and grasped it again to keep from falling.

Why not? her weary mind argued. Just for a minute.

It couldn't hurt. One hand on the tailgate, she grabbed the side of the truck bed with the other hand, and pulled herself up and over. She slid to the metal bed with a thunk.

Violet hesitated at the door to Tony's hospital room. She hadn't seen him in over two months, ached to see his handsome face, but wouldn't it seem funny for her to visit?

It wasn't strange in Mexico.

But then, she'd been with him when he was hurt. Natural curiosity, a reason to care.

She had to see him. Needed to, ever since his picture was on the news last week, when he'd been found half dead in the river. A shudder coursed through her. She didn't know why, but the river—any water bigger than her bathtub, but especially the Great Miami—had always scared the wits out of her. At least it had, as long as she could remember. And to think Tony had almost died there. She couldn't shake the feeling she had something to do with it.

Ridiculous. It was because she'd had one of those awful dizzy spells earlier that night. They always frightened her, even though they lasted only seconds and left no lingering effects.

Tony was going to be all right. She'd heard people talking in the cafeteria line.

But she needed to see him herself.

Just do it, Stephanie and Timmy would say.

She strained to hear voices. If he already had visitors, she'd move on. But she heard only the low buzz of the television. She squared her shoulders and walked in.

He was alone. His eyes were closed.

Still looking at him, she turned around, started to tiptoe out when his eyelids fluttered open. "Violet?"

Jitters surged through her. Lord, he was beautiful. Even in a hospital gown, with tubes stuck in his nose, and his hair all mussed up. Déjà vu struck her. Somewhere, sometime, she'd heard him say her name in that same, sleepy mumble.

She forced her voice to steady. "Hi, Tony. I- I was just here for a follow-up on a procedure I had done, heard you were here, thought

I'd stop by..."

Oh, drat. Why had she told him that? Surely he didn't care.

"Come on in." His voice was thin. He lifted his arm in a weak wave. "Sit down, if you want."

She thanked him and smoothed her skirt as she sat. "I'm afraid I don't have any Jim Winter novels for you this time."

The corners of his mouth tipped. "I've read them all anyway." He squeezed his eyes shut tightly, then turned away, as if it hurt to look at her. He stared at the television mounted on the wall opposite the bed. "I'm glad you came. I've been wanting to ask you something."

Her breath caught. Had he found out about... whatever she'd done? Something terrible. Something to do with lots of blood, and the horrible vision that had invaded her thoughts when she saw him on the news. Herself, gripping a bloody knife while Tony lay choking for breath beside her. Water all around...

Absurd. She couldn't have stabbed Tony. She'd been at home with Stephanie watching television when he was apparently attacked. Still, the feeling she'd done something unforgivable *(killed a man)* had grown stronger since then...

"...your family from around here?" Tony was asking.

She inhaled sharply. "Nope, 'fraid not," she said with a false lightness. She'd created a background for herself to use in situations like this. "At least, not as far as I know. I was adopted, so I can't be sure about my birth family, but... why?"

Could he have some clue to the mystery of her real past?

"I found a picture of a woman in my great-grandpa's stuff. She looked just like you."

Good Lord, what if it was her grandmother? *Calm down, Violet! Count to ten. Don't let him see.* "From... how long ago?"

"Oh, I don't know, I'd say nineteen-twenties, early thirties." His hand slipped on the bed rail, and his left eye twitched. Like he was lying. But why?

"That's interesting." She focused on his face and kept her eyes steady. She couldn't let him see her nervousness. "But probably no relation. My parents didn't know much about my birth mother, but I think she was from near where we lived, in southern Illinois."

Lord, she wished she had a cigarette. Not that she'd be allowed to smoke in the hospital. She reached up and twirled a lock of hair around her finger.

Thankfully, he let the subject drop and moved on to ask about work, people they both knew.

She had trouble concentrating on the conversation. Who was the woman in his great-grandfather's photos? Did Tony know something? If he found out Violet's past before she did, would he turn her in to the police?

She'd kept her promise to Stephanie and given hypnosis another try, but the session had yielded no more results than the other times. Most likely, the photo was a coincidence. He couldn't know anything. His gaze had held no malice, no accusation, only... sorrow?

She forced herself to rise. "I have to go now, I promised my roommate I'd look at her computer." Strangely, Violet had an affinity for them, though she was sure she'd never touched one before she'd come to live with Stephanie, her then-husband Vince, and her brother Timmy. "I'm glad you're doing better."

Tony mumbled his thanks and she walked out, encouraged by his seeming gladness to see her. After he was well enough to return to his job, she'd work up the nerve to ask him out, like Stephanie and Timmy were always telling her to do. At least ask him to join her for a cup of coffee after work.

A loud clang. Something slammed, jostling her. Then a low rumble. Vibration beneath her, and all around. A wad of silk—pretty dress with violets on it, she remembered—clutched in her fist. The acrid fumes of exhaust. A metallic, scraping noise and a sense of motion as something slid past her face—a tool of some sort. The rumble lowered in pitch, and another tool slid by and banged into the first with a clink. She opened her eyes a slit... darkness. More rumbling and motion. She slipped back into unconsciousness.

Over the next two days, Tony grew stronger. His parents visited each day, as did Bethany. Even Dora stopped by again.

And Lisa. He'd never been so glad to see anyone in his life. Everything. Fixed. Except for Charlotte, and there was no fix for that.

Keith Lynch stopped by the day after Tony woke from recovery. "Thank God you're all right," he said as he slid into the guest chair. "When I heard the news, I feared the worst."

"It won't happen again." Tony hoped his boss didn't ask him how he was so sure of this.

But Keith regarded him with warm, honey-brown eyes full of concern. The same color—and shape—as Violet's, Tony realized with a start. And Charlotte's. "You're one hell of a lucky guy," he said.

"Guess so." Tony didn't feel lucky. He was relieved when Keith left without pressing him for answers he didn't want to give.

He found himself thinking of Violet. A lot. He'd always liked her, enjoyed talking to her, but her almost constant presence in his thoughts now had to be because of her disquieting resemblance to Charlotte. It wasn't just her appearance, but something more, an inner beauty, a self-acceptance that transcended the harsh reality of being an overweight woman in today's image-conscious society. Charlotte hadn't been heavy, but she was the same height, and she'd possessed that same inner strength, that same confidence. Violet had to be related, though since she was adopted, chances were the connection would forever remain a mystery. Maybe once he got his head straightened out, went a few months without warping, he'd ask her out—

Footsteps in the doorway, a light knock on the open door. "Tony?" A man's voice he recognized but couldn't quite place. More footsteps, then the face. Ubiquitous smile, black ponytail flipping behind the man's shoulder.

"Everly. What do you want?" Tony tried to make his voice harsh, but it only sounded wheezy.

"I saw you on the news last week." Everly took the guest chair. "Wondered if you might reconsider—"

"Go to hell."

"I take it that means no."

Tony glared at him and grabbed the remote, his finger poised over the nurse call button.

"A body in the river." Everly shook his head and made a tsk tsk noise. "Jeez, Tony, first the flood, and now you go back and get tossed off a bridge. Don't you want—"

"I jumped," Tony said without thinking. Why did he tell Everly that?

"Christ, are you trying to kill yourself? I told you it's for good if you do yourself in, didn't I?"

"Better that than what Pippin would've done—"

Everly recoiled. "Theodore Pippin? What's he like? I heard he was like McCarthy—oh, shit, you weren't in his book, were you?"

Fear coursed down Tony's spine, clamped an iron fist around his ribs. Had he endured death a third time, let Charlotte take the fall for him, only to find himself at the Society's mercy in his own time? Was there no escape? "Get out."

Everly didn't move. "You—"

Tony jabbed the nurse call button on his remote.

Everly rose, held up his hands, palms out. "Chill out, Tony." He dropped his hands. "You did something, didn't you? Changed something."

He doesn't know. "Get out," Tony repeated. Where was the damn nurse when you needed one?

Everly rose, his Cheshire cat smile finally gone. "Listen, Tony, I don't know what you did, but be careful. I don't agree with Pippin's fanaticism or his methods, but there are others who want to return to those ways. And their numbers are growing. I have to admit, they may be right..."

Something about the knit of his brows abated Tony's anger.

"About what?"

"The effects of changing the flow of time. If you'd listened to me—"

"What?" Now Tony wanted to know.

Everly spoke slowly, deliberately. "Rips in the fabric of time, re-member?"

Tony stared at the sheet over his lap, the contour of the new scar on his belly visible through his hospital gown. Had he created a new universe by saving Bethany? By leaving his calculator in 1933? By *(leaving Charlotte to die)* going back for it? No wonder the Society was so opposed to changing the past. If the fabric between universes was stretched thinner every time someone made a change, the result would be...

Utter chaos.

Everly leaned against the door frame. "Some people believe that's what happened to Pippin's wife."

"That psycho was married?"

Everly shrugged. "Some say Mrs. Pippin just got tired of her hus-band's jumping into the past for weeks at a time, and left him. But he wrote in his journals that she disappeared through a rift in time."

Tony stared down while his mind tumbled around the possibili-ties. Killer mosquitoes. Bacteria. Viruses thought to be eradicated, that humans no longer were immune to. Larger animals, even people. How would he feel if someone else's messing in the time stream took Bethany from him again? He lay his hands flat on his lap and looked up at Everly. "Well, you don't need to worry about me any more. I'm through."

"Through what?"

"Through with this time travel crap. You told me how to stop it, that's all I wanted."

"Don't give it all up, Tony. It's wonderful. Observe and learn. But be careful." Everly moved toward the door. "Because they're watch-ing. Everywhere. Every*when.*"

Everly almost bumped into someone as he walked out the door. "Oh! Excuse me, ma'am." Tony couldn't hear the feminine acknowledgment, but he'd heard the rapid click of toenails on the tile. Seconds later, a beagle mix crossed the doorway—a pet therapy dog—with a golden-haired woman on the other end of its leash.

The dog lady? "Hey!" Tony said. She smiled at him as she walked past, but didn't stop.

He'd gotten a closer look at her than ever before. Her blue eyes twinkled, and though no wrinkles marred her model-perfect face, he sensed she was much older than she looked.

And she was indeed the woman who'd cut him off on the way to the airport in Boston.

"Alpha?" Tony hauled himself upward and almost yanked the IV drip from his hand as he slid out of bed.

Another detail snapped into memory. The time when he was ten, he hadn't just climbed into a car with a stranger, she'd pulled a knife on him. A polished silver knife, with an image of the planet Saturn engraved in its handle. "My God," Tony breathed. Did he have a guardian angel? From the Saturn Society, of all places?

Pulling the IV stand behind him, he hobbled to the door, no easy task with his energy still low. Recovery with a life-threatening injury must be more draining. But when he got there, the dog lady was nowhere in sight. "Excuse me," he called to a passing nurse. "Is there a pet therapy person around here?"

"We don't have anyone scheduled for today." The nurse frowned. "And you have no business being out of bed, Mr. Solomon."

"Please..." The energy he'd expended getting up was almost all he had. "I need to talk to her. Did she go into another room?"

The nurse gave him a stern look but stepped inside each nearby room to look while Tony leaned against the wall. "There's no one here, Mr. Solomon. Now let's get you back into bed."

"If you see her, come get me." His energy spent and hope gone,

Tony let the nurse help him back to his room. "Tall, thin but not skinny, blond hair... and usually with a dog." The nurse assured him she would, but Tony suspected she was patronizing him.

He'd find that dog lady. Somehow, he'd find out where the hell his guardian angel came from—and when.

Oily smells. Chemicals of some sort. Metal beneath her hand. She rubbed it, yawned, looked around. Where was she?

She squinted, and her eyes gradually focused. Light filtered in through narrow, grimy windows. She was lying in... she patted the ridged metal again, gazed around. A metal trough, with a windowed enclosure at one end. She was in the back of a truck. In someone's garage. How had she gotten there?

Something rumbled overhead. She looked up. A motor, with a belt. The garage grew brighter. Her head whipped around. The motor was making the door go up.

"...dang pipe wrench! Gotta be in the truck." A man's voice, each word carefully enunciated. Footsteps on concrete as the voice grew louder. "Ain't in the house. Ain't in the shed, done looked all over." She sat up, her energy returning, when the footsteps came around the truck. *Please don't let him hurt me,* she prayed. She saw him first, a skinny fellow with horn-rimmed glasses. His eyes lit on her and he jumped back. "Whoa! Wh- who are you?"

"I'm..." Her tongue stuck to the roof of her mouth. So dry... how long had it been since she'd had a drink? "I'm..." Terror crushed the air from her lungs. *Good heavens, who am I?* No name came to mind. No idea where she might have come from. "I'm..." She spied a pipe wrench lying in the truck bed. "Is this what you were looking for?" She held it up.

The man's eyebrows went up, then a smile spread across his face. "Yeah, that's it!" She crawled toward the tailgate and handed it to him. "Thanks," he said. "Vince'll be madder'n a hornet if I don't get that leak under the sink fixed afore he gets home." He started to turn around.

"Um, sir!" He stopped and cocked his head at her. "Please," she asked, "could I have a drink of water? And perhaps... use the necessary?"

His face went blank. "Necessary what?"

The fellow wasn't firing on all cylinders. "The toilet."

"Oh! Sure." He waited while she scooted to the truck's tail. His eyes riveted on her dress as she stood. "Wow, that's a doozy of a stain."

She looked down, bit off a scream. She couldn't move. Couldn't breathe.

Blood. Lots of it. Dried, crusty, brown. All down the front of her dress. Not hers. She was tired, hungry, stiff from sleeping—for days, it seemed—in the back of the truck. Where had the blood come from? So much, she must have killed someone...

"Hey," the man said. "Did you have one of them double fudge sundaes from Freezy Delight? Man, they're good, ain't they? I always wear a bit of mine, but you must've spilt the whole thing. That sucks."

"Um... yes." Definitely a bit slow. But kindness filled his eyes as he held out his hand, so she took it and hopped down from the truck.

He went to a couple of big, shiny black bags by the garage door, tore one open, and started rummaging through it. "That dress is ruined. Maybe there's something in here you can wear..." He pulled out a shirt, shook it, and held it up. "Here, try this..."

She put her hand to her chest. "Oh, I couldn't—"

"It's all right, Stephanie's just gonna give all this stuff away anyhow." She took the shirt while he continued pawing through the bag. "There's gotta be some sweats in here too..."

She held up the shirt. A white undershirt, with words printed on it. Dayton Daily News 10K Run. Well, at least she knew what the *Dayton Daily News* was, if not a 10K Run. "Thank you," she said as he thrust a navy blue wad of clothing at her.

Pants. Cotton knit, with a drawstring waist. Pajamas?

She didn't normally wear pants, she realized. But if anyone saw her in that bloodstained dress, they'd ask questions. Questions she couldn't answer. She had killed someone, she felt the certainty down to the marrow of her bones. But who? And more important, why? "I'd... could I change now, if you don't mind?"

"Oh. Oh, sure! Just come on in the house when you're done." After he left she slipped out of her dress, but as she dropped it onto the truck bed, something small and flat fell out of the pocket.

She picked it up, staring at the little, numbered squares... *Calculator.* That was what the device was called. One of the red chips that absorbed the sunlight was missing, and the metal case was scratched and crimped in places, as if someone had taken it apart, then hastily reassembled it.

A sense of ill flooded her, and she almost dropped the device again.

She had to get rid of it. Something terrible would happen if she didn't. She didn't know what, or how she knew it, but the certainty was so strong she was barely able to lay it aside long enough to put on the clothes the man had given her. They felt funny, but comfortable.

Better to be seen in pajamas than look like a murderer.

I killed someone. Whoever it was, he had to be dead after losing so much blood. And the calculator, strange as it seemed, had something to do with it.

She spied a sledge hammer in the corner of the garage. After scanning the back of the house to make sure the slow-witted man was nowhere in sight, she laid it on the floor and lifted the hammer. Two swings left it a mangled mess of plastic and metal. Satisfied, she scooped it off the floor, wrapped it in her dress, then walked toward the house, dress wadded up in her hand.

The yard and back of the house were deserted, thank heavens. A tall, wooden fence bordered the yard, and a picnic table sat on a concrete porch alongside the one-story brick house. Flies buzzed around three green, barrel-like containers near the door through which the man had disappeared. The lid had fallen off of one, and as she neared, the odor of garbage stung her nose. She glanced around once more. Perfect. She stuffed the dress down the side of the container, relief washing over her the instant it left her hand.

She knocked on the door. The man had told her to come in, but it didn't feel right. "Sir?" she called.

"In here." He hunkered under the sink, his head hidden beneath the cabinet. "Bathroom's down the hall…"

She found the washroom, though like everything else in the house, it looked… strange. The lavatory sat on a big, wooden cabinet, and magazines with names like *Cosmopolitan* and *Glamour* atop the toilet tank showed such scantily clad women, it made her face heat. Strangest of all was the air gun lying on the sink. At least that's what she guessed it was, with a name like Conair printed on its side. The urge to pick it up and study it racked her body, but she feared it might be dangerous and best left alone.

She wanted to explore the rest of the house, see what curiosities it held, but… *Shame on you, you know better than that!* It wasn't polite to nose through people's things, especially after the kindness the man had shown her, so she returned to the kitchen.

Books and papers, keys and unopened mail littered the small wooden table—along with a newspaper. She picked it up.

Dayton Daily News. Fifty cents.

Fifty cents? For a newspaper? Not even a Sunday edition?

The man bumped his head on the cabinet door as water sprayed out. "Dad burn it!"

She jumped up. "Are you all right?"

"Yeah, but…" He backed away from the sink as the stream of water kept spraying.

He'd loosened the wrong joint. Strange as so much else in the house was, the pipes at least looked familiar. "Here, let me…" She reached behind him and found the shutoff valve. "I'll help you fix this, if I could just get a drink—"

"Oh man, that would be fantastic." Rubbing his head, he climbed to his feet and yanked open the icebox. "I think we got some pop, unless Vince drank it." He rummaged around, then held a green and silver can out to her.

Pop? She took it, eying the unfamiliar print. Mountain Dew? As in moonshine? But surely no one sold that in a printed can. "Th-thank you, sir." He watched, expectantly, while she turned the can over. "Do you have a can opener?"

He chuckled and took the can. "Whatd'ya need that for?" He sat the can on the table and pushed a little lever on the top, and miraculously, a hole appeared. Grinning, he handed it to her.

As she reached for the drink, the newspaper caught her eye. The date on the masthead read Monday, June 7...

That couldn't be. She reread it.

June 7. And an impossibly distant year.

It had to be a mistake. "Hey!" The man thrust the Mountain Dew at her. "You want this, or no?"

She took it from him and sipped from the hole. Not moonshine, but a soda, sweeter than even Coca-Cola. And it was delicious. Nothing had ever felt so welcome as the cool wetness coursing down her throat.

But that paper... She let out an ahhh as she set the can down on the table, wiped her mouth with the back of her hand, then pointed to the newspaper. "Sir, how old is this paper?"

He looked curious. "That ain't old. It's today's."

His words faded as a rushing sound pounded in her ears. *That can't be right!* She'd gotten something mixed up, she didn't know what, but the date should not be after 2000! She didn't know what it should be, or how she knew it wasn't right, but—

"My name's Timmy," the fellow said. "You shore are a pretty lady. What's your name?"

What *was* her name? Panic lanced through her. She tried to concentrate. *Think!* If she didn't come up with something fast, he might call the police, or take her to a hospital.

All she knew was the pickup truck. Mountain Dew. This slow-witted, but kind man. And blood. All over that beautiful dress, with its lovely, purple violets... and there was a word she'd seen somewhere, in big, lit-up letters.

"Violet," she finally answered. "Violet Sinclair."

It wasn't her real name, but it would do.

Violet sat alone at a table by the window in the company cafeteria, watching fat, fluffy snowflakes fall from the January sky. She'd taken to sitting there after Tony had gone on leave of absence the past summer, because it reminded her of him.

It was where he'd always sat.

Unable to keep her mind on the computer manual she'd brought to read while she ate, she finally gave up and pushed it aside.

He'd come back that morning. She hadn't seen him, but she'd heard Mr. Lynch telling one of the other executives as they'd walked past the tech support department.

Those six months Tony had been on leave had been the longest she could remember—not that she could remember anything further back than the day she woke in Stephanie's garage and helped Steph's brother Timmy fix the plumbing.

Nothing would happen. There was no reason her relationship with Tony would be any different than before the trip to Mexico, almost a year earlier. Professional, friendly, polite, nothing more.

She just wanted to see him, that was—

"Violet?"

Sparks shot through her body. She could hear his voice, could feel him behind her...

Footsteps clacked on the tile floor, and a man's well-filled-out dress shirt and slacks came into view. *Who*—

Her eyes traveled up his body. "Tony?"

His blue eyes sparkled behind his glasses, and his mouth curled into a thin smile—the word *wary* came to her mind, though she couldn't fathom why.

He rested his hand on the chair across from her. "Mind if I join you?"

Rational thought fled, and her fork tumbled to the floor. "Uh... of course."

Heavens, he must think I'm a doddering fool. She bent to pick up the fork as he pulled out the chair and sat. She took as long as she could get away with to pick up the fork, hoping her face wasn't flaming red by the time she straightened and thought of something halfway intelligent to say. "I'm glad to see you're feeling better." She did her best to rein in the sappy grin that threatened to steal onto her face, tried not to look too excited. *He* was sitting with *her?*

"I'm glad, too. And glad to be back. I was bored out of my mind, not working." He squeezed a packet of crackers and dumped the crumbs into his chili.

Violet let her gaze linger on him. He definitely filled out his shirt more than before. Must've been using the gym, spending all that extra time on his hands lifting weights.

They talked of inconsequential things—the weather, the news, people they both knew. Finally, he ate his last spoonful of chili, and scooped the cellophane cracker wrappers into the empty bowl, then reached into his breast pocket and pulled out a small envelope. "My sister gave me a couple of tickets to the opera... not really my thing, but..." He turned the envelope over in his hands.

Was he going to offer her the tickets? Maybe she could interest Stephanie in going.

He kept his gaze on the envelope, turned it over once more. "Her son's playing in a basketball tournament that night, so they can't go. I was wondering... would you like to go?"

"With you?" Her breath hung up in her throat. Surely he wasn't—

"Well, yeah." His brows pressed down and his mouth tipped up as he met her gaze.

Violet pressed the back of her hand against her mouth before she could say anything stupid, like how much she wanted a cigarette, even though she'd quit months ago.

Finally, the man she'd dreamed of, watched, longed to know, was asking her on a date.

It was what she wanted. The chance she'd been waiting for.

With that thought, her jitters faded, and warmth slowly coated her. She slowly lowered her hand and let her smile, the one she wanted to give him, come out. "I'd love to."

Author's Note

Many thanks for allowing me to share Tony and Charlotte's adventures with you! Your time is valuable, and this is a privilege I don't take lightly.

My goal is for every Mythical Press story to provide an excellent reading experience. To that end, if you've spotted a typo or other error in any Mythical Press book, please let us know so that we may correct it. You can either contact the author through her website, www.jenpowell.com, or email publisher@mythicalpress.com.

If you enjoyed *Time's Enemy*, I'd greatly appreciate it if you could take a minute to post a review on Amazon, Barnes and Noble, Smashwords, Goodreads, or other venues; or simply mention it to friends and family. Reviews and word of mouth are vital to an independent publisher, and your opinions matter! Posts on Facebook, Twitter, blogs, forums and other social media is also a great way to get the word out and help independent publishers keep producing stories.

Time's Fugitive, in which Tony and Violet's adventures continue, is slated for release as an e-book in December, 2011, with a print edition to follow. To stay informed of this and future releases, please stop by my website and blog at www.jenpowell.com, or connect with me on Facebook and/or Twitter. I look forward to seeing you there!

~ Jennette Marie Powell

About the Author

Jennette Marie Powell is the author of several time travel and paranormal romance novels. A lifelong resident of the Dayton, Ohio area, she likes to dig beneath the surface and find the extraordinary beneath the mundane, whether in people, places, or historical events. While she has no desire to change the past, she enjoys learning about local history, particularly the early 20th century. Her preferred places to time travel are from her computer or Dayton's Carillon Historical Park. By day, she wrangles data and websites in between excursions to search for the aliens and spacecraft that legends say are stashed away on the military base where she works.

Jennette lives with her husband, daughter, two Rottweilers, and assorted small critters. When not working or writing, she enjoys spending time with her family, learning about local history, cruising in her Camaro, and riding her Harley.

Visit Jennette at www.jenpowell.com, or connect with her on Facebook or Twitter.

About the Authors

Felicia Barker is a queer, trans writer who escaped the faerie realm as a child and was raised in the wild by feral computers. She's been a hobbyist writer for many years and is just now dipping into professional publication. After fleeing the wilds of the North, she has been at home among the idiosyncratics of Bristol for six years, where her day-to-day life revolves around helping manage the Hydra Bookshop co-operative, a radical nonprofit community bookshop for Bristol.

Andy Bigwood is an artist, author, draughtsman, bookbinder, cartographer, illustrator, and 3d modeller from Trowbridge, Wiltshire. Trained in Technical Illustration in Bath (shortly before the evolution of computer aided design), Andy has provided cover art for a variety of fantasy, horror and science fiction novels, twice winning the BSFA Award for best artwork for the anthologies *disLOCATIONS* and *Subterfuge*. Andy is also a published author with six short stories in print. His short story in this book is a direct sequel to the one in *Airship Shape & Bristol Fashion*.

Stephen Blake lives in Cornwall. When not bemoaning his ability to procrastinate with the very best, he works, teaches T'ai Chi, and generally does whatever his cat masters instruct him to do.

Five years after his very first story was accepted for *Airship Shape & Bristol Fashion*, he has since had horror, science-fiction, and children's stories published.

He'd like to use this bio (don't you just love writing in the third person) to thank Cheryl, Jo, and Roz, for giving people a chance, for helping them learn a bit about story-telling, and being part of the Airship Shape family.

Tanwen Cooper wrote her first story about a family of mice at the age of seven while sitting under her bed. She has been spinning tales of magic and mystery ever since.

By day, she is an astrophysics expert and space journalist (yes, that is a real job) writing under the name Elizabeth Pearson. She currently works on *BBC Sky at Night Magazine* and regularly appears on radio and television as a 'talking head' expert on all things space. She is currently working on her first non-fiction book about planetary exploration, which will be published by The History Press in October 2020. She currently lives in Bristol, playing board games and counting the days until she can finally get a dog.

Julia Hawkes-Reed is a Unix hacker by day. By night, too, if it's been one of those sorts of weeks. Her origin story involves finding the big yellow Gollancz hardbacks in Winchcombe public library, the 'Making a transistor radio' Ladybird book and the John Peel programme. The 2006 Viable Paradise writer's workshop was something of a life-changing experience, and she has been quietly emitting stories of varying length since then. Some of those stories can be found in the anthologies *Airship Shape & Bristol Fashion*, *Colinthology*, *Dark Spires* and *Future Bristol*. She is fascinated by cold-war architecture, islands and stationary engines. Julia owns too many books and not enough tractors.

Maria Herring: Besides reading, writing, and teaching English, I am known for:

1) taking great long hikes up the side of mountains so I can chat to the trees

2) drinking a small fortune in coffee

3) drawing maps

4) dropping stuff

I live in the Mont d'Or with my partner, Fab, and Bilbo our cat, but we can often be found in the UK visiting family. The first installment of my brand new fantasy series, *The Healing Glass (Age of Academicians 1)*, became an Amazon #1 bestseller in its opening fortnight. That was nice.

Pop in and see me at either of these places – the kettle's always on!

https://www.facebook.com/MariaHerringAuthor/

www.mariaherring.com

Sarah Higbee: Born the same year as the Russians launched Sputnik, Sarah expected that by the time she reached adulthood, Humanity would have a pioneer colony on the Moon and be heading off towards Mars. She was at a loss to know what to do once she realised the Final Frontier wasn't an option, so tried a lot of jobs she didn't like and married a totally unsuitable man.

Now Sarah has come to terms with the fact that she'll never leave Earth, she has a lovely time writing science fiction and fantasy, as well as teaching Creative Writing. She lives in Littlehampton with a wonderful husband and a ridiculous number of books.

Gareth Lewis has self-published a dozen novels in a few genres, including fantasy, science fiction, and thrillers. He lives and writes in South Wales. On Twitter, he's @gdlewis23.

Scott Lewis is a Bristol-based journalist, writer, photographer and casual adventurer with a penchant for pulp and weird fiction. He has awful time management skills, and will one day get around to finishing his first novel if chronic procrastination doesn't kill him first. Until then he intends to amuse himself by writing more short stories, rummaging around old bookstores and libraries for obscure myths, legends and folklore, and gallivanting off to far-flung parts of the world on 'research trips'. He and his fiancee live under the iron paw of Nala (short for Nyarlathotep) the cat, who occasionally deigns to let them pet her.

Amanda McLachlan lives on a wind-blasted hill in Somerset. From spring to autumn she rears orphaned wild animals. She hibernates in winter

Ian Millsted is a writer and teacher based in Bristol. His non-fictional exploration of *Doctor Who*, *Black Archive 8: Black Orchid* was published by Obverse Books and he writes regularly about comics for *Back Issue* magazine and about sf and pop culture for *Infinity*, *Retro-Fan* and others. His short stories have appeared in *Challenger Unbound*, *North by Southwest*, and *The Hotwells Horror & Other Stories* among others. He has been shortlisted for the Bristol Short Story Prize. His western novel *Silence Rides Alone* was shortlisted for the Peacemaker Award. With Pete Sutton he co-edited *The Dark Half of the Year*.

Cheryl Morgan writes mostly non-fiction. She has contributed to *Locus*, the *SFWA Bulletin*, *Foundation*, *SFX*, the *SF Encyclopaedia*, *Vector* and many other outlets. Most recently she had an essay in the British Fantasy Award winning, *Gender Identity and Sexuality in Fantasy and Science Fiction* from Luna Press Publishing. Her most recent fiction can be found in the anthologies, *The Hotwells Horror & Other Stories*, and *Rainbow Bouquet*. Cheryl's writing can also be found on her blog, *Cheryl's Mewsings* (http://www.cheryl-morgan.com/) and in her fanzine, *Salon Futura* (http://www.salonfutura.net/).

Ken Shinn is now 55 years old and still resides in Bristol with his two cats. Since his published fiction debut in the original *Airship Shape & Bristol Fashion*, he's gone on to have short fiction and other pieces published in some 18 other books, most recently *Me And The Starman*, *Tales From The Graveyard*, and *One More Lifetime: A You & Who Miscellany*, and has more due to appear in the upcoming *You On Target*, *UNIT Fanthology/Fannual* and *The Unofficial Master Annual*. He has now completed his first novel, an expansion of his original short story "Case Of The Vapours", and needs only a publisher to finally unleash it upon the World. "Let A Mountain Be His Gravestone" is another building block of what he hopes will, one day, become the 'Vapourverse'.

Pete Sutton has a not so secret lair in the wilds of Fishponds, Bristol and dreams up stories, many of which are about magpies. He's had stuff published, online and in book form, including a short story collection called *A Tiding of Magpies* (Shortlisted for the British Fantasy Award 2017) and the novels *Sick City Syndrome* and *Seven Deadly Swords* (Longlisted for the Not the Booker). Pete has also edited eight anthologies and is a member of the North Bristol Writers.

On Twitter he's @suttope, and he's published by Kensington Gore and Grimbold Books.

Piotr Śweitlik was born in the Silesian City of Chorzów, Poland but currently resides in the lovely town of Frome, where he is busy working on his first novel. His stories appeared in the first volume of *Airship Shape & Bristol Fashion*, "Kraken Rises", on *365 Tomorrows* and in *This Twisted Earth*. He's half-responsible for the *Final Frontier* radio show. He is also the creator of the *Sphere* RPG and is currently working on an educational board game for kids.

One of his stories has been compared to Roger Zelazny's work, which set his ego loose on the world. He's still searching for it.

Deborah Walker grew up in the most English town in the country, but she soon high-tailed it down to London, where she now lives with her partner, Chris, and her two teenage children. Her stories have appeared in *Airship Shape & Bristol Fashion*, *Nature's Futures*, *Lady Churchill's Rosebud Wristlet* and *The Year's Best SF 18* and have been translated into more than a dozen languages. Her first novel, a space opera, *As Good as Bad Can Get*, was published in 2017.

Ben Wright is a bioinformatician currently living and working in Oxfordshire. Currently he is releasing science-fiction and fantasy stories on Wattpad and through Patreon. He has written and performed for local theatre companies and spends a great deal of time playing or writing different kinds of tabletop games. He holds a doctorate in statistics, which is about as exciting as you imagine. He's just old enough to remember *The Adventure Game* on BBC2. If he ever finds out exactly what being a bioinformatician is supposed to entail, he'll be sure to let you know.